PUNK

Punk

AMY Q. BARKER

Punk

Cover design by Charlie Alolkoy

www.amyqbarker.com

ISBN: 978-1-7353581-1-6
Library of Congress Control Number: 2020922246

Printed in the United States of America

For Grandma Q.,
whose 1932 diary inspired this story

Chapter I

I remember that day like it was yesterday. I was so young and fresh. I looked at the camera, but I was really looking at the adoring eyes behind the lens. I wanted to pinch myself because I had never been that happy before.

"Didi, take your cap off so I can see your hair!" he urged, hollering above the sound of the waves breaking against the surf.

I whipped off the cap and stood there posing in my new bathing suit. Then I ran up from the water to tease him, poking his side and dodging around him to plop down on the sand under the umbrella. He was there beside me in an instant, one hand holding the camera in the air and the other on my waist, kissing me until we fell back breathless and laughing.

After spending some time lounging in the sun, we went for a walk down the beach to find our friends, who were tossing a ball near the water's edge. We stayed back and watched. It was a magical day—the sound of the waves, the laughter, the salty sea air, Paul's hand in mine. I grinned up at him silently, and he leaned down to kiss me. The sun, a big white circle in the sky, pricked our skin with its heat, and our eyes glowed with the vigor and warmth of youth. I thought, if only I could capture this moment in a jar and save it for all time.

Alas, the circle in the sky slowly descended toward the distant horizon, and the day came to a languid end. We caught the streetcar home, and Paul told me he loved me until my heart ached with happiness. Every single moment of that day etched itself on my soul, rich and full, teeming with possibilities.

Of course, I couldn't have known then what was to come. It's funny— when you're young, no one tells you that life isn't as it seems, that the

future is never as you planned it. That life has its own way of moving for-
ward and traveling down a road you never considered or wanted. In fact,
sometimes life doesn't take you into account at all.

Sometimes, life has its own mind.

❦ CHAPTER II ❧

How to Slash the Spunk out of Punk:

Step One: Exile the deviant to her bedroom. She must contemplate her *behavior.*

Step Two: Take away entertainment, livelihood, comfort, ease, intellectual stimulation, communication, kindness, caring, love, and the will to live.

Step Three: Confiscate car keys, phone, laptop, earbuds, tablet, television, video console, record player, makeup, mirror, lashes, blow dryer, straightener, curling iron, and all cool clothes in closet (including most splendiferous metal studded black leather jacket).

Step Four: Fill remaining dialogue with rancor, malice, challenge, confusion, anger, resentment, and antipathy.

Step Five: Set social media to pause, as in a fast-acting horse tranquilizer dart.

Step Six: Push everything to a volcanic, frenzied state of boil so that said punk is forced to escape out a second-story window, crawl across the porch rooftop, and fall to the ground, only to ruin a perfectly good radical-ruby-red manicure and to discover her mother's firmly planted feet awaiting below.

Now you ask, did it work? Was this the proper formula? Did the alchemist mix the right fixins and stir in the right amalgam to sock it to the sicko? Were all forms of rebellion stripped from the defiant child? Was the lobotomy complete? Was the spunk sufficiently removed from the punk? Was she back to her pure, unblemished form—soft and clean and warm, like a newborn?

Hmmm...um...NO.

CHAPTER III

THE SUMMER BETWEEN MY JUNIOR AND SENIOR YEAR of high school, I traveled back in time to 1932. It all started with an assignment from Mom. Her latest punishment. The usual steps had been executed (see Punk Desk Reference—steps one through six in Chapter II). I hadn't been on social media for months. I was irrelevant, inconsequential, and invisible. However, Mom was still not satisfied. During her latest rant, she even had the balls to remove my bedroom door! Took it right off the hinges and stowed it down in the basement.

Fast-forward a couple of weeks, and I was on my bed reading *Rebecca*. You see, the one thing I had left was my books. My lifeblood, my panacea, my soul. I guess Mom figured, how much trouble could she get into with a book? It was a hot Tuesday in June, late afternoon. Franklin (my high school) had just let out the week before, and despite Mom's histrionics, I was enjoying a summer of leisure. Eating, reading, sleeping. Lather, rinse, repeat. Suddenly I heard Mom marching up the stairs and yelling like a cat in heat.

"Delia? Delia? Where are you? I want to talk to you!"

I didn't bother to reply, but I did look up disinterestedly.

"Delia!" she repeated, irate, out of breath. "Why don't you answer me when I'm calling you?" Stepping into my open, gaping, lack-of-door bedroom entrance, she regarded me with a shake of her head. "You can't just say 'Hey Mom, I'm up here'?"

Clearly no reply was necessary, so I waited. She was standing over me with her hands on her hips.

"Are you going to respond?" she asked as I rolled my eyes. "Okay, I guess not. Then let's just get right to it. Delia, do you have something you want to tell me?"

Why do parents always start with this? Like we're going to spill the beans right off the bat. I paused and replied slowly, "What do you mean?" Then, based on her annoyed look, I said, "No."

"Are you sure? You have one opportunity to confess." Apparently, only one chance to plead my case for a stay of execution.

"Confess what? Come on, Heather, I give up. What's this about?" I tried to hurry her along. I was at a critical juncture in *Rebecca*.

"Spare me the attitude, Delia. And *don't* call me Heather. I am your *mother*."

I stared mutely.

Exasperated, she asked, "Don't you know?"

"Know what?" Okay, so maybe I *did* know, but I wasn't about to guess and get it wrong. Actually, it could be a number of things...

Her nostrils flared like a bull's.

"Okay, let's see...where do I begin?" She loved to start like this (the first step in our intricate ballroom dance). Sarcasm. "Hmmm, let me think... what might you have done *this* time? Oh, I know, you're volunteering at the local soup kitchen. No, that's not it—let's see, you're sewing clothes for the needy. Um, no, wait, I have it—you're hosting a camp for wayward youth. Am I getting warmer?"

I gritted my teeth. Wouldn't *I* be the recipient of that last charity? I started to smile.

"Wipe that smile off your face, missy. So, nowhere close, eh? Shocker," she said, pacing the room. "Here I am, exhausted after working all day, while you're sitting here doing...um...wait, *what exactly are you doing?*" She paused and stared as my eyes turned wide and innocent. Her mouth pinched, she continued, "Anyway, I decided to run to the grocery store to pick up a few things, thinking I'll buy some fish to grill because I know it's your favorite and boil up some salt potatoes on the side. Maybe steam some broccoli—again, *your* favorite. You know I hate broccoli." She regarded me significantly. Lovely. Guilt. Then, "And I'm thinking how great you've been lately—sort of on a roll. I mean, you've managed to finish your junior year with halfway decent grades, you're finally done with *that boy*, not to mention the fallout from *the incident* with *that boy*. You haven't snuck out of the house in at least, let's see, three weeks. You haven't stolen cash out of my wallet (as far as I know). You haven't been wearing my clothes—although that *is* my T-shirt if I'm not mistaken—please put that back! And you haven't broken curfew. I was beginning to think things were looking up." She paused for effect and concluded with, "But I should have known better, shouldn't I have?"

As she was getting more animated, I noticed the most fascinating thing—this vein in her neck grew large and throbbed, almost as if some type of alien lived there. I began to imagine it would pop its head out and start talking to me. "Hello, Delia. I'm the alien living in your mom's jugular. I come in peace. Please feed me.

I enjoy salted wafer crackers with sour cream and caviar, and don't forget a glass of chardonnay."

When she paused, the vein slowly reduced to a normal size, and my eyes flickered back to her face. I was sitting up in bed now, waiting patiently for her punch line and wondering absently why she could never use Greg's name. Almost a year dating him, and she still called him *that boy*, as though he was *that insect* or *that rodent*. That rat. That slug. That ant. Granted, he turned out to be *that cockroach* with a capital *C*, but I wasn't about to give her the satisfaction of knowing she'd been right. We usually avoided the topic like the plague. I was beginning to wonder where this conversation was going, thinking *it* was like the plague, spreading and dying like a slow black haze.

Besides, why was she throwing *the incident* in my face? Yes, certainly monumental, as in Ox Bow or Three Mile Island, but I would like to have a break from thinking about it. Didn't she know I lived with it, steeped in it, every moment of every day? Wallowing, wallowing, wallowing. It wasn't as if I'd ever forget it. There was no way to forget it. It was there, always, within me, like an atrocious, deathly, lingering hangover. Would she ever let it go? Would *I* ever let it go? Was there any letting *it* go?

The standoff. She was waiting for me to flinch or choke or blink or fess up or pass out. Something. But I simply sat quietly. She hated this.

After two long minutes, she broke. "I should have known! It was *all* too good to be true! I swear your goal in life is to torture me, isn't it?! Tell me!"

Yes, Mom, that is *my goal in life*. I said out loud, impatiently, "Mom, would you get to the point?"

"The point? *The point!*" she screamed. Eiyeiyei. Let the screaming commence.

"Yes, the point! What is *the point*?" I repeated.

"The point is, the point is…," she stuttered in her anger, "that I ran into Stephanie's mom in the grocery store, and I mentioned how great it is that both you and Stephanie are keeping busy this summer working at Panera. Well, wasn't I looking foolish and like a *complete idiot* when Dottie tells me that you got fired from Panera weeks ago, and didn't I know that? Didn't you tell me that? Didn't *my own daughter* tell me that?!"

Oh, so that was it. Amazing she just noticed now that I had barely left the house in weeks. Anyway, about the job, big whoop. That was old news. I turned my attention back to *Rebecca*. Mom snatched the book out of my hands and flung it across the room. "Don't you dare!"

"Hey!" I cried. Dang it, she lost my place.

"Don't you 'hey' me! Tell me what happened. How did you lose your job? Actually, on second thought, *don't*. I'd rather not know. What good is it to know *anything* about you anymore, Delia? Bad news after bad news after bad news. Once again, I am so disappointed in you. Is that what you want to hear from your mother? That I'm disappointed in you? Here I am, struggling to put food on the table and provide for you, and all I get in return is your disobedience and disrespect. Do you hate me that much? Do you? Why, Delia? Why?"

As if she figured into my existence that much in the first place! Seriously? The tears welled up in her eyes as she sat down on the edge of my bed, spent. Now, the crying. I sighed. Crud. She was never going to get out of my room.

She lightly touched my hand. "Delia. Oh, Delia," she sighed. "Why are you always so...so *difficult*? Why can't you at least attempt to get along with people? To be *disciplined* once in a while? You are a bright, beautiful, strong young lady, and yet all you seem to do is cause trouble. Why is that? I *know* you can do better. I know you're meant for something *better*, Delia. I do. When I held you in my arms the day you were born, I thought, here is a girl who will take on the world! Yep, that's what I thought..." She let another tear escape down her cheek. Finally, she couldn't take my silent treatment anymore. "Would you please say something? *Speak*, please, before I start to lose it."

Start to...! Anything to get her out of my room. "What do you want to hear?"

"What do I want to hear?" she repeated, deflated. Finally, inevitably, the defeat. "I'm afraid if I have to tell you, then this conversation is over."

"Okay, then." I said, thinking, great, I can get back to *Rebecca*.

She paused for a moment, regarding me with a strange look. A look I didn't like. A look with an idea behind it.

She said. "Get up. Come with me."

Uh-oh. "Why? Where are we going?" Were we skipping the addendum steps in our ballroom dance (rebound, retreat, relief)? Surely not!

"Just get up," she replied flippantly. She wiped her tears away and grabbed my hand. Well, if this will make her go away...she'll probably show me some innocuous thing, like that photo album from our trip to New England or a dress she wants me to try on, and then I can get back to the rhododendrons and azaleas of Manderley.

Or so I thought.

She held my hand tight as we went across the hall to the attic door. Holy crap, was she going to take me up in the attic? I stopped, regarding her with wide eyes. She knew I hated the attic.

For my entire life, we'd lived in an old house out on Spencer Street. Right down the road from Kodak. Yes, *that* Kodak. Sure, it went bankrupt, but it was still there—sadly, just not the same as in its heyday. Rochester, New York. The place where you went for "a plate" (as in a garbage plate) at Nick Tahou's, Charlotte Beach (emphasis on the "lotte," not the "char") on Lake Ontario, Genesee Brewery, U of R, RIT, Eastman School of Music, the falls, the lilacs, the Erie Canal, the parks, the Finger Lakes, the music, the people—and so much more, but advisedly, not in that order. Or in that order, if you liked your hot sauce with a side of Tums. Our house (if you could call it that) was built in 1900, completely wood, inside and out, and completely needing a hundred repairs. Mom, my brother Tyler, and I had a system—anything leaking needed a bucket and a fan, anything malfunctioning needed a wire hanger and duct tape, anything groaning needed a kick and a prayer. Believe it or not, this system worked about forty percent of the time. For the other sixty percent, Mom tried to get a member of her boyfriend-of-the-month club to assist. We lived in a constant state of decrepit discombobulation.

Tyler and I used to beg Mom, "Can't we move? We hate this house!" Mom would reply, "This is the Diamond family home. We can never move. This house must always be possessed by the descendants of the Diamonds."

Possessed being the operative word. I was never quite sure if she meant owned or right-outta-Amityville. Based on the things-that-go-bump-in-the-night cries, creaks, and clangs originating from the attic, I speculated the latter. Why couldn't the descendants rest in peace already? Mom talked a lot about the Diamond legacy, which was probably why they were still haunting us. I thought the legacy was about as drab and long since forgotten as a dirty old two-dollar bill. The "D.D." was originally named after my great-great-grandfather, Dennis Diamond, who built it. He worked at Kodak as a chemist and carved these words into the cement floor in the basement: "D.D. c. 1900." Tyler and I spent many bored hours devising more accurate depictions of the acronym: Death's Doorstep, Den of Disrepair (or Den of Despair), Diamond's Dunghole, Dire Dookie, Dirty Ditty, Death's Dynasty, Dour Doom, Dumb Dumb, and so on. For whatever reason, though, the D.D. name stuck, despite our disdain and despite the house having long since passed down to Diamond daughters with non-D married monikers.

Holy crap, that was a lot of D's. Sorry to disappoint. ;)

Mom opened the attic door as it bucked and creaked, then started up the grumbling steps. I hesitated. I needed to think fast. There must be a legitimate reason I couldn't follow, and it couldn't just be that I was scared half out of my wits. I said with hurried panic, "Mom, it's like a hundred and fifty degrees up there! Are you crazy? We could die of heat stroke." Lame, Delia, lame.

"Oh, be quiet. Come on, get up here," she pressed. "This is not a request."

As I ascended the dark, cramped stairwell, the hair stood up on the back of my neck. Although our attic took up the entire top floor of our house, it still felt closed and cramped. There was only one tiny dormer window. The rest of the space was jam-packed full of junk. Five generations of junk. Junk shoved into every corner and crevice, under the eaves, and floor to ceiling. Junk. Junk. Junk. A hoarder's paradise.

When we reached the landing at the top of the stairs, Mom pulled the chain to an exposed light bulb. It was like the sun—you couldn't look directly at it. It shed thin beams of light into the claustrophobic, narrow recesses and caused shadows to spread and display grim reapers onto the nooks and crannies of the back walls. I glanced around, hovering an inch from Mom's back.

"What are we doing? Cut to the chase, please. This place creeps me the f out."

"Watch your mouth, Delia," she replied. God, Mom, irrelevant. Then she stated, "Okay, pay attention. I have an assignment for you."

"What?"

"Since you managed to lose your job *again*, I decided your punishment will be different this time. As of today, you are officially grounded. And cut off from the Bank of Mom."

Well, the grounding sentence didn't faze me—I had already been unofficially grounded by virtue of her taking every single thing of value away from me. But I didn't like the idea of being without coin (did she mean no allowance, nothing?). I began to protest, but she put up a hand.

In her most-mom voice, she continued, "*I'm not done.* And—stop rolling your eyes at me. Here's the deal: you're going to clean out the attic."

I think the look on my face said it all, but to verify, I screamed, "No freakin' way, Mom! It would take me twenty years! Plus, this has to be breaking some type of child labor laws." I paused to think, then said, "And...and besides, I'm supposed to spend the rest of the summer at Dad's, remember?"

"Well, as a matter of fact, I've already spoken with your father," she said, smugly. OH NO. "He has agreed—wholeheartedly I might add—to this little arrangement."

"What?!" Grrrrr! That Benedict Arnold! "Give me your phone! I need to call Dad!" My voice was shrill and hysterical.

"No, no, nuh, nuh...not so fast. You can call him later. Right now, I need you to focus on my instructions. Here's how you're going to tackle this. First—"

I cut her off, "Mom, are you out of your mind?! There are probably bats and rats and raccoons and who knows what else up here! I'll need a rabies shot or tetanus or HPV or something...plus, what if I pass out from the heat?"

"Enough, Delia. I'm sure you'll survive. You're young and healthy, and I have no worries about you spending a summer doing hard work for once in your life. Stop sputtering. Listen, you can open that window and bring the fan up from Tyler's room. And I'll buy trash bags and plastic tubs. You'll need to sort everything into piles. You know—trash, donations, heirlooms, keepsakes, dead bodies."

She smiled, gloating. Haha, Mom. HA. HA.

Meanwhile, I was imagining whacking her across the head with a dead rat's body, swinging it by its little dead-rat tail. Whoosh, thunk!

My eyes narrowed as she droned on, "When I get home from work each day, I'll check on your progress. I don't want you throwing anything away until I've given the A-OK. I'm afraid you'll get rid of something valuable. Oh, and that's the other thing. Since you have no job, you're welcome to sell whatever you find (after I've said it's okay) by whatever method you want and pocket the proceeds. I don't want you to sell any family stuff, but the other miscellaneous stuff is fine. So, see, it's not so bad, is it? And when you're done, yes, only when you're totally *done*, only *then* can you go to Dad's. Got it? Nod your head if you hear me. Blink once for yes or twice for no. Very funny—now you look like you're having a seizure. Okeydokey, you can start straightaway. I'm going to run to the store and get the supplies. I'll be right back. Any questions?"

Amid my blinking, fuming, and breathing hard, I thought of something. I said, "Hey, I'm going to need my phone back and a car to do this."

"What? Why?"

"I'll need my phone to sell this crap—there are like twenty good apps for selling old-people stuff. And I'll need my car to deliver the stuff I sell."

"First of all, it's not *your* phone or *your* car. You've lost your privileges to both—"

"Technically, the car *is* mine," I cut her off. "Dad bought it for me."

"Well, that's neither here nor there. And I bought you the phone."

"Yeah, the piece of junk...," I murmured under my breath.

"...which is a perfectly good phone. Anyway, forget about it. You're not getting either back anytime soon. I have a different plan."

"What do you mean?" I shuddered to ask.

"I thought we'd do this together!" Oh, the light in her eyes.

"How do you propose we do that?"

"I'll be here with you, in the trenches, after I get home from work. It'll be fun. And we'll use *my* phone and *my* car. What do you think?"

"Uh-huh," I said incredulously. "Mom, you're never home!"

"Delia. Always with the exaggeration…I *am* home. I don't know what you mean. Anyway, if you're worried, I'll make a point of being home."

She put her arm around me and gave me a squeeze, making me shrug. I had one word: "Hot."

"Come on, we're going to have a great summer." She let me go and tapped my butt, saying, "Okay, hop to it. I'll be back in a bit. And you'd better have made some progress."

"Or what? You'll send me to military school? I mean, what's left? Waterboarding? Dismemberment? Draw and quarter me?"

"Don't tempt me. Go!"

She was off, and I was left to a fate worse than death.

My philosophy in life: procrastination pays off. I went back to my room, picked up *Rebecca* from the floor. Now where had I left off? I found my spot, plopped down on the bed, and began to read. Wouldn't you know it, not two paragraphs in and that sneaky snake, Mom, came tiptoeing up the stairs and jumped into my room, scaring me half to death, hollering, "Delia! I leave you alone for five minutes! Apparently, I need to treat you like a two-year-old and stand over you until you get moving. Get up! Go!"

Busted! There she stood, hands on hips, tapping her toe. I threw my hands in the air, got up, carefully placing a bookmark in *Rebecca*, tossed my hair up in a messy bun, and stomped (loudly!) up the attic stairs as she watched. A few minutes later as I rattled things around, I finally heard her triumphantly trek away.

Damn. She definitely won round one. I breathed a sigh of stifling air into my defeated lungs, thinking this was going to be the vilest summer ever. My white flag was up. Well, my goal would be to finish quickly so I could get to Dad's. Two minutes after I heard Mom drive away, I went down to grab Tyler's fan from his closet. It might help, but I doubted it. I went back up, opened the dormer window (which took some elbow grease, let me tell you!), plugged the fan into the frayed extension cord hanging from the light bulb (hello, electrical hazard much?!), put it on high, and leaned my head over into the fan's open mouth. Ahhhh-ah-ah-ah-aarrrgh-grrrr. Helicopter blender.

Okay, Delia, what's the fastest, easiest way to zip through this project? It didn't have to be perfect. I wasn't submitting it for a grade. I just had to rearrange the deck chairs to make it look as if I had actually done something. That should be easy enough—I mean, the place looked like a hornet's nest wrapped in a beehive shoved into a ball of twine. The first step would be to clear a path through the crap to get to more crap. I stacked a few boxes on top of each other. Then I unhooked the clothes and other items hanging from the eaves (hello again, recipe for towering inferno much?), folded them into a pile, and laid them in one corner. That helped. Some of the shadow grim reapers disappeared into the background. I wondered if, at the end of this, I'd find a chunk of cheese waiting for me.

I decided to do my favorite formula for random equations. Works every time!

Eeny, meeny, miney, moe,

Catch a tiger by the toe.

If he hollers, let him go,

Eeny, meeny, miney, moe.

Pointing at seven different sections in the attic, I landed on the spot to the left of the window—the tallest spot in the attic (of course!) and therefore the most fully and densely packed. Oh well, I guess if I tackled it first, the rest would be easy in comparison. I opened the first box, which was filled with old toys and clothes. The relics of my childhood. I had to admit, when I saw my old stuffed rabbity-head Elmer, I felt a twinge of nostalgia. Awww, he'd been such a faithful friend! I rubbed his silky ears and wished I could go back in time to the days when both Mom and Dad would tuck me into bed and read me a book as I squished Elmer into my face and neck. After a moment, I stood up and threw Elmer back in the box. Those days were over. Back to business. No sentimental mumbo jumbo. I closed the box and sailed it down the stairwell runway. Ahoy, matey! Snap decision: all boxes and unbreakables would sail or fly, depending on the aerodynamics of the object. And everything else would wait up here in the dungeon. Several other boxes went by way of the first.

An hour went by, then two. Really, Mom, did you need to keep *every single* onesie that Tyler and I ever had? And elementary school projects? And Halloween costumes? And ski pants, hats, boots, photo albums, dolls, dog collars, craft supplies, Christmas trees (three!), wreaths, umbrellas, golf clubs, soccer balls, toboggans (those *really* sailed down the stairwell!), books, doorknobs, trash cans, tables, magazines, plastic pumpkins, clothes, clothes, and more clothes? And three sets of *Encyclopedia Britannica*, which apparently is some type of wiki from the Paleozoic Era. Sadly, those were too heavy to sail and instead tumbled down like a box of bricks.

By the time I heard Mom come back, yelling at me to stop throwing things down the stairwell, I could only see her left shoulder and the top of her head behind the pile that had accumulated at the bottom. Then I heard her talking to herself (per usual), "Okay, wow, that's a lot of stuff! Let's see, hmmm, how to tackle, how to tackle? Let's put the clothes over here and the toys over here and oh, look at that—aww, Tyler's onesie *Mommy's #1 All Star.* That was my favorite! Wasn't he the sweetest little baby? So good, always with those big blue eyes staring up at me."

God, gag me.

I walked to a corner so I didn't have to hear her anymore. There was a large oval standup mirror. I assessed myself in the glass. Here I am: Delia Marie Elliott. If I had to come up with one word for myself, it would be *cute.* Not beautiful. Not ugly. Not statuesque. Not wiry. Not stumpy. Not short. Not tall. Not fat. Not thin. Just cute. Long, straight brown hair. Brown eyes. Average-girl height. Average-girl weight. Average-girl chest, hips, stomach, legs. Cute. I put my hands on either side of my face, did a slight dip and a twirl, and said out loud, "Aren't you cute?"

After that, I treaded lightly toward a distant niche in the back. I noticed that the light from the dormer window was starting to dim. It was dusk, and I was hungry. Time flies when you're having fun. Maybe I should have stopped, but just then I heard a light shuffle in the back right recessed corner where the roof sloped down over the eaves. My heart skipped a beat. What on earth was that? *Or maybe not on Earth.* Shiver. Probably mice. Right? I wished I had a flashlight. Even with the exposed attic bulb, this area was dark and shadowy. I debated hollering down to Mom but decided against it. I kicked aside a few more items, then slowly came upon the spot where I thought I'd heard the noise. There was a huge green wool army blanket lying across something short and squat. I whipped the blanket off quickly and stopped to listen, but the only sound was the fan whirring in the distance. My eyes swept across the limited exposed floor. Nothing moved. I breathed deeply. Okay, it was nothing. Jeesh, Delia, paranoid much?

As my eyes came into focus in the dark, I saw what lay under the blanket—some type of wooden table or box. I couldn't quite make it out. It was approximately three feet tall and a foot and a half wide, square with a door that opened in the front with a brass handle. It almost looked like an end table you'd find beside a couch in a living room except for the fact that it was too tall for that purpose. Heck, who knew? It was probably some type of strange bookcase. Anyway, it was too dark to see it clearly, so I picked it up and brought it over to the light. I opened the door and peeked inside.

No books, but four things came directly into view. I pulled each item out and inspected it: a Kodak eight-millimeter video camera in a black-and-gold Kodak box, an oval glass bowl wrapped loosely in newspaper, a shoebox full of black-

and-white photographs, and a leather-bound book wrapped in a blue silk ribbon. I held a few of the photos up to the light. Three people sitting on a porch drinking iced tea out of large bubble glass tumblers. A black dog held on a leash by a man on a sidewalk (was that the famous Dennis Diamond?). An elderly woman rubbing her hands on an apron as the blurry image of a child ran up to her. Three people and a horse standing on the front lawn of the D.D., stock-still, staring directly at the camera as if it were a foreign object (which, back then, I suppose it was!). A man in a fedora and a long, dark wool coat with a fur collar ice-skating on a pond. I studied them, wondering who they were. My hands were sticky from the heat and sweat and dirt, so I placed the photos carefully back into the shoebox.

Then I pulled out the glass bowl from the newspaper and felt along the bumpy rim. The newspaper was dated July 27, 1945. Whoa. Old. I remembered a few years ago when Mom and I had gone exploring and ended up walking through an antique store and saw a display of this type of glass in all different colors. She had called it "Depression glass." The bowl was a pale-yellow color, like watered-down lemonade. It was heavy and solid for such a small piece, but also delicate and fragile. Putting the bowl back in the newspaper, I laid it aside. I lifted the leather-bound book. I cautiously untied the ribbon and turned it over to reveal the gold-embossed title "Daily Journal." I opened the pages and saw tightly knit handwriting scrolled in intricate detail on every page and even bleeding over into the margins. Wow, whoever wrote these pages had a lot to say!

Suddenly, I felt a flash of cold air and what I could only call a thin, wispy breath of a specter as it flew out of the strange wooden bookcase thing, right into me, through me, and back out again.

I gasped!

A moment passed when I could not move or think or breathe. What the—?

Then I heard a whisper: *Delia!*

I was frozen to the spot, my heart pounding out of my chest.

Just then, as if a joke were being played on me, I sneezed three times in succession. At the end, I groaned and stood up straight, hitting my head on the eave. Ouch! I put my hand up to the eave to hold on and cursed.

Holy crap, I'm losing my mind! Although, thankfully, nothing could wake the dead like a good sneeze. Or put the dead back to sleep, as the case may be, and I hoped the case *was*. I needed to get a grip. Seriously. I exhaled and closed the diary, tying it back up with the ribbon and tucking it into the elastic waistband of my shorts. I put the rest of the items back in the bookcase thing and closed the door. Good riddance, whatever you are!

Out the dormer window, the front yard was black, and the cicadas were as loud as a concert, singing like weeping sitars. Mom yelled up the stairs that dinner was ready. I closed the window, turned off the fan, pulled the light bulb chain, and navigated carefully down the stairwell obstacle course. Right before I hit the bottom step, I felt a whoosh of air hit the back of my neck, giving me goosebumps. I jumped over the pile and ran into my room. Mom, who had been kneeling down over a box of clothes, stood up abruptly and asked me if I was okay. I grunted something in response, shaking my body from head to toe as if to expel a crawling tarantula. Damn the D.D.! She shrugged and told me to come downstairs and eat. I hid the diary in my dresser drawer. Then I washed my hands and face in the bathroom sink and went downstairs.

On nights like this, we ate at the kitchen counter on the barstools instead of sitting in the dining room. Mom was in a good mood because she had won the standoff at the O.K. Corral. I was tired and felt as though all forms of liquid had evaporated from my body because of my unholy attic spa sauna treatment. I pounded down four glasses of water quickly and dug into the food. Mom chattered on about the contents of the piles awaiting decommissioning upstairs. I asked her about the wooden bookcase thing—she said it was probably Dennis Diamond's cherry music stand. This description did not enlighten me, so I stared at her blankly. I said something like, "That thing plays music?" She rolled her eyes at me and explained that it was used to hold sheet music. Once again, the "duh" look. Finally, she said, "Those pieces of paper you see people using while playing the piano." "Oh," I replied, feeling like a dolt, but then also feeling like, how was I to know? Didn't piano players use tablets now?

Anyway, she rattled on about other things, and I feigned interest, mostly distracted, thinking about the diary. I wondered whose it was and when it was written and what it said. Mom seemed a little disappointed when I finished eating so quickly and abruptly stood up, telling her I was tired and wanted to get to bed. She reluctantly let me go, watching me leave the room with a faraway look on her face. I ignored that and dashed upstairs, changed into my pj's, grabbed the diary out of the drawer, propped myself up with a pillow, and began to read.

☙ CHAPTER IV ❧

1932
Delia "Didi" Marie Diamond
Birthday: February 29, 1912
12 Spencer Street
Rochester, New York

January 1

(Friday) New Year's Day. Decided to start a diary. New Year's is a time for new beginnings, right? I hope it will be for me. I've been stuck in a rut lately. Work, family, friends, life. It's been a year and a half since I graduated Franklin, and now I'm looking for a new adventure. I think Mom and Dad would like for me to meet a nice boy and settle down. I would like that too. We had company last night (Harold, Vera, baby), which was fun, but then when I woke up this morning, I looked out the window at the snow and wondered what the future would bring. I went to Frances's in the afternoon and met her cousin Paul. After a while, we went to the Riviera and saw Rich Man's Folly *and* Sidewalks of New York. *Not exactly fireworks for the start of 1932, but at least I didn't sit home and cry.*

FYI, y'all, this is Delia. My commentary on these diary entries will be posted in my own handwriting so you'll know where the sarcasm comes from. Enjoy! So Didi's feeling a little blue. Hey, I can relate. Hang in there. That's what I've been doing—trying to tread water. Sometimes, that's all you can do. I wonder what the Riviera is...a theater? For plays or for movies?

January 2

(Saturday) Worked in the office on the bills and helped Sam with the lay-offs and extra pay. I should probably explain my thoughts on Sam. He's

nice, but not so good at math. In fact, I don't really understand why they keep putting him on the books when I'm the one who knows how to balance them properly. He always miscalculates, and I have to come fix them. Also, I think he wants to ask me out on a date because he stares at me something awful. He's not my type, and sometimes when I see him getting nervous and red, I excuse myself to the ladies' room so he won't get the chance to ask. Is this bad? I don't want to hurt his feelings, but I also don't want to go out with him! After work today, I went to Bernice's for supper. While we were getting ready to go out, Roy came and made a date for the morrow. Then Bernice and I went dancing until 11:15. Danced with so many boys, my feet hurt and I got a headache.

Wow, worked "in the office" in 1932! And showing Sam how to do it too! I wonder if she got any credit for fixing his mistakes. Probably not. Back then, I thought women were only allowed to be wives, mothers, nurses, or teachers. Good to know Didi proved that theory wrong, even if Sam is taking credit for her work. Yet she danced with all the boys. Kind of working that angle from both sides, eh? Gotta love it—what a woman! Is "the morrow" the same thing as "tomorrow"? Some type of leftover language from the British? Seriously, how is that expression still being used in 1932?

January 3
(Sunday) A headache still in the morning. Went home. Skipped dinner and slept until 2:00. Woke up and washed my head. Decided because of the New Year, I would style it differently, with a finger wave. New year, new hair, new life, right? Bernice came down for supper. All the kids have been going to the Genesee to bowl lately, so there we went too. When we walked in the door, it was the same crowd as always, so I was a little disappointed, but then I saw Frances's cousin Paul across the room with Roy and Barney. I hadn't noticed before (at Frances's house the other day) how tall and handsome Paul is. He has the most sparkling blue eyes. On the one hand, I wanted to stare at them all night, and on the other hand, I had to look away because they are almost too intense, especially when they fix on me! Such a strange feeling. And he said he liked my hair. He was swell. He even laughed when my bowling ball accidentally slipped out of my hand and landed on Barney's foot. Barney jumped up so quickly and with such a loud girl's scream that we couldn't help but laugh. Barney still bowled a 170 and beat us all, even with a sore toe!

Who knew they had bowling back then? Washed her head? Not hair? So strange. And that was something to note in her diary? Although the finger wave sounds interesting—was that like Betty Boop? Or Betty Grable. Va-va-voom. New hair, new life...I ought to try that! If and when I ever get my phone back, I'm gonna check out some YouTube videos on hairstyling. Couldn't hurt to mix it up.

January 4

(Monday) Went to work. Helped Sam with the ledger. He said, "Say, Didi, you're smart!" What a line! Didn't know what he meant—my new hair or my brains. Then before I got out of there, he asked me to the show on Friday, but I told him I was busy. "With whom?" he asked. I said, "I couldn't say." He said, "Why can't you say?!" and I just told him he was being rude and to leave me alone. Now I better figure out a way to be busy on Friday! I hoped Paul might call. Frances said he asked for my number after bowling, which made my heart pound. Minnie came down for supper with Eddie and baby Hotcha. We played pinochle and listened to Amos and Andy.

OMG, who names their baby Hotcha? Didi's kind of funny, blowing off that Sam dude with her little white lie. Although I can't figure out exactly where she and Sam are working—a bank, an office, a store, a what? And what is "Amos and Andy"? Some type of TV show? Oh wait, TV didn't exist in 1932, did it? Or much of anything else. Everyone was basically broke during that time, weren't they? Wow, life must have been so boring. Kind of like my life now. Holy crap, did I just compare my life to the Great Depression? Ugh. Someone shoot me.

January 5

(Tuesday) Roy called at 10:00. He wanted to know if he and Paul could make a date with Bernice and me for dancing at the Manitou on Friday. Aces! I think I wished for something so hard that I made it come true! This time when I looked out the window at the snow, I smiled because it made me think how lovely the white was against the dark, leafless trees. I didn't even mind the cold because Mom made me up a hot water bottle for bed and because thinking about Paul's eyes warmed my heart as I fell asleep.

Aces! That is an awesome expression. I'm going to use it in a sentence this week. I like it with totally, as in "I just won the lottery—totally aces!" In fact, I wish I could use it with *that* sentence this week, but since I have no money or car or phone, winning the lottery's looking about as remote as my popularity. Anyway, at least it looks like things are starting to heat up between Didi and this Paul guy... Speaking of heating up, using a hot water bottle—how did that work? Did you really take a *bottle* to bed with you? No plastic, so it must have been a glass bottle. How did it stay hot? And weren't you worried about kicking the thing off the side of the bed in the middle of the night and it shattering on the floor and waking up the whole household?

Come to think of it, though, how *did* they heat houses back then? With fireplaces? I mean, I'm looking out the same windows that Didi looked out of, here in the D.D.—maybe even the exact same bedroom window (I wonder, was this Didi's bedroom?), and I'm thinking brrrr. These windows are barely caulked at all around the edges, and certainly there's no insulation in the walls. Sometimes in the winter, I can hear (and feel!) the wind coming right through the cracks. When that happens, I just holler at Mom to turn up the furnace, but what did Didi do back then? Turn up the coal? Wood? Blankets. Lots of blankets. And quilts, probably. Didn't everyone use every last scrap of cloth in the house to sew together intricate quilts for warmth? Mom took me to the Susan B. Anthony Museum and House (a few miles away from our house), and they had this display about how Susan sewed a LeMoyne Star quilt by hand when she was fifteen and how it took her four years to finish! I remember thinking, wow, she had a crapload of patience, determination, and perseverance. I guess it boded well for her and for the rest of us that she did, and I don't just mean for that quilt!

January 6
(Wednesday) Worked half shift at switchboard and half in the office. Sam was there and tried to make a date, but I told him I was already going out with Bernice. He wanted to know who else, but I didn't tell him. Told him to mind his own beeswax. He didn't like that.

Who knew Great-grandma was a player? She had Sam on a string and Paul on a leash. What a badass! Made me laugh. She must have been something else.

January 7
(Thursday) I embroidered my lunching cloth. Vera and baby came down for supper. We played flags and rummy. Frances called and wanted to know if she could come down, but I told her we had company. I told her about tomorrow night, but she already knew from Paul. She said she would be there with George. I asked her about Paul, if he had a gal. She said he was free and that he asked about me too!

I guess they played a lot of cards back then. Definitely no TV then. Now she's using "tomorrow"—how did they know when to use "on the morrow" versus "tomorrow"? Like learning another language. What is a lunching cloth anyway, and why on earth would someone spend time embroidering it?

January 8

(Friday) I nearly dropped the ledger on the floor of the elevator when guess who got on with me? Paul! He told me he's working at the Stand now—that lunch counter on the first floor of the Powers Hotel, and his mom is the new manager. His brother is also helping out. I thought, oh, that's the fancy hotel down the street. That's a great job! And he'll be so close that I can stop by and see him during my breaks. He smiled as if he'd read my mind and said he was looking forward to tonight. After work, Bernice came down and we put on color. Paul and Roy were waiting by the streetcar. Paul said he liked my dress. Sam got on at Dewey, which was an odd and unexpected coincidence. I introduced him, and when Paul shook his hand, I noticed he gave Sam a sort of angry stare. I wasn't sure what that was all about. At the Manitou, Sam stayed near us and asked me to dance, so I danced with him three times. Paul seemed mad and asked me rather forcefully for "all the other dances." He really must like me!

First of all, that's hysterical when Didi says the Sam meetup was just a coincidence. I can't tell if she's that naive or being sarcastic. Since she's my greatgrandma, I'm going to guess the latter. Second, what's the deal with Paul? He seems rather possessive right out of the gate. She's taking it all as flattery, which maybe it is, but for me, I'd have my guard up. I mean, weren't these dances more like group dates—kind of share-and-share-alike activities with the young folk back then? Paul's definitely taking it to some new level. I'm gonna keep my eye on this guy. Okay, my final observation on this entry: "put on color"? Like actually painting the stuff on. Yowzah. Made me think of *Gone with the Wind* and how only the prostitutes wore makeup. Was Didi a rebel? Although, this diary was written after the roaring twenties, so maybe all the young ladies were "putting on color" by this point. Can you imagine if she saw what kind of "color" I put on every day?! Somehow I don't think charcoal black eyeliner was in her repertoire.

January 9

(Saturday) Woke up at 11:30. Went to a show with Frances at the Webster. It was snowing, so we took the streetcar to her house after the show and played

hearts with her parents. In the evening, we listened to Baron on the radio.
Stayed at Frances's. Asked her more about Paul—she said he's a real nice
cousin. His dad died of a heart attack in '24. His mother had to take over the
restaurant they had down there in Penn., but it didn't work out, so they came
up here to stay for a while. I found out his brother's name is Burrows. I asked
her if she thought I should date Paul, and she smiled and said, "Well, I know
he wants to date you!" We giggled and I confessed that I had wished for a
new adventure in the New Year and how maybe this was it. She agreed. We
stayed up whispering about her boyfriend, George, and about my prospects
with Paul and didn't fall asleep until who knows what time.

Interesting to learn more about Paul. I guess it's a good sign that Frances is
cool with him dating Didi. Too bad, though, about his dad dying. Life expectancy
was probably like thirty for men back then. So sad. On a different note, I guess it
is radio they're listening to. And now instead of the Riviera, it's the Webster. Must
be movie theaters because there just couldn't be that many plays going on around
town, not to mention, how could they afford that? Playing cards, radio, movies,
out dancing, sleepovers, double dates, and family suppers (or was it dinner?)—
she was definitely in the thick of things. Very social! How old was she? 1912 to
1932 = 20. She's definitely got more game than I have, at least in my current
state of barren wasteland nihilism.

January 10

(Sunday) Still snowing. Frances came home with me for a late dinner. Dad
said Paul called and left a message to come see him at the Stand. Frances
and I rode the streetcar there and visited with Paul and his brother. Paul's
eyes were on me again, and I had to pretend to read the menu because I was
blushing so. He told me he really enjoyed dancing with me and that we'd
have to go again sometime soon. I just nodded. We didn't stay very long at
the Stand because the snow was coming down thick by that time, and sure
enough, when we got to the streetcar, it was stuck in the snow, so we had to
walk home. My feet got wet. Wrapped them in newspaper and wool and
went to bed early to get warm.

What is a "streetcar" anyway—a bus, a trolley, a taxi? It wasn't something
drawn by horses, was it? Naw, that couldn't be. Weren't there any cars back
then? And why would you wrap your feet in newspaper? I mean, I can't think of
a more porous, thin material, but maybe the wool helped. Weird.

January 11

(Monday) Went to work. Some of the streetcars weren't running because of the snow, so I was late to my desk. Manager said I had to work an extra hour tonight to make up the time. Worked on the ledger with Sam again. He still hasn't figured it out, and my patience is running thin. Then he asked me about Paul. Wanted to know if we were going steady. I didn't answer, so he tried to make a date for Friday, but I put him off, saying it was only Monday and I didn't know what I'd be doing tonight, let alone on Friday. He's said, "Yes, that's why I'm asking you now.*" Some boys just don't get the hint. During my break, I went to the Stand to see Paul. Told him what Sam said. Paul said, "Rotters!" under his breath, and I laughed. Then he asked me to the show on Friday, saying Sam should buzz off. I thought I might jump for joy, I was so happy! I went back and told Sam I was busy Friday, and he just sulked and said, "I thought you didn't know what you were doing* tonight.*"*

Boy, Didi's working that jealousy angle to the max, isn't she? Gotta hand it to her—apparently it was effective.

January 12

(Tuesday) Slept until 9:45. Bernice came over, and we washed our heads and played cards. She wanted to know if she and Roy could come to the show with us. I told her I'd ask Paul. Just then, he called! I told him what Bernice said, and he said yes. Bernice left, and Harold and Vera came for supper with the baby. It was fun bouncing the baby on my lap in the kitchen. It made me wonder what it would be like to have my own baby. Earlier in the day, when I was talking to Bernice about Paul, she said she probably couldn't give me any advice because she and Roy had been together for so many years that she didn't even remember what it was like when they first met. All she could remember was that she sat next to Roy in third grade and he put a frog in her desk just to get her attention, which of course it did! He said they'd been together ever since, but Bernice recalls it took several months of cooling off after the frog incident before she would endeavor to talk to him again. She laughed and said he'd been making it up to her ever since, and that was the way she liked it!

Holy crap, the last time Didi "washed her head" was on January 3rd! Eeesh.

January 13

(Wednesday) Worked on the switchboard all day. I was glad because I didn't have to see Sam. Paul called late last night and told me he wouldn't be at the Stand today. He said his mom wanted him to spend the day cleaning their place and chopping wood for the fireplace. I missed him, so I spent my break thinking about what it would be like to have him in my arms dancing with me again. I wondered if he was thinking about me too. After work, I played on the Daisy Machine. Went to bed early. It was so cold, Dad said the thermometer outside froze!

Okay, I give up—what is a Daisy Machine? And can a thermometer really freeze? Also, I guess that answers my question about heating a house—firewood. At least for Paul's place anyway. As far as I know, the D.D. doesn't have a fireplace unless it's hidden somewhere, so it's still a mystery how they kept warm in this drafty dungeon.

January 14

(Thursday) I stayed in bed until 11:30. Frances came over for supper, and we went to the Young People's Meeting. It was crowded, and we ran into Glenys and Gail. The speaker was Mabel Hale, the author of Beautiful Girlhood. *She talked to us about organizing for the greater good. It was interesting. Frances and I stayed up late talking about it.*

Who is Mabel Hale? Sounds like the name of a Holy Roller. And what is a "Young People's Meeting"? Some type of thinly veiled kiddie communist organization?

January 15

(Friday) Worked on the books with Sam. He didn't get a single thing done on them while I was on the switchboard and home. What am I going to do with him? Oh well. After work, I bought a new dress. Home by 5:00. Bernice's dad dropped her off, and we rode the streetcar to meet Paul and Roy. They got on at Lyell. Paul said, "Wowee, you look like candy!" Bernice and Roy thought that was funny. I blushed and told him he was too much. We went to the Palace and saw Consolation Marriage *and* The Public Enemy. *Paul held my hand. I don't remember either show because I was so focused on the feeling of his hand in mine. It was soft and strong and warm and wonderful. On the way home on the streetcar, I told*

Bernice about the Young People's Meeting, and we decided to make flyers this weekend.

I would have dumped Paul immediately. Candy. Really? Ugh. And flyers? For what? God, I hope nothing about Hitler or Stalin or any of those shitheads. This was before their time, though, right?

January 16

(Saturday) Woke up at noon. Bernice left after supper. Dad's birthday. I gave him a scarf I knitted. He put it around his neck and ran out in the front yard to show me how warm it was. What a card! We had company for dinner (Minnie, Ernest, Eddie, Hotcha, and Grandma). Mom made a devil's food cake. It was good, and now I know where it gets its name! I talked to Grandma about Mabel Hale, and she gave me a few ideas for the flyer.

Mmmm...devil's food cake...yum.

January 17

(Sunday) Woke up at 8:00. Paul called. James answered and wouldn't give me the phone. Mom took it from him and gave it to me. I stuck my tongue out at him behind Mom's back, and he pulled my hair. Cripes! Brothers. Paul said he and Burrows were going ice-skating at Highland Park. I called Frances, and we took the streetcar there together. George met us. Paul helped me on with my skates and held my hand. Afterward, Frances and I went back to my house. Bernice, Glenys, and Gail were already there talking to Mom. We made a hundred flyers.

Brothers, indeed. I understand. I have a Tyler. Ice-skating in Highland Park! I've been ice-skating there—with Mom and my friend McKenzie. It's really beautiful there in the wintertime—right out of a Jimmy Stewart movie. Pretty cool that some of the things Didi's writing about are still alive and well here in Rochester. Makes me rather proud of my flower city! We're like the little engine that could when it comes to cities—small, stalwart, snowy, steady, and strong.

January 18

(Monday) At work, I distributed twenty flyers to the ladies working the switchboard and in the shop. Most said they would come to the meeting. I told them it will be a great opportunity for us to contribute to society. After

work, Frances and I walked around the neighborhood to hand out flyers to the ladies from school. I was so cold and tired by the time I got home, I didn't have the energy to call Paul back. James said he'd called three times while I was out.

Alright, what's the deal with these flyers and this meeting? Wait. Wait one minute—I found something! Stuck between the pages of the diary. This:

Young People's Meeting
Thursday, January 28th
7:00 pm
The YWCA at Kent Hall

Crying out to the Young Ladies of Our Community – Come One, Come All!

"Womanhood stands for all that is pure and clean and noble. She who does not make the world better for having lived in it has failed to be all that a woman should be."

~ Mabel Hale

Agenda:
Discuss how America can live up to its ideals of economic opportunity, democratic freedom, and equality.

Hmmm, so nothing about Hitler, but still a little vague. Maybe a splash of religion mixed with a smidge of politics. But heck, I gotta hand it to her—she was getting involved and trying something new. Maybe this would be her new adventure instead of Paul. Quite honestly, I'm glad she gave Paul the stiff for one day—I mean, give it a break. Focus on this charity/social gathering thing instead.

January 19–21
(Tuesday–Thursday) Woke up sick on Tuesday and stayed sick. Mom said walking in the cold didn't do me any good. I rubbed my throat, tied it up, and gargled with kerosene, but it was still sore. Paul called every day. Asked how I felt. I said okay except for my throat. He told me he missed me. He said George and Frances were going to the show tomorrow night, and did I

want to go? Probably not. I told him if I felt better, I would probably hand out flyers with Glenys instead. He said it would be better on my throat to go to a show. I didn't say anything, so then he said he had to go and would call me later. He seemed mad, but I didn't know why.

Good Lord, gargling with kerosene?! What is kerosene anyway? Isn't that some type of gasoline or heating oil? Thank goodness for modern medicine! What does she mean she rubbed it and tied it up? I'm so confused. Anyway, this Paul dude seems only worried about himself and not so much about Didi. I mean, sure he's calling every day to check on her, but that last bit about him wanting her at the show instead of handing out flyers probably had nothing to do with him looking out for her welfare and everything to do with wanting her close. Some of that shit reminds me of my ex, Greg. Big trigger for me, makes me squirm. I hope Didi's not headed down the wrong path.

January 22

(Friday) Woke up at noon. Only worked Monday this week. My manager wasn't happy with me. Glenys called and then Paul called. I told them both I was still sick. Paul said he would go stag to the show. His brother, Burrows, was going now as well, with his girlfriend, Stella. I feel sad that I can't go because I want to see Paul very much, and I'm also starting to get worried about the meeting next week. Will we get enough ladies to come? Gail called and said she made twenty more flyers herself and handed them out and posted them at the student union.

All those old-fashioned names, like a bowl of sour radishes—Glenys, Frances, Roy, Gail, Vera, Burrows. Thank goodness Mom had the sense to name me Delia after Didi. What if Didi had been a Pearl or a Florence or a Gladys? Scary. Dodged a bullet there.

January 23

(Saturday) Throat finally better today. Mom told me to stay in anyway. Played on the Daisy Machine. Wrote a letter to Betty and Flora. James played rummy with me. Paul called. I asked him if he talked to any other girls at the show. He said yes and did I mind? I said, "No, as long as they were ugly." He laughed and said, "Two of them were very pretty indeed." I just responded, "Well, well, well..." We were quiet for a few minutes after that because I wasn't really sure if he was kidding or not. After a pause, he

said he wanted to see me tomorrow. My dad said I shouldn't go out, so I asked Dad if Paul could come for dinner, and he said yes.

Yeah, I'm sure it was the kerosene that fixed her throat.

January 24

(Sunday) Woke up early. Finally warmer out today. Washed my head. Helped Mom clean up and set table. Paul came with Frances and Frances's parents. Mom said, "My, how tall you are!" Paul replied, "Yes, ma'am." Even James looked short next to him. Dad asked him about growing up in Penn. He said he liked it, but he liked Rochester better. He winked at me after he said that. Everyone laughed. After dinner, we went out to the Nantucket for a while. I showed him my notes, and he thought they were swell. He asked if I was planning on being the next Molly Brown. I said, yes, unsinkable!

I won't even go back and calculate the last time she washed her head. What the heck is a Nantucket? A bench, a bar, a restaurant, a patio, a lanai, a deck, a porch, a chair, a hammock, a table? A what? At least I understand the Molly Brown reference—she was the brassy redhead from the *Titanic* movie.

January 25

(Monday) Sam and I worked on the ledger together. During my lunch break, I visited Paul and Burrows at the Stand. I met his mom, Mrs. Miller. She said hello, but she didn't smile. Paul made a date for Wednesday. After work, I went to Bernice's. Gail and Glenys were there. We went through our notes for the meeting together. Both Gail and I are going to be the speakers.

January 26

(Tuesday) After supper, Paul called and said he didn't have enough money for a show and could he just come over tomorrow night? I asked Mom and she said yes, he could come for dinner. I told him about how Sam was coming to the meeting with his sister. He didn't like that. First he said, "Why do you talk to him?" I said, "Because I have to work with him." Paul told me to ignore him from now on. I didn't know what to say to that, so we were quiet for a while on the phone until he said he would see me tomorrow and hung up. I don't like it when he gets quiet. I wish I knew what he was thinking.

Ride your horse, Didi—ride it! Oh, and by the way, you don't need to be listening to Sam or Paul in this situation anyway—just do your thing, girl, and screw both of them!

January 27

(Wednesday) The workday was long. I was having difficulty concentrating on the ledger, getting nervous about my speech tomorrow night. Luckily, Sam was assigned to a different job, so I didn't have to deal with him too. When I got home, I changed into a different dress. I went to meet Paul at the streetcar stop, and he took my hand and said, "I'm sorry about the call last night." I said, "It's okay." He smiled at me with those big blue eyes, and I couldn't help but smile back. He still held my hand on the way into the house, causing James to whistle and Paul to drop my hand quickly. Mom made stew. Paul ate two bowlfuls. Dad asked him about his job at the Stand. He said it was fine. Said his mom was strict but fair. We played pinochle. I wanted to ask Paul more about his past, especially if he had dated any other girls before, but we never got the chance because the whole family was with us. Maybe next time.

January 28

(Thursday) Woke up at 10:45. Paul called and said he had some gas on his stomach. He took some baking soda to cure it. He wished me luck at the meeting. Bernice and Frances came to the house, and Dad drove us all over to the YWCA. I spoke for a full half hour. I was nervous but used my notes when I stumbled. Everything came up aces! We have a lot of work ahead of us, but the meeting was a great success! When I got home, I went right to bed because I was so happy.

Baking soda, eh? Once again, thank god for modern medicine. Sounds like Didi kicked ass with her meeting, so that's cool. I'm a horrible public speaker—I had to get up in front of English class last semester and talk about my analysis of *The Red Badge of Courage*. I literally don't remember a single thing from that entire day. It was as though my nerves caused the synapses in my brain to overheat and break—a complete system failure. Total void. Somehow, though, I managed to get a B+ on the paper and presentation. Utter mystery. Looks like Didi was much my superior in many ways, although the jury's still out on her taste in men.

January 29

(Friday) I went down to the Stand at break, but Paul was busy. His mom frowned at me and told me not to come back. She's not very friendly. Went to a show with Bernice and Roy and Sam (who invited himself!). Halfway through, Sam tried to kiss me! I turned my face. Paul called late and I told him. He was mad! Said he was going to slug Sam.

First of all, that Sam dude, he's got quite the nerve! *She* should have slugged him! And I can totally see why Paul would be jealous in this situation. However—*big* however—I'm still feeling worried for Didi because Paul's jealousy reminds me of my psycho ex, Greg. If only I could reach back in time (à la Marty McFly in *Back to the Future*) and have a chat with Didi. It would go something like this: "Didi, listen, I know you're jonesing for this dude, but hey, a hot bod and some sweet-talking ain't the be-all and end-all. I know from firsthand experience. Sparkling blue eyes don't necessarily equate with smart, caring, and secure. Speaking of eyes, don't be blind. Watch your back, my friend. The way he's acting, he could go postal at any time." Of course, after that conversation, Didi would probably say, "Um, who are you? And who is Jones? What's a dude? Also, why do you say Paul is hot when it's the dead of winter in Rochester, New York? Plus, I don't know why you would suggest that Paul go to the post office. I'm very confused by you, future Delia robot girl." I would ignore that and then add one last thing: "Didi, also, let's be clear, Paul's mom sounds like a total bitch."

January 30

(Saturday) Woke up at 11:30. Paul came to the house, and we walked to the streetcar stop together. He was still sore about Sam and said, "I haven't even tried to kiss you yet!" Then he asked, "What if I tried?" I responded, "Don't know 'til you try." Then he kissed me right there on the street. It was wonderful and all was forgiven. We went to the bowling alley. While the men were bowling, I asked Frances if George was ever "moody." She said, no not really—only when he was hungry. That made me laugh. I told her sometimes Paul was jealous, and she just said, "Oh, that's natural since you just started seeing each other. I'm sure it will be better after a while." That made me feel better. I slept like a rock, thinking about that kiss.

So much kissing, Didi—get a hold of yourself! Very risqué. I thought they only held hands before marriage back then.

January 31
(Sunday) All the ladies came over for tea and scones so we could look at our notes from the meeting. In the end, we decided to plan a dance marathon. We think it will benefit the most young people because it will provide food and shelter for a whole weekend, not to mention potential prize money to the winning couple. We also thought it would increase the number of supporters for our Young People's group—we want to bring in new participants in advance of the presidential election, which is obviously later this year.

Hmpf, so maybe it will be a political thing in the end, this Young People's group. Still sounds a little like socialism to me, or communism, or maybe just some jacked-up religious group. Already thinking about the presidential election—another thing for me to look up on my phone someday...I have to say, it doesn't surprise me they're going with a dance marathon—seems as though they all really like to dance. That was probably the only way boys and girls were allowed to touch each other back then.

Chapter V

As I sat at the kitchen counter watching Delia retreat up the stairs, I wondered what I was doing wrong. It seemed like no matter what I tried, her life was still spiraling. And now, losing the job at Panera? Ugh. There may have been more to that story than she was letting on, but I'd be damned if I could discover the full truth. Dottie said she didn't know, and Delia didn't reveal a thing other than that it was no big deal. That's the way it's been lately. She used to talk my head off. Now she kept it all inside, a quiet little brown-headed mouse in the house.

Sometimes I wondered if many of Delia's troubles stemmed from the divorce. It had been seven years since Johnston and I had split up, but I still had a lot of guilt, and I also realized that no matter how good or bad any divorce is, these type of childhood traumas tend to linger. She was seventeen now, and I foolishly thought with maturity would come a sort of grace and understanding, but that was naive of me. I think those feelings of confusion, abandonment, and displacement never truly go away. I should know. It was hardly like I had a stellar upbringing myself. But Delia was such a clever girl. If she could just get past this horrible *incident* with the evil ex-boyfriend, I think she could become something extraordinary. She really was smart as a whip and not likely to date any jerks again, and she had so many possibilities. Maybe she could be a future blogger or one of those newfangled social influencers. She certainly had strong opinions about things and talked intelligently about current events and the most popular stuff on TV and in books. I guess in the meantime, though, I would need to bite my tongue when she lashed out or spent time (maybe rightfully so) torturing me (intentionally or not). She knew just where to poke—my soft spots, my vulnerabilities. My troubles with men, my drinking, my life choices, my lack of parenting and of being around. But could I blame her? Much like her and like the teenager I wasn't but still acted like more often than not, I was still working on myself and didn't have all the answers.

When it came down to it, more than anything I just wanted Delia to succeed in life—to be happy, responsible, and kind. And yes, I wanted her respect. Of course, at this juncture, what I was getting was the usual challenges to my authority, questions about my disciplinary methods, and pushing my limits and my buttons. Ultimately she was undermining her own success, but she didn't see it that way. Of course, it was crystal clear to me—I was the queen of self-sabotage, so I could detect the signs in someone else from a mile away. Just like me, she thought she was making all the right choices, all the right moves.

It's funny: people don't tell you when you're pregnant that it's just the beginning of a lifetime of worry. Oh yes, and joy, blessings, and happiness. And sometimes also unappreciated toil, blame, and drudgery. I remember when she was a baby, I held her like an egg or a piece of spun glass, and when I wasn't with her, I wondered if she was okay. When she started walking, I followed around behind her to make sure she didn't run into anything or fall on her head. I cuddled and coddled and coerced her into being my sweet little precious baby girl. I was going to make everything perfect for her and her brother. They were going to have the upbringing I never had. I wouldn't let anything hurt them.

When Delia was about three, she fell off one of the barstools in our kitchen, and her two front teeth went straight through her tongue. I'd stepped away for a second and there it was—the blood, the horror, the screaming, the wailing. I nearly passed out. But then I got myself together, scooped her up in my arms, pushed a wet washcloth into her mouth, raced to wake a surprised Tyler from his nap, plopped them both like rag dolls into their car seats, and drove like a maniac to the emergency room. After all that, the doctor said he wasn't going to even bother with stitches—he thought it would heal on its own within a few weeks, and sure enough, it did.

No amount of me protecting her kept her from hurting herself. Or healing herself, for that matter. I sighed. I was tired. All these years later and so much for my well-laid plans. I was exhausted and completely inept at navigating this irate, irrational, illogical wolverine, otherwise known as the teenage daughter. I got up, opened a bottle of wine, and sat back down to drink a glass. And what about Johnston? Why was he blameless and spared the drama of Delia? Well, maybe not totally—she'd spent that messy month with him following *the incident*. I bet that wasn't much fun for him or his new wife. I tried not to think about them too much. Or about the divorce. When it came right down to it, he was the one who left me, not the other way around, and it still rankled when I thought about him walking away and me having to hold the family together after that. Granted, maybe the divorce was warranted. Maybe I did some awful, horrible—unforgivable—things, but still, it took two to tango. Or in our case, two to torment. It was honestly better for a while after we split up. So many arguments with each other and in front of the kids were taking their toll.

Now it was mostly water under the bridge, and the only time I was super bothered by it was when I had to deal with the new wife. She was nice enough, and we were certainly civil with each other, but still, it was so *awkward*. For example, last year she presented Delia with a new car. I had an overwhelming feeling (maybe my own insecurities) that she did it to make me feel small. I mean, of course Johnston paid for it, but he let her present it, like handing over the ring to "my precious." Big red bow, all leather interior, shiny, black, slick, sleek. She even bought those all-weather floor mats! That was enough to send me right over the edge. I can hear her now: "These will be so helpful when it snows. You know, to protect your Uggs."

God! I growled, drank my wine, and thought, enough about them. Why was I spending a second of my time thinking about them anyway? I was forging my own way in this crazy, mixed-up, nonsensical world. Sure, one could look at me and think, on the one hand, what did I have to show for myself? This house? This leaky, dilapidated mess of a house? Two children who, let's face it, mostly hated me, or at least didn't think about me much at all. A boring, crummy job. Oh, I just turned fifty last year too. That wasn't exactly a fun transition. But, on the other hand, I did have a ton of things to be grateful for. Home ownership (the Diamond family house at that!) was nothing to shake a stick at (even in its current state of disrepair, where a stick may actually knock the whole thing down), two great kids (who were also great works in progress, but aren't we all?), a stable job that provided excellent benefits, great friends (the kind who stuck with me through thick and thin— including a yucky divorce), and great health (not even a single prescription medication!), so what was there to complain about? Nada. Good. I held my glass up to myself and said, "Cheers!"

And I'd been dating a nice guy on and off for a while now—someone from high school—and it was going well. Heck, the whole colossal nightmare with

Delia really was on the mend, despite how it looked with this latest debacle. I wasn't sure why, but I had this realization (even as Dottie was standing next to the limes and grapefruits relaying the news that Delia no longer worked at Panera) that it wasn't the right job for her anyway. She always came home even more miserable and withdrawn. I thought the job would allow her to socialize with the right kind of kids, but I guess I was wrong. Wasn't the first time and wouldn't be the last. At least she finished her junior year with good grades, and maybe now she would burn off some steam (literally and figuratively) up in the attic.

Back to my big five-oh. My cursed birthday a year ago. So funny, as in odd, not har har. I bought a new dress, got a blowout at the hair salon, put on my sexy red pumps to go with my sexy red panties, and went to meet my sexy red hot date (ironically, he had very rosy cheeks) at the local Italian restaurant. His name was Tony—my friend Tammy's brother. She told me his wife died of ovarian cancer three years ago but that he was lonely and "single and ready to mingle." Based on that, I figured my chances of getting lucky were at least seventy-five percent, plus it was my birthday, so I might get a free dinner out of the deal. When I walked into the bar, there he was: cute, dark, tall, a nice smile. He stood and kissed me on the cheek. He said the hostess could seat us any time, but I asked for a glass of wine at the bar first (I was nervous!).

"Sure, sure," he said. We had some small talk. Where did he work? Kodak. Of course. Didn't everyone? Story of my life, story of my family. He'd been there twenty-eight years. Said he was just one of a handful left after the bankruptcy, and he didn't know how long his job would be around. I said something empathetic, or pathetic—I don't remember. I told him a little about my job at the post office. Then we rattled on about our kids—how many, how old, the usual. Then the dreaded moment of awkward silence...tick-tock-tick-tock-tick-tock. Thankfully, the hostess came over like a mirage, thank you very much, and asked if we wanted to be seated.

Dinner and the wine loosened us up a bit. By the time my tongue was tickling the coffee bean at the bottom of my Sambuca glass, I was thinking, this birthday's going swimmingly. He was sweet and handsome and funny. And he was wondering if I'd like to come back to his place for an after-dinner drink. I said sure. We headed to his bachelor pad—really, literally, like a small prison cell in the form of an apartment. The fridge had a jar of olives, a stick of butter, and a twelve pack of beer, one of which he offered me. Okay, I thought, who cares, as long as the place is clean. And it was! We made out on the couch and eventually headed to the bedroom. My face felt flush, and I was all squishy inside.

Then, as we hit the bed and proceeded to endeavor something more substantial, I heard the strangest noise emanating from the bottom of his throat. I was thinking, this is great—he's already groaning. But wait. That was not a groan. Oh no. Oh no, no, no, no, no. I pulled back and peered into his face, obscured by the darkness. Was that a tear in his eye? Rolling down his cheek? I asked, "Is something wrong?" He couldn't even talk, he was so choked up. He was trying to apologize, but it came out in a croak. He was a mess. I got up and grabbed a tissue from the bathroom.

I shook my head. Didn't it figure.

Great. Now I'm making men cry.

He was sobbing into my shoulder, explaining that it was the first time he had tried to "make love" (is that what we were doing?) to a woman since his wife died. And then he proceeded to tell me that this was their actual bed. He had kept it for sentimental reasons. Good Lord. That was about the fastest way to make me jump up. I apologized, telling him I was getting more tissues, but when I came back, I reached a long arm out to him, handing them over like one of those mechanical crane toy dispensers. I muttered a few soothing words as he poured his heart out. Several minutes went by, me hovering awkwardly halfway between the bed and the door, him a bereft puddle in a pillow. Finally, I managed (as politely as I could) to make a hasty escape, hollering back at him, "So sorry for your loss. That must be so hard. I can't imagine. Thanks for the wonderful evening, you take care of yourself, you hear? Okay, yep, hang in there. I'll...I'll...um, I'll pray for you, yeah, um, my condolences...yes, uh-huh, so sorry, again, okay, bye now, yes, okay, bye."

I snuck out of there like a thief in the night.

Jeesh, nothing like ringing in my second half-century with a bang. Couldn't I have signed up for a root canal instead? A trip to the DMV? Stuck in traffic on the freeway in a snowstorm? Forced to suck a mouthful of Lemonheads? That was a year ago, and I still thought about Tony sometimes. My friend Tammy told me he was still struggling. Poor guy. Is it bad that my first words to myself as I drove away from his apartment were, "Damn, and I thought I had it bad! My life looks like a cakewalk compared to that." I know, I'm horrible. Don't judge. It's kind of like that feeling you get when you hear about someone your own age who dies of a massive heart attack. Okay, alright, yes, I first think, oh my god, that's awful! But then my second thought (admit it, you do it too!) is, shit, my life's looking pretty good right now. Heck, things aren't perfect, really maybe even a mess, but I'm still here!

On my fiftieth, one of my friends sent me a card. It had a funny picture of a woman standing over a man, her hands on his shoulders in comfort, his head in his hands. It said, "You're 50. You're not dead." I laughed out loud. No, I was still alive and kicking, even if my kick was slower and older.

And here I sat. As I chugged my wine, savoring the burn down my throat and pondering these greater issues, my phone dinged.

Brian. Texting. My current love interest. A man. See, this was a perfect example. This was what life had come to. A man texting me on a weeknight, in my lonely hour. I should have stood up and shouted, "I don't need you! I don't need anyone!" Instead, being the needy, hypocritical, Pavlovian dog that I was, I perked up. Darn it, Heather. Pathetic.

"Hey," his text said.

"Hey," I wrote back. Profound. I snarled at myself and shook my head, thinking, Heather, you aren't going to solve the world's problems in a day, especially not while sitting your fat ass down on this inconsequential barstool, tipping back a few as you contemplate your irrelevance. Maybe for now, just make lemonade out of lemons.

"What are you doing?" Brian asked.

"Drowning my sorrows. You?"

"That good? Well, don't get choked. I'm watching TV."

"Anything good?"

"Sports. Mostly flipping channels. Want me to come over?"

"No, can't. Delia's here. Grounded again. Or still. I honestly can't remember."

"Bummer. What was it this time?"

"Got fired from her job. One thing after the other. I've got her cleaning out the attic."

"Yowzah. Good one!"

"Yeah, I've had to get creative. Run out of every other punishment. Nothing left!"

"No doubt. Soooo, a booty call's out of the question then? :)"

"Haha, yep, sorry, Charlie. I'll text you this weekend. Maybe we can grab a bite."

"Ok, sounds good. Later."

"Bye."

Brian Napier. Such a nice guy. And rather naughty. I liked that. And he did stem the tide of loneliness sometimes. I was glad to have an excuse to turn him down tonight, though. It didn't come easy for me. He had become a bit of a crutch for me lately. And that really wasn't fair to him, or to me.

We went to high school together, but he was two classes behind me, so I didn't get to know him until a few years ago. My friend Andrea and I were out for drinks one night in Pittsford, and she saw him across the bar. He was with a few other guys. She walked up to him and introduced us. Oddly enough, he remembered me—said he didn't need the introduction and that he used to have a huge crush on me when I was on the girls basketball team! I felt bad. I didn't remember him at all. Apparently, we were in the same home economics class too. Looking into his warm brown eyes as he flirted with me, I thought, how could I have missed this guy? He was cute.

So, we started to go out, a little. Sometimes three times a week. Sometimes not for two months. It was a strange relationship—if you could call it that. Once I called him on New Year's Eve. Ironically, we were both home alone, watching the ball drop from our respective couches. We talked on the phone through the whole ordeal, making little kisses over the line when midnight struck. It was rather silly and maybe totally pathetic, but at the time it seemed surprisingly cozy and fulfilling. Like me, he was divorced, except he had two girls—also teenagers—so we commiserated a lot. He told me up front that he would never marry again. He had been burned by his wife, who left him for his best friend and moved to Oregon. She never saw the girls, and he was left to pick up the pieces. I told him briefly about my divorce and said I wasn't rushing to the altar either.

Lately, I found myself thinking about him more than I should. It wasn't that I didn't want to take that next step with him. After all, he really was a great guy. It was just that I had such a blighted history with men. Unintentionally (or was it? I could never quite figure that out), everything (and everyone) I touched seemed to turn to hell in a handbasket. I was playing it safe this time. I didn't want to get too close and ruin what we had, as undefined as it was.

Back to reality. I picked up the kitchen and headed to bed. Another thing about turning fifty that no one tells you: sleep is not your friend. Why is that? The thing I used to cherish most in the world—laying my head down on a super-soft pillow at the end of a hard day to embrace that sweet oblivion like an oasis in the desert. Ahhhh…

What a joke! Sleep was like a dirty rotten scoundrel now—seemingly kind and caring, only to pull the wool over your eyes at the last minute. Or never to pull the wool over your eyes, as the case may be. Always resisting my companionship like a fickle friend, wanting more and more from me and offering nothing in return. I lay there, staring at the wall, at the clock, at the ceiling, and thinking, thinking, thinking (over-processing; if I had been a computer, my motherboard would have exploded every night at about this time). Tossing and turning, clenching my teeth, until finally, mercifully, around two thirty, I drifted off.

The next morning as I was getting ready for work, I peeked in on Delia. She was sleeping, but I shook her softly until she opened her eyes and reminded her about the attic. I told her I'd be home this afternoon to help with the sorting and selling. She nodded groggily. Then, as I was about to head downstairs, she called me back and asked me the strangest question:

"Mom, what was Grandpa's name?"

"My dad? Ken Jacobs. Why?"

"No. Not *my* grandpa. *Your* grandpa. Didi's husband."

"Oh…Didi's husband? What? Why?"

"Just curious," she answered mysteriously.

I shrugged my shoulders. Strange child. I said, "Ronald. I mean, I called him Grandpa Ron, but his full name was Ronald Culver. He was a tough guy. Very strict. I think he had a rough childhood and then, well, you know, the war came and that made it worse…I think he was—"

"Ma-ma-Mom, okay, alright, I don't want the whole family history, I was just curious about his name, that's all."

"Okay. Fine. Well, it was Ron. Did you find something up in the attic about him? I think some of his war medals might be up there and maybe some of his Kodak stuff too. Did you come across…?"

"Um, no, no, nothing like that. I'll let you know if I see anything. Okay, thanks, you'd better get to work. I'm going back to sleep. Talk to you later."

Odd. Okay. "Alrighty, don't sleep in too long, I want to see some progress when I get home. Bye."

"Okay, bye."

I drove to work thinking about those photo albums. I loved looking at the photos of Tyler and Delia when they were toddlers. They were so pudgy and cute, really scrumptious, like cinnamon rolls—you couldn't help but squeeze and eat them up. Tyler's hair was a particular shade of red, like mine, that everyone commented on. Thick and dark auburn, reminded me of caramel molasses. And Delia had the chunkiest rolls in her thighs, with chestnut brown hair spilling down her back. I'd be out walking with them in the double stroller, and people would stop us to comment on how adorable they were. Tyler usually giggled, but Delia scowled at people defiantly. She was a little spitfire, even back then.

She reminded me sometimes of her namesake, Didi. Didi was in a bunch of those photos too, looking young and strong and happy, with her parents and friends, her aunts and uncles, people I didn't recognize or know. She was cute like Delia, with dark hair and dark eyes and something strong and solid about her. It was strange to think about what components made up a face: sometimes you could see how a family member had the same nose or lips or hairline or eyes. Yet at other times, when you looked at each individual part, they were really nothing alike. How did it work that a face that had no individual feature the same as someone else's could still be called a clone? The sum of the whole was somehow more than the parts. This was like Didi and Delia—so many individual features different, yet their overall look was the same. It was like a trick of the mind—their faces—no one could deny they were related, but you couldn't pinpoint how or which feature made it so.

Of course, I was thinking of Didi when Delia was born—my grandmother had been a forceful influence in my life, and I knew that if I had a girl, she must have her name. But now that Delia was growing up, I wondered sometimes if I had made a mistake. The strength of Didi was showing itself in the rebelliousness of Delia. I laughed. As if the heritage of their personalities was a given, an inevitable trait passed down through the generations. Certainly, I was being silly. One was not necessarily connected with the other. I was reading into things and trying to find my way. That was all. I should just give it up and realize we are all individuals, created uniquely, with the mystery of our true selves concealed at birth and sometimes lasting a lifetime. Thus, the foolhardy need to analyze the humans in our sphere. Isn't that what life was all about? The drive to solve the mystery of ourselves and those around us? God, it was never-ending! And yet it often led to so much lack of understanding in the end. Humans were so complex…

I sighed, still contemplating this as I walked into the back entrance of the post office. I overheard Tom talking to someone, so I quickly threw my purse in my locker and headed over to where he was standing.

"Hey. Morning," I said to Tom while looking curiously at a young woman standing next to him.

"Hey. This is Ashley. She just started today."

"Hi, nice to meet you." I shook her hand. She was tall and thin, with long blond hair. My first thought: you poor thing, don't you know that the P.O. will suck the very marrow out of your soul? Run. Run!

"Hi," she replied with a radiant smile. I tried to smile back. Okay, so maybe I was being too hard on the P.O. It really was a good, steady job, and when I went home at night, I didn't have it hanging over my head, like some of my friends who walked around in a stress bubble that was on the cusp of bursting at the least provocation.

Tom said, "I'm showing her the ropes back here in the sorting area, but Rob requested she sit with you at the counter to observe."

"Oh, he did, did he?" I hated training newbies. "Okay, sure, no problem. You just come up when you're ready, Ashley, okay?"

She nodded. Tom was probably over the moon. An ugly old bachelor, he loved socializing. Fresh meat. When I started as a young, naive new employee, he asked me out the first week, but I was married at the time. Of course, after the divorce, he was right back at it. I put him off, told him I wasn't interested in dating, which was true, not that I would have considered him anyway. Thankfully, he got the hint and left me alone. I wondered absently if he was still a horndog. Watch out, Ashley!

I went to my counter with a wry smile on my face, got the keys from my drawer, looked at the time (eight o'clock), and unlocked the doors. There was always at least one person out there waiting. Today it was Mr. Parsons. He was one of our regulars. He had a thriving eBay business selling antiques and miscellaneous vintage paraphernalia. He shipped packages several times a week. He always came in early.

"Hi, John."

"Hi, Heather."

"Going to be a scorcher today, I think."

"Yep, looks like it."

I went around to my counter and weighed his things. "Anything interesting this week?"

"Storm troopers."

"Huh?" I queried curiously.

"You know, *Star Wars*. All the rage. Bought a bunch of the figurines, or action figures, you know, from an auction out in Honeoye last week. A big cache of them. They're selling like hotcakes."

"Wow, great. Yeah, I think I used to have a Princess Leia. I don't know what ever happened to her…"

"Well, if you ever find her, let me know. She'd be worth a lot today!" As I finished his transaction, I had a thought. "Hey, John, I've got Delia cleaning out the attic this summer. I suspect she might find some good stuff, maybe even valuable stuff. Our attic is really old and really packed. If she finds anything, maybe you could help me sell it?"

"Sure, sure, I could do that," he said, nodding. "Of course, it depends on what it is, but yeah, I could look it over and assess what you have. If it's anything worth selling, I'd be happy to help. I must warn you, though, I take a thirty percent cut."

That seemed like a lot, but then what did I know? "Okay, great. Delia has this grandiose idea that she knows how to sell these things on one of those newfangled apps, but I'm afraid she has no idea what she's doing. I'm worried she'll just give away our family heirlooms, you know?"

"Yep, I hear ya. That's why I don't let my grandsons see the stuff I'm working on. They look and think they're toys. If I buy something at an auction or garage sale, I sell the good stuff and give the rest to them—they're none the wiser."

"Probably not, haha. I bet they love it." I adhered the mailing stickers to his packages and placed them in the big bins, turning back to swipe his card. "Well, you're all set. Have a nice day."

"You too. I'll be back in a few days, and we can arrange a time to look at your stuff. Tell Delia to be careful. Broken items aren't worth anything."

"Got it. Okay, will do. Take care, John."

As he walked away, I smiled sadly. He may have been right about that for family heirlooms, and sometimes I wondered if it was true of their owners as well.

CHAPTER VI

AFTER MOM LEFT FOR WORK, I lingered in bed for an hour or two, rereading Didi's diary and thinking about who she was and what kind of good stock I came from. Who knew? Total shocker. Why did Mom never tell me? I tried to remember anything she had ever said about Didi, and the only thing I could think of was that Didi helped raise her and Aunt Mary.

As I willed myself to get up, I stretched and screamed a tiny prayer to the sun gods, "Please let me not melt today." I went downstairs to get breakfast, casting an evil eye at the attic door as I walked by. Mom had left the upstairs hallway in total chaos. She was going to be the one to help me on this project? Uh-huh. Right. Sure.

Even though it was only ten o'clock in the morning, the thermometer hanging off the back window said it was already eighty-five degrees out. Let the roasting begin. I wolfed down a bowl of cereal and walked back up the gangplank. I decided to head to the corner where I'd found the music stand (isn't that what Mom called it?) to see what other treasures might be waiting there. The fan's whir kept the crypt's heebie-jeebies at bay. No talking heads today. Thank god. I found several crates filled with hints of days gone by. Mostly wool coats and silk scarves and other ancient, moth-eaten garb, but then I hit on a scrapbook tucked underneath a lace tablecloth. It was chock-full of photos, quotes, flyers, notes, scraps of paper, clippings, and stickers, glued with thoughtful arrangement into a stiffly bound, thick black paper binder. I set it aside for perusal later.

A few minutes after that, in another box, I found a different diary—with dates from the sixties. It was a spiral-bound notebook with angry, widely scrawled handwriting inside. The name on the inside flap was Ann Aster Culver. Hmmm, I think that was Mom's mom. The grandmother I never knew. The one who went crazy—or as Mom always corrected me, "was mentally ill." Mom never gave me further details, so I was left to speculate on what she meant. Maybe that notebook held a clue as to why Didi raised Mom and Aunt Mary instead of her. I laid it on top of the scrapbook.

Hours went by. Steadily, steamily, I unpacked, sorted, tossed, sailed, and rearranged. I threw fifteen large stuffed animals over the banister of the upstairs hallway and down into the front foyer; they needed express delivery to the donation center. Just about the time when it was getting too crowded to move around on the attic stairs, I heard a male voice. I jumped half out of my skin. Was I hallucinating again? OMG, it was back! "Hello? Is anyone here?" I stood stock-still, a stack of board games in my hands, listening. That was definitely a real person's voice saying my name.

"Delia, is that you? Are you up there? Holy crap, what is going on in this house?"

Oh! It was Jake. The neighbor. Damn my overactive imagination! Defibrillator, please...breathing again. Heart out on a stick, get back into my chest.

When I had my breath back, I hollered over the fan, "Jake! I'm up here. Hang on, I'm coming down."

I navigated my way through the tangled mess, landing on top of a rolled-up rug at the bottom of the stairs. I felt such relief at seeing him, having thought him a ghost, that I grabbed him in a bear hug.

I pulled back and said, "Hey! How's it going?" He stared at me with the hugest grin. I added, "Man, you are so tan! What have you been doing? Laying out?" I looked up at his dark face and green eyes, with his shock of blond feathered hair, and realized with a gasp of admiration how tall and lanky he was. When had he grown up?

After a second or two when our eyes were glued to each other and our smiles mirrored the sun and each other, he laughed and said with a wry quip, "No, I haven't been laying out. Do I look like a girl? I'm lifeguarding at the RCC." Then a moment later, breaking our stare, he casually started examining a tub of balls at his feet. He said, "Whoa, this is a lot of stuff. What is all this?"

I rolled my eyes and answered, "Oh, Mom's got me cleaning out the attic. I feel like I'm filming an episode of *Extreme Hoarders*."

"I'll say. Wow, sucks to be you, dude."

"Tell me about it." I shrugged.

"Can I take these balls?"

"Sure, have at 'em," I replied. "One less tub I have to worry about. Just leave the empty tub or bring it back when you're done. I'm using empty tubs to haul stuff away."

He stood up to face me with a tennis ball in his hand. "Sure. Thanks. This is great. What about these books? You gonna do anything with these?" He rifled through a few hardcovers and paperbacks.

I said, "Actually, I was going to look through those. Might be a few good ones. But whatever I don't keep, you can have. You read?"

He gave me a sideways look and countered, "Nope, totally illiterate." Then he returned, in good humor, "Of course I read. I'm halfway through Ken Follett's *War* series right now."

I raised my eyebrows and said, "Ken Follett? Wow, you *do* read! I love his stuff."

"Yeah, he's great." He smiled a wicked grin and said, "I love the historical stuff, plus he certainly knows how to weave a strong story, doesn't he?"

I caught his drift and laughed. I raised an eyebrow and stated, "Dirty."

He confirmed, "Yes."

We stood regarding each other in mute understanding.

It was about this time that I began to think I was having some type of heat stroke because I found myself sinking into the green flecks of light emanating from Jake's eyes, and I had the strangest revelation: This boy is totally gorgeous. And something more. What was it? A flash in his eyes, a reticence to reveal what was behind the flash and the secret that lay there. I narrowed my eyes to decipher the cryptic code, but before I could crack it he blinked, and the flash was gone. Then I stepped back, realizing I was acting just like Didi with her sparkling blue-eyed guy, Paul! Oh, good Lord. I spent a second wiping my sweaty forehead, shaking off that déjà vu feeling, and pushing my hair back into its sloppy bun.

Disarmed and stuttering, I asked, "So, wha-what's up with you?"

He paused for the briefest of instants to watch me watching him and then said, "Not much. So, hey, I was wondering, is Tyler around?" He looked toward Tyler's bedroom.

"Naw, he's still at school—he's got an internship this summer."

"Okay, bummer. We could've used him...oh well, I'll see if Mike Reiser's around..."

"Used him for what?""

"Pick-up games, down at the pitch."

"Oh?" I asked, curious, a little too eagerly, "Co-ed?"

"Well, uh," he said thoughtfully. "Um, no, not so far...but I mean, there aren't any rules or anything, really—just whoever shows up gets to play." He paused and then asked incredulously, "Why, would you be interested?"

"Anything is better than this! When do you play?"

"Well, we don't exactly have a schedule or anything, but most days at three."

"Shut up! That sounds awesome! Would your friends mind?"

"The guys? No, not at all, definitely not." He regarded me with a fully arched smirk, which sent an unexpected spark down my spine. I felt a flush rise on my face, which made him grin even more broadly.

"Okay, cool." I tried to act casual.

"I'll text you in a bit."

"Don't bother. No phone. Mom took it. Just swing by and get me, if that's alright."

"Okay, sure. Wow, you *are* in trouble, aren't you?" He laughed as he grabbed the tub of balls and started down the stairs.

I called after him, "Hey, so...I haven't played in a while. Are they going to destroy me? Who's going to be there anyway? Do I know them?"

"Naw, you'll be fine. I doubt you'll know them, but then again, maybe...they're from the neighborhood."

I started to get a tightness in my chest. "Yes, but...but...do they *know* me?"

Catching the change in my voice, he stopped on the stairs and looked back. Suddenly, significantly, I noticed something click in his brain. His eyebrows came together as he answered slowly, "You'll be fine. They're mostly from Aquinas. I'll tell them to take it easy on you. And Delia?"

"Yes?"

"I've seen you play. I don't think you have anything to worry about."

I exhaled with a small smile. "Okay, good. See you later then."

He skipped down the rest of the stairs and out the door, shouting back, "Later."

At least it didn't scare Jake away—that was an unexpected blessing. "It" was the usual: *the incident*. Again. It wound a tight cord around my life—like a viper—no matter how hard I tried to squash it.

Maybe I shouldn't go. Soccer was my absolute favorite, but still...Would they stare at me? Would they *know*? What if they assumed things about me? How should I act? What should I say? What should I do?

Damn Greg Ashworth! Sometimes, I thought it was left in the past. After all, it had been so many months now. Yet, it was still there, just below the surface. I sat down on a tub and let the memories, horror, and guilt wash over me. It was the only way—steep myself, then purge it from my system. Like a drug detox. Until it came back to visit. Always like this, out of the blue, when things were feeling stable and normal again—bam! Back into the dark vortex. Dig into it, Delia, like a grave. And while you're at it, down in that deep black cavern, shovel a pile of dirt on your head—you deserve it!

At times like this, my first thought was always: why did I stay? Someone please remind me because I swear it makes no flipping sense. How could I stay with someone who said they loved me more than life itself and yet criticized *every single thing* I did? Every word out of my mouth, the way I walked and styled my hair, my clothes, my friends, my family, my house (well, that one I understood), my body (my thighs were too big, my knees were too pointy, my toes were too long, my eyes were too boring, my hair was too straight), too this, too that, too, too, too. He even used to say I blinked too much—what? How does someone blink too much? Seriously.

Oh, but he was crafty. Yes, he was. He would temper all of that dumping on me with over-the-top professions of love and adoration. Or was it *possessions* instead of professions? He would tell me he loved me more than anyone else, that he was the only one who knew me, who could take care of me, understand me the way he did. He told me I was everything to him. That he wanted to be with me for every waking moment of every day. If I wasn't with him physically, he wanted me to text him and send him photos or call him. I confess there were times when I told him I was vomiting or on the rag just to get a break. Usually these situations ended with him coming to my house to check up on me, realizing I wasn't sick, and exploding in a furious, seething rage that included demeaning me for hours until I apologized and begged for the chance to make it up to him. Which he made sure I did.

Then after almost a year, he breaks up with me! Said he found someone else who wasn't so needy! OMG, WTF! The *dick*. Being the foolish weakling he had molded me into, I pleaded with him to come back, so he finally left the other girl in the dust, much to my satisfaction. I thought the world was back turning on its rightful axis again. All was well. But then we had another blowout. He saw me talking to a boy in school—I was innocently asking him about a homework assignment. This sent Greg into a tirade, saying I was cheating on him and that I didn't know what was good for me, how he shouldn't have ever gotten back together with me because I was just a stupid, ugly, fat bitch. This all happened in plain view of everyone standing in the school hallway gawking. I cried and implored him to calm down, to be quiet, but he wouldn't listen. It was mortifying. I think some people knew about our tumultuous relationship, but now they knew the full extent of it. Greg screamed his final words, echoing off the walls, "We're done this time. For good. And you're gonna pay for it this time, you hear? Just you wait, you little bitch!"

I left school in the middle of the day, went home in fear, and cried my eyes out. I couldn't imagine what he meant. It was probably good that I couldn't imagine it because it ended up being much worse than what seemed in the realm of possibilities.

As I was driving to school the next morning, I thought it was odd that I hadn't heard from Greg. Usually when we were fighting, he would write me angry, heated, irrational texts for hours. Instead, there had been radio silence. It sent a chill down my spine—what was he up to? I didn't think we were over. Yes, he said we were, but it wasn't his style to simply let it drop, so I figured he was letting me stew a bit. When he said we were done for good, that usually meant done for a short period of time during which I was made to feel like shit and he was made to feel as though he deserved my repentance. Basically holding me off until he felt I was good and miserable. Then he would come back like a knight in shining armor to tell me I was forgiven and make it all better. I was sure that was it. Then, trying not to overanalyze, thinking I was being ridiculous, I took a deep breath and sang along with a song on the radio. Surely I would see him in a few minutes in class and all would be forgiven.

Then my phone started to light up. There we go, that had to be him. Text after text after text. I glanced down with a smile on my face. But my smile faded quickly when I saw it wasn't him. It was friends, lots of friends. And then people's numbers I didn't know. Whoa. Weird. Before I could think, my phone rang. I picked it up. It was my friend McKenzie, who asked if I was sitting down. I told her I was driving. She told me in an urgent voice to pull over. "Why?" I asked. She said, "Just do it!" I replied, "Okay, okay, I'm pulling into a church parking lot."

Then she blurted it out: Greg had texted photos of me to tons of people—intimate photos, private photos, photos that were for his eyes only. Fifty people, maybe a hundred, she wasn't sure how many. She forwarded me the photos. They were labeled: "Delia Marie Elliott, the biggest whore at Franklin."

As I sat in my car, I actually saw stars. Like they show in the cartoons when someone gets hit over the head. Stars in front of my face, floating around in my vision. I had the strangest sensation of wanting to pass out and throw up at the same time. I sat there like that for a long while—I don't remember how long, maybe two minutes, maybe a lifetime. When I could breathe, I took my seat belt off and opened the window.

Now, all these months later, I sat on a tub of antique mementos, flogging myself with the oh-so-modern memory of *the incident* that unraveled and ruined my life.

After *the incident*, there was *the fallout*. My life went totally nuclear. Within a few hours, pretty much everyone in my entire school and my entire town had seen the photos. Including my mother. And my father. And my brother. And my dentist. And my nursery-school teacher. And the bag boy at the grocery store. And every single person I had ever known in my entire life.

I was a colossal hot mess—mortified, inconsolable, suicidal. Mom sent me to a counselor, Doctor Peterson, who thought the best course of action was to get into a normal routine again, so after a week, Mom insisted I go back to school. It was a torture of the rawest, acutest kind. I felt every snub, sneer, and leer like a hot, burning fire poker to my psyche. I heard the whispers and giggles. I saw the boys (and even the teachers!) look me up and down. It was awful. Dad went to the police to see if he could get a restraining order, but they said there was no overt threat. He also talked to a lawyer to press charges, but they said when I'd originally shared the photos with Greg, I'd given him my implied consent in the first place, and there was nothing to be done. Dad wanted to talk to Greg's parents, but I told him that would be a waste of time. Greg's dad wasn't in the picture, and his mom worked three jobs and was never around and mostly expected Greg to raise himself. Dad was frustrated and irate and impotent, and eventually gave up trying to seek containment. Like my life, he realized (and I realized and Mom realized) that *the incident* really was nuclear, with radioactive toxins that would continue to leak out like a never-ending stream of poison that can only expand over time, and there was nothing we could do about it.

So I did what all rational human beings do in the face of abject hopelessness— I doubled down. Granted, prior to *the incident*, I had hardly been a Pollyanna or on a life course meant for valedictorian and Ivy League bliss. I spent most days with Greg—skipping classes, smoking, drinking, doing drugs—whatever he wanted, whenever he wanted it. After *the incident*, I figured what was the point of even showing up (for anything, for life)? Forget just skipping school, I skipped *every-thing*. I ran into some scummy new friends at the convenient store and disappeared with them for days. It was all kind of a blur, like a hazy, lazy, stoner-filled fog. I don't remember much, but I do remember hooking up with several boys, maybe more than several—sure, why not? A self-fulfilling prophecy—or a Greg-fulfilling prophecy, as the case may be. Isn't that what everyone assumed anyway? I was a lot of fun. Or not. I enjoyed the numbing sensation. And the dumbing sensation. The sensation that no matter what I did, I was always going to be the girl everyone had seen naked. No brain, no brass, no basic human rights of any kind. It was a wonderful feeling. Can you blame me for self-medicating?

Mom was frantic, desperately trying to reel me in. She locked me in the house. I escaped. She took away my electronic devices. I stole them back. She sat me down and talked to me (and talked, talked, talked until she was blue in the face), but I didn't give an inch. What was the point? Talking wasn't going to change anything. Finally, exasperated, she shipped me off to Dad's. That lasted one month.

He said I was making Beth (the wife) nervous with my quiet, gloomy, dejected presence, moping around the house in dismal despair and sleeping twelve to fourteen hours a day. Swift boomerang back to the D.D. and Mom's ever-present, ever-pathetic attempt to help me *move on.*

Then one day, out of the blue, I had an epiphany about the whole thing—*the incident* and the aftermath. It was this: Fuck him! Excuse my French. No, really. Don't. Because I mean it—fuck him! Fuck that son of a bitch Greg Ashworth. Why was I letting him ruin my life? Why was I letting that asshole *define* me! Why would I give him the satisfaction, the power of knowing he made me self-implode?

#MeTooFuckYou.

I decided (much to my mom's consternation—what was Delia up to now?) to do an about-face. I removed my piercings, covered up my tattoos, avoided contact with my prior nasty acquaintances, sobered up, and tried to pick up the pieces of my broken life. I went back to class, and instead of groaning when my teachers called on me, I answered. Much like Mom, they thought, wait, what just happened—did Delia Elliott just answer that question, and correctly?

When I was home, I stayed inside, away from people for a long time, like months. Finally, I got up the nerve to approach my old buddies and former friends from B.I. (Before Incident). It wasn't easy. Everyone had moved on with their lives, and I was a used piece of toilet paper flushed down the rusted pipes of a toxic landfill. At best, they were in a state of resentful reserved suspicion. Why was I talking to them now when I had been absent for so long? Not to mention, why would they associate with me when my reputation was so distasteful and appalling (for reasons justified and not).

If only I could have announced over the P.A. system: Please wipe all prior knowledge of Delia Marie Elliott (including unmentionable text and subsequent actions) from memory banks and begin anew. Coming soon to a theater near you: The New Delia. It's a thriller, keeps you on the edge of your seat, no one knows how it will end.

Okay, so I hadn't turned into a complete psychotherapist or anything, but I did try to step outside myself and understand how I got to this place. Self-reflection and introspection were good, right? Of course, so was self-recrimination. In retrospect, I may have been a needy, blind, rebellious teenager doing what teenagers do—crying out for attention and getting it in all the wrong places. I would never admit this to Mom, and I hated to admit it to myself, but all the disdain I used to hold for other weakling girls my age went right out the window. What right did I have to judge anyone when I had been a sniveling idiot playing right into the hands of that domineering, controlling, manipulative dickhead? Ending in the biggest, most heinous humiliation brought on by my own insipid, vapid, urge-to-be-loved carelessness.

Yes. Mine. ME. Oh sure, Greg was mostly to blame, but I was the fool who sent him those photos. I was the pathetic parasite who stuck to his side when he made me feel like crap about myself. What did he offer me in return? Criticism, hatefulness, shame. And now I was trying to figure out how to dig myself out of the hole of horror. And stand on my own two feet. Why wasn't there a way to go back and redo entire portions of my life? WHY? I was on a road filled with potholes and divots. It was a long, bumpy road, and I was only about a half-skip down it, but all I could do was keep moving forward and make that road something *different* in the future. Something better. At least I was at the bottom—there was nowhere to go but up.

I often mumbled this mantra to myself: "Keep it moving, Elliott, no stopping, no looking back, no looking to the side or to anyone else. Just look in the mirror and look ahead. That is all you can do. Period."

My words to live by. My words to survive by. By a thread.

A very thin, tiny, taut, twisted, transparent thread.

℘ Chapter VII ℘

February 1
(Monday) Woke up at 9:15. My birthday month! Paul called, and I told him my birthday was on leap day and I was going to be 5 years old! He said I looked fantastic for my age. I said he had 28 days to think of something good for a birthday gift. He said he already had a few ideas. Bernice came over for an hour this morning to plan the meeting for Thursday night. Today I worked noon–8:00. Inventory. Went to bed right when I got home. I was tired.

Wow, Didi was a leap year baby—not something you hear about every day. I'm not even sure why we have a leap year in the first place. I mean, it's sort of illogical, like how the new moon really means no moon and how when we have bad weather in February, we have to take our "snow days" in June. On a different note, I honestly can't keep track of all the jobs Didi does at this place—office, ledger, payroll, layoffs, books, register, switchboard, inventory. I'm exhausted just reading about it. And I still have no idea where she works.

February 2
(Tuesday) Worked all day on the inventory. Sam was there, asking me questions. I ignored him (mostly). Went to the Stand to visit Paul. He couldn't talk long because it was busy. His mom gave me a look, so I left. Paul called at 9:00 tonight. He said I looked nice today. Wanted to make a date for Friday, but I told him I would probably be too tired because of the inventory and the meeting. He suggested we go to the matinee show on Saturday instead. I asked if he was coming to the meeting on Thursday, and he said yes, if his mom would let him leave before closing. He asked me if Sam was still trying to kiss me, and I said, "No, but he is still annoying me." He said, "Well, don't let me near him. I'll knock his block off." Honestly, it's funny

to picture that because Paul has to be at least five inches taller than Sam. Sam wouldn't stand a chance.

February 3
(Wednesday) Work, work, work. Too tired to write.

February 4
(Thursday) Meeting was a success! Paul was there (with Burrows) and said I was amazing. We told all the ladies to invite their men this time—brothers, cousins, boyfriends—and they did! We had a large crowd, so that helped with the planning of the dance marathon. Just like last week, Glenys wrote on the board and Bernice wrote in her notebook. We have the longest list of tasks, including figuring out the date and location of the dance marathon, but at least we'll have a lot of help. The only thing that was kind of odd was that Paul came up to me right afterward, put his arm around my waist, and tried to steer me outside. He said, "There are too many people in here. Let's go get some air." I went outside with him for a few minutes and he kissed me, which sent me to the moon, but then I told him I wanted to go back inside since I hadn't yet finished making arrangements with Gail and Glenys. As I started to walk back toward the door, I thought he would follow, but instead he walked away down the street without saying goodbye. Inside, Burrows and Stella asked me where he was, and all I could do was shrug my shoulders. I'm going to have to talk to him because I don't understand.

Shit, these kids were organized! And double-shit, Didi, you've got one psycho ex-boyfriend in training there. Greg used to always rain on my parade too. The happier I was and the more fun I was having, the more he would make sure I was removed from that equation, STAT. Oh Didi, I'm afraid for you! Question: Does it make me totally jaded and cynical that I now see all men as selfish, self-absorbed, arrogant a-holes? Hmmm, I'll need to think on that...

February 5
(Friday) On my feet all day with the inventory. Stella came by and asked to help with the organizing. She couldn't come to the meeting last night but still wanted to assist. I assigned her to food and told her how we were planning to provide a nearly continuous supply of food throughout the weekend (day and night). She laughed and said, "Wow, maybe I should request

*another assignment." When she left, I was counting scarves in a box, but
I was thinking about the whole undertaking of the dance marathon and
wondered if we had bitten off more than we could chew. Didn't see or talk
to Paul.*

Last year at my high school, they did a dance marathon to raise money for the
senior trip. The whole shindig was from Friday night at 7:00 pm until Saturday
morning at 7:00 am. A measly twelve hours. These young people of Didi's are
planning a dance marathon for the *whole weekend.* My feet hurt just thinking
about it, not to mention my bladder and my bowels. You gotta wonder if that's
totally legal. I mean, imagine the liability, like, how would that work from a medical
standpoint? Wouldn't people pass out or vomit or cry or hallucinate? Did they just
let them fall to the floor and leave them to fend for themselves? Have ambulances
standing by? I wonder...

February 6

*(Saturday) Woke up at 11:30. Paul called first thing and wanted to know if
we were still going to the matinee. I said, yes, that was fine, but I wanted
to talk to him afterward. He paused before saying okay. He hadn't even
mentioned the other night, as if it hadn't happened! Although he said okay,
I began to be afraid to bring it up myself. Frances came over, and on the
way to the streetcar to meet George and Paul, I told her everything. She
said she thought Paul was just getting used to being in a new town with
all new people and probably didn't like the fact that I knew everyone and
everything. She said, "Boys don't like that. He was probably just intimidated by your popularity." I said with a grin, "Well, I can't help that." She
laughed and said, "True." I thought about our conversation all through the
show. He didn't try to hold my hand, and it was almost as though we were
strangers sitting side by side. Finally, when it was over, George and Frances
said they had to go visit George's parents and left in the other direction
while Paul and I went to a diner to eat wieners and fries. After a lot of
silence, he said he was sorry and told me he didn't like for me to be around
so many boys. I told him that in a matter of time, he would get to know
these boys and become friends with them, and then he would realize he had
nothing to worry about. He said okay but looked very dejected for the rest
of the meal. At the end, we parted at the streetcar stop. He leaned down,
gave me a kiss, and said he would "try to be better next time."*

Apparently, men were Didi's weak spot. That's all I can think of, and I guess I can relate. Why did Mom never tell me about this Paul dude and Didi? She must have known about him. I mean, it seems as though they're pretty serious in the diary, but I realize this was long before Mom was even a blip on her radar (or her daughter's radar), so maybe something happens to change the course of things. I honestly hope so. Of course, I could always ask Mom. But then I'd have to tell her about finding the diary. We haven't exactly been in a "sharing mood" lately. And I also kind of want to get through the rest of it and see where it goes before I start grilling her about it; then she'd probably spill the beans on everything before I've had a chance to figure it out myself. Hmmm. Mum's the word, I think, or rather no-Mum's the word.

February 7

(Sunday) I felt so good about my talk with Paul that I got up early and made breakfast for the family. I called the Stand at noon. Burrows answered and said Paul was busy and couldn't talk. He called me back at 2:30 and wondered if he could come down for supper. Dad said yes. He came, and Dad asked him questions about the Stand. Paul told him it was busy sometimes but not always. The weather was warm, so we spent an hour or two on the Nan. He told me what it was like growing up in Pennsylvania. The restaurant they owned was for the miners, but when his dad died, his mom had trouble keeping it going. She didn't want the miner's life for her boys (apparently her dad and grandpa both died in a mining accident in 1910), so when his mom's sister (Frances's mom) said they might find work in Rochester, they sold their place in Penn. and moved into an apartment up here on Lyell. It was nice to hear more about his life. Now I think I know why he hasn't invited me over to visit his place because it sounds rather small. I walked him to the streetcar stop. He kissed me and said I was the prettiest, nicest, smartest girl he'd ever known. I asked him jokingly if I was the only girl he'd ever known, and he smirked and said no, of course not. Then I had to get serious and ask if he'd dated a lot of girls in Penn. His face suddenly became dark, and he said softly, "Just one." I didn't want to pry, so I said, "Oh." Later, I had trouble sleeping, wondering what she was like.

Didn't Mom say that Didi's husband's name (Mom's grandpa) was Ronald Culver? Then how did Didi go from this Paul dude, who obviously worshipped her, to ending up with Ron Culver? I mean, there must be some major breakup coming, right? Did people really break up back then? I figured it was always meet someone, fall in love, get married, and you're done—stick a fork in you. So strange. Of course, I'm rather rooting for a breakup because I'm seeing a lot of red flags. We'll see...

February 8

(Monday) Sam and I worked on the payroll until lunchtime, then he insisted on going with me to the Stand. Paul came around the counter to kiss me, which made Sam red and made me laugh. I love it that Paul doesn't mind kissing me in public. Although we've never officially talked about going steady, it seems as though we must be when he kisses me like this. He told me he had to work late every day this week, so I probably won't see him much, which made me sad. Bernice came over and we started organizing for Thursday's meeting. She said she and George had already created several potential flyers and wanted to bring them to the meeting to ask everyone's opinion. I said that sounded grand. Glenys and I are going to scout locations this weekend.

February 9–11

(Tuesday–Thursday) Weather got cold quickly. Sam and I worked on the books all week. He teased me about the kiss. Jealous. I bought a pound of Fanny Farmer's for Sullivan (a bet). He paid me 15 cents for the milkshake he owed me. Paul called and I told him about the candy, and he didn't like it. Said he didn't like me being gay with other boys. I told him, "I only like one boy." Glenys and I picked four locations we want to visit this weekend: Elmheart, Phoenix, Summerville, and Glen Haven. Meeting on Thursday went well—everyone made progress on their tasks. After we pick a location, we can pick a date. George's flyer design is perfect. A lot of details still pending, but many hands make light work!

I guess "being gay" meant something entirely different back then. Otherwise, that sentence makes no sense whatsoever. Btw, who the heck is Sullivan? Didi certainly *did* have a lot of "friends." Maybe Paul had a reason to complain. Although, she seems to be only interested in Paul, so what do I know? Maybe girls back then kept all their options open until some dude put a ring on it. Btw, fifteen cents for a milkshake sounds awesome. I could really go for one right now. These places they mention for the dance marathon, I wonder if any of them are still around. I'll need to check on that. My lack of Google and Wiki right now is about to kill me. Totally stymied.

February 12
(Friday) Bernice was here at 2:00. Roy called and wanted to know if the three boys could come down. When they came, we had lunch and wrote down more notes about the dance marathon. Paul called and said he couldn't come out until tomorrow due to work. Went bowling with Bernice and the boys at the Genesee. Roy bowled a 220! Stayed all night at Bernice's.

February 13
(Saturday) Met Glenys at the streetcar, and we visited the Elmheart. I think it will work because it's big and open and beautiful—such pretty details on the walls, the moldings around the doors, and the whole house-like feel of it. Plus, it's down on Manitou Beach, so dancers can take breaks and walk out by the water if they like. It's so close to the streetcar stop too! The only problem is that the owner wants 50% of ticket sales. We tried to explain that we need a larger portion of the money for food, drinks, prizes, and decorations, and also some left over for our Young People's organization. He didn't seem to want to listen to two girls, so I told Glenys we would go to the other places tomorrow and then have more leverage for renegotiating. Glenys came home with me for dinner. Paul came over, and we all played hearts. Glenys left at 8:00, and then I walked Paul to the streetcar stop. He told me he'd missed me all week. We kissed and I told him I appreciated him not getting worried about me when we weren't together. He laughed at me and said worried wasn't the word he would use, but thanks for appreciating it. I wanted to ask him questions about his past and the "just one" girl, but the streetcar came and we had to say goodbye.

February 14
(Sunday) Helped Mom in the morning because we had company for dinner (Homer, Leona, and their kids). We played coffee pot and pinochle. I met Glenys at 1:30, and we went to Summerville and Glen Haven. Summerville wasn't big enough, and Glen Haven was booked for both of our proposed weekend options. We still asked about prices, and they said they only take 20% of ticket sales. The Elmheart is too much! We still have to see about Phoenix. Paul called and asked me to be his valentine. He said he'd give me my gift if I came to the Stand tomorrow. I made him a card.

I've heard of pinochle, but what the heck is "coffee pot"? Sometimes, I swear I'm deciphering a foreign language with this diary.

February 15

(Monday) Work was busy—I was on the register all day and couldn't get to the Stand. When I got home, James told me Paul had called three times. When I called him at home, Burrows told me he was still at the Stand, but when I called the Stand, his mom said he'd just left. Finally, he called late, and Dad answered and came to get me out of bed. Paul was mad or sad or something—I wasn't sure—said he'd wanted to give me my gift but we'd missed each other. I'm beginning to notice that Paul can be sensitive. Went back to bed but couldn't sleep.

Sensitive? Puh-lease. It's more than that, girl.

February 16

(Tuesday) Back on the ledger today with Sam. He said Paul had come by the day before, but I had already left. Apparently, Sam decided this was his chance and asked me to go to the Manitou on Friday night. Of course, I refused, but he said he'd wait to see if I changed my mind before he asked another girl. I told him to go ahead—I wasn't going to change my mind. Paul didn't call, and I didn't see him. I guess he's mad. Doesn't make sense—why is he mad at me? *Just because I'm not always available to him? Frances and Gail came over to plan for Thursday's meeting.*

Gotta hand it to Sam—he's persistent. But he needs to take a chill pill at this point. So does Paul, for that matter. Didi, can't you see how insecure he is? I wonder why...she needs to probe a little more into that ex-girlfriend from PA situation. Maybe that'll unlock something.

February 17

(Wednesday) Paul called. I didn't have to work, so he came over on the streetcar in the morning before he went to the Stand. Said he was sorry, that he didn't mean to be jealous of other boys. I told him again there was only one boy for me. He kissed me and gave me my valentine—candy and a card that said, "Sweets for my sweet." He liked the card I made him. We're better now, and I'm trying not to remember how we weren't getting along earlier. He said he can't come to the meeting on Thursday because of work, but he and Tony were going to visit several five-and-dimes to see if they would donate prizes for the dance marathon. That was nice of him. Tonight when I looked out the window at the snow, I prayed that we would stay this happy forever.

A bit of a roller-coaster. Sticking your head in the sand won't make it go away. Once again, I'm having flashbacks to my ex. Puke. Always with the apologies and repentance and promises to do it better in the future. I remember I used to tell Greg, why don't you just not do these bad things in the first place, and then you won't have to apologize for them afterward and shovel up a bunch of empty promises? He would always say for every bad thing, it was the *last* bad thing. Ya, right. I talked to my dad about it once, and he said, "Good intentions do not guarantee good results." Ain't that the truth.

February 18
(Thursday) Worked on the ledger and told Sam to buzz off. I left early to get a permanent wave. James said I looked like a poodle. Brothers! Paul called, but I didn't tell him about it—wanted it to be a surprise. He said Burrows and Stella were going to the Manitou tomorrow night, and did I want to go too? I called Frances and George, and they're going. We made a lot of progress at the meeting, but most everyone is waiting for Glenys and me to pick the location. Without the location, we can't finalize the date or ticket prices or flyers or anything! I told them how sorry I was—with work, it was too hard to visit every location. Glenys and I agreed we'd need to finalize our choice on Saturday.

Permanent wave = a perm?

February 19
(Friday) On the switchboard all day. Frances came down and helped me style my hair and put on color. We met the boys at the Manitou at 8:15. Paul said my hair looked swell. We danced for hours until my feet hurt. I told him this is what it will feel like at the dance marathon. Sam came over and danced with me. Paul gave him a dirty look and was mad when Sullivan came over and asked to dance too. After that, I took Paul into the other room so we could talk. I asked him why he was always so jealous. He denied it and said it was because I was always favoring other boys. I ignored that and probed, "What happened to you? With that other girl in Pennsylvania?" His bright blue eyes went so black that I was a little scared. He looked away and said, "Nothing." I grabbed his hand and said, "Come on—we shouldn't have secrets. Please tell me." Finally, he looked back at me and answered, "She was a girl...I grew up with, and...and..." He stopped and I felt my heart in my throat as he finished, "...we were engaged."

Engaged! I took my hand away in shock. When I could find my voice, I asked, "What happened?" He only stared off in the distance with an angry (and hurt?) scowl and replied, "I don't want to talk about it." No matter how I cajoled him after that, saying that nothing he could say would make me like him less, he was steadfast and refused to say another word about it. The rest of the night, he was quiet. I went home and cried something terrible.

Whoa! Dun, dun, dun. The plot thickens…

February 20

(Saturday) Woke up miserable. I'm still not sure what to make of Paul's confession last night. On the one hand, I really want to hold him in my arms and comfort him. Last night, he seemed like a lost child to me—and I wanted to make everything better. But then on the other hand, I wanted to know what happened between him and that girl, and he wouldn't tell me, which made me frustrated. I think if I knew, I could find a way to talk through our difficulties. In the meantime, though, I couldn't take any more time this morning to think about it because Glenys and I had our day mapped out—to finalize the location of the dance marathon. We decided to go straight back to the Elmheart and negotiate with the owner. We explained how the other locations only charge 20%. He said, "Well, go use them—I'm trying to run a business here." Glenys looked so mad she could have burst, but I simply said, "Sir, think about the number of young people we're bringing into your establishment. Sure, you're right off the streetcar stop, but if people don't know your place is here, they won't come. After the dance marathon, they'll know, and they'll only want to come here to dance." His eyes narrowed at me, and he said, "40." I replied, "20." He said he couldn't do any better than 30 no matter what, but Glenys chimed in meekly, "Sir, I heard that you're a fair man. You wouldn't want to take advantage of two young women trying to make the world a better place, would you?" He sighed and stared at her so hard, then said, "25. That's my final offer." We nearly screamed but resorted to shaking his hand heartily and left before he could change his mind. Happy, happy, happy!

Good for them—they didn't let that old miser take 'em for a ride—nice! With regard to Didi and Paul, she's so noble to try and comfort and fix him. I just don't know if it's worth the effort or not. Maybe stick with the charitable stuff instead.

February 21–25

(Monday–Thursday) Busy week at work. I've been on the switchboard. Only got a few minutes for lunch, so didn't see Paul until Wednesday night—he came over and we listened to the Ku Ku Hour on the radio. He still wouldn't talk about the girl in Penn. and instead told me he had something special to give me on my fifth birthday. Meeting on Thursday was aces! Everyone liked the Elmheart location and the deal we brokered. Date for dance marathon is weekend of March 25, 26, 27. Weather bitter cold this week, so went to bed early every night.

I found an old radio up in the attic—gotta be the same one they listened to the "Ku Ku Hour" on (and "Baron" and "Amos and Andy"), right? I wonder if it still works. I'm gonna take it down and see if Jake can help me with it.

February 26

(Friday) Woke up late. No work today, so I washed my head and did patch-work. Bernice came down with Roy. We worked on the flyers and talked about going to a show, but Paul called and said he had to work the Stand because his mom was sick. He made a date for the morrow. Roy invited the boys over, and we played rummy until late. Bernice stayed over.

February 27

(Saturday) Met Paul, Bernice, Roy, Sullivan, Henry, Fleming, and Pearl at the park to ice-skate. Paul held my hand, and we tried a flip and a jump but fell down. He's too tall for me! He said I'm no Sonja Henie, which made me laugh. Bernice and Roy helped us up. They fell several times too. We left late after our hands and feet were numb. Paul was in such a good mood (maybe because of his confession?), I feel like I can't rock the boat, so I'm not asking any more questions—just enjoying our time together.

That's great. Ostrich much? Can I blame her, though...I was just as bad with Greg. When the bear's calm and well fed, don't poke it, right?

February 28

(Sunday) Spent all day working on the flyers with Bernice. Went home for supper. I was on the Daisy Machine for a few hours. Paul called and said he and Tony had trouble with the prizes. Stores didn't want to donate. He wondered if we could provide homemade items. I thought that might

work. Told them we would talk about it at the next meeting. I said most couples want to win the first-place prize money, but I thought the other couples should get something too. However, maybe it didn't matter much. We would ask and see what everyone wanted to do.

February 29

(Monday) My birthday! I worked the books with Sam most of the day, which wasn't such a great birthday gift. I went to the Stand at lunch, and Paul said he would come over after work. When he came, we had cherry pie. Mom and Dad gave me a new sweater and wool gloves. James gave me a scarf. Eddie and Vera gave me a broach. Paul waited until we were out on the Nantucket. He gave me his signet ring! Told me he loved me and would I be his girl? I said yes and what took him so long? Went to bed in the clouds.

Well, I guess she got her birthday wish, so I'm happy for her, no matter how misguided that wish was. Once again, though, WTF is a Nantucket?

Chapter VIII

As you might imagine, my epiphany came as a shock to people. Including myself. No, not the part where I realized I wasn't going to let the jerk ruin my life anymore, but the part where I was a changed woman. That doesn't happen overnight or even after months of self-flogging and ruminating on the stupidity of my own actions. Let's just say I was a work in progress. Clearly. Here I was, months later, still cleaning a cluttered, stinky, cobwebby attic and sleeping in a bedroom without a door. *Trust* was the operative word. Did anyone trust me yet? Did I trust *myself*?

After what seemed like an hour but was probably only ten minutes, I stood up from my self-reflecting, self-wallowing plastic tub and willed myself to shake off the darkness and oppression. No one ever promised me a rose garden, did they? Wasn't that a book? I needed to look into that...Hey, on another note, if Taylor Swift could sing, "Shake it off. Shake it off," then I could, couldn't I?! I sang the song out loud as I wiped away my worthless, penitent, pointless tears.

I headed back up the rickety stairs to the attic and spent several hours rummaging, sorting, and stacking. Sometime in the early afternoon, I stopped working to make a sandwich, heading out to the front porch swing to eat while listening to the sounds of cicadas and sprinklers. I realized I hadn't been out of the house in days. I was becoming quite the recluse, but look what I was missing—it was beautiful out. There was a nice breeze, the sun was shining, and the birds were singing. I tried not to notice that the lawn needed mowing. Since Tyler was gone, this task had fallen to me, but I tended to put it off until the grass was so high that a bushhogger would be more appropriate than a mower. Ho hum. Maybe tomorrow.

After a few minutes of contemplating the wonders of the great outdoors of suburbia, I had a flash thought. I put my sandwich plate down on the wicker table, knelt down beside the swing, and tipped it up. A-ha! Underneath its belly, it read: "The Nantucket. Fine Quality Front Porch Swings. Made in Tell City, Indiana." Well, that solved one of Didi's mysteries! I smiled as I sat back down. I suddenly felt so connected to her—here I was in the same house, out on the same porch, swinging on the same swing, thinking about Didi almost ninety years later. She had sat here with Paul and kissed! Even with our modern-day vast stores of technology and newfangled gadgets, our world hadn't changed much, had it? There was still the simple pleasure of swinging on a porch swing and watching the world go by. Not to mention the intimacy of canoodling on what was basically a moving love seat. I smiled as I thought of Didi and Paul, his arm around her shoulder, her head leaning against him.

Still in my happy reverie, I glanced around the neighborhood and munched on my sandwich, thinking gosh, I was pretty lucky. This really was a great place to grow up. I guess I hadn't thought of it before. Down the street, three boys rode their bikes out onto the road and then circled back into their driveway, popping wheelies. A dog barked in the distance. Mr. Zewlecki, two doors down, adjusted his sprinkler into a higher, fuller stream on his west yard. Across the street, Mr. Morris whacked down his mole holes with a shovel while Mrs. Morris pulled weeds in her vegetable garden. Jake's little sisters (he had four) sat out in their front yard playing with their dolls and trying to dress their cat Diggers in a *Frozen* costume. I smiled. Come to think of it, poor Jake—all those girls and he the oldest and a boy—it was no wonder he spent his days working at the RCC, playing soccer on the pitch, or hanging out with Tyler when he was home.

I finished my sandwich with a sigh. I realized I felt almost normal again, sitting out here like this, observing the world and realizing I was just a tiny cog in a big wheel, and did my big bad blunder really matter in the grand scheme of things? After a while, I went in, grabbed a bottled water from the fridge, and ascended the stairs, only to realize when I hit the second floor landing that there was literally no space left in the upstairs hallway for another thing. I grabbed an empty trash bag from the roll Mom had placed on the stair post. Every single hideous, outdated, fraying outfit from my childhood (and Tyler's), not to mention clothes that hadn't fit Mom in at least ten years, went into the bag, and then another bag, and another. By the end, I'd heaved eleven bags over the stairwell and down into the front foyer. Good riddance.

Somewhere about the time when I could start to see patches of the hardwood pine floors again, there was Jake, my soccer savior, bounding up the stairs and asking if I was ready. Suddenly I thought, would I be okay playing with the boys? It had been a while since I'd even touched a ball. I'd quit the varsity team mid-season last year. Not because I wasn't good. Heck, Coach Andrews cried when I quit. She actually *cried*! I was her star midfielder. It wasn't so easy to find someone who could run like the wind, had awesome foot skills and passing precision to die for, and never got tired. Not to mention, my foot—I could score from the thirty-yard line, lefty or righty. Certainly nothing to shake a stick at. But (wah-wah) I was dating Greg then, and he said soccer was taking time away from him and he didn't like the way the boys looked at me when I played. So that was the end of that. Dick.

To Jake's inquiry, I answered, "Hey! Not quite." He was looking at the remaining piles on the floor. I laughed at his face and said, "Believe it or not, this is way better than it was an hour ago. I gotta change. Meet you down on the porch? I'll be quick."

"Okay, cool," he said absently, investigating a box of pots and pans. He asked, "Can I take these? Mom would love them."

"Sure, take 'em."

"Great—I'll bring the box downstairs and retrieve it when we get back."

"Cool, be down in a sec."

I ran into my room to change, grabbing my cleats out of the back of the closet. I felt a slight flutter in my stomach—was that nerves about soccer or about Jake? So strange! Up until now, I had found Jake an annoying nuisance. When we were young, he would stop by unannounced to play with Tyler anytime day or night. Jake, being a few years younger, worshipped Tyler and made me gag with his fawning. To make matters worse, Jake always seemed to find time to torture me—pull my pigtails, pinch my arm, steal my toys, or simply be a typical boy: arrogant, disgusting, and unwelcome. Coincidentally, he was completely and purposefully (or diabolically?) oblivious to my nudges, grunts, and shoves. I would physically (and vocally) ask him to leave me alone, but he would just laugh and do something else obnoxious.

Once when I was seven or eight, he snuck up behind me and put gum in my hair. Mom spent hours trying to untangle it and finally had to cut off a huge chunk. I cried so hard and got worked up into such a state that Mom lost her temper and screamed at Jake (who was already volubly repentant and nearly crying himself). She actually yelled, "Jake, go home and don't come back!" We didn't see him for a while after that, and I had to admit I felt a little bad about it afterward. I don't think he realized the consequences of his actions, nor the chemical epoxy effect of gum and hair in combination, nor the chemical effect of a girl who loves her hair and has been forced to amputate a large portion of it due to a boy's stupid prank.

As I pulled on my soccer shorts, I thought back to all the little games, taunts, and tricks from our childhood and rolled my eyes at my current state of lunacy.

What was wrong with me? How could I see Jake as anything but a silly, childish boy? Granted, he was the same age as me, but in the grade behind me since his birthday was after the cutoff. He seemed younger. Like the baby brother I never had or wanted. Boys matured slower than girls, didn't they? But then he was a reader—that surprised and fascinated me. It showed maturity and brains, neither of which I had expected from him. And he had hair under his armpits—such a ridiculous thing for me to notice when he wore that green shirt with the cut-off sleeves. But I did notice. Very manly armpits, not boy armpits.

When I came downstairs, he stated, "Nice" as he looked me over with a grin. Had he guessed my non-brotherly thoughts? Was his mind roving in that direction too?

I smiled as we headed out the door and walked toward the pitch.

He asked if I'd found anything interesting in the attic.

"So far, no Monets or Shrouds of Turin, but there's still time."

"*Antiques Roadshow?*"

"Maybe *Flea Market Finds*, with more fleas than finds."

"What exactly did you do anyway?" Jake asked.

"Today? Not much, really. Mostly bagged up clothes."

"No, dummy, what did you *do*? To be on attic duty."

"Oh, that. Yeah. I got fired from my job at Panera and sort of forgot to tell Mom—or anyone else, for that matter."

He laughed. "How'd that happen?"

"What? The firing or the memory loss?"

He grinned. "Both."

I shrugged. "I'm kind of over the wrath of Mom, you know, so I just let it slide and hoped she'd be none the wiser. It actually kind of worked for a few weeks, but she ran into someone at the grocery store who spilled the beans."

"Bummer," he said. "What exactly happened at Panera?"

"You know Danny Pike?"

"Senior? Stocky wrestler?"

"Yep, that's the one. Lughead. The other girls think he's 'like totally dreamy,' but I think he's a total dick. He works there, and he was constantly touching me. Grop-ing, really. Mr. Handsy, if you know what I mean. All hands, no brain. So, one day, I may have kneed him in the balls. Oopsie. Sorry, not sorry. I mean, he deserved it—there's only so much a girl can take of that crap. The little suck-up baby, he complained to the manager, so they fired me." I shrugged again. The continuing saga, a day in the life of Delia Elliott.

He frowned and exclaimed, "Wow, what a jerk!" A few seconds later, he added,

"Remind me not to ever get on your bad side."

I gave him a crooked smile in response.

"But, seriously, that sucks."

"Yeah, whatever."

"So...so you didn't tell the manager what really happened?"

I gave him a "duh-yeah-right" incredulous look. "Like I said, the other girls in there think he's great. And the manager's son is on the wrestling team with him, so who do you think he's gonna believe? His word against mine. I mean, no biggie. Serving bagels and schmear wasn't exactly on my most-treasured career aspirations list anyway." I looked away as we walked, thinking about what I wasn't telling Jake—how Danny would constantly pull up the infamous *incident* photos on his phone, brandishing them in front me like a weapon. Then he would proceed to grab my breasts or my ass and grab himself down there. I would try to get away because he truly made my flesh crawl, but inevitably he would get his dig in and make me feel like worthless shit before someone came along and interrupted his fun. I would run to the ladies' room and cry, trying to pull myself together. I knew it was just the price I had to pay for *the incident*, but still, it never got easier. When I finally took the matter into my own hands—or my own feet, as the case may be (thank you, soccer skills!)—I kneed him so hard, he actually doubled over and spit on me. It was the most satisfying firing I'd ever had.

"Too bad," he said sympathetically. "Did you tell your mom what happened? I mean, what *really* happened."

I chuckled mirthlessly. "Are you kidding me? In her mind, no matter what, everything is Delia's fault. Kind of pointless for me to explain. Not that I haven't given her reason to blame me for everything, but honestly at this point, I'd rather let her imagination run wild. Makes our home life so much more interesting."

"I bet," he chuckled, scrutinizing my face with a mixture of interest and skepticism. Then he puffed himself up and said, "You need me to kick Danny's ass?"

I laughed and smiled at him. So sweet. "No, don't waste your time. He isn't worth it. Plus, I took care of it myself. I suspect he was walking funny for a few days."

"Phew," he wiped his brow and continued in a high-pitched soprano voice, "that guy would hurt me. I bruise very easily."

"You do?" I challenged and pinched his arm. He cried out like a slaughtered piglet. We both laughed.

"Well, do you want a job at the RCC?"

"Huh? Really?"

"Yes, really. We have openings right now."

"Oh my god, that would be awesome...although I don't know if Mom would give me back my car. Maybe...if I could convince her I was serious."

"How did you get to Panera?"

"My friend Stephanie drove me."

He nodded. "Well, let me talk to my manager tomorrow. If you needed a ride, maybe we could carpool."

"That would be great. Hey, thanks," I said, this time punching his arm softly.

His voice pitched up in the higher octaves again as he ran ahead of me, screeching, "Noooo, please, you brute, please don't...hurt me!"

After he finished his charade and came back, I noticed his kind green eyes with their strange, warm sparkle lighting on me. Again I felt that strange déjà vu about Didi. I looked away self-consciously and pointed to the pitch as we approached. "Whoa, this is it. Been about a hundred years since I've played over here."

"You'll be fine," Jake said as one of the guys walked up to shake his hand.

Jake introduced me. I said "hey" as the guy noticed my gear and asked, surprised, "You playing?" I nodded, and he grinned and exclaimed, "Awesome!" Then, without another word, he ran out to the middle of the field to pass and juggle the ball with the rest of the guys.

None of them looked familiar, thank god, but then one turned and pointed at me. I had a quick sinking feeling in my stomach.

Jake quickly said, "Hey, don't worry, they don't know you...or know of you... they're just shocked that a girl wants to play with us."

I nodded skeptically.

He said, "They'll underestimate you on the field, then you'll open a can of whoop-ass on them, right?"

I tried to laugh and said, "Yeah, sure. Thank you for that encouragement from 1991. I feel better already."

Jake moved closer to me and in a slight, swift motion took his forefinger and thumb and smoothed out the tight knot that had formed in my forehead. I found myself smiling up into his green eyes, which were laughing at me. I pondered absently that he smelled good—like a sweet, salty pretzel.

He said, "You'll be fine. And don't hate on my old-school lingo."

I gave him a sideways grin and he was off. I put on my cleats, shin guards, and socks, and stretched while watching the guys pass in the distance. Okay, some self-talk, Delia. These guys aren't going to give you a second thought. I was just another player to fill in on the field. That sounded like heaven to me, so I smiled and stood up. I juggled the ball for a few minutes by myself, trying to look and act more confident and nonchalant than I felt.

Just then, a girl I didn't know walked up to me and said hi with a sort of challenge in her voice. I said hi back. She was little, blonde, perky—you know the type, your typical nightmare-slash-pop-U-lar cheerleader—and was wearing cut-off short shorts and a pink tank.

I looked away and asked her as a sort of joke, "You playing?"

"God, no," she answered definitively with a leveling glance at me. "I came to watch."

Before I had a chance to think, I said, "Really? Why?" I mean, after all, it was just a pickup game, hardly worth spectators.

She replied, "Well, that's my boyfriend over there." She pointed at the gaggle of men, so I wasn't sure who she meant. Not that I cared.

I squinted at the group and nodded. "Oh."

Then she challenged, "Is one of those guys your man?"

I said with disdain, "Um, no. I'm here to play." That was just the kick in the ass I needed. I ran out onto the field, not looking back. I started passing and doing other warm-up exercises. Jake was there—first talking with his buddies, then watching me and tossing the ball back and forth with me. After a few minutes, he came over and handed me a pinnie. As I put it over my T-shirt, I joked, "What, we're not playing skins versus shirts?"

His eyes widened with a white-hot glint, but he replied mildly and with a forced casual tone, "Funny. Um, no, let's stick with pinnies."

"Okeydokey, coach," I said innocently. I could see he was guarded in a way he hadn't been a few minutes before. What had he been talking about with those guys? It made me slightly self-conscious, and I had a momentary regret about the pinnie joke. He shrugged his pinnie on, pointing me to the left midfield position, which was perfect for me—how did he know that? I was glad to see we were on the same team. While we were waiting to kick off, I noticed the blonde had planted herself in a folding chair on the sidelines, and after a minute, another girl, a redhead, walked up and started talking to her. She unfolded her own chair and plopped down beside her.

One of the guys blew a whistle and started the time on his watch. My heart began to pound out of my chest. I had forgotten about the adrenaline rush! It all came back to me, and I flushed with the glow of it. The feel of the sticky grass under my cleats, the surge of blood in my veins, the sweat breaking out on my forehead, my thighs pumping, the sun baking the top of my head. Like a shook-up pop bottle being opened. I smiled from ear to ear.

The first ten minutes or so, I probably looked like a chicken let loose in a coop full of coyotes, running around aimlessly toward everything and nothing in particular. And no one would pass to me, so that was starting to piss me off.

Then it happened—Jake tossed me an easy one—right at my feet. Suddenly, I was having an out-of-body experience. It was as if all of my muscles, joints, and tendons were connected symbiotically, like magnets being slammed together in perfect harmony. I was apart, yet in step with each perfectly placed player, like a chess board—watching, assessing, adjusting, maneuvering, thinking, processing, juggling. I possessed the ball and it possessed me. I weaved in and out of two startled opponents (oh yes, I did giggle at their pinched, irate, surprised faces as I flew by them, which maybe didn't help the situation, but I was having too much fun to care). I dodged toward the corner as I saw Jake (was he reading my mind?) position himself directly in the center of the goal box. I kicked a high, neat, soft ball toward him, and as the keeper made a full-throttle dive directly at Jake's feet, Jake scooted aside with a tidy side step and headed the ball neatly into the goal.

Scccccooooorrrrre! I heard the announcer's voice in my head, like a megaphone—the full arc of the words—and I couldn't keep the perma-grin off my face. I was stopped short (in a good way!) when Jake slammed against me in a full-body bear hug, raising me off the ground as I laughed and screamed. After only an instant, he dropped me roughly in a manly way, and I thought that was even more hysterical—too typical of soccer players—passionate and tough, but putty underneath. Several of the guys came up to high-five me. I glanced back at Jake and noticed he was breathing hard and grinning broadly at me.

As we all got back into position, I noticed that the blonde and her friend were sending me flaming daggers across the field—what was their problem? Whatever, witches—go back to your hair and makeup.

The floodgates opened after that. The guys started passing to me, and my mad skills and intuition came back. It was as though I had never left soccer. And I didn't care that they were boys and I was a girl. I didn't care when one of the opposing players shoved me to the ground, hard—I jumped back up and stuck my tongue out at him. He turned back to laugh.

Finally, when I felt the sweat pouring out of my pores and my legs dragging, the whistle blew and it was over. What had been hours seemed like five minutes. I came off the field smiling, joking around with the other pinnies, grabbing a bottled water from a cooler. Suddenly, on the sidelines, the smile was wiped off my face when the cheerleader came flying out of her chair, wrapped her arms around Jake, and kissed him full on the mouth. It seemed forced and staged. One of the guys coughed uncomfortably and spit on the ground nearby. I walked away, pretending to shake my legs out. After a few minutes, I glanced back curiously. Jake had pulled her aside and was talking to her in an intense whisper. She looked peeved, and he looked politely restrained.

I stalled and tried not to notice, sitting down on the ground and slowly taking off my shin guards, socks, and cleats. One of the pinnie guys was sitting next to me, doing the same, and we talked amicably about the game. After a few minutes, I got up to leave, saying goodbye loudly. Jake didn't stir from his intense conversation, so I headed home alone. During the five-block walk, my ecstatic mood waned as the endorphins wore off and I began to process the reality of the Jake-slash-blonde combo.

So much for my two-day crush on the boy next door. Apparently, it was over before it began. Oh well, I needed a relationship right now like I needed a hole in the head.

Then again, wouldn't it be nice to fill the landfill-sized hole in my heart?

CHAPTER IX

DAMMIT, DELIA! I got home and she was nowhere to be found, the slippery snake! The house looked as though a bomb had gone off. I thought about calling a few of her friends but then realized I didn't even know who her friends were anymore, so I called Johnston instead. He didn't know where she was and promptly made me feel (intentionally or not) like a horrible mother because I was clueless as to her whereabouts and because I didn't know the first place to start looking for her.

So I'm thinking, here we go again. Same old routine, and I'd thought she was doing better and that the attic was helping! Stupid me. My blood was boiling.

Right around the time I was about to blow a gasket, she moseys in, all nonchalant, with a sullen, sweaty face and her cleats in her hands. Not a word of explanation. I gathered she was at the pitch, but she didn't think to leave me a note? I hollered at her, "I thought you were kidnapped, raped, in a gutter somewhere!" In between gulps of milk directly out of the jug (really?!), she stood staring at me quietly, with bored, tired eyes. As she grabbed three granola bars and a box of raisins out of the cupboard, I accused her of not caring or even considering. I followed at her heels, up the stairs, quickly realizing my cause was lost and pointless when she went directly into the bathroom, closing the door in my face and turning the shower on. I yelled through the door, "Mature, Delia, really mature!"

Is child abuse legal in New York? Under what circumstances? Really, there must be a loophole. What else is left?

Spent, I sat down on a plastic tub in the upstairs hallway, fingering a shoebox full of loose photos near my feet. After a minute of fuming and slowly deflating, I picked up several photos—of me, my sister, my dad, my mom, cousins, aunts, uncles. All right there. Stuck in time. Back when we were young and carefree. We had some good times back then. And some bad.

There was a book of poetry under the shoebox. I picked it up, and a photo fell out of the seams. It was Didi with a tall, handsome man—not Grandpa Ron, but someone else. His arm was around her waist, and she was looking up at him with unadulterated adoration and worship. She seemed sweet and radiant—like a butterfly suspended in the hot summer sun. I wondered absently who this young whippersnapper was with my Grandma Didi. I must admit, she looked better than she had ever looked with Grandpa Ron. Curious.

I headed down the stairs, gathering up the bags of clothes tossed like collapsed beanbags all over the foyer, and threw them in my car. I drove as fast as I could to the donation center and handed them over, wanting to get back before Delia could sneak out again. Johnston called me on the way. Oh, I guess I forgot to call him back—whoops. Delia's fine, I told him—she was just playing soccer on the pitch.

Then, unrelated, startling me, Tyler called. He wanted to know if I could pick him up in a few weeks from college after his internship was over. I said, yes, of course. I would just need to know if I could come on a weekend. Otherwise, I would need to take a day off work. He said he'd let me know. Then he mentioned something that stunned me into silence. It was news I decided to process later because I wasn't sure how to react, so I changed the subject, telling him about Delia's attic project. He laughed and said I would have more success if I just burned the house down. I chuckled at that and said, "Now, now." We chatted for a while longer about miscellaneous stuff and finally said goodbye and hung up.

Back home, I noticed Delia had tacked up a sheet over the entrance to her bedroom. Fine, be that way. I could hear her in there chomping on her granola bars. Imagine the crumbs. Ugh. That would need vacuuming, along with the rest of the house, assuming we'd ever see the floor again. Which reminded me, the air conditioning wasn't working—it never seemed to get cold enough. I'd have to call about that tomorrow.

Sorting through the attic memorabilia, I gingerly wrapped several antique knickknacks, placed them in tubs, and carried them down to the trunk of my car. I figured I'd have John look them over the next time he was at the post office. Heck, maybe they were worth something. Wouldn't be the worst thing in the world to have some extra cash. I smiled to myself, envisioning John holding one of my treasures and stating with enthusiasm, "Yes, in fact,

this item is a rare Tiffany blue-and-white bud vase that's worth five hundred thousand dollars!" That could happen, right? Then I remembered that I
didn't have any vases like that, or probably anything else of value either. Not
to mention I remembered that millennials didn't buy antiques—they spent
their money on "experiences." So who was going to buy this crap? Old-timers
like myself? Maybe. I sighed. It was nice to dream, wasn't it?

I was suddenly jarred awake from my fruitless reverie by a barrage of texts
from my friend Donna:

"SOS. I need you."
"STAT. 911. Help me."
"Must. Get. Wine."
"Lost. At. Bottom. Of. Well."
"Send Lassie."
"Or Fabio."
"Or cabernet."
"Or chocolate."
"Or all of the above."
"NOW."
"Why haven't you responded yet?"
"Can't you see I'm having a crisis?"
"I can't wait any longer."
"Crickets. Seriously."

I rolled my eyes and laughed. Oh Donna, Donna, Donna. My chummy,
offbeat, off-kilter, blond bosom buddy. She really was too funny sometimes.
And maybe a little bipolar too. We fit together like salt and pepper.

"STOP. Remain calm," I wrote back. *"I'm here. What's up?"*

*"I need a drink. Andy should be home in 5 minutes. I already told him I
needed a girls' night out. You down?"*

"Sure. What did you have in mind?"

"Brunkers. 6:45. See you there."

"kk."

"kk."

I let Delia know (through the sheet) that I was going to dinner with Donna. I told her there was leftover cold pizza in the fridge. She grunted back. I
changed my clothes, looking wistfully at the half-finished attic project on the
hallway floor as I headed down the stairs and out the door. At least the downstairs foyer was cleared out now. Better that than nothing. And in the words

of Scarlett O'Hara, "After all, tomorrow is another day." Insert meme here.

When I got to Brunkers, Donna was swiveling back and forth on a bar-stool, tapping her fingers on a glass of wine, reaching in and out of the snack bowl, and erratically fiddling with her hair like a Kardashian on crack. I sighed. She wasn't kidding about the SOS. The night had just begun, and I already felt tired.

"Hi, sweetie," I said as we hugged.

"Oh, thank god you're here. You need to talk me off the ledge. For real."

"Can I order a wine first?" I laughed.

"I suppose," she replied, rolling her eyes in mock impatience. "Steve, we need a wine over here. Cab, I presume?"

"Yes, that's fine, size grande, por favor," I said to Steve. Poor guy, he'd probably been listening to Donna's sob story for half an hour already.

"So, whazzup, girl? I want the full story. No, wait, I take it back. Give me the abridged version. CliffsNotes, please."

"What?!" Donna screeched, indignant.

"Alright, then, the *full* scoop. Just keep your voice down—not everyone wants to be part of our reality TV show."

Being Donna, she raised her voice to a scream. "Why not? Come on, join in! I don't care who hears it! I've got nothing to hide."

Oh boy, she was drunk already. I would need to catch up. I smiled calmly with a small wave to the patrons staring at us, mouthing, "Sorry, so sorry." This was going to be a long night. To Donna, I said, "Okay, okay, calm your hormones. Tell me what's going on, but please try not to get us arrested or kicked out of here." She rolled her eyes and got quiet, defiantly crossing her arms in front of her. Then I said soothingly, "Go ahead."

She waited a half-second, trying to decide if I was worthy of her story now that I had rebuffed her, then launched into, "Okay, so Andy calls me from work today, all casual, you know, like he does when he's delivering bad news. He says Holly wants to know if we can keep the girls for the rest of the sum-mer. Keep in mind, we've already planned to have the girls for the first half of the summer, not to mention most of the school year. I mean, what kind of mother is she?! Don't answer that—I already know the answer. She barely sees them as it is, and I told Andy I can't take it! An entire summer?! As if we didn't have any other plans. This is not what I signed up for. We had an agree-ment. He's reneging and he knows it. He brought me flowers tonight, that son-of-a-bitch. Who does he think he is? And do you know what kills me?

I mean, really kills me? The girls constantly tell me how great their mom is. Mommy took us to the mall, Mommy did this, did that, Mommy, Mommy, Mommy." Donna did the universal gagging finger-down-the-throat sign.

"Then why doesn't Mommy ever want to see you girls? Tell me that. Why doesn't Mommy ever want to feed you or clothe you or help you with your homework or do anything with you? Why doesn't Mommy take you to the dentist or the doctor or for haircuts? Tell me that! Mommy makes me want to spit fire! AND they think her new husband is sooo dreamy. Chris is so nice. Chris took us out for ice cream. Chris went to Build-a-Bear with us. I didn't tell Andy about that—I think it would kill him. For real, though, this guy's in their life for like a hot second and they're already saying he's the best guy ever? Meanwhile, when they finally do see the girls, of course, there are absolutely no rules of any kind. Oh noooo! Andy and I have to do all the dirty work—they leave all of that to us because they don't want to spoil anything for the girls. I'm like, what?! They just want to spoil them, period, not spoil everything for them. Don't they realize that this is what being a parent is all about? You're not supposed to be their friends—you're supposed to set boundaries. That's how children learn! And to make matters worse, the girls come back to our house and have whiplash—they're all indignant that Andy and I make them follow a routine, clean up after themselves, and go to bed on time. Basically, they end up hating us. It's enough to make me want to scream!"

I looked at her empathetically, trying to think of something positive to say. I replied lamely, "Well, if they're with you the whole summer, at least they'll have to get used to your routine and rules."

"Sure. Right. I'm sure they'll jump right in line. Ha!" she scoffed. Then after a moment, she said, "No, I told Andy I'm moving in with you. Do you mind? You have that big old death trap, basically empty, with plenty of space for me. What, like, four bedrooms, and only two of you living there…right?"

"Hey! Don't mock the D.D.! Sacred ground, you know. And, actually, Tyler's coming home in a few weeks. I just talked to him. But you can have the fourth bedroom if you want, although there's a hole in the floor, the window's busted, the wallpaper's peeling off, and the ceiling's covered in old water stains." I laughed pitifully. "Oh, and the A/C's on the fritz."

"I'm not kidding, you know. I mean it," she replied menacingly.

"I know. I'm not kidding either," I countered soberly.

I smiled because I knew this was all a boiling kettle—once the steam was released, Donna would be back to her old self.

I asked, "So, why exactly can't Holly watch them?"

"Oh yeah, I didn't tell you the best part. You're never going to believe it. Makes me sick to my stomach. Just take a guess."

"I have no idea."

"No, guess. You will die!"

"Um, I don't know. She's sailing around the world in a yacht. She's headed to Monaco for gambling season. She got signed to the William Morris Agency. She's joining the circus. I give up. What?"

"Ha, good guesses, but NO. You will die!" she repeated, her voice slightly slurred as she started her second, third, or fourth wine (hard to say exactly what number...my drunk-dar was pointing to, hmmm, let's see, *fourth*). "They're spending the entire summer in, wait for it...Hawaii! Seriously. Hawaii!"

"What? No way. How can they afford that? Doesn't he work?"

"YES, that's the kicker. It's for his job!"

I countered, "Doing what?"

"Apparently he works for the electric utility company, and there's a power plant on the Big Island," she answered with bitterness. "They need an engineer to run some project down there for a few months. Heck, I don't know... lifestyles of the rich and famous."

"Why can't the girls go with them?"

"Oh yeah, Holly told Andy that things were so expensive down there, there was no way the girls would be able to come. Apparently they're staying in a tiny apartment. And she said they were really 'stretching' it by allowing her to go with him and that she was going to have to pay all her own expenses while they were there."

"Gee golly, I feel so bad for her, having to pay her own way," I said with sarcasm that Donna appreciated with a head nod and lip curl. "I assume his company's paying for their room and their food, so what expenses will she have anyway? Probably just shopping."

"I know, right? She told Andy that Chris shouldn't be held back from this opportunity because of her and the girls. Blah, blah, blah, BARF! Like Andy gives a shit about Chris. I said WTF, why can't she just let her man go, and she can stay back here and be a mother for once in her life? Andy told me to sit down because my face was turning red."

I noticed her face was quite pink even now. I tried to speak as calmly as I could. "I'm sorry—that really stinks." Then I looked into her eyes and said sincerely (knowing the steam was out of the kettle now), "You know, those girls love you."

She paused mid-drink and stared at me. It was funny because her face went from anger to rebuttal to acceptance to love in a split second. I had to laugh, and she did too. She said simply, "I know. And I love them too. They're my everything." She paused and, for effect, said with fake menace, "The little terrorists."

I smiled and added, "Anyway, I wish I had something to suggest or offer, but I don't..."

"Oh, but you do, sister, remember? A bed. Or a padded cell, as the case may be. Hey, do you wanna get some food?"

"Yes, let's."

"Hey Steve, bring us menus—we're gonna order food. I think I need something in my stomach."

"Ya think?" I said to Steve, winking. He smiled and came back after a few minutes to take our order.

Donna paused, drinking her wine and looking into my face. "So...my friend, sorry, I've been monopolizing the conversation. What's going on with you?"

"Oh, you know me, boring." I shrugged. I paused, quietly, holding my breath, wondering if I should take the pin out of the grenade I was holding. "Although I do have a bit of news..."

"You do? What? Shoot."

"Hold onto your glass."

"My goodness, what?"

"Beth is pregnant."

"Oh. My. God. NO."

"YES."

"How did you find out?"

"Tyler told me on the phone today. He said Johnston called him this morning. I was driving and I swear, I nearly swerved off the road."

"What is the matter with that man?! Fifty years old, right?" Donna asked, incredulous.

"Fifty-two, actually. I know. Can you believe it? I guess that's what you get when you marry someone twenty years younger than you. I'm surprised they waited this long."

"So Johnston never got the snip-snip after Delia?"

"Nope. You remember Delia was C-section? Cantankerous, even back then." I grunted. "After they pulled her out, they tied me up, killing two birds with one stone, so to speak."

"Oh yeah, I forgot about that. Smart. I'm still on the pill, which I realize is insane at my age. I'm the crazy one hoping menopause comes sooner rather than later. So hey, what did Delia say about the news?"

"She doesn't know yet. She's grounded. Cleaning out the attic as punishment right now. And she still doesn't have her phone, so she hasn't talked to her dad in a few days. I suppose she'll need to call him...I almost want to hold off for her sake. I'm not sure how she'll react. I think she's still so fragile since, well, since *you know*...Although lately, it's the strangest thing...I thought she was doing better, but then she got fired from her job, and now I don't know what's going on with her. She's a mystery to me, tied up in an enigma, tied up in a box of marbles. And my marbles are what I'm about to lose with her."

"Aren't your marbles already gone?" Donna asked with a tilt of her head. I laughed. She added, "Teenage girls are simply unfathomable." Her enunciation of *unfathomable* came out like "unfam-am-able," so I chuckled. Dear, sweet, drunk Donna.

"It's funny," I continued. "Tyler's pumped. He thinks the baby will be a boy—you know, a little mini-Tyler."

"Aww, that's kind of cute."

"Yeah, I suppose...I think he was also worried I might be upset by the news."

"Well, are you? And by the way, I am so sorry I've been blabbing on and on about my problems when you're dealing with your own Chernobyl."

"Oh no, don't worry about that. I think I'd rather keep it off my mind anyway. I'm not sure how I feel about it. It's not like I'm envious. I can't imagine what Johnston's thinking, at his age. Doesn't he remember how much work it was? Heck, still is." I shook my head.

"No doubt. Hello! Like never-ending. He's cray-cray, that's for sure."

Our food came, so we stopped for a while to chew and contemplate. After a few minutes, I said thoughtfully, "Donna, did you ever wonder what the heck we're doing here?"

She choked a little, then chuckled and said, "Here? Eating French dip and frics?"

"No, you ninny—seriously. Not here. I mean, *here*, on Earth, you know. Like what our purpose is."

"As humans? As a species?"

I sighed, exasperated and amused. I put my sandwich down. "No, not that. Although that's an interesting question too. No, as me, Heather Elliott, and you, Donna Peters. What's our purpose?"

She thought about that for a minute and said slowly, "Well, I was clearly put here to rule Andy's world." I laughed. "That man would be lost without me. And the girls, too for that matter. I organize everything for them. They would probably never get out of bed if I didn't get everything all ready for them. Not to mention, they would most certainly starve to death."

I grinned and agreed, "Word." We high-fived. "Well, you're lucky. And more importantly, *they're* lucky to have you. But yeah, I guess for me it's a bit different. I've been thinking lately that I can't figure out what I'm doing here. I'm like a boat without a rudder, you know? Oh, don't look at me that way—I don't have the suicide hotline on speed dial or anything. It's just… well, I'm older now, and Tyler's away and Delia's…being Delia right now… and soon she'll be away…and Johnston's off living a whole new life with someone else…and I don't know…I guess I'm confused."

I paused, trying to figure out how to articulate my feelings. I continued feebly, "Heck, I went to a movie a few weeks ago and had a revelation—I was invisible!" I laughed mirthlessly. "How did I realize this? Not because I was there alone—oh no, I'm totally used to going to movies alone. It was because there were six movie trailers before the movie even started, all of which targeted eighteen-year-old boys. Science fiction, fantasy, alien invasion, robots, superheroes, astronauts, action, adventure, nudity, oozing body parts, special effects, farts, cursing, drugs, death, destruction, war. Everything except complex real women, mature women, women with real-life troubles, happiness, relationships, connections, struggles, striving, strife, life, and love. Where are those movies? Where are *we* in the stories of today? I mean, aren't women fifty percent of the population? Then why are we removed (oh so conveniently) from the equation? From the consciousness of the modern world? Are we so easily forgotten, annihilated, vaporized?"

Donna was nodding in commiseration, then alternately shaking her head in indignation. She felt what I was saying—she got it. She exclaimed, her drink in the air, "Let's storm the theaters!"

I burst out laughing. "Can you imagine? We'd frighten the ticket counter boy so much, he'd probably pee his pants."

"Serves him right!"

We laughed together for a while. I took a few more bites and then said, "You know, it made me so stinking mad! It made me wonder what I could do about it and if there was some course of action for the average middle-aged woman to sway our world in the right direction. Sure, the women's movement in the '60s and '70s, not to mention the more recent #MeToo movement, has helped move the needle, right? And that's a blessing, for sure, but it still seems as if we're not meeting the mark, you know?"

All Donna could say by way of sympathy and understanding was, "Right. Uh-huh. Exactly. Totally agree."

Then, trying to sift through the fuzzy matter that was percolating in my brain—back in the dark recesses—I brought something into focus and said, "Did I ever tell you that my grandmother helped raise me?"

Donna garbled, her mouth full, "Uh, um, not sure…wait, is that Didi?"

"Yes, exactly. Delia Diamond."

"Delia?" Donna asked, confused for a second.

"Yes, that's who Delia's named after—my grandma, but no one ever called her Grandma or Delia—she was always just Didi. It's funny that we've all lived in the D.D. and her name was Didi. There were a lot of D's back then and still are now, I suppose."

"Darn tootin', darlin'," Donna countered. We both giggled.

I set my wine down and continued slowly, "I don't know if I've ever told you this, but did you know my mom was taken away from us in a straitjacket?" Donna's face pulled back in shock. I guess that answered my question. I went on, "Yeah, she came after me with a knife when I was twelve. My hands got cut up pretty badly, and she nicked my shoulder. Thank god Dad was there—he intervened and probably saved my life." I paused, remembering the incident with vivid, horrific clarity. Then I said sadly, "Of course, he was already dying of cancer by then, so our lives went into a complete tailspin after that. First they put my sister and me in foster care for a year or so—that was a nightmare—then eventually we ended up back at the D.D. with Didi and Grandpa Ron. It's really crazy because I have whole portions of my life, like years and years, that I don't remember. It's like a void. I simply can't remember. I don't know why. I don't think it's normal. I mean, you remember your childhood, right?"

Donna was trying to absorb what I was saying, still slightly drunk, her face a mask of consternation and feeling. She answered thoughtfully, "Yes, for the most part."

I said, "You see, I just don't. I was just looking through some photos Delia brought down from the attic—of me and my sister when we were girls—I don't remember myself then. It's like looking at a photo of a stranger."

"Oh, Heather," Donna said, rubbing my shoulder, "I didn't know…that sounds awful…"

"Thanks. Yeah, it's just strange. I probably should have had counseling or something. I try not to think about it, but sometimes, like today, it pops back into my mind and I'm left feeling confused and a mess all over again."

"I bet," Donna sympathized.

"Looking back now, though, the one gleam of light was Didi. I don't know what we would have done without her. I mean, she was amazing. Such a strong woman. I think she had to be—Grandpa Ron was a total tyrant. He was against taking us in. He wanted us to stay in foster care—said we'd be better off. Ha, if he only knew…! But Didi put her foot down after a while—went and grabbed us out of that bad situation and brought us back to the D.D. In fact, one of the few things I do remember from that time was Didi saying over and over again that even if she couldn't 'save everyone,' she could darn well 'save us.' I still don't really know what she meant by that, but the impression I got was that she was trying to right some wrong from her past."

"Well, thank goodness for that. So, things got better then?"

I smiled glumly, admitting, "No, not really—well, a little. Didi was great, don't get me wrong, but Grandpa Ron was resentful and mean. If Mary or I misbehaved, he paddled us or used the belt or whatever was handy. He took an iron skillet to me once. That hurt like hell. Sometimes he'd lock us in the attic for hours—or days if we were really bad. Or he'd take away our food. We would go for whole weekends with nothing to eat—only water and sometimes milk that Didi would sneak us. I remember during the school year I'd be so happy it was Monday morning because at least I knew I could get some food at school."

"Holy shit, Heather—that's horrible! You should have reported him!"

"Ya. Right. Please. You remember how things were back then? There was no reporting stuff like that. Plus, we'd just come from foster care, and we were happy to have our own beds to sleep in. I tell you what, it definitely gave me perspective on my mom's mental health. Mary and I were only there with Didi for a few years because as soon as we could, we graduated and moved out, but Mom spent her entire childhood in that house with that man! I guess it's amazing she didn't go off the deep end sooner. Not to mention Didi. I don't know how she survived."

"So, you don't believe in nature over nurture?" she proposed.

"Oh, jeesh, I don't know. Maybe a little of both. My mom definitely had some type of chemical imbalance, that was for sure, but I don't think being raised by Grandpa Ron helped the situation. He was so callous and unfeeling—that couldn't have been good for a girl who was slowly going through an emotional breakdown."

"No doubt. So awful." Donna's eyes were kind. She was quietly thoughtful.

We both drank more wine. I wondered if those photos had triggered something in me. I hadn't thought about Didi or Grandpa Ron in years—or my mother, for that matter. I must have blocked them all from my consciousness—thus the void in my memory. Maybe some type of survivor's serum.

I continued, "You know, I always wondered why Didi married him. She was so kind and fun loving, and he was so dour, and sour, and mean. They were complete opposites. And I knew they fought a lot, especially over us. I think she saw the effects of his actions on my mom, and maybe that's who she couldn't save. But I never knew for sure, and sometimes I think it ran deeper than that. It was so strange because she seemed oddly powerless in the face of his cruelty. She tried—she'd distract him and cover for us when she could, but ultimately he was like a heat-seeking missile—he always knew when we were out of line. And for some reason, she went along with his ways. I never quite understood the whole dynamic of their relationship. She seemed to be...*obligated* in some way to him—like she owed him something. But then she wanted us to feel safe. I don't know. She was caught between a rock and a hard place."

Donna reflected, "Well, you know how it was back then—you were supposed to be subservient to your man—love, honor, and *obey*. Maybe that's why. Not to mention, come hell or high water—you stuck it out. Till death us do part and all that. It's a good thing we women are liberated now. We don't have to put up with shit like that anymore."

"Thank god. Yeah, I suppose it could all be related to that," I replied skeptically, still trying to work it out in my mind.

"What? Do you think it's more than that?" she asked.

"Maybe...who knows? I guess I wish I knew more about Didi so I could figure it out. In the meantime, it just makes me think that women's lib taught us to be strong, independent, confident women, right? And taught us how to work. How to bring home the bacon and fry it up in a pan."

We stopped to sing the jingle from the old Enjoli ad and giggle.

I went on, "Exactly. Our mothers taught us we were supposed to grow up and have it all. You know—the career, the husband, the family, everything. But don't those expectations set us up for failure? I don't know about you, but there's no way I can live up to them. First of all, my mother loses her mind and is institutionalized, so there goes that role model. Then my dad dies. And Didi raises me, but I feel like I'm watching a woman who's a puzzle with some pieces missing. Mom kills herself and I jump right into marriage with Johnston when I know nothing about keeping a husband happy—or keeping myself happy, for that matter. The kids come and I'm left flailing in the deep end. I'm working at the post office—relegated to sitting on a stool for the rest of my life, saying, 'Would you like a book of stamps with that?' I get a divorce and suddenly I'm a single mother raising two kids with no instructional manual and no net. And as far as dating goes, I'm either completely invisible or a complete pariah. So, yeah, in conclusion, lately I guess I've just been wondering what on earth it's all about."

Donna frowned and said, "Sister, here's some more wine. I think you need this more than I do. Wow, Heather, I had no idea about any of that. I'm so sorry. It's just awful what you went through. No wonder you're struggling." She leaned in and hugged me, then paused as we sipped our wine, each lost in our own thoughts. Finally she put on a stiff upper lip and said, "Okay, now, I have a thought. Get off that ledge, look deep into my eyes, and listen." I sat up expectantly and stared at her, starting to grin despite the remains of the heavy conversation lingering in the air. "The meaning of life is this—are you ready?" I nodded, my eyes widening. "A healthy colon," she burst out laughing, her head shaking and falling nearly to the table, overcome by her revelation. Before I had a chance to react, she began to stand up and twist around, saying, "Would you like to see a healthy colon?"

Oh, Donna, Donna, Donna. I whispered to her (laughing and suddenly frightened, seeing Steve and some others at the bar turn our way), "Sit back down, for goodness' sake, you crazy cuckoo!" That's what I get for trying to have a serious conversation with Donna.

She sat back down reluctantly, and I quipped, "You think I haven't already seen your colon?" She smirked and nodded knowingly, which made us both laugh. I continued, very soberly, "It's a thing of beauty. And you're right.

Although you didn't quite state it this way, you're right that we both have our health, and that's the most important thing. We can't take that for granted."

"No, we can't!" Donna agreed. We clinked our glasses and smiled at each other. Then she said, "Now Heather, listen to me—no, really, seriously this time, I swear. Scout's honor." She held up three fingers, turned them around to face me, and said, "Read between the lines." More laughing, the nut job— she was going to need an Uber home. Finally, she forcibly rubbed her cheeks downward with her hands, peeling the grin away, and relayed this, "Sweetie, life is really about this: a midweek date with your best friend, a good glass of wine (or two or five), and venting about life's mysteries with someone who will listen and care."

I smiled, saying, "Truth."

"And hanging out with good friends who *get* you, inside and out. Savoring that time together. And knowing that no matter what has happened in the past, the other great thing about life is that you can start rewriting it today if you want, or tomorrow or the next day. Nothing is set in stone. Nothing is irreparable. We're not defined or locked in by our past or by the people who raised us. We make our own futures—no one else. You got that?"

Wow, I thought, all of a sudden Donna's actually spouting off something of value. My little drunken guru. I said, "You know, you're making a whole lotta sense. Why is that?"

She put her hands on my shoulders and looked at me, deep in my eyes, saying, "I think I might be a genius. Hmmm. Or it's because I really need to pee. Can we hit the head on the way out?"

And just like that, the moment was gone. I grinned. "Yes, dear."

We paid Steve and gathered our things. On the way to the bathroom, I said, "I really do hear what you're saying about making our own futures—I'm definitely going to work on that. No matter what's going on with the kids, I know that I need to do my own soul-searching—more introspection about what I want out of life and how to get there. And in the meantime, be more present with the kids. I haven't exactly been mother of the year. I gotta work on that. Also, I was thinking about exploring something else with my career. I just feel as though I'm at a dead end, and instead of bitching about it, I need to *do* something about it. I'm not sure what yet, but I'm going to figure it out."

"Yes! You go, girl," Donna said, nodding.

"I know we're talking about the future and all, but I might explore a little

more of my past too. I'd love to understand more about Didi and my mom…
I don't know…I'd love to solve the mystery of them both. In the end, it
might help me understand myself. Maybe I can chat with my sister—she
may remember more than I do. Heck, maybe Delia will find something up in
the attic. There are so many relics and heirlooms up there. Who know what
treasures might be revealed…"

"That's the spirit. Maybe she'll find a trunk full of cash. Anyway, that all
sounds like a good plan," Donna said hurriedly, rushing into a stall.

When she came out and we were washing our hands side by side, she said,
"Listen, no matter what the plan is, I'm here for you, okay?"

"Thanks," I said, "that means the world."

Donna pulled up the Uber app on her phone as we walked out of the
restaurant and had one final thought, "Speaking of the world, have you seen
the *Wonder Woman* movie? I mean, I know you were just talking about all of
those superhero movies, but that's one I can get behind, you know? She grew
up on an island of only kick-ass amazon women. Why don't we just recreate
that world instead?"

"Hmmm, I don't know…can you imagine if all of our periods started to
sync up."

Donna's eyes grew wide as she pronounced, "Whoa."

"Exactly," I agreed, and we both fell into a puddle of laughter.

CHAPTER X

OKAY, SO DON'T JUDGE, but I kind of skimmed through a whole crapload of Didi's diary entries. All that stuff about the ledger and payroll and meeting her friends and relatives—that started to swim together in my mind, and I couldn't figure out where it was headed, so boom, I skimmed. Come on, you know you do it with books too. I'm not the only one. Plus, I really wanted to know what the scoop was with Paul. For a few entries, she didn't even mention him or the whole "engaged" thing, which I found very rude and inconsiderate of her. So, can you blame me for shooting through a few boring entries? Anyway, for your benefit, I'm only including the interesting entries and tidbits below. You can thank me later.

March 4
(Friday) Ran into Sullivan and his friend Hollis. They had just left the diner and were going down to Clive's house, so we went. We played Ping-Pong in his basement until midnight. They're all coming to the dance marathon.

Okay, this entry wasn't exactly interesting, but still, Ping-Pong in 1932? Who knew?

March 5
(Saturday) I went to Bernice's house and spent the night. We took turns reading Shadows on the Rock. *Went to bed at 1:25.*

Really, no mention of Paul yet? Wonder what *Shadows on the Rock* is. A book? I need to look that up.

March 7
(Monday) McCurdy's called and told me they didn't need me to come in today. A little while later, Sam called and told me they asked him to stay home as well. He wondered if we should be worried. I said, how am I supposed to know? I went back to bed. Later that evening, Mom, Dad, James, and I played rummy and talked about the Lindbergh kidnapping. There are some bad people in this world. Paul called, said he's sick, but his mom still needs him to work, so he won't be able to see me all week.

McCurdy's!! Didi's finally said where she worked. I think that used to be a department store in Rochester. I vaguely remember it. I'll ask Mom. Okay, so I'm sure I should know this, but what is the "Lindbergh kidnapping"?

March 9–11
(Wednesday–Friday) Frances called and said Tommy got the Democrat & Chronicle—*they're going to come out to the marathon with their society page reporter! On Friday, I met Paul at the streetcar, and he kissed me, said he felt better. He squeezed my hand so hard on the walk back, I had to let go. He said he loved me that much! Bernice and Roy came over, and we put up flyers everywhere. Afterward, we played murder, a guessing game Roy taught us about music.*

I bet he squeezed that hard trying to keep his thumb on you because you've been apart for a while. No question about the girl back in PA. WTF. But hey, wow, awesome that the D&C was the newspaper back then and still is today!

March 13
(Sunday) I worked on five decoupages and twenty embroidered napkins. I called Paul at the Stand, but he was busy. The Mrs. answered and told me not to call again. Paul mentioned yesterday that she was mad at him for missing so many hours when he was sick and didn't want him to "waste" any time with me this week.

Once again, I think the "Mrs." is a complete bitch. What is her deal? Another red flag, Didi!

March 14–17
(Monday–Thursday) Back on the ledger with Sam. Clara and Will came over for supper on Tuesday night. They said their son, Lloyd, was doing

well in Utica, making $17 per week. He's living with three other men in a tenement down by the river. Paul called and said he misses me. He's all better and wants "to come see his ring" on Saturday. I talked to Bernice on Tuesday about her man, Roy. I wondered how they were doing. She said swell. I told her a little about Paul and how jealous he was. She said Roy wasn't like that. Made me wonder about things a bit. I didn't tell her about the girl from Penn. because I still don't know any more about it. I've been having some trouble sleeping lately, and I think it's because I'm worried about Paul's past, but I'm afraid to ask him about it when he's been so sweet to me lately. Mom told me the other day that I'm twenty now and have to be thinking about settling down and making a home of my own. She said I'm a young woman now and need to start acting like one. I said, "I'm trying!"

$17 a week!!! OMG, how did people live back then? On a different note, Didi's finally taking stock. Interesting. I wonder if she'll shove Paul to the curb. I can't tell if her mom is implying she should go forth and make hay while the sun shines or dump his ass. Maybe that signet ring triggered something, finally.

March 19

(Saturday) Paul called from his break at the Stand. Said he wanted to take me to a show. He said Burrows wanted to come too, with his gal, Stella. We went to the Webster, but they ran out of vanity ware, so we left and went to the Palace instead. I brought home a yellow bowl. Paul held my hand and told me he loved me. We kissed a lot. I don't remember the show.

Sounds like no curb for Paul yet. And no explanation of the mysterious engagement. Ugh. Vanity ware? Is that the pale yellow bowl I found in the cherry music stand? I need to figure out if Depression glass is the same thing. God, the need for a phone is acute!

March 20

(Sunday) Today I spent some time talking to Dad. He sat me down and asked me a few questions about Paul. He wondered how I felt about him. I said I thought I loved him. Then he asked what Paul's intentions were, and I said I thought he might want to marry me someday. Dad said, "Sweetie, you're twenty years old now—no longer a little girl. Your mother and I want the best for you. We like Paul—he's a nice boy—but have you thought about how he would support you?" I couldn't answer because I

didn't know. He said, "The Stand doesn't seem like a long-term plan. Your mother and I want you to think through these things before you get too serious." I nodded, but I didn't know what to think. I love Paul and he loves me, and I'm sure we can figure it all out together. Right?

Good job, Dad! Finally, someone pressing on the brakes. Maybe it'll spur her to ask him some questions. Plus, why is she putting all her eggs in this one basket? She has so many other prospects, not to mention the fact that Paul is so possessive. I want something more for her! And have I mentioned that reading Didi's diary is making me realize I want something more for *me*?! Even with the whole horrendous way it all went down, I still thank my lucky stars every day that Greg and I ended things. He seemed dreamy to me in the beginning, but now I wish he would fall off the face of the earth. It's funny to think how love and hate are only a sliver away on a razor's sharp edge. Granted, Paul isn't a total shithead like Greg was, but still, that doesn't mean he's right for Didi.

March 21–24
(Monday–Thursday) I went to the Stand on Monday during my lunch, but Paul came over and said he couldn't talk because his mom was there. He said the Mrs. was mad at him and Burrows for going out last Saturday and spending money. I didn't see him the rest of the week because we were busy planning the dance marathon.

March 25–27
(Friday–Sunday) The dance marathon was a success! Everything came up aces! We sold more tickets than we could have ever imagined! 119 couples entered, and we paired up 67 singles. After the D&C article came out on Saturday morning, the spectators kept coming and coming until we had to turn them away at the door. We had couples who entered from Buffalo and Syracuse, and even one couple from Erie, Penn.! Didn't see Paul all weekend. I was too tired on Sunday to call him and went to bed at 8:00.

Wow, that was a lot of people for a dance marathon. Good for them! I feel like they should start a business or something. They're so organized. I mean, it sounds like they just fed and housed the entire young adult population of Rochester for a whole weekend. Keep it up and they could just about find a way to end the Depression.

March 28
(Monday) Work was so tiring that I fell asleep on the ledger. Sam nudged me back awake.

March 29
(Tuesday) Finally started to feel okay again. Paul called and said he want-ed to talk to me, so we met at the diner after work. He said he only had an hour until he had to be back at the Stand. He wanted to know who I danced with at the marathon. I told him no one. He looked angry and finally said he heard that I'd danced with a few boys. I asked who told him that, and he wouldn't say. I admitted that yes, we were supposed to be stand-ins for the women on the floor when they took a break, so I had done that (just like all of the other volunteers), but that was it. He looked furious. I said, "I don't like that you're being suspicious of me. And I don't see how you can be when I've done nothing to make you so!" We both sat there fuming for a few minutes, and then I pressed spitefully, "Besides, I'm still waiting to hear all about your girl back home and the big engagement. Don't you think I have a right to know more about that?!" He stared at me with such anger...I've never seen his blue eyes so dark. I immediately regretted it and started to apologize when he abruptly stood up and walked out the door. I was so humiliated, I left soon after (I had to pay!), feeling my cheeks on fire and my tears stuck like daggers in my throat.

Now we're finally getting somewhere. Please, Didi, keep pressing, or alterna-tively, walk away—better yet, run.

March 30
(Wednesday) Paul called me at work three times, but I had Sam tell him I was busy. Sam kept asking me what was wrong, but I didn't tell him. None of his beeswax. As I was leaving the building on my way to the streetcar, there was Paul, waiting on the sidewalk. He walked with me for a while without saying a word. Finally, a block away from the streetcar, he asked, "Can we talk? Over there, on that bench in the park?" "Okay," I agreed, a little afraid. He started by apologizing, but I'd heard that before, so I didn't say anything and waited. Then he began again with, "Her name was Gertrude, but we all called her Gertie. Her parents and my parents were friends, and we grew up together." He paused as if that was it. I gave him a look and he continued, rather reluctantly, "I was in love with her, and

it was expected that we'd get married, so I proposed the day we gradu-ated high school. We were due to get married in the fall." He looked away, his eyes a mysterious shroud. What was going on in that head? Finally, he looked back at me, right in the eyes, with such sadness and something else (humiliation?) and said, "A month before our wedding, she told me she was with child." I gasped! Oh! I think I turned beet red and looked down at my hands. The implications were staggering—I didn't know how to respond. Then I was even more aghast when he continued with, "It wasn't mine." My hand flew to my mouth, and he simply nodded at my look of horror. I could see the entire trajectory of his experience, interwoven with the agonizing hours since, written all over his face.

Holy shit! Wow, so that explains his jealousy issues. Oh man, what a mess. Poor Paul! Poor Didi! Now what are they gonna do?

March 31

(Thursday) I barely slept a wink last night. Work was extra busy today on the switchboard, thankfully. I called Paul at the Stand and told him I would pray for him and that we would talk again soon. When we said goodbye yesterday, he buried his head in my shoulder and I felt his body shaking against mine. I still had so many questions, but I told him they could wait. Tomorrow, I leave for Niagara Falls with Mother, Dad, and James to visit Uncle Louis, Aunt Edna, Lydia, and Abner. I told Paul I would call him when I returned. I didn't tell him that I was relieved to get away from him for a few days so I could think about what he'd said.

Good, she's going on a trip—timing couldn't have been any better. In my own mind, I can't decide if this news excuses his behavior toward Didi. Yes, of course, the PA chick cheated on him and got pregnant by another dude—btw, whoa, in the thirties—wasn't that, like, grounds for the guillotine? Totally scandalous! So you can sort of see why he's all *Fatal Attraction* with Didi. I wonder how he knew the baby wasn't his. Did she tell him? Or maybe they never did the dirty deed. Anyway, so then what happened? Did she come to Paul and want him to pretend to be the daddy, or did she call the engagement off and go be with the other guy? I assume there was no such thing as abortions back then, so did she give the baby up for adoption? What happened to the baby? And what happened to them? Plus, weren't the parents freaking out? And the town gossips...! Oh my! So many things unanswered...

Chapter XI

MOM WOKE ME UP THE NEXT MORNING to tell me she'd be late getting home that night. She was meeting Tanya and Christine after work. Shocker. It was the beginning of day three of this attic project, and she had already bailed on me twice. Who did she think she was kidding? Whatever, Heather—have fun with your gang of desperados in search of the perfect glass of wine accompanied by the elusive and (just as) desperate handsome divorcé.

As she stood in the entryway of my bedroom, I was thinking about Didi and wondering how to open up Pandora's box just a crack. I sat up in bed and said (as casually as I could), "Hey, Ma—I've been seeing a lot of old photos in these boxes, you know, and I wondered a little about...well, about Didi and Grandpa Ron and your mom and dad. You don't talk too much about any of them."

She frowned at me. Apparently, I couldn't have confused her more if I had asked about her favorite song or the weather in Tibet. She said warily, "Um, okay. What do you want to know?"

"I guess I have a bunch of questions, like what was Didi like when you knew her and how did she meet Grandpa Ron, and did they always live here in this house? I mean, wasn't it kind of weird, them moving into her parents' house instead of having their own place? And how old was Didi when they got married and had your mom, and what were they like when you and Aunt Mary lived with them? And what exactly happened to your mom anyway? And to Didi?"

She pulled her face back and knitted her brow, "Whoa there, Nelly. That's a lot of questions." She paused, a sort of reticence and evasiveness clouding her face. Maybe I had unknowingly poked a soft spot. Weird. She said slowly, "Um...listen, I have to get to work right now, but how about we get together this week sometime and talk. It's been a while since we've done anything together, just us. What do you think?"

Oh well—so much for unsolved mysteries. I shrugged and said, "Okay."

Then, starting to leave, she came back and said, "Listen, if you're going out today, can you leave me a note this time so I don't have to call in the national guard?"

"Sure thing, Mummy," I agreed with a thumbs-up. Throw her a bone—the woman looked haggard. Between the late-night drinking and me bringing up painful memories (apparently), she was clearly off her game.

"Good," she replied. "And mow the yard please. Someone's going to report us to the city."

I nodded with false earnestness. Like I cared.

She paused a minute. Her face made a funny twitch as she sat down on the side of my bed. I swallowed. Dang, now what?

She said slowly, "Delia, have you talked to your dad lately?"

"No, why?" I asked, feeling a bubble rise in my chest. I reminded her accusingly, "I don't have a phone, remember?"

She ignored that. "Can you give him a call today?"

"Sure, okay...why? And how?"

She sighed and regarded me with a slight caginess before saying, "Well, I'm debating about leaving you your phone."

I sat up and screeched! As I nearly knocked her off the bed, she stood up and shook her head at me. I may have overplayed my hand and quickly tried to recover, saying as casually as I could, "That would be cool. I could start posting some of the attic junk for sale."

"Yes, yes, that would be good," she responded, not really listening, handing me my phone from her pocket, very slowly, and keeping her hand on it as I tried to pull it from her grasp. She said, "But call Dad first, okay?"

"Sure, sure—whatever you want," I said with my best fake smile. Jeesh, what was going on with Dad? She let go of the phone, and I formed my fingers around it like a portkey—take me away! I was breathing hard and smiling from ear to ear.

"Okay. Don't sell any family heirlooms, okay? And don't spend the whole day on the phone. Remember what Doctor Peterson said. And I want to see some progress around here when I get home, do you understand?"

Uh-huh, like she was gonna notice progress at drunk o'clock tonight. And god, why did she have to bring up that quack, Doctor Peterson? My one-time counselor who had this ridiculous theory that we should all get rid of our cell phones. Revolutionary, Einstein. Like that's gonna happen. I think the dude had this dream that it would be just like the fifties again and everyone would be tossing their phones (like banned books) into a huge bonfire and singing "Kumbaya."

Right. Seemed completely plausible, like Cait Jenner becoming Bruce again or One Direction getting back together.

"Got it, I'm on it," I assured her with my most productive, compliant daughter face.

"Good," she said, somewhat distracted, looking around my messy room. "Maybe I should stay home tonight..." Her voice drifted off.

"Why? Are you worried about me tossing out the photo from your eighth-grade dinner dance with Tibby Thornton? Never fear—I've already memorialized it in a shadowbox, complete with dried flowers and a wreath made of human hair."

Mom smiled, despite her distraction, her eyes back on me. She squeezed my shoulder and said, "Oh Delia, how can someone so smart and so funny have such a stick up her butt?"

"Hey!" I yelled. "That's for pleasure only. Maybe you could use one yourself."

"Delia! Enough! Ewwww!" She went out of the room with her hands over her ears, reminding me again not to be on the phone all day and to call my dad right away. Repetition—Mom's elixir of life. I'm not a complete idiot, Mom—I heard you the first three times.

After she left, I sat in bed for an hour in a complete trance, scrolling through my missed texts, phone calls, and everyone's social updates. It was rather disconcerting to realize that I had been completely off the grid for months and ninety-nine percent of my friends hadn't even noticed. Was it possible that everyone's lives had gone on without me? Not even a blip on the radar. F-ing sucked.

I spent another twenty minutes or so looking up stuff from Didi's diary. A lot of those places and things didn't exist anymore—like a world gone by or simply disappeared. Made me wonder, would someone look back on our time in ninety years and think, what were they doing with their time back then, and what were those stupid phones and TVs and tablets all about? Except maybe in my case, with the way the world was changing on a dime now, it would be ten years instead of ninety. Kind of scary when you thought about it.

Anyway, I finally tore myself away, stretching my neck and wrists. The sun was shining through my window directly on my cleats, and I smiled. Yesterday had been a perfectly awesome foray back into the game, set in motion by the angels of soccer heaven. Why was I worried about the world inside my phone? My mind wandered to Jake. God, that boy was good-looking. I remembered that at one point in the game, I'd noticed the swift, strong movement of his thighs as he was running. And I liked how the cowlick sent his bangs over the left side of his forehead. And his eyes were like the sun-streaked speckles of a forest reflected on the surface of a lake. Mmm-hmm-yum. That bear hug—like being enveloped in a sweaty sea of warm goo, but not the gross goo—more like a vat of aloe vera or something.

But what was he doing with that blondy-blond bubblehead? She didn't seem to be his type. Vacuous and voluptuous, in all the wrong places. Or in the right places, said every boy everywhere. Ho-hum. I guess I wasn't his type. Of course, how would I know Jake's type? Up until a couple of days ago, I thought of him as the annoying boy who put gum in my hair. Now I found myself imagining him leaning in to tuck a piece of hair behind my ear. And touching my cheek. And putting his hand on the small of my back. And pulling me into an embrace. And pressing his lips to mine.

Ert. Brakes, please. He's got a girl, and a jealous one at that. And maybe I was wrong about the bubbleheadedness—maybe she was a perfect Madame Curie under the corn-silk hair—who knew?

Anyway, Delia, better let that ship sail.

I went downstairs and ate a bowl of cereal. Then, being the dutiful daughter I was feigning to be at the moment, I mowed the yard. Afterward, I remembered I had stashed away that black scrapbook and the spiral-bound notebook. I looked at the scrapbook first. It was jam-packed with photos of Didi and Paul, all black and white, secured with corner squares and labeled with cute little expressions like "Paul swimming for the Olympic trials," "Paul trying out for his role in the pictures," and "Paul sweeping me off my feet." There were strategically placed heart and cupid stickers throughout—it reminded me of a sticker album that a sixth grader would put together. Funny, here she was twenty, yet acting like a lovesick adolescent. Maybe kids matured later in life back then.

I found the flyer for the dance marathon in there. It had a hand-drawn picture of a couple dancing and all the particulars Didi had mentioned in her diary. God, how did they make hundreds of copies back then? Must have traced them by hand. Can you imagine?

I began to wonder what had happened between the photos in this scrapbook and the Didi who raised Mom. Such a mystery—she was obviously madly in love with Paul, but she ended up with Grandpa Ron. Paul gave her that signet ring—wasn't that like a pre-engagement ring? I guess I'd have to keep reading (or skimming) to figure it all out. I held one of the photos up to the light in the hallway. It was quite the fetching shot of Didi standing knee-deep in the water, a bathing cap in her hand, a smile on her face. She looked young and happy and free. What happened to that girl?

I put down the scrapbook and shuffled through several open boxes. I was struck by the number of photos we had in this household. I swear, the D.D. was a warehouse storage facility for Kodak. Pretty much everyone throughout our family's history had worked there, starting with Dennis Diamond. Mom used to talk about it a lot. How Dennis and then her Grandpa Ron and then her dad and then my dad had all worked there. Plus, Mom (before the P.O.) and her sister Mary (summer internship during college) as well as basically every living and dead person who had ever passed through the D.D. at one point or another, had worked at Kodak.

Crazy, though, how a company so big, old, and influential can go down the tubes in a heartbeat. Something for the business pundits to ponder for all eternity. In the meantime, I was drowning in the colossal Kodak archive that was my attic and now the upstairs hallway, contemplating what to do with five generations of still frames—snapshots frozen in time. You can't sell them. You can't throw them away. You can't donate them. So what do you do? Keep them. To take up space. Lots and lots of space.

Incidentally, there was some crazy family story that Grandpa Ron invented color film. Or was it that he was the first to use color film? I'm not sure. As per Mom's usual exaggerated dictation on D.D. family lore, there was some embellished ditty about Grandpa Ron being a film tester back in the thirties and taking color photos before color was even around. I suppose it was at least somewhat plausible. Maybe I would find some color pics mixed in with these black and whites. Of course, there was also the other crazy family story that Grandpa Ken (Mom's dad, who died before I was born) saw the video of a man walking on the moon in a super-secret Kodak test lab years before it ever happened in real life. Um, what? Sure. I know. Certifiable. Hereditary line clouded with all kinds of muck. Lucky me. At least I'm half made up of Dad's stuff. Thank you, Johnston, for saving me from *Girl, Interrupted.*

Speaking of family muck, I went back into my room to look through the spiral-bound notebook. It had the name Ann Aster Culver written in large letters across the inside flap. No date. My mom's mom. Unlike the Diamond family legacy, Mom didn't talk about her mom. Hardly ever. Other than to say she was "mentally ill" and "institutionalized." I guess I could see why, flipping through the angry scroll-work describing "the rise in robot density" and the role of "artificial intelligence" in "replacing human activity." Then there was the bluster detailing "microtechnology," including "recircuiting" of "electrical devices" into miniaturized "sensors" and "actuators" for "insertion in brain stem" to "increase throughput and reduce errors," thereby "eliminating the human factor."

It all seemed highly intelligent, actually. Like an engineer trying to solve an electrical problem. But it definitely bled over into paranoia and psychosis. I flipped through the remaining pages, trying to decipher the dark poetry, ramblings, black-inked artwork, and incoherent soliloquies, but finally gave up. It wasn't logical or chronological or *anything* "ical," and it seemed as if no amount of time spent on it would lead to an understanding. It was like trying to find the coordinates of a ship on a sea that hadn't been discovered yet. Cryptic, disjointed, discombobulated. I gave up and set it down. Enough exploring the bowels of my family's innards.

I called Dad.

"Delia!" he answered, surprised. "You got your phone back?"

"Yes, well, I believe it's on some type of temporary visa program, but yes. How are you? Mom was very insistent that I call you—I'm not sure why...?"

"Oh yeah, that...well, hang on, I'm at work...let me go find a room...one sec."

I waited with a strange feeling in the pit of my stomach. He sounded serious. Why did he have to go to a room to talk to me? I had a flash that he and Beth might be getting a divorce. God, history repeating itself! That would be awful. I really liked Beth, and I couldn't imagine him going through another divorce. Right when we finally had a good routine all worked out. And Mom being (relatively) stable. It would certainly be a hot mess. My cereal churned in my stomach.

"Okay, I'm here. Hang on, let me close the door. I thought you were on attic duty."

"Yes, still am. By the way, thank you for that!"

"Hey, you gotta pay the piper sometime. It was Mom's idea, but I didn't think it was such a bad one. Why, how's it going?"

"Stellar," I answered flippantly. "That's about all I wanna say about that. So, what's the fire drill all about?"

"Are you sitting down?"

"Yes. What is it, Dad? Spit it out."

"Beth's pregnant."

"What? Holy shit!" I screamed, shocked.

"Yep, it's true. The Remington is still shooting real bullets. Can you believe it?"

"Dad! TMI, jeesh. Wow, though, congrats—that's awesome. So...so...are you excited or what?" I was think-talking...I mean, the guy was old...how was I to know? Was he happy about this? Did he plan it?

"Of course I am! What kind of a question is that? Yes, we're both very excited. I was a little worried...well...how you and Tyler would react...though... I wasn't sure..."

"Wait. Tyler knows?"

"Yes, I called him the other day. I would have called you too, but, well...no phone."

"Of course, I'm the last to know."

"Well, don't worry about that...Beth's only like eight weeks along, so you haven't missed anything. What do *you* think about it? I mean, how do you feel?"

"I don't know..." I had to screw my eyes back into their sockets. "I'm shocked, of course. I didn't realize you guys were even thinking...or trying...but yeah, it's cool. Why not? A baby brother or sister...wow!"

"Yep. Crazy, right? I can't wait for you and Tyler to be big brother and sister. You can change his diapers, feed him, teach him how to ride a bike, teach him how to curse...actually, come to think of it, can you *not* teach him certain things...there will be ground rules..."

Ignoring that, "So, it's a boy?"

"Oh, no. Well, I mean, I don't know—we don't know yet. Beth wants to find out during the ultrasound, but I don't. I'd rather be surprised, like it was when you two were born. But we'll see..."

I predicted they would know the sex in exactly one month. I laughed and said, "Well, either way, it's great, Dad. Really great. I just can't believe it. Are you... scared at all? I mean, you'll be, what? Like seventy or eighty when the kid goes to college...right?"

"God! Leave it to you to throw my age up in my face," he said laughing. "Yeah, I've done the math—it's not pretty. But I don't care. I'm in great health, still fit as a fiddle. And my grandma and grandpa lived into their nineties. Heck, look at Mom and Dad—they're in their late seventies and doing great. So I figure, I should be fine...of course, I could get hit by a bus tomorrow, but other than that I'm up for it. Why not?"

"Okeydokey, Pops—I'm proud of you. And say congrats to Beth for me. I'm really happy for you both."

"Thanks, Delia. That means a lot to us. Love you, girl."

"Love you too, Dad."

"So, hey, before we hang up, you're coming to stay in a few weeks, right?"

"Depends..."

"Oh yeah, the attic. Fun, fun...well, we'll play it by ear then. No worries, we have your bed all ready."

"Okay, I'll let you know. What about Tyler?"

"I only talked to him for a few minutes the other day, but he told me he planned to come on the Fourth of July and stay for the month. We'll see."

"Okay, cool. Maybe I'll come then too."

"Alright, sweetie. That sounds good. Hey, you been okay...lately?"

"Yep, fine, good."

"You sure?"

"Yes, Dad, I'm fine. In fact, I played soccer yesterday, and it was awesome."

"Mom told me about that—she thought you disappeared again."

"Wah-wah, you know Mom..."

"No seriously, Delia, cut your mom some slack, okay?"

"Uh-uh."

"Really. Okay. I better let you go. I'll talk to you again soon. Love you, sweetie."

"Love you too, Dad. Bye."

"Bye."

I hung up, thinking, holy crap! Another Elliott on this planet. That was wild. I loved babies as much as the next person, but seriously, my dad was so old. How on earth was he going to handle that? Diaper duty and spit-up and no sleep? Wow. And he was still paying child support to Mom for me and paying for Tyler's college. That man was certainly stretching the Bank of Dad for many years to come. Oh well, not my problem. Thankfully he had a good job. He'd left Kodak before the bankruptcy and became an executive at Bausch and Lomb. Better get the Roth IRA in gear, Daddy Warbucks.

The baby would be good for Beth. I think she'd always wanted kids. So far, she'd been great with me and Tyler, even when we were (and maybe still are) bratty and undisciplined. She'd always been patient, kind, nurturing. You could kind of understand why Mom hated her. She was probably broiling with the news.

I was a little curious, though, how the new baby would affect my relationship with Dad. Would I ever see him anymore? Wouldn't all the attention go to the new baby? Although...maybe that wouldn't be so bad. I didn't really need a magnifying glass on me at this particular juncture in my life. What he didn't know didn't hurt him. Not that under my new and improved Delia plan I was expecting to continue down my former highway to hell, but still, everything was rather fragile right now, so maybe having the heat off me for a while was a good thing.

Speaking of staying under the radar, even though I had my phone back now, I decided not to post anything. My social media could stay quiet, and I would remain in stealth mode. Better to observe and get the lay of the land first. Instead, I dug into attic work. I downloaded several selling apps and posted a few ads for old furniture. I used creative, vivid, catchy descriptions and uploaded snazzy pics to accompany the details (i.e., Aunt Ida's Truly Heinous Tangerine Silk Flowered Couch, Two BarcaLoungers Complete with Perfectly Paired Bodacious Butt Imprints, Desktop PC Awaiting Decommissioning from the 1996 Smithsonian Asset Recovery Vault). Speaking of cash or my lack thereof, I needed it, and fast. I was so broke! Maybe these sales would give me some ready coin. After I finished posting, I decided to call my friend McKenzie.

"Hello?" she answered tentatively.

"Zup, homey?"

"Um, who is this?" Mock annoyance.

"Guess."

"Come on, who is this?" Still with the farce.

"I'll give you a hint."

"Yes?"

"I was sent to the principal's office three times."

"That doesn't narrow it down. Can you be more specific?"

"One of those office visits was for writing "Beee-atch" on your locker in magic marker. Now do you remember?" As if she hadn't seen my name pop up on her phone the moment it rang. I continued with a chuckle, "Aren't you the little thespian."

"Haha, you know it. Like my acting? 'I coulda been a contender!'" she said in her best Marlon Brando. Then, "Hey, I had to give you some razzing. I mean, how long has it been? Like freakin' months, girl. So...Miss Delia, the invisible. Where the heck have you been? You know, we've all been wondering if you were alive or dead or in juvie."

"Military camp. You know, whips and chains."

She grunted. "Sounds like my kind of camp. We thought it was rehab."

"Same difference."

"No, seriously. Where have you been?"

"The usual. The D.D. Mom's got me cleaning the attic."

"Whoa, sucks to be you."

"No doubt. So, what are you doing today? Wanna come over?"

"I gotta work."

"When?"

"Two."

"So, come now, just for an hour. I'm dry as a bone. I need gossip. Unabridged. Hook me up, girl. Come hither. Now."

"Hang on, let me see if I can."

I heard her talking to someone in the background, and then she said, "Okay, be there in a few."

"Cool. Bye."

Awesome. I felt myself renewed with teen spirit already. I went to the porch to wait on the Nan. The neighborhood was already abuzz with mowers and kids hollering out the windows. It felt like summer. I smiled to myself.

Fifteen minutes later, McKenzie pulled up in her Prius, beeping the horn and screaming, "Delia Elliott, get your lazy ass off that swing and get to work!"

I laughed and went to greet her with a hug. It was good to see her. We sat on the swing. She was tall and tan and blond with dark brown eyes.

I immediately grilled her. "What's been going on? Who've you seen? What've you been doing? Where've you been? What've I missed?"

She laughed. "Chillax, girl. Jeesh, you know this town—I mean, seriously, you haven't missed much."

"Well, what have I missed?"

"To begin with, a certain someone was asking about you."

"What? Who?" I couldn't imagine who she meant.

She gave me a knowing frown, and I chucked her shoulder.

"Who?" I thought she was joshing me and that there really was no one asking about me. Keep in mind that I hadn't talked to anyone in months.

"Greg, you dummy."

"Oh," I said flatly. "No way. That ass. Where did you see him?"

"At the movies."

"With who?"

"I don't know...some skank."

"What did he say?" I gulped. Did I really want to know?

"He said, 'Hey, McKenzie. Looking fine.' So slimy. You know. Anyway, then he chats me up a bit and says, 'Hey, where's Delia? Is she with you?' I told him no, and he wanted to know where you were. Always checking up on you, I swear. I told him I didn't know. I didn't want to tell him I hadn't talked to you in months... otherwise, he'd probably get full of himself, thinking he had something to do with that, the asshole. Would you believe it—he told me to tell you to call him."

"He did not!"

"Yes, he did!"

"Fuck," was all I could think to say.

We sat in silence for a while, swinging.

I asked quietly, "So, are people still talking?"

She waited to answer...thoughtful, reluctant. "Not as much as before. It's definitely died down, but well...you know how people are..."

I regarded her soberly. "What do you mean?"

"Well, I mean that I don't hear much about it anymore, like barely ever. But, well, sometimes..."

"Tell me, McKenzie. *Right now.* What do you mean?" I repeated my question, knowing the Band-Aid had to come off. Better now than later out in public somewhere.

"Okay...I don't know. God, I hate to tell you, really I do...but anyway, Alicia and I were at Tully's the other day getting ice cream, and we overheard some kids talking about you."

"Who? Kids? What kids? What did they say?"

"We didn't know who they were, and by the way, if this eases your mind, they didn't know who you were either. They just knew about you and knew your name, but they didn't know you. They were talking about the girl whose photo had circulated. Apparently they had all seen it. The girls at the table said how horrible it was, and the guys said...well, the guys were typical guys—you know, dicks."

"God!" I put my head in my hands. It would never really end, would it?

McKenzie put her arm around my shoulder. "I'm so sorry, sweetie. Just ignore them. They suck! They all suck!"

We sat like that for a while. Finally, I raised up on the swing and said, "Well, now at least you know why I've been off the grid for months. How can I go out with shit like that happening at every turn? How?"

"I know, I know...it's awful. Awful! I wish I could make it go away for you. I do."

After a few minutes, I resignedly changed the subject and told her about Dad's news. I confirmed, "Yep, the old guy's still doing it."

"Ewwww. Wow, though—*wow.*"

"Yeah, totally bizarre. I'm going to have a baby brother or sister. I mean, I remember wanting one of those when I was like three years old, but not now, for shit's sake."

"No doubt. Totally Alec Baldwin."

"Yup. I mean, it's cool—I'm happy for him. Just strange, that's all."

We sat contemplating and swinging.

Then I said, "Wanna come inside and see the tornado?"

"Sure. Do you have anything to drink? I'm arid."

I got her a glass of orange juice and walked her around the house, giving a tour of the masses. She found a small lamp in one corner that she liked. I told her to take it. It was dark blue with yellow stars and said, "Twinkle, Twinkle, Little Star."

At some point, I asked her, "Hey, by the way, where are you working?"

"Starbucks."

"You are? That sounds cool. Do they have any openings?"

"No—where were you like a month ago? They filled all the summer jobs back then."

"Bummer. Figures. Oh well. Hey, do you remember Jake Freimuth?"

"Sophomore?"

"Yes, well, now going to be a junior. Lives down the street."

"Yeah, yeah, I know him. He's dating Chelsea."

"Blonde? Cheerleader type?"

"Yep, that's the one, but she isn't a cheerleader. She's a swimmer. In Penfield."

"Dang, girl, how do you know her?"

"She goes to our church. She's friends with my sister. Why?"

"Well, okay, I guess I didn't know...not until yesterday anyway. Jake and I played soccer over at the pitch, and she was there. And well, before she was there, before I knew he had a girlfriend, I was kind of...like...kind of crushing on Jake a little." I bit my lip.

"What the heck, Delia? You go right from the flames into the fire."

"I know, I know. Don't get me wrong—he doesn't know...I'm not going to pursue him or anything, especially if he's got a girl. I was just curious, I guess." I deflected, "Anyway, he said he might get me a job at the RCC."

"That would be cool. I hear they pay fifteen dollars an hour."

"Really? Didn't know that, but that would be awesome. We'll see..."

She shrugged and asked, "So, what else has been going on?"

"Nada. Squat for me. How are you and Justin doing?"

"Good—going strong. It'll be six months on Monday. Can you believe it?"

"No way. That's great."

She stayed for a while longer, and it felt great to catch up. It had been so long, on my survivor island, sequestered, and I hadn't realized how much I'd missed human interaction. Eventually she left to get to work, and I went back up to the attic. I posted seven more items for sale and responded to inquiries on the earlier posts. One guy said he'd stop by to pick up an old bookshelf that night, and some woman said she'd be over to get a large gold mirror. Then I sold three dressers, two silver serving trays, and a cherry desk, so more pickups tomorrow. I was already set to make three hundred twenty dollars, and I was flying high. Cha-ching.

Right around the time I was completely absorbed in assessing the chipped veneer of an antique bookcase, wondering if I could cover the exposed chips with Old English, I heard a welcome interruption. Jake, running, not walking, up the stairs, screaming my name.

"Hey," I said, with a smile.

"Hey," he replied, with an unexpected (and oh so welcome) hug.

"What's up?" I asked when he let go and looked at me with such a glow in his green eyes that I had to look down for a second to avoid revealing my own glow.

"You down for the pitch?" he asked.

"Sure thing, hang on..." I pulled out my phone.

"Whoa! You got your phone back?"

"Yep, but I'm still wearing the ankle bracelet. Let me text my parole officer and change my clothes, and I'll be right down." He laughed and left me.

I texted Mom, *"Heather, I'm going to soccer with Jake. I know you won't be here, but I wanted to let you know so you won't put my face on a milk carton."*

She texted back, *"Thank you, Delia. I appreciate you letting me know. Did you call Dad?"*

"Yes—we'll talk about that later."

"Okay. Have fun! Don't let those boys push you around."

"Those wusses? No problema, señora. Later, gator."

She returned with a plethora of heart emojis.

Chapter XII

WHEN I GOT THE TEXT FROM DELIA, I felt a smidge of comfort in my heart. Was Delia progressing? Three days in the attic and she was already texting me her whereabouts, playing soccer, and hanging out with Jake Freimuth. Promising. I really liked that boy and his whole family. Maybe attic duty was working. I hated to take credit, but well…why not? I was feeling about twenty-five percent confident about the turn of events. Maybe, just maybe, the fuselage of the plane that crashed all those months ago was slowly being reassembled. I sighed. Or maybe it was just a mirage.

At work, I noticed that Tom had brought Ashley up to the front to teach her how to check people out. She sat with me the other day, but just as my shadow. Today she was actually getting some hands-on training, and Tom was loving being her mentor, saying little nuggets like, "Now, when a customer goes to leave, don't let him out that door before you ask if there's anything else you can get him. You'd be surprised the additional sales you generate with that simple question. For instance, I usually point out that we sell greeting and gift cards (pointing to the display), which are great for the last-minute shopper. You know, it's so helpful to have a one-stop shop so folks can bundle their errands." Ashley nodded dutifully while I tried not to let them see me rolling my eyes. During a quiet period, I overheard her say to him that she was engaged to be married. That was nice. She really was sweet. Out of the blue, somehow Ashley's presence made me remember the other millennial who had most recently (and most unceremoniously and uninvitedly) popped back into my consciousness—Beth. I couldn't believe Johnston was having a baby. The announcement made me feel yucky inside. I wasn't sure why. Certainly, he was a great father to Tyler and Delia, despite our issues, so I guess it was good for him to be starting on this new adventure with her. It was just the idea that he was so settled and sure-footed, and I was so…well, not.

Don't get me wrong—I wasn't jealous. Not of the pregnancy. Oh, no. I'd been there, done that, and I was good to go. For sure. I remembered back then, when Tyler was born, I would call Didi nearly every day to get her advice. Was the baby supposed to take one nap or two? How would I know if he was getting enough milk when I was nursing? When was the right time to put the locks on the cabinets and those plastic safety covers on the outlets? She was great. One time, when Tyler was colicky and I couldn't get him to stop crying, I called Didi in the middle of the night in desperation, saying I was about to lose my mind from exhaustion and frustration. She came right over, held him and cooed to him, and finally rubbed something into his gums (to this day, I'm not sure what it was). Miracle of miracles, he was quiet after that—went right down and fell fast asleep. I laid my head down on the daybed beside his crib and didn't remember a thing after that until morning. Didi must have let herself out and gone home—a phantom angel of stealth selflessness.

Now I was trying to picture Johnston's new world in my mind. Probably so different from the one we'd been in during our twenties, learning how to raise our children from scratch. We had no idea what we were doing. Now it was so different…with this new baby and new relationship, he would already know so much. For instance, I assumed there would be no traditional separation of duties. Back then, I was always expected to do everything for the baby (feeding, diapers, development), plus housework, laundry, cooking, cleaning, and my real job, while he was expected to go to the office and come home again. During one of our frequent arguments, I remember screaming at him, "Do you think fairies come in the night to vacuum and do the dishes and buy the groceries?!" I think he sorta did.

But these young women nowadays, they expect equal rights in the workplace *and* in the home. Lucky them. Johnston would probably be equal partner and parent for the next eighteen years. And let's be honest, for the next *forever* number of years. Wow, that's a lot of years to contemplate. Oh well, he made his bed (literally and figuratively!), and now he had to lie in it. It would be interesting to see how it all worked out. For my part, I still wasn't clear on the direction of my life, let alone creating a new one. And yeah, maybe at my age that was slightly pitiful, but one thing I knew for sure—I was happier being in my shoes than his right now.

As soon as my shift was over, I jumped in the car and drove to the bar, Lock 32, to meet Tanya and Christine. It was a beautiful night on the Erie

Canal—the sun reflecting off the water, and the boats, kayaks, and canoes swishing by in the lazy summer heat. As I waited for the ladies to show up, I went to the bar and ordered a beer, taking it and sitting down on a stool overlooking the water. I smiled. I thought about my conversation with Donna from the night before. I remembered her thoughts on the meaning of life (not the healthy colon part!) when she said it was all about enjoying friends and savoring each precious moment. Sure, Johnston was having a baby, but heck, I had something better—freedom! To meet my girlfriends on a weeknight, to drink where I wanted and with whom I wanted and as often as I wanted and as many as I wanted (okay, so maybe these weren't stellar life goals, but still…). And I could date! I could flirt! I could go to chick flicks! I could eat ice cream out of the container! I could sleep in on a Saturday! I could drive to Canada! I could go boating! I could hike a mountain! I could read naughty books! I could date hot guys! I could break their hearts! I laughed, thinking, so what if I didn't actually do many of these things? The point was, I *could*!

Tanya walked up and said with a grin, "You look like a kid who's been caught with her hand in the cookie jar."

I laughed and replied, "Maybe I am! And you look like a fourteen-year-old girl who's ready for the cotillion ball!"

"Thank you—I'll take that as a compliment."

We hugged and laughed.

She pulled back and challenged, "What, you don't like my dress?"

"Oh, don't get all huffy. I just meant you might be a smidge overdressed, that's all." She did look spectacular in a tight white sundress with an orange sash. I stood back and admired. I said, "Hey, I'd do you."

"Good," she said, grinning. "By the way, love that," she pointed at my top, a green V-neck flowy number.

"Thanks, chick—would you do me?" I asked with a pout.

"Eighty ways to Sunday, my friend."

"Ouch, sounds painful." We both laughed.

Christine arrived and before long we were sitting three abreast on the stools facing the canal, drinking our beer, and diving into our usual banter. Ever since high school, it had been like this for us—the three witches of Eastwick. That movie was big when we were in high school, and we had even dressed as the characters for Halloween one year, complete with all the hair and makeup. It went over like gangbusters. The boys loved it, and Tanya met her husband that way. We were juniors and he was a senior. He walked right up to her that day and asked her out. We died laughing at the time, but all these years later they were still married, with three grown children and a grandbaby on the way.

Tanya was loud and boisterous and fearless. Christine, on the other hand, was shy and introverted. I was somewhere in between. Christine had been so quiet for so many years that she didn't get married and settle down until she was forty-five. She was an engineer at the nuclear power plant, and her husband worked there as a physicist. They didn't have any kids, but they did have three horses, six barn cats, three dogs, and a large chicken coop.

"How's the P.O.?" Tanya asked me.

"Same shit, different day. How's Weggies?" Tanya worked as a manager at Wegmans, which just happened to be the most spectacular grocery store chain in the whole wide world, a sort of mecca-slash-tourist-attraction-slash-grocery-store. Crisp, clean, massive, and stocked to the brim, you had to see it to believe it.

"Ditto. Busy, but fine. You, Christine?"

"Good."

Tanya said, "Okay, glad we got the work talk out of the way. What else is going on?"

"Actually, speaking of work…," I said.

"Yes? Did I cut it off too quick? That's a first." Tanya was surprised—I never had anything interesting to say about work.

"Oh, sorry, don't get excited—it's not about the P.O. It's something else I've been thinking about lately. So…I've been watching a lot of home improvement shows—"

Tanya chimed in, "Oh, I love those! I watch them too! What I don't understand is how they're able to get those houses looking perfect in such a short period of time. It's just not possible…"

Christine said softly, "I think it's all just a ruse, you know? They hire like seventy-five people and spend a gazillion dollars. No regular, ordinary folks like us would be able to pull it off. They act like they snap their fingers and voilà, it's done!"

"Yes, exactly! It's ridiculous! Of course, I still watch," Tanya admitted.

"Me too," Christine laughed.

Christine asked Tanya, "Did you see the one the other night—that house in California with the rats crawling around in there? Oh my god!"

"YES!" Tanya exclaimed. "I saw that! Totally gave me the heebie-jeebies.

So that's a perfect example—do you really think the host of that show, what's his name and his pretty wife, are down in that muck exterminating those varmints? Of course not! They stage a couple of photos and head straight back to their penthouse suite. Total B.S."

Christine nodded, and I cleared my throat and raised my hand. "Hello? Ladies? Earth to ladies? I was trying to talk about something…"

Christine laughed and said, "Oh! Sorry about that. Please go on."

"Well, as I was saying, I've been watching those shows, and I was thinking about—"

Tanya cut me off again, "Oh. My. God. You're gonna renovate the D.D.! That is so awesome! I wondered when you'd get around to it! It *so* needs it! All these years and no one, and I mean *no one*, understood why or how you've managed to stay in that death trap."

"What?!" I said, shaking my head. "No! It's not that. Although that would be great, but I don't have the money or skill for that right now. Oh, and that reminds me, dammit, I forgot to call about the air conditioner! It's on the fritz again. Grrrr. Anyway, would you both just shut up for two seconds and let me talk?"

They smiled and did the zip-across-the-mouth sign, grinning like schoolchildren in trouble with the teacher.

I sighed and continued, "So, I was thinking…drum roll, please…maybe I'd get my real estate license. You know, sell houses. What do you think?"

"Really?" Tanya said, frowning. "Oh sorry, am I allowed to speak now? Wait, really? That sounds great and all, but why?"

Not the best opening. "Well, hear me out. I've been thinking about it for a while. Not this exactly…but wanting to do something else with my career… you know? The P.O. is great as far as a stable job and great benefits, but does it warm the cockles of my heart? Um…not. It mostly makes me want to stab a large serrated knife into the cockles of my heart. On a daily basis. And I want… well actually, I'm not sure what I want, exactly, but I want something *more*."

Christine nodded, trying to understand. She asked, "So would you quit the P.O.?"

"No, not right away anyway. I need to stay a few more years to get my pension. I figure I'd do the real estate thing on the side for starters, see how it goes…and maybe sometime later, if I'm successful, I'd retire from the P.O. But don't worry, I'm not fully counting on it all working out perfectly. I'm just going to take a stab at it."

Tanya stared at me with a crease in her forehead. She finally shrugged and said, "Stab? After what you just said about the P.O., I'm a little worried." She chuckled, then said, "Yeah, what the heck, why not?"

"Then why are you looking at me that way?"

Her forehead smoothed out, and she said, "What way?" She sighed and said, "Okay, so I'm a little skeptical, I admit it. Not that you couldn't do it—you've always been super smart and productive. It's just…well, it's just… is this the right thing for you to do *right now*?"

"What's that supposed to mean?" I asked, defensive.

"Don't get me wrong—I think it's a great idea, in theory. But in execution, wouldn't it take a ton of time? I think you have to study for it and take some big test and be available to people at all times, day or night—at their beck and call. I can't even imagine. I wonder if you've thought this through. Plus, with Tyler in college and Delia a senior this year—I remember those ages for my kids—aren't you sort of at *their* beck and call, too? Especially Delia. Wouldn't this new job take you away from them, from her?"

"Well, yes, I guess so…a little, but they're on their own already most of the time anyway."

"Yes, exactly." Tanya answered significantly, staring at me with big eyes.

"And what the hell does *that* mean?" Now I was pissed.

Christine jumped in, "Heather, listen. We love you. Both of us. We do. So don't take this the wrong way, but it seems like, well, it seems like you're barely ever home as it is, even now. I text you and you're out and about…a lot. Okay, so I know what you're thinking by your look—in other words, what do I know? Sure, I don't have kids, but still, I kind of agree with Tanya. I wonder sometimes about Delia being left alone so much…especially in light of…well, in light of the year she's had."

"Seriously? Seriously?!" I was about to blow a gasket. How did a conversation about real estate end up being a critique of my parenting skills? I pushed back. "Hey, I'm essentially a single parent, first of all. And I know I'm not perfect, but I think I've done a pretty bang-up job with both my kids." Okay, so I knew as I was saying this that I was totally negating Johnston's role, not to mention exaggerating the effect of my own parenting on my kids, but still, these gals—my best friends!—were really getting my goat.

Tanya took my hand, "Yes, of course. We agree. Those kids are great. We aren't trying to be judgmental…"

"YES, you are!" I felt the heat in my face. And then I dug myself in deeper and proceeded with this rant, "You have no idea how hard it is to be the one who has to make all the decisions all the time. Sure, Johnston tries to pretend like he's participating, but it's easy to be a great parent when you only see them on the weekends and during the summer. I get all the hard stuff, and he gets to be the fun parent. It sucks to be the hardballer, the disciplinarian. It absolutely sucks. And half the time it doesn't even work. So what if I go out and drink away my blues sometimes—wouldn't you? I feel like I deserve to let off some steam. And that doesn't make me a bad parent!" I paused to breathe and calm down, and then I said flatly, "Oh, and by the way, Beth's pregnant."

"Shit," Christine and Tanya replied in unison.

We all took chugs of beers, followed by silence.

After a while, I said, "You know, I was watching this program on TV the other night—about these macaws that have to eat clay in order to absorb the toxins in their food."

Tanya and Christine stared at me as if I were crazy. Then Christine smiled and said, "Are you saying you have to drink a lot of beer to swallow Johnston's baby?"

"Pretty much," I replied.

They both burst out laughing. I joined in and shrugged my shoulders.

Tanya said, "I'm so sorry, sweetie. You go get that real estate thing. It would be good for you. I'm such a dope—I shouldn't have said a word."

"It's okay," I said, touching her shoulder lightly. "It's really no big deal, the Johnston thing. I'm actually quite...happy for him. And of course, you're right about me. I've been so...so *absent* lately. From Delia. From Tyler. From my life. After Delia's *incident*, I guess I just sort of shut down a little, you know? I failed her. I failed myself." I paused, and gosh darn it, I felt tears well up in my eyes. I knew I had a reckoning coming, but did it have to happen here? And now? I couldn't stop them—there they were, those evil, accusing tears, falling down my face. My repentant, guilty, worthless face.

Christine pulled me into a hug and said empathetically, "Heather, come on—that's not true. These things happen sometimes. Maybe you did all the right things, you know? It's no one's fault."

Tanya agreed, "It's true. Half the time, I'm totally guessing how to raise the kids. They're each like their own Rubik's Cubes. I'm constantly trying to solve them and never quite succeeding."

I gave her the "uh-huh-ya-right" look, but Tanya continued, "Actually, I have a confession. Do you want to hear it?"

I pulled back, raised my eyebrow, and said, "I don't know, do I?"

"Yes, you do—trust me. So, when Sheila was little, a baby, she had that awful allergy to my breast milk, remember? Well, I didn't know what the heck was going on—I just knew she was completely miserable for the first several months of her life. Jacob had been so easy for me, so it didn't make any sense. What was wrong with this girl? The doctor thought I wasn't feeding her properly—kept sending me to those La Leche classes. Jeesh, I felt like a bad cow—put me out to pasture. I mean, it's supposed to be natural—totally easy, right? Sure! Anyway, when Sheila would start doing that crazy thing she did where she would rear up and arch her back like a horse that's been prodded, I would just take her and lay her down in her crib, unfed and crying her eyes out, and walk away. I'd close the door and go down in the basement so I didn't have to hear her. I left that starving child up there, by herself, not knowing when anyone would come back for her. I was a horrible piece of shit. To this day, I think she's still wary of me—she always goes to Tom before me. But can I blame her?"

I said, "I know you're just trying to make me feel better, but I'm certain that isn't true. Sheila loves you! And babies are hard. I remember Tyler didn't sleep through the night until he was nearly a year old. I've never been so sleep-deprived in my whole life. I actually have no recollection of his first words or when he started walking. It was like a year of amnesia. I'm amazed I survived it."

Tanya said, "I know…I know. I'm being silly, and Sheila's fine, she's fine now. I just still feel guilty about it, I guess. And my point is that we can do *everything* for our kids. I mean, I would lay down my life for those kids, take a bullet for them—I would! But no matter what I do or what they do, things will never be perfect. We'll let each other down, we'll screw up, we'll make a mess of the whole thing. But hey, you know, maybe that's okay."

Christine and I nodded. I said, "Yeah, it is."

We clinked our glasses.

After a few minutes, I said emphatically, "I'm gonna try harder to be around more, be a better parent, I really am."

"That's all you can do, sweetie. That's all any of us can do. And we'll be right here with you," Tanya replied.

I paused and asked with a wry grin, "So, are either of you interested in selling your house?"

Chapter XIII

April 1

(Friday) Woke up early because Dad wanted to get on the road by eight. The car ride was long. I thought a lot about my conversation with Paul. Of course, my family had no idea why I was so quiet. Mom asked me what was wrong, and I just mumbled, "Tired." What was I going to do? I loved Paul, but now I wasn't sure about our future. Was he permanently damaged from that broken relationship? If I were him, I'd be afraid to date ever again. And who knew what his thoughts were on engagements and marriage. Was he opposed to them now? I knew I didn't have the full picture yet. What happened to the girl and the baby? Where were they now? How could Paul be engaged to such a girl?! Did he still talk to her? My thoughts were so jumbled and confused that when we arrived at Niagara Falls, I decided to push it all out of my mind. Instead, I tried to enjoy our time visiting with family. It was good to see them. Dad and Uncle Louis took about a thousand photos with their Kodak Brownie cameras. There was still ice on the river, but the falls were rushing like a freight train. I couldn't believe the sound! We stayed at the Clifton Hotel. It was the cat's meow!

Good questions, Didi. I'm glad she's taking time to contemplate her relationship with Paul. What are the ramifications? I mean, you can't blame Paul for what happened, but I would still want to understand how it all went down. Didn't he know the PA girl was cheating? And was his anger toward Didi just a consequence of his (rightful!) jealousy toward the PA girl? Or was he controlling and jealous of the PA girl, and that's why she cheated? Not that I'm justifying her behavior or his, but there are so many unknowns. I hope Didi gets to the bottom of the situation. She'd better, before going back with him, full-bore, only to learn he's permanently damaged. On a different note, I looked up the Clifton Hotel. It burned down later that same year (in December of 1932). So sad. Didn't all those big wooden buildings eventually burn down?

April 2

(Saturday) We ate breakfast in the hotel, then checked out. We walked along the avenue, and I bought a silver spoon with a maple leaf. I sent a postal card to Paul saying simply, "I love you." Lydia sent one to her steady boy too, even though he only lives a few miles away. It was good to see my cousin—she's so pretty and kind. I hadn't seen her in four years. She was a lot taller, and her hair was styled like a Gibson Girl. She said she couldn't believe my parents allowed me to get a permanent wave. I said, "I used my own money to pay for it, so what could they say?" We laughed about that and ran ahead of the group to see the falls again. It was frigid, but we didn't care. We walked out on the ice as far as we could until they told us to get back. Later we went to the dance hall, and I danced with a stocky fellow named Leroy. He told me I had nice eyes. I had a sudden and shocking thought: maybe I should just date this boy and all my troubles would go away. Then a second later I thought, no, that isn't a good idea—I love Paul! What was I thinking? Lydia and I went to bed at 3:30 when Uncle Louis told us to "quiet down and go to sleep!"

I don't blame her. When faced with overwhelming complications and sticky issues that are not so easily processed or resolved, I often fantasized about running for the hills too—if only in my mind. Case in point, after *the incident*, one of my favorite pastimes was to read and reread all the *Twilight* series of books, fantasizing that some handsome, invincible vampire would come rescue me from myself and my life. Of course, no amount of dreaming made it happen, and I was left to face my own colossal shitstorm without the help of a bloodsucking hero. Wump, wump.

April 3

(Sunday) Mom woke us at 8:15. We bundled up and walked through the park for several hours, then packed up and drove home. When I got home, I called Paul, but he wasn't home, so I called the Stand. Burrows answered and said Paul had just left to pick up some supplies. Paul didn't call back until five. We met at the streetcar stop and talked for an hour. Here's the gist of what he said: (1) when Gertie told him, she also told him that her parents had decided to send her to a place for her confinement, and the baby

was to be given up for adoption; (2) she was never going to see the other boy or the baby again; (3) she still loved Paul and wanted to marry him, but they would have to postpone the wedding until the spring so she could "go on a trip to Holland with her Dutch grandmother" (which was really a screen for the confinement). He didn't give a lot of details and said he had to get back to the Stand to close, so we said goodbye. For the first time in a long time, he didn't hold my hand or kiss me. He said he would tell me more the next time we saw each other. I stayed up late in my bedroom, trying not to think too much but not succeeding.

Trouble in paradise. Heavy.

April 4

(Monday) Hard to go back to work after the weekend. Between Paul's confession and the trip to Niagara Falls, I was drained and irritable. To make matters worse, Sam was there to greet me at the door. He said we were assigned to spring inventory all week. Cripes! He asked about my trip and said he met Jean Lussier once. I asked who that was, and he told me a man who went over the falls in a rubber ball in 1928. I didn't know if I believed him about the man or about him meeting him. Both sounded fantastical, so I rolled my eyes, to which Sam said, "Really. I swear!" At about noon, Sam asked me why I was acting "all wet." At first I told him it was nothing, but then he was being nice and pressed, so I told him that Paul and I had been "having discussions" and that I was still thinking about them. He asked if our discussions were about marriage. I said, not exactly, why? He wanted to know if I intended to keep my job at McCurdy's if Paul and I got married, and I said no, of course not. He looked positively crestfallen. I wasn't sure if it was because he would miss our talks or because he would miss me helping him on the ledger!

So hard when practicality gets in the way of love, isn't it? I tell ya what, made me think to myself that I'm gonna make my own way in life and not rely on a man or anyone else. Then I can make my own choice of a life partner based not on necessity but on the stuff I truly care about. Btw, people going over the falls in a barrel—who knew that shit was real?! Or in this case, a rubber ball. Crazy fools!

April 5–8

(Tuesday–Friday) Inventory, inventory, inventory. A tough grind. Didn't hear from Paul until tonight (Friday). He came by and we played pinochle with Mom and Dad for a few hours, then went out to the Nan and talked. He kissed me and told me how much he loved me, and did I really want to be his girlfriend? I said yes, I did! But I also told him I needed to know more about what happened and to understand how it would affect our relationship. He was quiet after that for a while. Then he said, "You know, before she told me she was going away, she asked if I would still marry her and accept the child as mine." He stopped and stared at me with such conflicting emotions on his face. He said, "I couldn't do it, I just couldn't. I loved her still—I did—but the thought of her with that other man..." His eyes turned into that raging darkness again, and I could see the pain behind them. He continued, "I knew if I did that, I would grow to hate the child, and that wouldn't have been fair—to the child or to me. Or to her, for that matter." He looked off into the yard as he asked me softly, "Do you understand?" I took his hand and said, "Yes, I think so." Then I asked, "So she went away?" He looked back at me and nodded. "What about the wedding?" "We canceled it. It had been scheduled as a small family affair, thankfully, so we simply didn't have it." "Then what happened?" I asked. He sighed and shrugged his shoulders before saying, "She was gone, we moved here, and that was the end of that." We sat swinging for some time in silence. Finally, I asked him, "Do you still love her?" He looked at me with a funny smile and said, "How could I? I love you now."

April 9–10

(Saturday–Sunday) Worked both days on inventory. Went to a show at the Little on Saturday night with Paul, George, and Frances. We went for a walk after that, but it was cold, so we took the streetcar home. We're all getting sick of this cold winter. When will spring come? At the streetcar stop, I asked Paul if he still believed in love and marriage and happily ever after. He gave me a big hug and said, "Yes, with you, I do!"

Well, that's promising, but hmmm, maybe glossing over some things, Didi. I hope she's got the sense to dig a little deeper. We'll see what happens. Also, Didi, I hear ya on the weather. Rochester in April is like most other cities in December. Mom and I went to a movie at the Little Theatre a year or two ago. Such a neat old building—amazing that it's still around and still operational.

April 13

(Wednesday) Young People's Meeting is tomorrow, and we're trying to figure out what we should do next. I told Glenys I might not have as much time to help out for a while because I was so busy with work. She said that was fine because they would be needing me more when the presidential candidates were announced in the summer.

April 14

(Thursday) Working the register today. Before I went to the Young People's Meeting, I stopped at the Stand to say hello to Paul. The Mrs. was there, so I didn't stay long. Paul won't kiss me in front of his mom. I asked why, and he said after what happened in Penn., she doesn't trust girls anymore.

Okay, well, so now I think I understand the Mrs. a little better. I guess I misjudged her. Maybe she was just looking out for her son, keeping him from having his heart broken again. Of course, Didi was blameless in this situation, but still, moving to a new town with all new women buzzing around Paul, I can see how she would be suspicious of Didi and the others.

April 17

(Sunday) Helped Mom with the meal. Paul came at noon. James brought around his new girl, Adelaide, who was very nice. Afterward, I asked her why she would bother with my brother. She laughed, but James didn't. Paul and I played hearts with Mom and Dad until Paul and I went out to the Nan. I told him we needed to get serious and talk about things. He agreed but said he didn't want to talk about the Penn. girl anymore. I said okay, but I wanted know if he wanted to talk about us. He said, "Like what?" "Well, you gave me your signet ring, so you must want to be with me. Do you think you can be with me even when I talk to other boys or dance with other boys?" He looked down at his hands, trying not to let me see his face, then said, "I suppose. I'll try." I said, "Okay." Then I asked, "What type of future do you see for us?" He said with a laugh, "I hope a bright one." It was good to see him looking happy, so I laughed with him and agreed. Then I tried to get serious again, mentioning the talk I'd had with my dad a few weeks ago. Paul wondered why my dad was skeptical of him without really knowing his intentions. I said, "I think he just wants to be sure his daughter has someone to support her—in every way, not just in love. That's all. You understand?" Paul said sullenly, "Of course, he thinks

I'm beat because I can't even scrape together a five-spot. It's just so hard to get ahead..." I said, "I know." We didn't talk very much after that. He kissed me at the streetcar stop, and I told him it would all work out, one way or another. He nodded but didn't smile.

April 22

(Friday) Paul and I went to the State to see The Lost Squadron. *He held my hand the whole time. I think he was thinking about our talk the other night because he told me he loved me and wanted to marry me. He said he'd been putting his savings in a jar under his bed, and as soon as the jar was full, he would ask. He said he didn't have a father to advise him or provide for him and his brother and mother, and that was very hard, so he understood why my dad was wanting to make sure I was making the right choice. Then he talked about the fact that his mother never mentioned his dad anymore. She didn't like to talk about the past—or the future either, for that matter—just wanted to make sure everything was getting done right now. I felt bad for him and kissed him.*

April 23

(Saturday) Dad talked to me again about Paul. I told him about the jar, and he said, "A jar doesn't a life make." I said, "I know, but I love him." He was trying to be kind (and firm) with me and said, "Didi, I want you to make your own life, and if it can't happen with this boy, we'd rather you be on your own, living with us, until the right boy comes along." I cried a little and told him I didn't want another boy. Sometimes life is so hard. I tried to explain Paul's circumstances—not having a father and relying on his mother's initiative to keep the family afloat. He said, "Yes, this is noble and worthy of praise. She must be a strong woman to manage that counter and raise those two boys on her own, but acknowledging that, we must also look at the big picture."

Boy, can I empathize with that! I couldn't see the forest for the trees when I was with Greg. I didn't see the forest *or* the trees! I was blinded by love—by obsession really—for the man, as flawed and ridiculous and horrible as he was. Blinded! I think in our day and age, you can see how it happens too. We're shown all of these vapid TV shows and magazines (not to mention social media platforms) where everyone looks so polished, perfect, and airbrushed/plasticky, and we're supposed to be like that all the time, when in reality we're a sticky, ugly, heinous mess of humanity (oh the humanity!). No one wants to show their underbelly or air their dirty laundry, or when they do, it usually ends up being for a wildly popular publicity stunt (you know, under the mantra that no publicity is bad publicity). So how can we be expected to step back and say, my god, what is life really about? And why does everything seem so perfect from the outside (from our perfectly posed selfies on Instagram) when in reality most of us are completely miserable and have no idea how to fix our lives? How are we to know (and not just know, but actually digest, absorb, embody) the fact that ninety percent of what we're shown and what we're told to revere in this world is complete and total bullshit?! I mean, look at Didi. Back in her day, those old black-and-white movies she was seeing (the "shows") were always about some poor woman finding a rich man (and all her worries magically going away). Didi probably wished some miracle would happen for her and Paul. If only she could will their relationship to succeed. Heck, it seemed like she ended up being the same way with Grandpa Ron—doing whatever it took to make it work. She was definitely a fighter and stubborn, and a problem solver too. But I know from firsthand experience that you can't force something that isn't meant to be. And no matter what the world shows you as the perfect life, there is no such thing. Sometimes reality forces you to look at the big picture, even when you're diving and ducking away from it like a prizefighting boxer.

April 30

(Saturday) Paul came on the streetcar with Burrows and Stella, and we went to the roller-skating rink. Paul held my hand the whole time. We stopped after a few hours to eat a picnic and buy an icy. He said he was able to put $2.23 in his jar this week. I smiled and kissed him. I don't know why, but I didn't tell him about my talk with Dad.

Chapter XIV

Jake was swinging on the Nan when I got downstairs. As we started walking toward the pitch, he asked, "What happened to you yesterday? I turned around and you were gone."

"Dude," I answered with a smile, "um, let's see, I waited around for like twenty minutes, and you couldn't get your face out of that girl's sphincter, or vice versa... I'm not sure. Either way, it was time for me to skedaddle."

He laughed uncomfortably. "Boy, you just say whatever's on your mind, don't you?"

I nodded. "Just call me no-filter-Elliott."

He raised his eyebrows and simply said, "Well, that girl, as you called her, is Chelsea, my girlfriend."

"I know. I got the four-one-one. All good, Jakie—whatever tickles your fancy, or whoever tickles whatever you like tickled." I smiled obligingly.

Oddly, he frowned at me. He said, "She's really nice, you know. Very sweet—really, I swear. And we have a lot in common."

Golly, defensive much? My smile got smaller, but I said lightly, "At ease, soldier. Hey, sincerely—all good. I don't need the particulars. She seems like a lovely young lady. I'm glad she's glazing your donut. I've got nothing against her. In fact, I don't even know her...but I'm sure she's great."

Despite my little pep talk, he continued, "No really, she *is* great." Then after a few minutes during which I didn't say a word and stared straight ahead, he said, "So what if she's a little jealous sometimes? I mean, that's normal, right? She's really awesome most of the time, I swear, but sometimes she doesn't like it when I talk to other girls. She flies off the handle and freaks out. I'm not sure why..."

"Uh-huh," I said, nodding and thinking, uh-oh, are we headed down a tunnel of confessions? Stay still, Delia. Do not engage.

"Yesterday she was in one of her moods...," his voice drifted off.

I kept my head facing forward. And we're walking, we're walking...

Nothing. Not another word. I glanced his way. There it was: the invitation in his eyes, wanting me to probe further into something I wanted to run from, to the outer edges of Earth. I stupidly took the bait. I asked, "Really? Why would that be?"

"Well, because...because I was...because you were...well, because of you."

I looked up into those flashing, wonderful pools of green light—and just for an instant our eyes melted together. So that was the secret I had seen there that first day in the hall by the attic. I exhaled as the key clicked into place, thinking fifty thoughts at once and only saying lamely, "Oh."

He spoke quickly, "What do I do?"

"Jake..." How was I to answer that? I shook my head.

"Yeah, I know..."

We walked in silence for a while.

Finally, he asked again, "What do I do?"

I answered slowly. "Nothing. I mean, you just told me you two had a lot in common. Isn't she, um, some type of swimmer?" I wasn't going to be the iceberg to this *Titanic*.

"Yeah, pretty good, too, but the season doesn't start until November. In the meantime, she drags me to the mall with her. She tries on clothes for hours and makes me wait outside the dressing room so she can show me each outfit individually. It's really boring."

"Well, that doesn't seem so bad," I said, trying hard to leave the sarcasm out of my voice, which was (let's face it) impossible. "Maybe next time, bring a book."

"Uh-huh, right. You try that for, like, six hours." Then after a minute, during which he was breathing hard, apparently irritated at being forced into fashion hell, he mumbled, "It's enough to make a guy go batshit crazy."

I said as lightheartedly as I could, "Come on, maybe you'd only go apeshit crazy...that's not as bad as batshit, right?"

He laughed and grabbed my arm, making me look at him as he said, "You're making fun of me, aren't you?"

He regarded me strangely, a little bit hurt, so I felt obliged to explain, "Don't get me wrong—I totally empathize with your...situation. I do. But I'm completely maxed out, you know, on drama—for the year and maybe for forever."

"Oh," he said, nodding slowly with an awareness flashing across his face. After a minute, he looked at me with such understanding and sympathy that it was hard for me to look away as he said, "Hey, listen—that was just about the shittiest thing a guy could do. I've wanted to say something to you about it—how...how...

awful and wrong that was."

I tried to brush it off with a shrug. I couldn't handle the strange warmth his eyes sent into my soul. What was I going to do with that? I said nonchalantly, "Thanks. It certainly blew the big one." Sometimes it was better to put your cards on the table and hope you wouldn't fold too early.

He still regarded me with those kind eyes that were killing me softly until he could see that I had my wall up. In fact, a trick I had learned during my time in purgatory, after *the incident*, was to imagine a bricklayer building a wall around me. Like literally, a mason with his trowel and bucket of mortar in one hand and several bricks in the other, stacking them up around me, brick by brick by brick until no one could see me, touch me, or get to me. At the end, I felt like that nursery rhyme where the three little pigs end up in a brick house that the wolf can't blow down. I could stay in there, safely, forever.

My eyes flat and straight ahead, hearing the sound of the bricklayer clunking down each brick, one by one, I waited for him to look away, which he eventually did.

Oh well. Good. At least we got that out of the way. I had confirmation that he knew about *the incident* and didn't run away screaming. That was good, right? I almost felt as though with every new acquaintance (or in the case of Jake, re-acquaintance), there had to be this moment of acknowledgment of my past. It really sucked. Like I had a criminal record that had to be disclosed to a new employer. And what sucked the most: speaking about it gave it energy, credence, power—like a corpse coming back to life. It was a double-edged sword of confession and humiliation, all over again every time.

Mercifully (and maybe because he saw through my wall and didn't want to take it down yet?), Jake changed the subject and asked, "So, what are you reading right now?"

"Oh, we're talking books now?" I grinned. Anything to lighten the mood was A-OK with me. "We're gonna need more time."

He laughed and said, "That's what I'm hoping for."

I smiled and answered, "I'm reading *Rebecca*."

"Chick-lit?"

"What? No way. Du Maurier is for all readers. *Rebecca*'s like a spicy murder mystery with a side of intrigue and romance. You can borrow it when I'm done. It's good. How's Ken Follett coming?"

He said, "Good." We were near the field now, and he hollered hello to the guys, then turned to me suddenly and said, "Oh! I nearly forgot—I think I got you a job at the RCC, if you're still interested."

"Really? Sick! Yes!"

"Working at the front desk. Would you like that?"

"That would be awesome. Are you sure?"

"Well, you'll have to apply, but the manager said he had openings. You'd better go over there tonight or tomorrow and talk to him. His name's Ted. Tell him I sent you." And that was that. I guess the "more time" would come later. I shrugged. He was off, running to the middle of the field. I sat down on the grass with a smile. A job! Yeah! I'd make some extra coin and get to see Jake every day. Would I still be able to play soccer? Somehow he managed it. What about the attic? What about a ride to work? Details, details, details. I'd have to run it all by Mom tonight.

By the time Mom came home that night, I was almost asleep. I had finished *Rebecca* and was making progress on Didi's diary. My eyes were heavy as I reached for the light switch, but I paused mid-reach when I heard her steps on the stairs.

"Delia?" she said, peeking around the sheet.

"Hi, Mom," I answered drowsily.

"How's it going?" she asked, sitting down beside me on the bed.

"Good...tired. How are you? One hundred proof?"

"Very funny. No, we started early, so I quit drinking a few hours ago. I feel fine actually."

"Uh-huh, right-e-o, Momma. What did the real housewives have to say?"

"Oh, they're fine. Tanya's oldest is pregnant—did I tell you that? The one who lives in Albany. They're excited—first grandbaby and all. The baby shower's next weekend."

"Sounds bitchin'. The usual scourge of balloons, glitter, taffeta, and tirades. You going?"

"Naw, too far to drive."

I nodded and waited. She said quietly, "Speaking of babies..."

"Dad," I acknowledged, astutely and directly.

We stared at each other, nodding mutely. Then she looked around my room evasively, finally coming back around to my face and asking, "You okay with it?"

I shrugged. "You?"

She shrugged.

Silence.

She sighed and smiled. Apropos of nothing, she said, "Christine said they're thinking about buying a llama."

"A llama!"

"Yes, a llama. Or an alpaca. I can't remember which...wait, I think it was an alpaca."

"Wow, cool. What do you do with those?"

Mom frowned and chuckled. "Heck, I don't know. I think you can shear them or eat them or something. I don't remember what she said."

"No way—you can't eat them!"

We both laughed. Mom admitted, "No, I guess not." We regarded each other for a few minutes. It had been a while since we'd laughed together.

Again, I waited, more tired. She was so uncharacteristically chatty this evening. I wondered why. She asked, "How was the pitch?"

"Great. I scored."

"You did?"

"Yup, the goalie was pissed. He threw a little hissy fit. Couldn't take it that a girl scored on him. It was hysterical."

Mom smiled with a strange sort of prideful grin. "Good," she said. Then, "Hey, what are you doing tomorrow night?"

"Why?" I asked suspiciously, before answering. It was always wise to gather facts before answering open-ended questions.

She started, rather awkwardly, with, "Well, because if you're free, I think it would be great...to...I mean, only if you want to...maybe we could...I think it would be fun if we could...do something together."

So funny, as if she were trying on a new dress and didn't yet know if she liked it or not. Not to mention, it wasn't like Mom to give up a Friday night. I couldn't decide whether I was shocked or flattered or wary or confused. Maybe she had taken it to heart when I asked those questions about her childhood and Didi. It would be great to pick her brain a bit and get some answers. I asked, "What did you have in mind?"

"Golly, Delia, take that look off your face. You seem so shocked. I told you we should talk, so let's do it. Don't worry—this isn't an invite to a Tupperware party or anything." She smiled and then said, more thoughtfully, "I know it's been a while since we've had quality time together, and I think lately I've been..." she paused for a moment, reluctant to admit, "maybe neglectful and rather absent. I'm sorry."

"Lately?" I said accusingly, with a grin.

She rolled her eyes and laughed. Then her eyes softened as she tucked a strand of hair behind my ear. She added, "I guess I've been caught up in my own life too much. Will you forgive me?"

"Sure, Mom—it's not like I've been sitting here crying into an Orphan Annie bucket of lost hopes." Of course, she didn't know anything about my bricklayer, and she didn't need to know.

She didn't reply and kept looking at me wistfully. It made me uncomfortable and I was starting to squirm, so I deflected with, "What should we do?"

"Oh, I don't know, maybe just go for a drive or out to dinner. Whatever you want. What do you think?"

"Don't care. Whatever."

"Okay, I should be home early."

"Hey, do you mind if we stop at the RCC first? Jake's lifeguarding there and said there's a job opening for the front desk. I need to fill out an application and talk with the manager."

"Yes, of course. That's great news!"

"Well, I don't have it yet, but yes, it would be great...assuming...well, assuming you'd give me my car back. Otherwise, there's really no point in me applying."

"Oh," Mom said with a frown. "I hadn't thought of that." She paused. I saw her brain spinning, weighing the risks—did she trust me with a car yet? I had survived one day with the phone, and no major catastrophes had occurred (she assumed).

Finally, she asked, "How does Jake get there? Could you ride with him?"

"I'm not sure. I assume he drives or his parents take him. But I doubt we'll be working the same hours."

"Maybe you could ask the manager about that."

"Okay, I'll try. I mean, if we do have a shift together, I could certainly share a ride with him, but I don't think that's always going to be the case."

"Doesn't hurt to ask."

"Alright, I'll ask," I said, thinking it was unlikely that would work out. It had been such a pain bumming rides for the Panera job—now I was going to have to do the same for this job. Although this time with Jake. Smile. Much better.

She stood up to leave and pointed toward the hallway, saying, "So hey, it looks like you made some progress today—things are starting to clear out."

"Yep, I sold that couch—some old guy came by and got it with his son a couple of hours ago. And the recliners are gone, plus several lamps and mirrors."

"Wow, very quick work. I hope you didn't sell anything important. Hey, by the way, you didn't sell the bamboo whatnot, did you?"

"The what? Not?"

She chuckled. "An old shelving unit thing—it's made of bamboo and holds knickknacks and things. It's called a 'whatnot.' I want to keep that. It was Didi's."

"That thing? Yeah, I saw it. Still up in the attic. It was Didi's? Hmph, cool."

"Yes, it was something I remember being in her room—your room—when I was younger. In fact, let's move it back in here tomorrow."

"Okay, well, it doesn't match my décor," I quipped, putting my hand up to my chin in stoic observation, "but maybe I can make it work. I'll put books on it." Then I asked, serious now, "So, this was Didi's room?"

"Yep, as a child. Of course, when she got married to Grandpa Ron, she moved into the master suite (my bedroom), but I remember her telling me how important this room was to her. She left it basically the same, even when Mary and I came to live with her—we stayed in Tyler's room then and were told not to come in this room."

I'd wondered about that. Interesting. I nodded, channeling my inner Didi—the diary, the bamboo thing, the room. I felt the hairs stand up on the back of my neck. After a few minutes, Mom said goodnight and went to her room. I drifted off to sleep thinking about Didi, imagining her using that Daisy Machine thing to embroider the pillow cover my head was on.

When I woke up the next morning, I went full-bore into attic duty. I put the items for sale out in the garage. Then I threw five more bags of clothes down to the front foyer for donation. Finally, I rearranged the remaining items into properly labeled boxes and tubs: "Photos from Mom's Sordid Past," "Didi's Treasures of a Time Gone By," "Miscellaneous Old Crap," "Childhood Memories from Prince Tyler and Princess Delia," "The D.D.'s Relics of Repugnance," and so on. Those went back to the attic, stacked and rearranged by category. There were still a few furniture pieces I wasn't sure if Mom wanted to sell or keep, so those were in a corner, awaiting her assessment.

I found myself oddly satisfied and proud of the fact that the attic had whole sections of floor that were visible for the first time (no doubt) in thirty years (probably more like eighty or ninety). I couldn't explain the feeling other than sheer joy as I stood there sweating, my hands on my hips, surveying my work. It was a sense of release, rejuvenation, and accomplishment. It had only been four days, and sure, there was more to be done, but still...the progress was palpable. God, it was a metaphor for my life lately! Clean, purge, resell, release, rebirth, relief! Shazam!

Jake came by at the usual hour. I showed him the old radio—the one Didi used to listen to with her family. We weren't sure how to operate it, and I was afraid we might break it if we tried, so Jake said he'd drop it off at his house to see if his dad could figure it out. I said that sounded great, and then I explained about the date with Mom and going to the RCC to apply for a job.

He said, "So no-go on soccer?" He seemed so disappointed that I had to smile.

I asked him, "Any tips on the job?"

"No worries. You'll get it. Ted's cool—I told him you were coming."

"Will I be working the same hours as you? Because, well, Mom doesn't really want to give me my car back…she thought I might ride with you."

"Oh sure, that would be fine, although I work the early morning shift. You may not want that, and I don't know if that's the shift that's open at the desk. Ask Ted. It might be."

"What are the exact hours?"

"Seven to noon. I leave around six forty."

"Yowzah, that *is* early. But okay…I guess I can handle that…" Especially if I'm going to wake up to those big green eyes.

"Yeah, it sucks getting up that early, but then you have the whole rest of the day and night to yourself, so that part's cool. Okay, well, good luck. I'll miss you at soccer today. Who will be our ringer?" He smiled and chucked my shoulder. I smiled back. Then he hovered for a minute more, staring at me. Finally, I raised my eyebrows, waiting, until he said, "Hey, about yesterday, our little talk, are we… cool?"

My face cleared. I said, "Sure, of course. You? I noticed she wasn't there yesterday."

"No, she wasn't. I think I enjoyed it more," he admitted sheepishly.

I chuckled and said, "Naughty boy."

"Yeah, well, she's still mad at me. Who knows…I'm supposed to see her tonight."

"Naked and afraid?"

"Ha! No. Well, sort of, I mean, *no.*"

I laughed at his discomfort. I said, "Good luck with that."

"Uh-huh, gee, thanks. Okay, let me know how it goes with Ted today, alright?"

"Okeydokey. Later, gator."

"Later." He stood staring into my face for a few extra seconds before turning to go. I sensed he was attempting to siphon some misplaced courage from my countenance, but I forced myself to look at him straight and clear, not giving an ounce, thinking to myself, not my battle, not my man, not mine…

❧ Chapter XV ❧

May 1

(Sunday) Slept in a little. I was tired, and Mom said I could sleep as long as when I awoke, I washed my head and cleaned my room, which I did. We listened to the radio for a few hours and played rummy. Paul called late and said work wasn't very busy, but the Mrs. wanted him to stay late anyway. Said he loved me.

May 2–6

(Monday–Friday) The weather was fine all week, and people were shopping. I had to work the register. Sam was doing the books and came down wanting my help and because he was "bored." I told him, "No sirree! I'm busy enough without your work too." Didn't see Paul all week. He called every night. He didn't mention his jar at all. I'm not sure why.

Good for you, Didi, telling Sam to do his own work. Hmmm, that's not promising about Paul and the jar.

May 7

(Saturday) Woke up at 10:15. The week was a tough grind. Frances and George came over for dinner, and we took the streetcar to meet Paul. Went to see a show at the Century. Paul was so happy to see me (and me him!). He kissed me over and over until George said, "Say, aren't you two sociable enough for today?" We laughed and Paul kissed me anyway, just to let George know he didn't care what he said. Paul told me he loved me and didn't want to ever go that long again without seeing me. We didn't talk at all about our parents or anything important, and it felt wonderful.

Great idea, Didi, just put your head in the sand. That ought to work.

May 8
(Sunday) Minnie came down for supper with Eddie and baby Hotcha. I helped Mom with the food and played with the baby for a while. He liked my new scarf. I wrapped him up in it, and we went outside in the yard to play. Paul called and James answered. James teased him and said I wasn't home, but I grabbed the phone, and Paul said he was going to knock James's block off. I told him James didn't have a block! We laughed about that for a while.

May 9
(Monday) Sam and I were back on the ledger this morning. Sam met a new girl, Honoree. That's all he talked about—it was Honoree this and Honoree that. I finally said, "If you like her so much, why don't you marry her?" He said, "I think I will!" I laughed in his face, but he said he was serious. And he only just met her! I said, "A wedding costs money," and he said, "So does a marriage, but I've been saving." That made me quiet, and fast. How is it that Sam meets a new girl and two minutes later everything is coming up aces while Paul and I have been together for months and we're nowhere closer to our happily ever after? When I got home from work, I didn't hear from Paul, so I went to bed early. I cried a little into my pillow, wondering why life is so complicated sometimes.

Well, for as much as Didi gets annoyed by Sam, you have to hand it to him—at least he has a good job and a clear plan. Life is complicated, Didi, that's for sure, and not always easy, especially when you shove everything under the rug. It seems like that will make all the bad stuff go away, but in the end it usually doesn't.

May 10
(Tuesday) Went to see Paul and Burrows at the Stand during lunch. They talked to me for several minutes before the Mrs. came over and told them to mop the floors in back. Paul called after he got home and told me his mom wasn't happy because they'd had fewer customers lately (with the weather being fine outside). He said he hoped business picked up soon. He also said he talked to his mom about marrying me, but she said, "Don't get any of those newfangled ideas in your head. Remember what happened last time." He said he didn't know how to respond, so he let it drop. Coincidentally, my mom asked me tonight how things were going with Paul. I told her good, but she must have seen something in my face because she said, "Why

*don't you go out with some of your other friends this weekend?" I said,
"Mom, my friends are Paul's friends." She said, "Now come on, what about
your friends from Franklin and the ladies in the young people's group. You
haven't seen them in a while." I just answered, "I suppose. Well, maybe,"
and let it drop.*

Mom's intuition is kicking in. She knows things are off with her daughter but
doesn't know how to fix them. At least she's making constructive suggestions. I
doubt Didi will listen, though. I wonder if Didi will ever tell her parents about the PA
girl—or tell anyone else, for that matter. Probably not. I think there was (and still
is) some shame associated with any unwanted pregnancy, even if it's not related
to you. My friend McKenzie told me a story once about her great-aunt. I guess
at the funeral, this stranger shows up and introduces himself to the family, saying
he is the aunt's son. Before that, no one knew he existed. Apparently the aunt had
gotten pregnant and had the boy before she was married, and had given him up for
adoption. Then later in life, she found him and started corresponding with him and
calling him on a daily basis! No one knew a thing about him. She went on to get
married and have her other four sons, who now found out they had a half-brother
they never knew before. I mean, that situation was pretty shocking, and that was
just a few years ago. I imagine back in the thirties people barely spoke about pregnancy at all, let alone this Paul situation. So now Didi's friends and family won't
have the full picture (just like she didn't originally), and they're probably wondering
why Paul is so possessive and why his mom is the way she is and all other kinds
of whys.

May 11
*(Wednesday) The manager wanted me to work on the floor today because
the salesgirl called in sick. Sam came down and bought a broach for Honoree. I called Paul when I got home. He was still at the Stand and couldn't
talk.*

May 12
*(Thursday) The salesgirl was sick again, so I worked the floor. I tried to
call Paul at the Stand, but the Mrs. answered and said he wasn't available.
I always wonder if she gives him my messages. All the talk today at the
store was about the Lindbergh baby.*

I Googled—so awful! That Lindbergh baby was found dead after all those months of ransom and instructions and searching. I can't even imagine. There are some evil people in this world.

May 13–15

(Friday–Sunday) My back aches and my feet are sore. The salesgirl quit! I worked all weekend. The floor was crowded. I made a good commission. Paul called, but I told him I was awfully tired. I didn't see him or anyone this whole weekend.

May 16–18

(Monday–Wednesday) Paul called Monday and made a date for Wednesday. He said the Mrs. didn't want him to take a night off, but he said he would anyway. He said it hadn't been busy in days, so he didn't know why his mom was being so strict. Bernice and Roy met us at the streetcar, and we went to see a show at the Webster. Paul said he wasn't able to put any money in the jar because the Stand was so quiet. He didn't know what he would do. I actually insisted on paying for the show, which he didn't like, but he finally said, "Okay, just this once."

May 20

(Friday) James brought his new gal, Adelaide, around for supper. She's nice. I asked her why she likes James. James pinched my arm and said that wasn't funny. She laughed and said she disagreed, and that she finds me very funny. That made me smile. I stuck out my tongue at James. My pen pal Eleanor wrote and said she'd be coming in early June (Dad said I could invite her to come this summer, and now she is, and I can't wait—it'll be nice to see her). Paul called and said he had to sneak away from the Mrs. to call me and couldn't talk long but that he loved me. Mom asked me again tonight if I would be going out with "my other friends" this weekend. I said I wasn't sure yet.

Good for you, Mom! If only Didi would listen. I think she wants so badly for it to work that she can't listen to reason or even see reason when it's right in front of her face. Makes me think of a conversation I had with my mom a few months into dating Greg. She said, "You know, Delia, any boy who expects you to be available to him at all hours of the day and night is not the right kind of boy. You should have your own time to do with as you please and then be with him when you both want to be together. This incessant texting and calling and seeing each other is unhealthy. Why don't you set up some time with your other friends this weekend and give it a rest with Greg?" Of course I didn't listen. I didn't want to hear that. I thought I knew better—after all, our love would only grow stronger if I made more time for him, wouldn't it? Oh, Didi, if only you could know what I know!

May 21

(Saturday) I made thirty-five sales. I like the job now, but my feet hurt at the end of the day. Frances called and wondered when I'd be able to go dancing. I told her maybe Thursday or Friday. To make my mother happy, I called Glenys and asked how the Young People's Meetings were going. She said they had stalled out a little as of late but were hoping to pick up more in the summer. She said with so many people still out of work, it was hard to find new ideas to spur the economy and help the young people. She thought the presidential election might be their only hope. She said Hoover wasn't doing anything for the average Joe, and everyone needed a change. I asked her about going dancing with Gail and the others, and she said maybe next weekend.

May 24–26

(Tuesday–Thursday) Slow on the floor this week. They said I have Friday off and they would let me know about Saturday and Sunday. I was glad. The time goes so slow when no one's shopping. Paul called but couldn't talk long. Told me Burrows went to Penn. to visit their grandparents and see if he could find a job down there. He said the Stand is doing poorly, and his mother asked Burrows to leave. Paul was worried he was next. He said this week he had to take money out of his jar to pay for the streetcar. He sounded sad and downtrodden. Said he missed me and would come by tomorrow.

May 27

(Friday) Paul came at 6:00 and asked to speak with Dad. They went in the dining room and stayed for a long time. Mom and I were in the kitchen, and my stomach was filled with butterflies. I had no idea what they were talking about! Finally, Dad came and said they had "reached an agreement." He wasn't smiling, but Paul was, so I had no idea what to think. Dad said, "Paul would like to marry you, Didi, but we first need to assist

him in finding a way to support you. He doesn't feel the Stand is going to work out, and he's not sure where else to turn. I told him we could do a trial engagement, work toward the goal of a new job, and see how it went." I jumped in Paul's arms. I was so happy, I cried. George and Frances showed up at 7:30, and we told them the news. Then we went dancing. It was the best night of my life!

Good Lord, how is *that* going to work out? What did Paul say to the dad to convince him? I'm floored. Maybe Dad felt sorry for him. After all, Paul really is kind of like a lonely lost soul, isn't he? Trying to figure things all by himself. That mom of his isn't any help. At least he's showing initiative, but I'm still concerned. What if they can't find him a job? Plus, I know Paul and Didi are getting along pretty well now, but what happens when the next boy comes along and flirts with Didi? Somehow I don't think Paul's going to be all copacetic with that situation when he was so irrational and angry before. Isn't this just a Band-Aid?

May 28

(Saturday) I woke up with hugest smile on my face! Like a dream! I'm going to be Mrs. Paul Miller! Paul called from the Stand and told me he loved me and couldn't wait to be my husband.

I guess all thoughts of seeing Glenys and her other friends have gone out the window now. Ho hum.

May 31

(Tuesday) Mom and I sat at the table most of the afternoon and made wedding arrangements. Paul came for supper, and Dad took him out to look for a job, but they didn't have any luck. Clara and Will were here yesterday. They said Lloyd lost his factory job in Utica. They didn't know what he would do. They said times are tough everywhere and just keep getting worse. It reminded me of what Glenys said and also of Paul's situation. I just don't know what's happening in our world that it's so hard to make a living. I tried not to think too much about it when Bernice and Frances came over to spend the night. We stayed up for hours looking at the latest issues of McCall's, Ladies' Home Journal, *and* Good Housekeeping.

Chapter XVI

AFTER JAKE WAS GONE, I took a quick shower and got ready, taking extra time to straighten my hair and put makeup on. I guess an interview at the RCC was worthy of some extra effort (was it an interview when you simply applied and handed over your form to the manager?). Anyway, when I got downstairs, Mom was on the phone, and I pointed at my watch. She held up a finger, said a few more words, and hung up.

"You look adorable," she said, taking my face in her hands. "God, you have the best hair. I wish mine looked half as great as yours."

"Well, it's all the mayo I put in it." I said facetiously, regarding her red hair poofed up around her face as large as a lion's mane, thinking no amount of product would tame that.

She dropped my face, shaking her head, and said, "You ready to go?"

"Yep."

We drove over to the RCC. The manager was a middle-aged guy, tall, trim, nice. I told him about Jake, and he brought over an application. As I filled out the form, Mom asked him about the hours and pay, and if I would get free access to the facilities. He was polite, and when I handed him the final application, he asked me a few questions about my experience and then offered me the job. He said he didn't think I'd get the same shift as Jake every time, but he might be able to work it out for some shifts. I said that was cool and we'd figure out the rest. I shook his hand and thanked him. He told me to come at one o'clock tomorrow so Tina could train me, and after that he'd get me on the regular schedule starting Monday. Sounded perfect. We said our goodbyes and were out the door.

Mom said as soon as we were in the car, "Well, that was easy."

"Yes, it was," I agreed. Then I asked, "Where we goin'?"

"I was thinking maybe we could go to Schaller's and then walk out on the pier at Charlotte. What do you think?"

"Sure."

As she drove along, we were silent for a while. There was always this mild strain between us now. It hadn't existed before (when I was a girl). I used to tell her everything. She was my best friend, and I loved being around her. We spent hours and hours together, watching movies, shopping, driving, eating, talking. Even during the divorce, we cried in each other's arms. I didn't understand why they had to split up, and I tried (in my ten-year-old way) to process the loss and to console her. I followed her around and wiped her tears away and told her it would be okay. In retrospect, maybe she was relying on me a little too much—after all, weren't our roles slightly reversed back then?

Then when the teenage years hit and I spent my usual half-time at Dad's house, I realized what a stable, normal household felt like. Dad and Beth enforced rules, chores, a routine, discipline. Okay, so I'm not saying I loved that right away—in fact, in the beginning, it was a total pain in the ass. I was chafing under the bit, pushing back and arguing against every rule with my own personal war chest of rationalizing excuses. But after a while, seeing that they didn't give in under the pressure and knowing I'd lost the battle, I finally got in line (for the most part). Over time, I found myself having less anxiety at their house, which was a shock to me and unexpectedly pleasant. I slept better. I ate full meals during normal mealtimes and relied on the two of them to help me with the scheduling, organizing, and over-all management of my life. It was like diving into a warm, comfortable (competent) pool of love and reassurance after having been tossed around by an erratic, scattered wave of confusion and unpredictability.

On the other side of the coin, as much as I loved Mom, she was clearly still "finding herself," which didn't lend itself to her being an overly giving, instructive, or capable mother. Sometimes (especially since *the incident*) I found myself on edge, riddled with nerves and anxiety, trying to keep it all together—school, homework, sports, activities, friends, food, support—by myself. During the rare times when she was around, it was more as an enforcer and disciplinarian, which I realize was necessary after everything I'd done, but still, some days I felt my spirits dragging under the weight of our current uncomfortable relationship.

Don't get me wrong—if Mom heard these thoughts in my mind right now, she would say I wasn't being fair, that she was doing the best she could under the circumstances. She would probably blame Dad and Beth—they had all the advantages: the money, the house, each other—and she was a single mother living in a dump with a boring job and two kids to raise. She would probably also say I was the cause of our current tectonic fracture. I was the one getting into trouble all the time—how could she be blamed for that? She taught me right from wrong, so why did I continue to choose wrong?

Regardless, it was all a bit of a cluster. Anyway, here we were, in a car together, alone, for the first time in months—cautious, treading lightly, slightly closed off, guarded, quiet. I wasn't sure how to break the large chunk of thick ice between us or why I was always the one who had to do the breaking. I remained stubbornly mute and waited.

Finally, after fifteen minutes, she asked, "Guess what?"

"What?" I took the bait. Her voice sounded upbeat, so she was making a conscious effort to stay on neutral territory.

"I brought that box of antiques to the P.O. today because this guy comes in a lot who sells stuff like that."

"Uh-huh, the box of mothballs and candy canes?"

"Very funny, no, the good stuff. Anyway, he looked it over and said he'd give it a go—post it on his site and see. He said some of it wasn't worth very much, but we might get a few hundred for that Japanese figurine and the antique mantel clock. Oh yeah, and that old knife and the carved wooden panel, he thought those might fetch something."

"Wow, cool. So, the D.D.'s finally paying it forward." I didn't bother to tell her that I had already made a couple hundred on the furniture. After all, she had said I could keep the profits from what I sold but didn't say anything about telling her how much I made from what I sold. I was planning a delightful spending spree on Amazon as soon as my sentence was over.

"Yeah, I mean, don't get your hopes up," she said, smiling. I nodded. Then she mumbled, "Not that it matters—probably already spent on the air conditioner anyway."

"Speaking of that," I cried, remembering, "What's the deal? I've been in the ninth layer of Dante's hell this week."

"I know, sorry about that...I promise to call tomorrow and have someone out."

"You must. I swear, I feel like a Shrinky Dink about to be baked down to the size of a pea."

She laughed and said, "Alright, alright, I'm on it."

"Thank you!"

When we walked into Schaller's, I got that awesome whiff of chargrilled deliciousness like a punch in the face. It was the most exquisite smell ever! My mouth started to water as I stood in line at the counter. It was kind of packed, so by the time we sat down to eat, I was really starving. I tucked into my burger like a lion cracking open a water buffalo. Mom grabbed us extra pickles, which we scarfed down with equal gusto.

After a while, I said abruptly, "Hey, by the way, about the stuff in the attic..."

She looked up with curiosity and said, "Yes? Did you find something?"

"Um, well...," I paused. Should I tell her? It was like a sunken treasure I pulled up from the deep, and I wasn't sure I wanted to share. But then I had a lot of questions. She might have answers. First I started with a softball and told her about Jake taking the radio to his dad.

In between bites, she said, "Oh, that's a great idea. I bet he'll have it in working order in no time."

I nodded. A few seconds later, after she had swallowed, I went in for the kill. "I found some diaries."

"Really? Whose?" she asked quickly.

"Didi's. And your mom's."

"No way! Where were they?"

Ignoring her question, I asked, "Did you know about them?"

"Well, I knew about Mom's. I read hers a long time ago, but it was very hard to follow—like reading hieroglyphics or William Faulkner or something—total stream of consciousness, actually more like total stream of chaos. Impossible, really."

"YES!" I confirmed, excited, but then I said. "I gave up on those within an hour."

"I bet. Sad, really," she said slowly, and my enthusiasm faltered.

"How old were you when...when she passed?" I asked curiously and cautiously.

"Twenty-one," she answered quietly. "I hadn't seen her in a long time. Didi would go to the hospital once a week, but Mary and I only went on Thanksgiving, Christmas, and Easter. It was a depressing place—people sitting in the hallways drooling on themselves, screaming for no reason, or totally comatose. And she was so medicated, she couldn't really communicate with us. Anyway, when she... killed herself...Didi said it was a blessing in disguise because she wasn't leading any kind of life in there."

I nodded and asked softly, "How did she...?"

"Hung herself with a bedsheet."

I didn't say anything for a while. Finally, "Sorry."

She nodded grimly, then said, "I didn't know about Didi's diary. What did it say? Did she talk about us?"

"No, no, the diary is from the thirties, before you were born. Before even your mom was born. I've only read a few months' worth so far. It's kind of cool...how people lived back then..."

"Hmm. You mean during the Depression...?"

"Yes, sure, a little about that—making ends meet and all—but more about her activism and group dates and riding streetcars and going to see movies, which they called shows. Stuff like that..."

"Ha! Really? Interesting. You'll have to let me look."

I responded, "Yeah, I will, definitely." Then I paused before I said, "So, also, um, here's what's weird, Mom. This diary, it's all about some guy Didi was dating named Paul—not your Grandpa Ron."

"Oh?" she said, surprised. "That's funny. I vaguely remember her talking about 'having a string of beaus' when she was younger. She didn't mention any of them by name, though. Was it serious?"

"Yes, definitely. Like, headed toward marriage. I haven't finished reading, but... do you think maybe she *did* marry him?"

"Oh no, I doubt that. How could that be? I only ever knew her to be with Grandpa Ron. And women rarely got divorced back then. Certainly I would have heard about that. But then again, there was a lot I didn't know about Didi. She was a strong, proud woman—a woman of discipline and order and conviction. But she never really revealed anything about herself and definitely not about her past other than stories of her dad, Dennis Diamond, and his legacy—you know, about coming over here from England, working at Kodak, and then building the D.D. and raising a family. Mary and I were left in the dark about pretty much everything else having to do with her."

"Wait. Didi's dad was from England?"

"Oh yes, and her mom. Haven't you seen that Staffordshire china I have in the walnut buffet in the dining room?" I looked at her blankly. "You know, the plates and cups and saucers with the pretty pink rose pattern? That came from Didi's mom. Didi served tea in it every day for Mary and me when we were teenagers. It was kind of a sweet tradition she must have inherited from her mom."

As Mom was talking, I was readjusting my thinking about Didi's dad and mom in the diary—I now pictured them speaking in English accents and having been uprooted from their home country to move to snowy Rochester, New York. Wow, must have been a big change and a challenge. Didi never really talked about that in the diary. I guess with her dad being gainfully employed at Kodak, they were really much better off than most during that time.

I asked Mom, "So she never talked about anyone named Paul? What about her brother, James? Or her friends Frances, Bernice, Roy, George, Sullivan—anyone?"

She shook her head and said, "Nope. None of them sound familiar. I mean, she mentioned once that James died in the war, but that was about it."

Oh, James died in the war! I wondered how many others from the diary died that way too. I had a flash—maybe even Paul! That might explain how Didi ended up with Grandpa Ron.

As I was thinking these thoughts, Mom was still talking. "Being my grandma, I rarely thought about Didi as an actual person, you know, with a life outside of my sphere. I never saw her with friends or family around. And I was your typical self-absorbed kid, so I didn't ask questions. Heck, there were photos of people in frames scattered all over the house, but I never once asked who was in them or what they were all about. And eventually they just ended up in those shoeboxes and tubs you've been cleaning out. I really wish I had asked more questions when I had the chance."

She frowned, then continued thoughtfully, "I do remember that once in a while, I would come in from a date or home from school and would find her sitting in a chair crying. It was so strange. I was almost afraid to let her know I saw her. She would always wipe away her tears quickly. Once I got up the nerve to ask her what was wrong, and she just said, 'Oh nothing, dear. Just reminiscing, that's all. When you get to be my age, you start to think back on your life, and sometimes the memories make you...sad...that's all.' I never knew what she meant. It seemed almost like she had a lot of regrets, but I could never figure out what they were. I asked my sister once, and she thought it might all be related to her marriage to Grandpa Ron."

"Huh," I said, nodding and wondering myself. I didn't know what to think. I couldn't even imagine the Didi from the diary sitting around and crying about anything. She was always so upbeat and focused. I also couldn't image her not having friends around—she was so social in the diary. What happened to *that* Didi? Seemed like a different person from the one Mom was describing. I asked, "She had it bad with Grandpa Ron?"

"I think so...he was...a hard man. I don't know if it was his own upbringing or if he got messed up in the war. Anyway, Aunt Mary and I, we didn't like him. I always sort of wondered if Didi married him...out of some sort of necessity or obligation. Not pregnant or anything—that came later with my mom. But back then, during the Depression, and during the war years, I think times were tough, especially for women. They were expected to get married and settle down and rely on a man for their happiness. It's hard to say what Didi had to face."

She paused and then continued, thinking out loud, "I may not know many of Didi's personal stories, but with regard to the Great Depression, I do remember the aftereffects of that. The fact that we could never, ever, under any circumstances throw anything away. That was definitely a mantra in the D.D. household."

"I noticed," I said, my eyebrows raised. "Yeah, I found this one shoebox filled with old, um, what do you call them? Those things you put thread on?"

"Spindles?"

"Yes, spindles. Or is it spools? Whatever they are. Anyway, who would keep those? And why?"

"That was Didi. She couldn't throw anything away. Grandpa Ron was even worse—he once took a strap to me when I tossed an empty milk jug in the trash."

"What? A strap? Like a belt? Come on." I laughed, thinking she was joking.

"Yes, sweetie, that's what I'm saying. A strap," she answered soberly, and the smile froze on my face. "A strap, or a switch, or a ruler, or a spoon—really, anything that was handy. The back of his hand always worked in a pinch. He was a mean, horrible man."

I stared at her face. Why had I never heard any of this? "Wow, I didn't know. That's awful. Why didn't you tell me? In fact, you haven't told me anything about your childhood." I began to feel like a bad daughter, just now realizing this. What else did I not know? I was as bad as she had been with Didi—never thinking of my mom as separate and distinct from me or having lived an entire life before I came along.

She sighed and said slowly, "The truth is, there's a lot I don't remember, and that's probably a blessing."

I frowned. Poor Mom.

She added, "I try not to think about it. Don't get me wrong—there were some great years too, especially when my dad was alive and healthy. He was the kindest man."

"What did he do?"

"Engineer at Kodak. Smart, handsome, dedicated, sweet. Mary and I tagged along behind him everywhere. Sometimes he would take us out bike riding through the neighborhood. We made quite the picture—Dad with his trim, dark hair and long legs, and me and Mary with our thick, curly red hair and big smiles. People would wave and holler at Dad, 'What beautiful girls!' He always responded, 'Yes, they are. You should see their mother!' And he wasn't kidding. She was beautiful and he loved her—worshipped her, really. He tried so hard to...to fix her, to save her from her demons, from herself, for years and years, but he just couldn't. And Didi couldn't either. They both tried, but Mom's demons were beyond saving. She was taken away, and Dad was diagnosed with cancer and died so suddenly. It was all just...such a waste—a crushing, horrific waste."

I watched Mom's face as she talked. She looked sad and defeated. I began to think that this was the first serious conversation we had ever had. I said, "Wow, Mom, that's awful. I'm really sorry."

It was as if she hadn't heard me. Her eyes looked haunted as she continued, "You know, Mary and I, we came home from school one day, and two strangers were sitting on our couch with Didi—these two elderly ladies, social workers. And as they talked to us, I stared at two neatly packed suitcases in the corner of the room. I knew it right then. They were there to take us away. We were never really given any explanation. Just that we needed to find a new home. Mom was in an institution and Dad was sick, so all I can assume was that Didi couldn't manage taking care of him and us anymore. My dad's parents lived in Wisconsin, so much of the burden of Dad's treatment and care fell on Didi. With Didi occupied, I'm sure Grandpa Ron had a hand in the decision that we were the ones who needed to go. He was conveniently absent that day. But we cried in Didi's arms as she told us to be good, strong little girls, and we were off to foster care."

She paused and I stared at her face, watching the tears well up in her eyes. This was all news to me. It explained a lot. I began to feel guilty about my own part in her frazzled existence. My accusing nature with her, especially these past few months, was not helping either of us, was it? Blame was such an insidious vortex—it sucked you in and made your own life a cool treat of rationalization. But that was not reality. As children, we assume our parents are born with the innate instinct to be perfect parents, and therefore that's the standard we hold them to. But isn't that ridiculous? It's not inherited or inbred—it's learned. I hadn't even thought about the fact that Mom's own upbringing (now revealed to be an insecure, unsuitable nightmare) may not have been the best breeding ground for an ample study in parenthood. She was actually doing quite well, despite her childhood, as far as I could tell.

I reached over and grabbed her hand. She regarded me with such warmth then, in a way that she hadn't in months. Then she smiled softly and squeezed my hand back, using the other to wipe her tears away.

I asked, "Ma, what happened then? I mean, didn't you tell me you ended up back with Didi at some point?"

"Yes, after a few years. Not right away, though. First Dad died. They didn't even let us say goodbye. We hadn't seen him for a month or two, and all of a sudden they were taking us out of school for the day to attend the funeral. There he was in the casket, all pale and plastic—like a wax doll. How is a girl supposed to get that image out of her head? Open caskets are truly dreadful, especially for a child. I think something in me kind of died that day because it was just after that when my memory goes blank. I remember we kept in contact with Didi—she would come pick us up for ice cream or lunch, once in a while, or we would talk on the telephone. Well, anyway, after a few years, she could see that foster care wasn't working for us. We were passed around to so many different houses, I don't remember them all. I'm not exactly sure how she did it, but somehow she convinced Grandpa Ron to take us in, and there we were, back in the D.D. again."

She said that last sentence with a sense of finality, faking a small smile. She took her hand away and crinkled up her napkin, placing it on top of her empty food basket. I guess we were done, so I finished my last fries. I was still so curious, though, I wanted to ask fifty more questions. Oh well. Baby steps. Clearly this was not going to be a once-and-done conversation. We threw our trash out and walked to the car. It was a beautiful night—warm, balmy, clear. I used the car ride to the pier as an opportunity to bring up one last tidbit about Didi because I wanted to get her thoughts.

I said, "You know what's so weird? This Paul guy, the one Didi's dating in the diary, he reminds me a little of...Greg."

That got her attention. She took her eyes off the road for a second and stared at me, wide-eyed. She said flatly, "Whoa."

"Yeah, exactly," I responded and tried to figure out how to explain. I began, "Don't get me wrong—he definitely loves her and is very serious about her— they're basically engaged—but he's jealous and always asking about other boys. And he's got a bit of a past. I don't know, just something about him...bugs me. Plus, her dad has been kind of warning her about him, and on the other side, Paul's mom doesn't like her—or any girls, for that matter. There are just all kinds of red flags." I paused and reflected, finally saying, "I guess it makes me glad that Greg and I didn't work out, even with everything that happened. I feel like I'm worried for Didi...I can't exactly explain it, but I don't want her to be stuck with this guy and have something bad happen to her like it did to me."

Mom said thoughtfully, "I get that. But for Didi, we both know she ends up with Grandpa Ron, not this Paul guy."

"I know, I know, but I guess I want to understand why. It seems like she went from one bad situation to another, you know?"

"Well, I can say from experience that love isn't always the way you plan it. Heck, neither is life, for that matter. Sometimes you start down one road, fall in love with the best of intentions, and then somehow it all goes south and you end up on an entirely different road. Then you look back, even years later, and don't understand why. I must admit, I feel a little like that with your father sometimes."

"You do?"

"Sure. We were young and in love. I naively thought we would last forever. But after you and Tyler came along, we were both working and so busy, and somehow we slipped away from each other. That initial bond just sort of...disappeared. And it seemed too overwhelming to try to put it back together." She paused and sighed, looking at me with a small smile. "We really didn't know what we were doing, but I tell you what, I will never regret it—I ended up with you and your brother. And I learned a lot along the way." She chuckled self-consciously and corrected, "Well, let's just say I'm still learning."

I smiled and said, "So that old adage is true, eh? You're never too old to learn new things."

She grinned and replied, "I think in my case, it might be more accurate to say, 'You *can* teach an old dog new tricks.' But anyway, I try. Listen, when we get home, I definitely want to see Didi's diary. Maybe I can figure it out. If there's one thing I know about Didi, she was a caretaker and a fixer—sometimes to her own detriment. You know how they tell you on an airplane to put your own oxygen mask on first and then assist others? Well, Didi didn't always do that."

I nodded and stayed quiet the rest of the ride. I kept thinking to myself, I survived my own situation with Greg (by the skin of my teeth), and I was definitely going to learn from my mistakes. Note to self: stay away from bad boys, no matter how much they reel you in with their overly confident rebelliousness and swagger. And I was going to stand on my own two feet, too, and never be persuaded to love with blind devotion again. I was going to put on my own mask first. But then I thought, there was no saving Didi, was there? That was the thing about looking into the past. You couldn't change it. For Didi, for me, for Mom. All we could do was absorb it, learn from it, and move on.

When Mom and I got to the pier, the sun was like a big orange ball on the horizon. The whole area was packed with people strolling along, savoring the summer air and the sound of the water lapping up on the beach and rocks. We walked beside each other, at first silent, absorbed in our own thoughts, people watching, and taking in the scene. Families, young kids, strollers, baby backpacks, laughing, running, yelling, tattoos, piercings, dogs, chains, hotdogs, watermelon, ketchup spilled on the cement, beer cans thrown over the edge, fishermen, boats, swimmers, sunbathers, beachballs, beach bags, towels, bikinis, tanks, baseball hats, and the smells of fried food and cigarettes.

Mom finally said, "I spoke with Brian last night."

"Napier? You did?" I asked, surprised and curious. She rarely talked about her boyfriends with me.

"Yeah, he called pretty late. We didn't talk very long."

I liked Brian. He was less mental than the others. In fact, he seemed like a nice, stand-up, stable, normal kind of guy. These were words I rarely used in association with Mom's amours. And I knew his daughters, sort of—we weren't friends or anything, but I knew them from school, and they seemed nice and normal too.

"How's he been?"

"Good, I think. I haven't seen him in a while. His girls are away this weekend, and he asked me to go boating with him, but I wasn't sure if I should..."

"Why not?" I asked.

"Well, of course I want to go...it's just I didn't want to leave you...alone again...I thought you might want me to help with the attic."

This was new. She was really trying, and that made me smile. Despite that, though, I didn't want her to miss out, so I said, "You're worried about me? Puh-lease, Mom. You're fine. I'm fine. Go. Have fun. Besides, I totally have the attic under control at this point."

"You really don't mind?"

"No worries, Mummy. Although I guess that means you'll be leaving me the car, right?" I asked with a smirk.

"Oh! I hadn't thought of that." She paused and I gave her my most innocent, pretty-please face. She laughed and said, "Okay, I might...I said *might*. If so, this will be on a trial basis only. This is not a free pass—hear me?"

I nodded mutely.

"You'll need to act responsibly. And I don't want you using it for running all over town—you are to take it to work and back, and that's it—understood?"

I gave her two thumbs up and said, "Yes, your honor." I stared at the beautiful summer sunset with the largest grin on my face, my heart and mind singing Queen's "Bohemian Rhapsody." I skipped down the pier, and she laughed after me. It felt like old times again—happy-go-lucky Mom and Delia. Wow!

❧ Chapter XVII ❧

So, I didn't tell Delia about the real estate thing. Maybe I should have, but we were having such a great night for the first time in a long time, and I didn't want to upset the apple cart. Maybe I was chicken. Maybe I wouldn't pursue the idea anyway. I didn't even know what it entailed. It was just a whim. Maybe it was over my head, too much work, too complicated. Maybe I was grasping at straws. Wanting more purpose in my life and thinking a career change would be the answer. Foolish, I know. And quixotic. Anyway, I didn't want to bring it up with Delia and have her think I was crazy and not be able to deny that she may be right. Yes, just plain chicken, but whatever the reason, I stayed mum and didn't regret it. The evening was magical.

After the pier, we went to Abbott's for ice cream sundaes and sat outside on a picnic bench eating them, feeling the warm, balmy air and watching fireflies dance around in the trees. The other tables were filled with families who, much the same as us, were soaking up the remains of the summer sunset and drinking in the night sky as it slowly filled with the twinkle of stars.

I was still thinking about that diary of Didi's and wanting to get my hands on it when we got home. I had always thought of Didi as an enigma. I remembered her being the strong, kind matriarch of the family. She was petite, gray, and wrinkled when I knew her, but somehow stalwart and steady, like a hearty reed in the wind. But then sometimes she was timid and quiet like a girl in church, showing deference to others as if her place was of no consequence. This latter behavior I mostly observed around Grandpa Ron as she acquiesced to his irrational disciplinary methods. During those times, she would slink out of the room with her head down, seeming sad and downtrodden, a ship without a port. I wondered if the diary held any clue to the duplicity. Although my imprint of her—the image of her face and hands—had faded over the years, I still was curious about her. What had her life been like before

Grandpa Ron? What had those early years been like—as a young girl during the Depression, growing up in this house? And how had she handled things later, when her only child spiraled down the path of madness? Had a piece of her gone down with her daughter? Maybe her stand against Grandpa Ron to get us out of foster care was her way of gaining back some small semblance of that disjointed, broken story, even if only to descend into her old role of subservience after the triumph. Utterly confounding—I wasn't sure I would ever know. But maybe the diary would shed some light on the mystery.

Out of the blue, in the middle of my reverie, we were just finishing our sundaes when Brian texted. Delia and I read it together.

"Hi doll, we on for tomorrow?"

"He calls you *doll*?" Question from Delia—yes, always with the commentary. "Who are you, Doris Day?"

"Yes—we're old, and what's wrong with him calling me *doll*? I think it's sweet."

"What's wrong? Um, let's see—sexist, old-fashioned, degrading, derogatory…"

I rolled my eyes. My little feminist. I ignored her and texted back, *"Yes, looking forward to it. What time? What can I bring?"*

"Condoms. Lots of condoms," from Delia. I put my hand over her mouth, as if he could hear her.

"I'll pick you up at 10. You don't have to bring a thing, just your bikini and a towel."

"Preferably a yellow thong," Delia mumbled under my hand.

"Well, I don't own a bikini, so that's going to be tough, but I'll bring my bathing suit and several beach towels. You don't need me to bring food or drinks? Sunscreen? Koozies?"

"Koozies, Mom—seriously?" Delia again.

I answered her rationally, "Men don't think about these things, and I don't want to hold a warm beer in my hand the whole time."

Delia shook her head as Brian responded, *"Nope, I have all that. Bring a change of clothes, if you like. We can go for dinner somewhere afterward."*

"And after that, I'll take you to a place you've never been before." Delia with her insinuations. I told her to shush.

"Perfect. Can't wait, see you then," I responded.

"Me too."

I smiled and put my phone back in my purse.

Delia said, "I've seen that look before—Momma gonna get some."

"Delia, please," I said, with my best Mother-is-exasperated look.

She laughed and said, "What? Like you're not?"

"Never you mind if I am or if I'm not. You're too mature for your own good. Or immature—whatever shoe fits."

She rolled her eyes at that. Then she smiled and said, "Listen, really, I like Brian. I still haven't exactly figured out your relationship—if that's even what you call it."

I shrugged, uncertain myself. We had never tried to define it, and that had worked out just fine so far. I replied slowly, "I don't know. I like hanging out with him, but neither of us has actually talked about anything more serious…or about anything in particular."

"You mean, you haven't had 'the talk' with him? Like, yo, what's this thing we're doing here anyway? Are we boyfriend-girlfriend, going steady, pinned, or just booty buddies? Never asked?"

"Nope."

"Never?"

"Nope, I swear." I shook my head again.

"Well, aren't you apathetic. Or is it pathetic? I can't tell," Delia accused.

"Delia! That is not nice."

"Well, what word would you use?"

I pursed my lips. "Okay, so, we've been taking it slow, I agree…"

"Slow? How long has it been?"

"Since our first date? Oh, I don't know…maybe two or three years…I don't remember."

"Years?! Glaciers move faster than you two. Make it official already! What's the holdup?"

"I'm not sure what you mean by 'official,' but if you mean dating monogamously, I don't want to pressure him to do that. He had such an awful divorce, and he's very busy with his girls. Did you know that his ex never sees those girls? He's their only breadwinner and parent. I think his plate is rather full…I don't want to add to that."

"Excuses, excuses. Come on—his girls are my age, so they take care of themselves. And screw the divorce. You're divorced too. That's no excuse."

"I know. It's just that I know he's been hurt and that it's hard for him to be…vulnerable again. Plus, for all I know, he's seeing five other women besides me. We have a sort of don't-ask-don't-tell philosophy."

"God, Mom! You haven't wanted to know? Not even a little?"

I gulped—jeepers, the third degree from Delia. "Well, yes, I suppose I've wanted to know…sometimes, but then I'd also rather not know…or not think about it too much, especially if he *is* dating five other women. What good would that do me?"

"Well, um, let's see—it might make you want to have a conversation with him to figure it out."

"Okay, okay, enough. Maybe you're right. I'll chat with him tomorrow. Put some feelers out, see how he reacts. I like the guy. And he seems to check all the right checkboxes."

"Exactly. He's great. Stop putting it off. Who knows? You might be pleasantly surprised."

"Maybe…thanks," I said as we grinned at each other. It reminded me of when she was a baby and she would smile up at me as I bathed her—an expression of love and contentment, mixed with connection and trust.

Was I mistaken, or were we bonding?

And then Delia stuck her tongue out. I laughed and sighed. Spell broken. Ho hum.

❧　❧

The next morning, I peeked in on Delia, still sleeping soundly, hugging her stuffed bear, sweet and fresh like a little girl, with her hair matted down on her cheek. I smiled as I tiptoed downstairs to make myself coffee and toast. As I sat on the stool overlooking the backyard, I remembered back to the time when I would sit on this very stool and listen to the robins sing in the backyard as Didi busied herself at the stove. The bacon would smell mouthwatering in the iron skillet, and Mary and I would be at our wits' end with hunger and impatience. Didi was always calm as she deftly drizzled a spoonful of pancake batter on the griddle, telling us both to "hold our horses" and "simmer down." We would laugh and try to knock each other off our stools. We couldn't get enough of her home cooking, and more so, her love and attention. Delia told me last night when we got home that I couldn't have the diary yet—she was still reading it. She waved it in front of me, and I took it from her for a moment, scrolling through the pages of tight, neatly packed writing. My interest was piqued but then quickly blasted as Delia grabbed it back into her hot hands. I smiled. I would have to wait.

I looked at my watch and saw that it was nine fifteen. I quickly got ready, packing a bag of clothes, beach towels, shoes, sunscreen, and yes, koozies.

Delia was awake now, sitting up in bed. I showed her my koozies and said, "So there!"

She laughed. "Do what you gotta do, Ma. No sweaty drinks for baby doll."

I grinned, zipped up my bag, and laid her car keys down on her dresser.

She put her hands together like she was praying, crying, "Yabba dabba do!"

"Yes, you'd better yabba dabba do nothing to that car, and I mean nothing. Not a scratch or dent or hiccup, as far as I'm concerned. Understand? And no friends riding around with you. Just go to work and come back, do you hear? Don't think I won't find out if you try anything funny."

"I swear, I won't be funny. When am I ever funny? Wah wah wah, I'll be fine, Mummy. No worries. You go do your thing and don't worry your pretty little head about it."

I sighed. Like asking the moon not to shine in the night sky. "Okay, please don't let me down. I'm trusting you."

Delia nodded with a deadpan look. She hated it when I said that.

"I'm off, then. Text or call if you need me. Work a little on the attic before you go, okay? And have a great first day at work."

"Yes, yes. Have fun with Brian. Don't forget to have *the talk*."

"Well…maybe…we'll see."

"Do it. Like Nike says. Just do it. Don't be chicken."

"Bawk, bawk, bawk," I cried, smiling, elbows in the air.

Delia shook her head, saying, "Dweeb."

"Okay, bye."

"Buh-bye." she responded, puckering up her lips with air kisses. Such a beautiful mouth, that one. I laughed and blew her a kiss, heading down to the porch.

As I swung on the porch swing, I found myself getting nervous. So stupid, Heather. I was a grown woman. And I had been out with Brian more times than I could count, but he still had this effect on me. Not the breaking-out-in-a-sweat, want-to-die kind of effect—more like the excited-will-he-hold-my-hand kind of nervous. He gave me flutters! Like a teenager. Ridiculous. I shook my head.

And there he was—pulling into the driveway in his Jeep Wrangler—looking all kinds of hotness. Tall, muscled, tan with that sexy bald head. Gotta love a smooth cue ball. And those eyes—warm, kind, brown with that naughty little twinkle. When the sun hit them, they lit up like lightning bolts, especially when he looked at me. It sent those bolts directly to my heart.

As I got in the car, he grabbed my hand and said, "Aren't you a sight for sore eyes."

"Who, me?" I said innocently, laughing. I was wearing rather tight jean shorts and a light blue T-shirt that matched my eyes. I'd left my curly red hair loose (large and in charge) and put on some new pearly pink lip gloss. "You look pretty good yourself," I said, squeezing his fingers.

He asked me slyly, "You want me to come into the house first? Top it off before we get started?"

"Oh, you naughty, naughty boy," I answered, laughing. If only we could! "Naw, can't—Delia's inside."

"Damn," he lamented. "Well, later then."

I smiled, silent, encouraging, mute, thinking, *hell yes.*

He headed out on the road, and I asked, "How've you been?" I felt along his trimmed fingernails and the crook in his thumb. I loved his hands.

"Good—busy, but good. Just been working like a dog. And hanging out with the girls. The usual. You?"

"Same."

"How's Delia's attic project going?"

"Actually, surprisingly well. We've already sold a few things and donated a bunch. And I'm even more excited because Delia just got a job."

"She did? That's cool. I thought you told me she was fired from her job?"

"Yeah, that was the last job—at Panera. I still don't know exactly what all went down with that. But this is a new job. Working the front desk at the RCC. God, I hope she can keep it for at least a week."

He smiled empathetically. "Setting the bar high, eh?" He knew my anxiety level on the Delia front, including the roller-coaster ride we'd been on for the past year. He never judged. He made me feel like everything was going to be okay. "How'd she get the RCC job?"

"Jake Freimuth—you know him? The boy down the street. He works there and helped her get an interview with the manager. Luckily, he didn't ask too many questions." I laughed.

"Well, I'm happy she's doing better."

"We shall see. Only time will tell. I gave her the car keys, which may be a mistake. If it is, it would be my own stupid fault. Or wishful thinking—I don't know. I had a nice date with her last night, and we sort of made up, so

I'm trying to cut her some slack. I feel like she's finally turning a corner on things. I can only hope and pray…"

"Don't worry—it'll be fine." It was nice to be with a guy who didn't feel the need to provide solutions or to fix me and my life. Brian had always been a great listener. So different from Johnston. He laid his hand on my knee, and I put my head back on the seat, looking over at him. His eyes were like warm pools of brown butter.

I asked, "How are your girls? They working this summer?"

"Yep. They're doing great. Nancy's working at Dora Lee, and Sam's out at the golf course again."

"Man, that's a nice deal Sam has. How much does she make doing that?"

"Depends how drunk the golfers are," he said, laughing.

"I bet."

"I'm not sure exactly, but I think she does pretty well. I was out there golfing a round last Saturday morning with some friends, and there she was, driving that cart all over the place. I think the tips go up as the day goes on. It was so hot last weekend, she said she sold out of Gatorade by noon. But then they all switched to beer—she said it was her best Saturday yet." He grinned.

"Nice. Is she still dating Derrick?"

"Yep, going on a year now."

"Wow, that's amazing, especially at her age."

"Yeah, I think so too. I'm kind of amazed. She was always my shy one— you know, nose in a book, and yet here she is, working at a golf course and dating Derrick—serious too. I would have never guessed it. And I really like Derrick—he seems to have a good head on his shoulders, and he loves Sam. Treats her very respectfully."

"God, I'd love to have Delia find someone like that…"

He nodded. "Someday she will."

"One can only hope. What about Nancy?"

"Single. Happily—for her and for me. She's just shoveling ice cream over at Dora Lee and getting ready to apply to colleges."

"Good for her."

"Yeah, they're both doing great. No thanks to me. Honestly! Don't look at me that way…okay, so maybe I had a little to do with it, but still, they're just great kids. I feel bad because I haven't seen either of them very much in the past couple of weeks. Work's been insane. And this weekend they're visiting their cousins in Cleveland."

"Yeah, I mean, that happens sometimes—life gets busy. So, what's been going on with work?"

"Oh, we were finally starting to make some progress on that five and twenty interchange when the engineers come back and tell us they're changing the design. I was like, are you f-ing kidding me? We're already halfway through the project! And now you want to change it?! My guys are all lined up, ready to finish it in a few weeks, and now they put the kibosh on it. And I can't make heads or tails of the stoppage. The engineers tell me that the original design was cutting through some type of environmentally sensitive area, and they didn't figure that out until just now. So, we have to redirect the exit and easement. They're not even sure how we're going to make it work. I was over at the engineer's office every night this week, standing over his shoulder and talking him through several viable options, but still nothing's figured out yet."

"Yuck. Sorry about that. Job security, though, right?"

He raised his eyebrow grimly. "I suppose. How's your job?"

"Oh, good. Nothing ever really changes at the P.O. Well, except we got a new girl this week. She's nice. That's about it. Tom's soooo excited."

"That old horndog still there?"

"God, yes—he'll never retire. He'll probably die in the back room, and we'll have to take him out on a stretcher."

"Probably," he said smiling. "What else is new with you?"

"Actually, I do have something I want to run by you, but first, would you please tell me where we're going? I have no clue. All I know is boating."

"Why do you need to know?" he asked defiantly.

"Oh, come on! You're not going to tell me?" I cried. That stinker!

"I thought you liked surprises," he challenged.

"Well, the last surprise I had was Delia getting fired from her job, so what do you think?" I answered with a grimace.

"Not all surprises are bad, you know."

"I'll hold out judgment on that, if you don't mind."

He shook his head and laughed. "Just you keep your panties on, missy—you'll know soon enough," he answered mysteriously.

"So, I take it this surprise won't entail my panties coming off," I retorted, laughing.

"I didn't say that," he clarified, "Don't put words in my mouth, you little vixen." His hand traveled up my knee a little, and I grabbed it before he went too far.

After a few minutes, he asked, "What did you want to tell me about?"

"I've been thinking about a side career," I said, looking at him shyly.

"Lingerie model?" he asked with a grin.

"Yes, that's later tonight." He liked that. I continued, more serious, "Naw, I was thinking about getting my real estate license."

"Oh, well, that's cool," he said, rather quickly. Then after a minute, "Sure, why not?" He was always so supportive—no hesitation. What a guy!

I continued, "Yeah, I mean, I might be crazy because I was looking it up, and it's going to take a minimum of seventy-five hours of training, and then you have to pass this monstrous exam, so I don't know…we'll see."

"Wow, that is a lot of time—how would you do that?"

"Not exactly sure yet. I can take the classes online, so that helps. I wouldn't start anything until Delia and Tyler are back in school in the fall, of course. It's just something I've been thinking about lately."

His eyebrows drew together. "Well, what brought this on? Unhappy at the P.O.?"

I sighed. How to explain? Without sounding pitiful or ungrateful. "No, not exactly. My job is fine, I suppose. It's not very exciting, but it pays the bills, and the benefits are good, so I can't complain."

"So…then what?"

"I don't know…lately I feel a little…lost, you know? Okay, don't judge. First of all, I'm old…haha, don't try to deny it—you know you're old too. The other week, I had to order progressive glasses! They make it sound like you're getting a party fit for your face—and then you realize it's just a fancy way of saying that your eyes are just as decrepit and pathetic as you are. Dirty swindlers! And let's be real—I'm not winning Mother of the Year. I have this dead-end job, I have no hobbies—wait, does going out and drinking every night count? No? Bummer. Okay, so like I said, no hobbies. I watch way too much reality TV, I eat crap most of the time, I rarely exercise, I have no future goals. I've been thinking about it lately, and I realize I have been here on this Earth for over a half century, and what do I have to show for it?"

The entire time I was talking, Brian's face was cryptic, masked, watching the road. After I finished, he looked at me. I held my breath. He smiled and said, "Well, you have me."

I grabbed his hand and kissed it. Those sweet brown eyes! "Do I?" I asked.

"Yes," he answered definitively. I smiled. Could this count as the Delia talk?

He continued, "You know, I have those thoughts too sometimes—I think it's only natural. But who knows the answer for any of us? Think about it—if an alien came down to our planet, it would think, what a bunch of strange and uninspired creatures! They sit in large boxes all day and stare at small devices stuck to their hands and or mounted to desks, and then they ride in oblong machines that drive them from one box to another box. They shove bits of kibble into their faces several times a day, then poop it right back out again a few hours later. They lie on squishy squares, completely inert, doing nothing for eight hours a day. What a lazy, inept species!"

I laughed. "No doubt. I never thought about it like that. You have a point."

"Please—the average ant can lift fifty times its body weight! What do we have to show for all our higher consciousness? We're obese, sluggish, weak, and slow. We put our energy into whining about politics and music and sports—hell, it's amazing we have the initiative to get out of bed in the morning, let alone be productive members of society."

I nodded, then said dryly, "This is some pep talk."

He chuckled, squeezing my hand and changing his tack, "Listen, all I'm getting at is that life isn't easy. It's hard to know the meaning or purpose, but all we can do is ride the wave, you know? The ups, the downs, and the in-betweens."

"Talking dirty to me, baby?"

He laughed. After a moment, he said, "That's the smile I want to see. By the way, if it makes you feel any better, I've had progressive lenses for five years already."

"Ha! See, I told you you were old too! I feel better." I regarded his face with something akin to love. He always made me feel like I was a better version of myself. How could I not love that?

After a few minutes, he said, "And hey, if you need help with the exercise or food thing, let me know. Don't scowl at me, deary. I'm not saying you need it, but I do follow a fairly regimented routine that works for me. I'd be happy to share some tips."

"You're so good. Way more organized and disciplined than I am—I really envy that."

"The key is not to tackle everything all at once—you get too overwhelmed. But small changes implemented over time can really add up."

"Totally. I know you're right. And honestly, I know what to do—I mean, it wasn't too many years ago that I was in great shape. I just need to get back into a routine again. Commit to it. Somewhere along the line, I slacked off."

"Yeah, that happens. Just start back up. No biggie." He paused thought-fully, then asked, "So, the real estate thing...?"

I laughed self-consciously and said, "Yeah...I don't know. Clearly, I need to think about it some more. That's why I'm running it by you. And my friends. And random strangers on the street. I guess I can't decide. It would certainly be a big commitment—seventy-five hours ain't nothing to sneeze at, that's for sure. Not to mention that after I'm certified, I'd have to work nights and weekends. That would be new. But then I look on the plus side, and I think it would be so interesting. Meeting new people, seeing all kinds of different houses, helping people find their perfect dream home. I think I'd be really good at that."

"Of course you would," he said openly, but then, with a pause, "And I could be a professional wrestler, but you don't see me going off and doing that."

"You would be great at that!" I said laughing. "But I see your point. I know...it's seems like I have ADHD or something, doesn't it?"

"Naw, that's not what I meant. Hey, you do what you want—I'll be here to support you, whatever your decision. I'm just saying that looking out-side yourself for the answers isn't always the way to personal fulfillment." He looked at me significantly and continued, "I should know—that was my whole bag in my twenties. And what did that get me but anger, frustration, and a divorce." He looked away as his face clouded.

"But you have two wonderful girls."

His eyes cleared slightly, and he nodded, saying, "I do at that. And even more, I have peace of mind. But I learned a hard lesson back then: only you can make you happy. Yeah sure, the external stuff—money, things, people—they can certainly enrich your life, but everything you need to feel complete is right here inside you." He reached his hand up to my heart and pressed his finger there. I grabbed it and smiled at him. Of course he was right.

Finally, I said with cheek, "So...let me get this right. What you're saying is...you can't always get what you want...but if you try sometimes...you get what you need...?"

He smiled and sang the rest of the lyrics as we both laughed.

For a while, I watched the country roads speed by, wondering at the beau-ty of the hills and valleys and farm fields. Then I noticed a small patch of blue off in the distance. "Is that Canandaigua?"

"Yup, that's it. That's where we're headed."

"Oh! I love Canandaigua Lake! Where'd you get a boat?"

"A buddy of mine from work asked me to house-sit this weekend. He's out of town and wants me to check on the cat and make sure everything's okay. He said I could use the house and the boat."

"Wow, awesome! Hey, there's a vegetable stand—let's stop!" I cried, feeling happy and excited. It wasn't every day that you could stop at a roadside stand.

"Alright...why not?" We got out and inspected the goods. They were so ripe and colorful, like a rainbow of healthfulness. He asked, "You like tomatoes? What about these? Peppers? Squash? Cucumber? Yeah? Let's get a bunch...we can grill some...what about these berries for dessert? I thought we'd go out for dinner, but maybe we'll stay in."

"Now you're talking..."

"You have any cash? Let me see...I have two tens. You have a few ones? Okay, great." After we slipped the cash into the metal box slot under the stand (honor system out here in the sticks), I laid the vegetables down in the backseat. As I began to turn around, Brian was behind me in a flash, grabbing my waist, twisting me around into his chest. He said with a growl, "Hey, give me a kiss."

I planted my lips on his as he enveloped me in his embrace. My heart was beating wildly as we melted into each other, and I heard some of the vegetables fall over onto the floor.

Chapter XVIII

I GOT UP AND FINGERED MY CAR KEYS, grinning from ear to ear. Last night it was "Bohemian Rhapsody," this morning it was Lizzo's "Good as Hell." I hummed the tune as I got ready. Heady power and freedom! Where to go? The beach? Naw, I was just there last night. The mall? Naw, too busy on a Saturday. Putt-Putt? Naw, too teenybopper. What about breakfast? Saaaweet! When was the last time I went out for breakfast? I should call McKenzie and see if she wants to come. What time is it? Ten already? Hmmm, too late for her. Screw it, I'll just go by myself. I'll bring a book. I don't need no stinking friends to prop me up—I'm fine on my own. Wait, what time is work? One o'clock? Okay, yeah, I'll be back in plenty of time. So maybe I won't get any attic work done, but now that I have the RCC job and have my car back, who cares? Whoops. Slipped into old-Delia mode there for a sec. Well, I can always work on the attic after my shift at the RCC.

I looked through my selection of books. Hmmmm, too early in the morning for Henry James or William Somerset Maugham. Maybe Edith Wharton? Nope, too melodramatic. D. H. Lawrence? Colleen McCullough? Too naughty in a public restaurant. I finally settled on Raymond Chandler's *The Long Goodbye*. Nothing like a little gumshoe to go with my vroom-vroom and woo-woo. It felt so good to be back in my car. My pinecone freshener still stunk up the interior. Made me realize with a start that I hadn't driven the car since winter. Holy crap! Crazy. I really had been on a bender, hadn't I? Well, no worries, I was free now. Free and clear—me, myself, and I. I turned the radio up as a Clash song came on. I sang at the top of my lungs, the windows down. The looks from passersby didn't faze me—I was on top of the world.

I decided to go to the diner out on Ridge—Mom and I had gone there once or twice, and the blueberry pancakes were awesome. When I arrived, it was packed, so I had to wait a few minutes on the wooden bench by the front door until a table freed up. I cracked open my book and started reading. After a few minutes, two

girls came in the door with their mother. I recognized them—they went to my
school, but I wasn't friends with them. They sat on a different bench off to the side
and waited. I felt their eyes on me, but I kept my nose in my book. Does one say
hello to a random person from school just because we happen to be in the same
place at the same time? Um...decidedly not.

Just then, the hostess called my seat. As I got up and followed her, I heard one
of the girls say, "Yeah, she's the one. Remember? From the text. *That* text. Mom,
you remember us telling you about it? That guy—Tammy, what was his name?
Gabe? No, Greg. Yeah, Greg. That's the girl." Then, "Whoa, shut up! That's her?
She's smaller in person. God, how awful. Can you imagine? I can't believe she goes
out by herself. She's got balls. I'd be afraid to leave my house. Isn't she a junior?
I heard she's been with like half the guys in school. I think she was in my French
class last year. What's her name again? Deanie or something weird like that. Wait,
let me look—I think I still have that text saved somewhere..." Finally, mercifully,
the mother whispered, "Sshhhhh! Shush, you two!"

I thanked the hostess and sat in my little booth, facing away from the front. I
tried to pretend I hadn't heard, but I felt the angry, frustrated, telltale tears begin to
well up in my eyes. Dammit! All I wanted was a nice, peaceful, anonymous breakfast to celebrate getting my car back, and here I was confronted (again!) with the
ghosts of my horrid past. I put the menu up to my face and swallowed my tears. I
wanted to rush out the door, back to my car, back to the sanctity of the D.D. It
was so unfair! I peeked around the menu toward the front—now they were getting
seated in the booth right by the front door. Well, I couldn't leave now. It would only
add fuel to the fire—then they would really have something to say about me. She
just got here and now she's leaving already? What's her problem? Plus, then they
could talk about me more freely, probably do a blow-by-blow of my body parts.

Gulp. I quickly wiped away a stubborn tear from my cheek and braced myself
for the waitress. I ordered pancakes and began my book, wrapping my hair around
the side of my face and leaning over the book in a sort of cocoon. I found myself
rereading the same paragraph over and over, not digesting a thing. And when the
pancakes came, I couldn't digest them either. I picked around the edges. I was so
mad. It made me hearken back to Doctor Peterson's words: "Anger turned inward
is sadness." Certainly, that's where the tears were wrenched from—my hopeless,
helpless anger at Greg, at those girls, at myself.

Why couldn't I live in a big old city somewhere far, far away? Like Detroit. Or
Chicago. Or Istanbul. Why couldn't I ride one of those transporter things from
Star Trek? "Beam me up, Scotty!" Or better yet, why couldn't I use one of those

mind-eraser things from that *Spotless Mind* movie? Duh, of course—the movie's whole premise is how that doesn't necessarily fix everything, but still...right now, it sounded like heaven to me.

The waitress broke into my thoughts, "Ain't it good, honey? You want something else instead?"

"What?" I asked, distracted. "Oh, no, that's fine. I guess I wasn't hungry after all. Can I just get the check?"

After I paid, I took a deep breath, seeing the dreaded booth still occupied. I sighed, got up, and raced by it, pretending to hunt for something in my purse—my head down, my hands occupied. I scurried directly to my car, shutting myself inside before the inevitable cathartic tears came gushing out. A waterfall, chest heaving, not a tissue or napkin to be found anywhere. F-ing hell.

I had to wait a few minutes until the first wave passed in order to see well enough to drive. I thought to myself how, once again, I had let it all get to me. It was like drinking a foul-tasting poison that ferments in your gut and seeps out, even more potent, over time. *The incident* still had this effect on me, all these months later, fresh as a daisy and stinking like a skunk cabbage. And it was my own poison I was drinking. I'd stuck that evil powder in a jar with sour vinegar, shook it up, and drunk it all down myself. No one else. All these months later, I was still imbibing it—ounce by ounce. I wiped the worthless, resentful, stupid tears away as I drove.

Okay, so what did that shrink always tell me? Try to focus on the positive. Raindrops on roses and whiskers on kittens. Bright copper kettles and warm woolen mittens. Brown paper packages tied up with string. Help me, Julie Andrews. Save me. Okay, okay, okay. The positive. Hmmm. I still had my room and my car and my friends. I had my books. I had soccer. I had a new job. I had Mom and Tyler and Dad and Beth. I was about to have a new baby brother or sister. I had YouTube and Instagram and Google and Twitter. I had the great outdoors and air in my lungs. I may have been scraping the bottom of the barrel, but I still wanted to jump into the barrel and disappear. Grrrrr...focus, Delia, focus!

Positive, happy thoughts...Jake...in a green T-shirt and short shorts...mmm, now we're getting somewhere. Come to think of it, Jake knew about my sordid past, and he hadn't made a big deal about it. He didn't think of me as a total pariah. I wondered if I would see him at the RCC. Maybe I would text him and ask if he'd be there. When I pulled in the driveway, I looked through my phone but realized I didn't have his number. Come to think of it, why would I? He was Tyler's friend, not mine. Right? Hmmm. Maybe I had adopted him, temporarily. Or more?

What time was it? Almost noon. Should I walk down the street to his house? Why not. Better than going inside the D.D. and wallowing for another hour. I dropped my book and purse in the hallway, stopping in the bathroom to blow my nose and look in the mirror, and headed down the street. Two of Jake's sisters were in the front yard running through the sprinkler in their bathing suits. See, now *that* was a positive image. If that wasn't summer happiness in a nutshell, I didn't know what was. I smiled.

"Girls, girls!" I came up to them, screaming through their delighted shrieks. The older one, Emily, ran over to me, breathless.

"Hey, Delia! We're mermaids! Do you want to see?"

I laughed. "Yes, of course."

Emily did a somersault over the sprinkler, and Kelly jumped over the spray, landing in a pool of hysterical laughter on top of her sister. Emily kicked her off and then tried a cartwheel, her back leg tripping over the hose so she landed upside down in a grassy pool. Kelly followed, doing a roundoff, successfully leaping the gulf and standing up proud with both hands in the air.

I hollered, "Amazing. I didn't know mermaids were gymnasts."

I tried to walk past them to the front door, but Kelly came and took my hand, saying, "No, Miss Delia—you have to stay here and watch us."

"Actually, I was looking for Jake. Do you know where he is?"

"Jake," she frowned and wrinkled her nose. She shook her head and said, "He's at work."

"Oh," I said, deflated.

Then she squeezed my hand with both of hers, grinning, and stated definitively, "Now you can play with us! Come on!"

As she dragged me over toward the sprinkler, the spray hitting my shirt, I protested and thankfully was saved by Mrs. Freimuth, Jake's mom, at the door, yelling, "Girls, leave Delia alone!" Then to me, "Delia, sorry, come over here."

I broke free with a shrug of my shoulders at Emily and Kelly.

"Hi, Mrs. Freimuth. How are you? I was coming by to talk to Jake."

"Nope, at work."

"Yup, I heard. I'm headed there myself in a bit."

"You are?"

"Uh-huh. Jake helped me get a job over there. I start today. Front desk."

"Well, I didn't know that—how wonderful!"

"Uh-huh," I paused for a moment, not wanting to leave, but not having a reason to stay. I looked away toward the girls.

She studied my face a moment and said, "You know, his shift actually just ended, so he should be here any minute. Why don't you take a load off and wait for him?" I looked back at her as she motioned for me to sit with her on the front stoop. I smiled gratefully and sat beside her.

She asked me a few questions about my family and then, "Jake tells me you've been playing soccer over at the pitch with him and the guys."

I nodded self-consciously. "Yeah, a little." I wondered what she thought about me being the only girl who played. Then I realized her sharp eyes weren't analyzing me for my soccer prowess but instead were looking into my soul with a high-precision microscope. You don't become a mother of five without knowing when someone's been crying.

She said softly, "Sweetie, how've you been lately?"

I uttered a short laugh and replied dismissively, "Oh fine, just fine."

She nodded knowingly and quietly. She prompted, "Delia, come on...what's really going on?"

I broke my face away guiltily from that caged stare, looking down the street toward my house. Could I make a run for it? Hmmm. Nope. I sighed.

I turned my head back to her, trying to meet her kind, knowing eyes. "I guess I'm having...a bad day."

She nodded and waited. When I didn't continue, she asked softly, "How so, sweetie?"

"Oh, the usual. Life sucks and then you die," I answered flippantly, trying to brush it off with a bitter laugh.

She wasn't buying it. She stated flatly, with gentle intent, "No, really."

I said, "I think I may have messed everything up. Already. For good. Is that possible? At the ripe old age of seventeen? I may have ruined my life." I grunted and swallowed a large lump that had formed in my throat. I continued, "I just don't know how to get back on the right track. I keep trying, but it's like I'm walking through sludge."

She reached around and hugged me to her side. Then the tears were beginning again, and I tried to stop them but couldn't hold them back. She spoke into my hair, "Oh sweetie, I wish I could take it all away. Life isn't always easy, that's for sure. But there's no way you've messed it all up for good. Don't you know, every day is fresh and new—a clean slate. It's you who must decide what gets written on that slate. Don't let anyone tell you otherwise. Nothing is unfixable, nothing is for good, until you die, my friend—nothing."

I nodded into her shoulder, rubbing my eyes.

She continued, "Heck, look at me—I'm surrounded by wild, screaming children, food stuck in my hair, diapers piling up in the trash, fifteen loads of laundry waiting to be done, a sink full of dirty dishes, and to top it all off, I officially weigh seventy-five pounds more than I did on my wedding day. So, take that and smoke it in your pipe, my dear!" She chuckled, throwing her hands up in the air.

I had to laugh. She grinned down at me and added, "Seriously, though, I have days just like you're having, when I don't want to get out of bed. But you know what, Delia? Guess what happens on those days?" I shook my head. "That's exactly when God throws me a bone. He sends an angel into my bed to say, 'Mommy, mommy, I love you,' or he sends my husband to me with breakfast in bed, or he sends me a message from my mother-in-law telling me she can't stop by today because she has explosive diarrhea." At this, she burst out laughing, causing me to choke. Too funny. Her daughters stopped their sprinkler games to stare, and she swatted her hand in the air at them, letting them know Mommy was okay.

After a minute, she calmed down, glancing into my eyes with kindness, "And that's when God sends me a girl from down the street who needs a sympathetic ear to tell her everything's going to be okay. Delia. Look at me. Everything's going to be *alright*. I promise. No, it won't be perfect, and no, it won't be easy. But you will get through this. Whatever it is, no matter how bad. You will have a day, maybe not today, maybe not tomorrow, where you will look back at this day and think, wow, I survived that and I'm doing okay. And if I can survive that, I can survive this day too and the day after that and the day after that."

I nodded. "Okay," I said.

She gave me one last embrace and then stood up as Jake pulled into the driveway. The girls ran over to greet him. He opened the door, oblivious to the urchins tugging on his swim trunks, and said joyfully, "Delia! Hi! What are you doing here?"

I smiled, stood up, and went over to him. It was those green eyes again, blazing their heat on me. I said with more strength than I felt, "Not much, just sitting here talking with your mom."

"I heard you start today."

"Yes, soon. I need to get going, actually."

"Yup. Ted told me. Well, I'm glad." He looked down at his sisters for a moment, fiddling with their hair, and then back at me. He scrutinized my face, and I began to blush—had he noticed the dried tears? Was he a sniper of emotions like his mom? I thought possibly so...

He said slowly, thoughtfully, "Maybe we'll see each other over there sometime."

I nodded and said, "My mom gave me my car back, on a trial basis, but I wondered...maybe...maybe we could carpool over there...together...sometimes. Save money on gas. I mean, if we have the same shift."

The girls ran back to the sprinkler, and Mrs. Freimuth answered for him, "Of course!" I noticed she was staring at us with a knowing smile. She was on to us, that one.

I turned to leave, and Mrs. Freimuth gave me a hug, saying, "You remember what we talked about."

I nodded, and Jake said, "Hey! Wait a sec. I don't have your number."

"And I don't have yours."

His mom said goodbye, discreetly heading back in the house while Jake and I stood on the front stoop exchanging our contact info.

At the end, he looked directly into my eyes, asking tentatively, "You okay?"

Dang. How did he do that? Made my heart skip a beat. I gulped and said as confidently as I could, "I will be."

As I started to leave again, he chucked my shoulder and said, "Call me."

I nodded, turning back for an instant to glance one last time into those green pools of light. Just like that, I had gone from the depths of despair to the highest mountain peak. I walked away with a small wondering smile, feeling the heat of his eyes on my retreating form.

❧ CHAPTER XIX ❧

BRIAN'S FRIEND'S HOUSE WAS SPECTACULAR. Not huge, but very modern and right on the water. We went inside, bringing in the veggies and our bags, and went hunting for the cat. Brian said his name was Squiggy. We called out to him for several minutes but never found him and finally gave up. He must have been hiding somewhere. We checked his water and food dishes, and both were full. Oh well—he would appear when he was ready to greet us.

We opened the sliding glass door and stepped outside, making sure to close the door behind us in case Squiggy had been waiting in the wings all along in order to attempt a cat caper. When I looked at the view of the lake just below us, I sighed, glanced at Brian, and said, "Wow." Rolling, shiny waves of crystal-clear water, a field of grapevines displayed in verdant relief against a distant hill, and two sailboats floating gracefully by, their masts like stalwart soldiers in the sun.

"Nice, isn't it?"

"Nice doesn't cover the half of it. How do you know this guy? Can I be friends with him too?"

He laughed and said, "Um...no. You're all mine, and I'm certainly not going to share you with Peter. He's a lady-killer."

"Oh, is he? All the more reason...," I said coyly, and Brian kissed me, effectively ending that conversation. I asked, "Where'd you meet him?"

"He's one of the foremen on my team."

"No kidding? So, foremen do pretty well then?"

He coughed and said, "Yeah, sort of, well, actually, not really...Peter's kind of special. Super-smart guy—he actually worked for IBM for thirty years, got full retirement, and then decided to start a whole new career in construction. I guess he wanted to use his hands more—get outside, that type of thing."

"Wow, jack-of-all-trades?"

"Something like that. You want to see his boat?"

"Yes!" We started down the steps that led to the dock. I asked, "So where is he this weekend?"

"I guess he met some girl from Albany. He was driving out to see her for the weekend."

I certainly was no expert on boats, but Peter's looked new, big, and fancy.

Brian stepped down onto the lift and began unbuttoning the boat cover, talking for a while about the boat's features and motor size, all of which were lost on me. I sat down on the dock, took off my flip-flops, and stretched my toe into the water. It was cold and wet and wonderful. I could see the rocks and seaweed underneath the surface, and then a foot-long fish slowly drifted by as I gasped, pulling up and pointing.

He looked and laughed, saying, "Whoa! That's a big one!"

"Oh-Hell-No-Sharknado!" I exclaimed with a giggle. "Jeesh, that one's going to take off a foot. Do we have fishing poles?"

"Probably, but let's do that later..."

"Okay, sounds like a plan. It's so beautiful here."

"Yes, it is," he agreed, smiling up at the blue sky and warm sun.

"So, where should we go?" I asked.

"Anywhere you want, baby. Why don't you go pack us a picnic lunch and get your suit on, and I'll be there in a minute to help."

"Gotcha!"

As I prepped the food in the kitchen, I thought, how lucky am I? Brian was such a good guy. How could anyone ever hurt this man? He had the warmest, most sympathetic brown eyes. What kind of woman was that ex of his? Didn't make any sense to me. Granted, I didn't know the whole story. I'd never asked details because I'd never wanted to poke that soft, vulnerable spot in him. And he'd never provided anything more than cursory comments on the whole debacle.

Of course, I had never told him any details about my divorce either. Maybe it was better that way. I often wondered about full disclosure versus complete historical obscurity—which was better when starting a relationship? Gory details, warts and all, or what they don't know won't hurt them? I mean, you couldn't leave out the major chunks—otherwise, who the heck were you dealing with—could be a scammer or a con artist. Thank goodness Brian and I knew each other from high school—there was no hiding anything from that crowd. In fact, I probably knew more about him before we started dating than what he had told me firsthand afterward. I guess he could say the same about me. Not that we were close in high school. In fact, I didn't really remember him at all, even though he says he remembered me, which of course, made me feel like an oblivious snob. But then fast-forward to years later, and before we went on our first date, I asked around about him (as I'm sure he did about me), getting the basics secondhand.

I gulped thinking about that. If he had gotten the basics on me, it was a miracle he wanted to date me at all! Did he know about my mom, my childhood? What about my divorce? I had only hinted at the sordid details. I wondered absently if he knew about the affair. Probably. I suppose the whole town knew. I was such a stupid, irrational, hormonal mess of a woman back then. And to jump into bed with that philanderer—what was I thinking? He was such a player, and of course he couldn't keep his mouth shut. And on top of that, he was awful in bed—those fat, sweaty, cattle-hoof hands, and it was almost always over in three baleful grunts. Pig. Why, oh why, Heather? You foolish, stupid young thing! Even if Johnston and I weren't getting along, even if Johnston didn't understand me, even if Johnston worked too many hours, even if Johnston wasn't there for me when I miscarried and wanted to crawl into a hole and die. Even if…even if…I knew there was no justification for it. I knew it deep down, and it still made my stomach hurt. Again and again, I badgered myself, how could I have? There was not enough remorse or repentance to take it away. It still washed over me sometimes, with the guilt, but I had to shake it off and move on. It was what I tried to ingrain in Delia too: some past mistakes couldn't be fixed or obliterated, but they could be learned from, they could be replaced by new memories, new ways of handling similar situations—more thoughtful, intentional, intelligent ways, or better yet, don't let yourself get into a situation like that in the first place, ever again. This was why I had taken my time with Brian. I never wanted to feel that weak and susceptible again. I never wanted to feel out of control of my own destiny or be a part of ruining someone else's.

As I cut fruit into a bowl, I had a revelation: well, shit, Beth probably thought the same thing about me that I thought about Brian's ex! How could this woman (me!) have hurt Johnston? We were none of us saints, nor hopeless sinners either, were we? Well, yes, we were all sinners. Only some of us did unforgiveable things and had to live with a brick in our stomach the rest of our lives.

I shook my head. I knew one thing for sure—I didn't deserve Brian.

Why was he dating me if he knew my past? Shouldn't he have run for the hills by now? Especially in light of *his* past? Delia encouraged me to probe Brian about our relationship—why had it remained so casual for so long? But maybe I already knew the answer. Why would he want anything serious with me? I was damaged goods. Wasn't it obvious without me asking him?

I was so lost in thought, I nearly jumped out of my skin when the cat rubbed his side up against my leg. Two seconds later, Brian came through the door like a breath of fresh air and asked if I needed any help. I shook off my glum expression and smiled back. I wasn't going to ruin the day—he didn't deserve that, or me bringing up something better left unsaid and unexplored.

"Nope, I think I got it. I found Squiggy."

He picked up the kitty and nuzzled him. "Yes, I see—he's a nice little guy, isn't he?" He was rubbing under his chin and saying, "You were hiding from us, weren't you? And now you're wanting some love. You're just a shy one, that's all." Rather proving Brian's point, Squiggy promptly pushed himself off his chest, clamoring for a release, and hit the ground running. He was off to his safe place, and we were off to the boat. Brian grabbed the cooler, and I grabbed the picnic basket and some towels.

Brian held the door for me and kissed my cheek as I walked through it. Then he smacked my butt lightly, saying, "Let's get this show on the road!"

I replied with a salute. "Aye aye, captain!"

We headed out onto the open water. It was a perfect boating day. Sunny, warm, clear, and not too busy. At first, we drove around the perimeter, looking at the houses and feeling the wind in our hair and the splash of the water on our arms and hands. Brian opened two beers, and I put the obligatory koozie on each, handing one back to him. As we sipped and enjoyed the scenery, I said, "God, it doesn't get any better than this!"

He smiled and nodded. After a while, he slowed down in the middle of the lake and turned the motor off, saying, "Let's get in."

I looked at him skeptically, "But it's freezing!"

"Come on—it's not that bad. Let's at least dunk our feet."

"Okay," I agreed, thinking that was manageable, but when I dipped my feet in, I squealed, "Ahgheesh, no way!"

Brian laughed and dove headfirst off the back. When his face popped up out of the chilly water, he screamed bloody murder with a hoot and a holler, splashing around and carrying on.

"Serves you right, you fool!" I said, laughing.

"Very…refreshing. And it's June!"

"I know, right?" I laughed. "Didn't you know the Finger Lakes were formed by glaciers? I think this is where they filmed the movie *Frozen*."

He said, "I don't doubt it. Come on, though, it's not that bad—get in with me."

Those sweet, adoring eyes. I shook my head and smiled down at him. Before I could think, in one swift movement, he reached up and put his freezing hand on my thigh as I cried out and jumped up. That was it—he quickly pulled himself out of the water onto the back of the boat and rubbed his drippy, icy body parts up against me as I shrieked. A second later, he had me in a bear hug, and we were leaning off the edge until whoosh! We were both in the water, laughing hysterically, our legs intertwined, our hair stuck to our faces. When I recovered from the shock, I socked him in the arm.

"Ohuuuwww, you!" I yelled, trying to keep my indignation but failing miserably since he was in my face with a toothy grin and dozens of wet kisses. How could I resist that? We laughed and kissed and swam around the boat. Several times, he tried to catch hold of me by my legs or my arms, but I skidded away underwater or pushed him away with my hands.

Finally, getting tired and out of breath, we hopped back on the boat, still laughing uncontrollably. There was no getting away from him then, and his hands were as sticky and multitudinous as an octopus's suction-cup arms. Before I knew it, we were lying flat on the bottom of the boat, and he was pulling my bathing suit top down. I tried to lean up, screaming through my laugh, "Wait! Someone! Help me!"

He mumbled through his occupied lips, "No one's going to save you now, my pretty—you're all mine."

"Oh noooo, it's Blackbeard come to plunder my virtue!"

His only response: "Aaarrrrgghhhh!"

His hands and mouth were on me like swarming bees, and everything seemed to be aroused very quickly. He wrapped himself around me, kissing my mouth, my cheeks, my breasts. I relaxed in his arms and succumbed to the heady feeling of lava bubbling up from my toes into my groin. He felt me relax, and I opened my eyes just long enough to see his knowing and encouraging grin.

Somewhere in the middle, we heard a boat go by, but Brian put his hand over my mouth and shushed me as I giggled between his fingers. He slowed his movements down and gathered me nearer to the inside panel of the boat.

I coughed into his hand with laughter until the motor passed. Then he took his hand away and kissed my laughing face as we both went gleefully back to business.

When it was done, he jumped in the water again, this time naked as a jaybird, the crazy fool! I put my suit on and stood up, watching him splash around. He kept saying, "Get in," but I shook my head. I eventually threw him his suit, and as he slipped it on, he told me I was a prude for not skinny-dipping with him.

I yelled defiantly, "A prude?! Where were you a second ago, during all that motorboating?"

"Ha! Ah yes, the motorboating...hmmm, nothing beats motorboating. And you have such lovely bumpers."

"All the better to beat you with. Would you get back in here?" I laughed and shook my head.

He climbed back in, toweled off, and sat in the captain's chair, grinning from ear to ear. He was like a happy puppy dog who's just been given his favorite treat. I maintained my false scolding look from the seat next to him. After a few moments, he finished drying off his hair and face, and I noticed he was thinking about something. His facial expression had changed, deepened somehow. I altered mine, raising my eyebrows as if to say, what now, you rascal?

He reached over and put his hand in mine and said, in all incongruous soberness, "You know something?"

"What?" I asked tentatively, taken slightly aback by his tone.

"I'm mad about you." His look was soft, like a child's, but there was a hint of humor still in his eyes. I thought, oh, he's pulling my leg again.

I laughed and said, "Well, I know you're mad, that's for sure. No one else in their right mind would jump in the lake like you just did. Twice!"

As I chose to look away from his joking eyes, I noticed with swift precision that they had changed, darkened, like a veil over his face. With a pang, I thought, had he been serious?

He said, looking down now, "No, I mean it, Heather. I'm mad about you."

I paused a moment, processing, staring at the top of his head. He was *mad* about me? I couldn't help it—I found myself doubting the sincerity of his words in the context of us. These past couple of years had been great—fresh, fun, light, airy, a wild ride. But not serious, certainly not intentional. His overwhelming state of reserve when it came to his emotions, his love, his inner self—I had always let that lay fallow, carefully preserved, untouched, and untouchable. I hadn't wanted to explore that. Neither of us had ever broken the seal on the bubble of superficiality that kept our relationship in squeaky clean, self-contained order. And yet, here he was, saying he was mad about me.

I sat in shocked silence.

After a few minutes, he looked back up, searching my eyes and seeing the perplexity there, swiftly snatched his hand back, swiveled himself around in the chair, and started the boat motor, pushing it into gear.

In an instant, I snapped out of it, grabbing his hand again, saying, "Brian, wait! Turn the motor off."

He regarded me warily and left the motor running. He said, "Forget it, okay? It was nothing. I'm sorry. I shouldn't have…said anything."

"Don't say that!" I cried, realizing the next words I brought forth from my lips could make or break us. More softly now, "Please…don't say that…I'm sorry—you just took me by surprise. Please…turn the boat off."

He complied, then stared at me, guarded and patient. I continued, "Brian, you must know I feel the same way! It's just…it's just…" Good Lord, I felt like I was taking my life in my hands! I whispered in direct, overwhelming sincerity, "I'm scared! Alright? There. I said it. I'm scared!"

He sat with a disbelieving look in his eyes. Then he smiled at me like I was a two-year-old who had just admitted she was afraid of the bogeyman. "Heather." He said my name so sweetly and consolingly. And with his heart in his eyes, he asked softly, "You're scared? Scared of what?"

Thank you for those adoring brown eyes! They gave me strength. "I don't know…we've been getting along so swimmingly for all this time. Pardon the pun," I laughed, my heart in my throat. "I honestly figured you weren't interested…in anything…*more*. And I always felt kind of okay with that. Wait! Don't pull away! It's not that. It's not that I didn't *want* more. Of course I did! But…but, don't you see? It's just that…well, you must know, can't you guess it…? Do I have to spell it out?"

"What?" Now he had a frown on his face, trying to figure out what I was saying.

I wasn't doing this well. How to get across to him without looking like an idiot? I took a deep breath and started, "Well, ever since I can remember… ever since childhood, I guess…everything, well, anything and everything I've ever *really* wanted, you know—love, kids, home, job, everything *important*…

well, I've jinxed them! I've ruin them, messed them up. Or they've become ruined. I'm not exactly sure how it happens, and I'm horrible at exploring the whys—I just know that everything I touch or come in contact with seems to wither and die, or at least go bad somehow." I looked down into our interwoven hands, wondering if what I was saying made me look like a superstitious fool. I willed myself to continue, "I think…I think…sometimes that God doesn't mean for me to be happy. Or maybe, well, maybe that's not fair to God. Chances are I just screwed everything up myself. No help or fate from God needed." I chuckled mirthlessly, still not looking up. I added sadly, "Paying penance for past deeds done badly, I suppose. And you and I, well, of course I've wondered if there was any future for us. I've dreamed of it—quite a bit actually." I regarded his face then, noting a puzzled look on it. I said resolvedly, "But then the cold, hard facts slap me in the face: I don't deserve you. There. Now you have it. You've tied your boat to an anchor. You may want to jump ship and save yourself."

I waited. His expression changed slowly from confusion to incredulity to understanding to resolve. He said simply, "You're ridiculous."

"What?!" I cried, letting go of his hand. Was I hearing correctly?

He grabbed my hand back and spoke so softly that I couldn't help but look directly at his calm, sincere face. He said, "Don't take it the wrong way, and get rid of that frown, you silly, silly woman! Listen to me. Heather. Everything you touch doesn't die." He laughed and said, "I don't know if you noticed all the things you touched a few minutes ago, over there on the boat floor, but clearly, I can assure you, none of those things were dying."

I rolled my eyes at him and he went on, "Seriously, though, dear Heather, you really are ridiculous. So what if you've had some failures in your life? Look around you. No one's perfect. Look at me—I'm hardly on the wall of fame for most successful life choices. And here's the thing—pay attention because I want to drill this into that beautiful, unpredictable, crazy red head of yours: I admire you. *And* your life. Just as you are, just as it is. In fact, what's more, I *respect* you and your life. You've been through it, and so have I, and we're both still standing, aren't we?"

He stopped. Whoa. That sank into my heart and soul like a tall drink of lemonade on a hot summer day. I stared, surprised and humbled. I didn't know how to respond.

He continued, "I've held back until now because I wanted to give you your space. But that's done. Starting right now. Got it?" He took a deep breath and pressed on: "So here goes: Can't you see what you are? Has no one ever told you before? Heather, you're a gem. Wrenched right out of the inside of a spectacular mountain. I saw you, and I was just like a prospector panning for gold—I noticed you as clear as day (exactly how you are and who you are) and that you weren't like those other miscellaneous rocks sullying up the pan—you *were* the bright, shiny piece of treasure. Just exactly how you are. With all of your past and present and future."

He said this so soberly and with such feeling that I started to cry. He smiled knowingly and continued, "I mean, this was a no-brainer. You're smart and sweet and kind and funny and caring, not to mention my dream goddess in the bedroom." I laughed through my tears, and he sat back a little, still watching me with those kind brown eyes. "And to be honest, you're being too hard on yourself. Sure, things in your past aren't necessarily all unicorns and rainbows, but no one's past is that way. And you have two great kids, and they love you (whether or not they say it or show it), plus a great job (maybe not super interesting, but still…), and a big house with loads of family memories, and don't forget, you have a great guy by your side who's explaining to you right now how you're a gem." He paused to make sure I was hearing this. I stared, reddening and teary-eyed. "Besides, don't you notice that we're all, every one of us, just stumbling along in this life? We're like a bunch of blind two-headed monsters—running into walls, breaking fragile objects, crushing things underneath. No one knows what the hell it's all about or how to make it work. No one is an expert. And if anyone claims they are, more than likely the next thing they will do is accidentally blow up Planet Earth. All we can do is learn from our mistakes and move on. That's all anyone can do. Keep moving forward."

I nodded, amazed at how I had been thinking the same thing up in the kitchen a little while ago. I said, "Yeah, but…but…aren't you afraid of the aftermath…of the pain, if something fails?"

He was smiling at me as if I were a child again, his brown eyes like warm layers of corduroy, deep and rich. "Yes, of course, we're all afraid of the pain, but so what? Pain is part of life. And if there isn't pain, how can you decipher and appreciate the joy? We have to experience both extremes to savor each of them properly, don't we? In life, you have to take a chance. It's all a crapshoot anyway, so why not try for something new, something more?"

I said quietly, "You're not afraid…I might hurt you?"

"*Are* you going to hurt me?" he asked flatly, staring directly into my eyes.

I said swiftly, "No...no, of course not. Well, I hope not. I would never *mean* to hurt anyone, least of all you. But...but sometimes I do stupid things."

Again with a laugh (that merciful, light, bright laugh!). He asked, half in jest, "What, you're not in command of your own actions? Is that what you're saying?"

I answered perplexedly, "No, yes, I mean, no...it's just...well, I can be needy, I guess. And scared, and sometimes I run when I'm scared. Maybe, after a while, you'll get sick of having to come find me and talk me down off the ledge."

He chuckled deep in his throat and responded, "You know, I'm no basketful of kittens either. Listen." He stopped to think and then said, "We can't predict the future. All I can say right now is that I pledge to try. To try to make you happy. To try to make it work. I pledge to care for you. To love you. To support you. What if we both just start with that and see where it goes from there?"

I felt myself falling into his eyes—down deep into that soft well of strength and comfort. I said, "Okay."

He pressed his lips to mine and then leaned over my hand and pressed his lips to the skin there. I watched him, marveling at the surprise discovery of an oasis there and the acceptance of that revelation.

I waited until he looked up again before saying with a joke in my voice, "So, when you say 'mad about you,' do you mean Belinda Carlisle mad or do you mean *One Flew Over the Cuckoo's Nest* mad?"

His eyes crinkled and then glinted with false menace. "I mean *Misery* mad. Bring me those feet!"

He reached for my legs as I squealed, jumped up, and scurried to the back of the boat. He was close on my heels, and I gave in, letting myself fall into his arms. He leaned me down softly on the boat cushions in order to kiss the top of each foot, grinning up at me mischievously as I watched with newly tender and loving eyes.

CHAPTER XX

June 1–2

(Wednesday–Thursday) Work was busy yesterday, but not bad today. I made 26 sales total. Paul came for supper tonight. After we ate, I showed him the things we cut out of the magazines to see if he liked them. He said he didn't care as long as I would be his wife. We decided on a wedding date: Saturday, July 30th. He thinks he'll have a better job by then. Dad is paying for the wedding but "on a budget," and then Paul will come live with us until we can afford an apartment. I told him I would save all my money. He kissed me and told me he was the luckiest man alive!

Why so quick? Probably antsy to get in her pants. I still can't believe the parents are agreeing to this. All I can figure is that Paul must be really good at convincing people. Heck, he got Didi to fall in love with him. Not much info about the Mrs., though. I wonder if she even knows yet. P.S. Can you imagine living with your parents right after you get married? Would make for a lousy honeymoon, that's for sure.

June 3–4

(Friday–Saturday) Worked Friday. 10 sales. We all took off work on Saturday, and Frances, George, Paul, and I spent the day at Seabreeze. It was sunny and beautiful and filled with people and fun. Paul won 2 cigars, a cane, and 3 boxes of candy. We rode the Greyhound, Leaping Lena, Honeymoon Trail, and Old Mill. Both Paul and George bought Panama hats. Frances stayed over.

First thought: Why are they spending precious coin on a day at the amusement park? Second thought: Maybe I'm being too hard on them. Third thought: Maybe they deserve a break and want to blow off some steam—after all, things have been rather serious lately. Fourth thought: What can I say? Seabreeze is awesome—I totally love that place! I haven't been in years, though. Last time we went I rode the Jack Rabbit, and I remember commenting to Tyler that I wondered how old the wooden roller coaster was. It's always a little dicey when you're on the thing and it's groaning and creaking like the floors of a rickety old house (like the floors of the D.D.!). You definitely say a little prayer in between your screams. I guess the Jack Rabbit wasn't around during Didi's time, because she doesn't mention it in her list of rides, but it certainly seems like it could have been. Fifth thought: I wonder what it would be like to go to Seabreeze with Jake. Would he win me a prize? Would he hold my hand on the Jack Rabbit? Would he kiss me in the photo booth?

June 5

(Sunday) Worked for several hours. Then Mom and I wrote a list for the trousseau: white satin wedding gown, tulle veil, going-away three-piece suit, afternoon dress, street dress of wool, coat in tweed, lace dinner dress with jacket, sweater, cardigan, skirt, evening wrap, two hats, shoes (street, evening, slippers, mules), negligee, gloves, bag, handkerchiefs. Dad said he will pay for the trousseau since I'm his only daughter. He's been so sweet, offering to pay for everything. Mom is giving me her cedar hope chest. Paul said he looked for jobs during his lunch break every day this week, but there's nothing.

Man, I want a trousseau. Never heard of it before, but it seems like a good deal. I think I just saw that cedar hope chest up in the attic behind the big black armoire. I'm gonna check that out. I wonder if any of those things she mentioned are still in there. I mean, do you keep the things in the chest, or do you use them? I'm so confused. Either way, I will say this: Dad's being mighty generous. I wonder if he thinks Paul will find a job and eventually it'll all work out. I wonder too. Doesn't seem promising.

June 6

(Monday) It was slow at work. Sam came down and said Honoree broke up with him. I asked why, and he said that she told him he was "too much." I had to stifle a laugh. Then I felt bad because he looked hurt. Paul called and said he finally told the Mrs. about the wedding. She wasn't happy, but what could she say when my parents are paying for everything?

Indeed. Why is it, though, that Didi's parents have sat her down and had the talk with her, trying to get her to see the seriousness of planning a future together, and yet Paul's mom hasn't. I'm not sure I get her. I mean, I understand her skepticism toward Didi and toward the wedding (for obvious reasons), but I don't see her engaging at all with Paul, Didi, her parents, or anything involving her son. Wouldn't she want to meet Didi's parents? Find out what kind of people they are? And why isn't she helping Paul find a job? Maybe too busy trying to figure out her own future, but still…she's seems more of a disconnected boss than a mother.

June 7–9

(Tuesday–Thursday) Frances and George came down to make a date for Friday. Paul said Burrows was back in town, but the Mrs. told him to go back to Penn. because she couldn't support him anymore. The Stand isn't doing well, and she said she already had too many mouths to feed. Problem is that Burrows is in love with Stella, and she's still up here in Rochester. He doesn't want to go back to Penn. He doesn't know what to do. Paul's in the same boat. I told him I would ask around at McCurdy's, and I thought we could go to the next Young People's Meeting and ask there too. We haven't been to the meetings in a while, so he thought that might be a good idea. Dad's trying his best to help Paul, but he said there just aren't any jobs right now, and too many other young men are looking for work.

June 10

(Friday) Paul met us on the streetcar, and we went to the Manitou with Frances and George. I told Paul I would pay for everything, which he didn't like, but he accepted. Didn't have a choice. It was packed with people, and we danced for hours until my feet hurt. Paul said he loved me over and over. Frances and George said they were envious of our "almost wedded bliss." Stayed at Frances's. Went to bed at 1:25.

Wonder why the other friends in her group aren't all getting engaged too. Probably they don't have any money either. Seems like they're being smart about it and waiting. What's the rush with Paul and Didi anyway? I suppose it was expected back then. Thank god for women's lib. I don't have to rely on marriage or a man— I can make my own way in the world without even considering a man. Of course, sometimes I do consider a man, especially a certain man with green eyes and feathered blond hair…

June 11

(Saturday) My pen pal Eleanor came on the train today, and Dad and I went to meet her. She's staying the weekend with us. It was great to see her again. We met two summers ago at Saratoga Springs when we went to take the waters. She lives nearby in Ballston Spa and works the baths. She'd never been to Rochester before, so we drove her around a bit. She talked to Dad about the Eagle Hotel fire a few days ago. It was quite a tragedy. Later, up in my bedroom, she told me about her beau, Henry. He's older than her and already has a house and a car! She thinks he'll propose in the fall. We stayed up until 2:00 going through my trousseau list and the magazines.

Just like that Niagara Falls hotel! Must have been like a daily occurrence back then. They needed to seriously start using brick or stone instead of wood to make these flimsy hotels.

June 12

(Sunday) Paul came for dinner and met Eleanor. We talked about the wedding. He's going to ask Burrows to be his best man, and I'm going to ask Frances to be my matron of honor. Bernice will be a bridesmaid, and Paul asked James to be a groomsman. Afterward, I took Paul out to the Nan alone before he left and showed him the trousseau list. He said he liked the negligee. We kissed a lot.

Typical guy. Horndog. Well, at least it sounds like they'll have a healthy sex life.

June 13

(Monday) Dad and I dropped Eleanor off at the train station before work. It was a wonderful visit with her. She said she'll write me as soon as she's engaged. She said she can't come to our wedding because of her job, but she'll invite us to hers. I told her we would try to go and maybe stay a week then. Paul came by after work. He said the Stand was so quiet that the Mrs. was talking about closing it. I asked what they all would do if that happened, and he didn't know. He said Burrows was already packing his things in order to head back to Penn. this week, and he thought the Mrs. might go with him. I tried to think of things to make it all better, but I couldn't think of anything. We sat on the Nan for a long time in silence.

June 14

(Tuesday) Work was busy. Sam came by and told me Honoree called him and now they're back together. I told him to scram. I had my own love life to deal with and didn't need to hear about his. He asked if I "woke up on the wrong side of the bed," and I said no, but maybe I did!

June 15–17

(Wednesday–Friday) Worked a lot and made 32 commissions. I offered them all to Paul, but he refused to take the money. He told me to save my money for our wedding and for afterward. He didn't have enough change to take the streetcar this week and had to walk to the Stand every day.

June 18

(Saturday) Bernice and Roy came by at noon, and we rode the streetcar to May's watermelon party. There were 11 girls and 7 boys. They were playing a game on the dining room table when the phone rang. It was Paul! He said he was walking there and wouldn't be there until 2 and not to talk to any boys. When he came, we played Ping-Pong and ate a lot of watermelon.

Wow, didn't know watermelons warranted a party, but okay. So strange how one day they're wallowing in the dire situation they're in, and the next they're at a watermelon party. But maybe that's how people survived back then—chin up, turn that frown upside down, put on a happy face—that kind of B.S. is probably what kept America going. I remember watching a Judy Garland and Mickey Rooney marathon on TCM once, and all those movies were like that; little Bobby and Sue are starving and Uncle Albert's drinking gin out of a jug down at the Piggly Wiggly, but let's ignore that and get the old gang back together for a show. Like somehow the "show" would feed the whole damn town with well-decorated tap shoes and a belting crooner.

June 19–23

(Sunday–Thursday) Mom and I shopped all day on Sunday for my trousseau. The rest of the week was busy. I asked my manager to schedule me for as many hours as he could, so he let me work the floor during the day and two hours each night on the ledger. I didn't see Paul.

June 24

(Friday) Frances came over and spent the night. We embroidered my wedding handkerchiefs. She thinks Paul will make a splendid groom since he is so tall. She wonders about George because he's only 5'6". I told her it didn't matter as long as he loved her. She said it didn't matter because George hadn't asked yet. We talked for a while about her aunt, Paul's mom, and she said she didn't know her very well because they had spent all those years in Penn., but she said her aunt never seemed "very sociable" and was often "not talking" to her mom "for various reasons." I told her about them potentially shutting down the Stand. Frances said she hadn't heard that and how unfortunate.

Sounds like the Mrs. doesn't even get along with her own family. She's a piece of work. I bet Didi was on the cusp of asking Frances and her family for help. She clearly wants to save Paul from his circumstances but doesn't know how. It's rather commendable of her. I think back on my relationship with Greg, and I never once felt sorry for him. Is that strange? I loved him, but I guess I was always so focused on making him happy and trying to comply with his every whim that I never thought too much about what made him tick. I remember he told me once that his dad "smacked" his mom around sometimes. I said that was awful, and why would he do that? He just said it was no big deal and "he only did it when she deserved it." After my shocked silence, I asked if his dad struck him as well, and he just looked at me and said, "Sure, what of it?" I always remembered the way he said it, like it was perfectly normal. Looking back now, what kind of household did he grow up in where that was considered okay? Thank god he never lifted a hand to me, although sometimes he would grab my wrists so hard that they bruised. He knew just where the line was that he couldn't cross, and he made sure to get as close to it as he could without going over.

Clearly Didi's seeing the holes in Paul's life—the lack of a father figure and a mother with a cold, hard way about her—of course, he would cling to Didi with her happy, open heart and kind, warm, caring nature. She wanted to make it all better for him. I guess I never tried that with Greg. I mean, don't get me wrong—I tried to make him happy in every way I knew how, but I never paid enough attention to his own life circumstances (outside of me) to see if there was something else I could do for him or some other way to fix his world. Maybe that makes me a bad person, but honestly, I don't think it would have worked anyway. You can't change a man who is most assuredly going to repeat a pattern, regardless of the fact that he had nothing to do with the making of it and probably had no recourse in defying it. Maybe I should have tried, though...

June 25–26

(Saturday–Sunday) I worked all weekend, double shifts, and my feet hurt. Paul came tonight for a few hours. He said he had to borrow change for the streetcar from the Mrs. and she wasn't happy. We went out on the Nan and kissed. I showed him the handkerchiefs that Frances and I embroidered. He said he might use them right away because he still couldn't find a job and didn't know what to do.

June 28–30

(Tuesday–Thursday) Paul called and said the Stand closed and that his mom and Burrows are moving back to Penn. on Saturday. One month until we are married. He said he was able to stay in the apartment until then—that the Mrs. had paid enough for July, thank goodness. But she wanted him to pay her back as soon as he got a job. He said he would sell his dad's pocket watch this week so he had enough money to eat. I told him not to sell it and to ask for money from my dad instead, but he refused. He is proud. I offered to give him money, but he wouldn't take any. I cried a little with him on the Nan.

It makes me sad for them both. Selling the dad's pocket watch for food had to be heart-wrenching.

Chapter XXI

I ROLLED THE WINDOWS DOWN IN THE CAR and let my hair blow in the wind on the way over to the RCC. I had gotten my cry out, and I felt better. Ted, the manager, met me at the front door. He gave me an employee T-shirt, an entrance pass, and a tour of the facilities. Afterward, he introduced me to Tina, who was going to train me. She was nice. She looked to be about thirty-one or thirty-two and said she had twin two-and-a-half-year-old boys. She told me Jake had come by that morning to tell her not to be too hard on me. He greased the skids, that thoughtful boy.

Tina explained how to scan people in, how to look them up on the computer, and how to sign them up for a new pass. After that, we spent several hours talking and laughing (in between folding towels and checking people in). It felt good to be myself and not worry about any preconceived notions (other than whatever Jake had said to her). She was friendly and funny. She told me all about her boys' potty training and how she was losing her "ever-loving mind." She said her house had turned into a state of international negotiation—for three M&M's, one boy would sit on the Elmo potty for an hour but still not go. The other boy required eight chocolate chips and was now going number one but not number two. Then they tried taking away both of their favorite toys, which led to a standoff wherein neither would go at all. She rolled her eyes and said they were running out of options because as of this morning, neither had gone number two in two days, including in their diapers! She was at her wit's end. I couldn't help but laugh, the way she told the story, and thinking in the back of my mind—wow, Dad and Beth would be dealing with this kind of stuff soon (bless their hearts).

At one point, Ted came by and said with a laugh, "Keep it down over here you two—the customers will think you're not working." We grinned and shrugged. He showed me the schedule for the coming week and wondered if my hours were okay. Sunday from noon to five, then Monday, Wednesday, Thursday from seven to noon, and Saturday from one to six. Jake must have worked some magic—

three days with the same shift as him! And I could play soccer in the afternoon. I told Ted it looked perfect. I had a slight qualm about later in the summer when I would be at Dad's. Would I still be able to do the job and soccer and the commute back and forth to his house? I'd have to figure that out. Also, I wasn't sure about having enough time to finish the attic. But then again, what could Mom say? I was gainfully employed, and all those tubs and boxes would eventually get sorted or sold. After all, I had already made a pretty good dent.

Tina said she was sad we wouldn't be working together again. I asked why, and she said didn't I know? I was being trained so I could replace her. She was leaving. She said her mother couldn't handle the potty training, so Tina was being "redeployed" back to "Poopopolis." I was bummed because she was so nice and, outside of Jake, the only one I knew there. Oh well. We didn't let it dampen our spirits and joked around the rest of the shift. She knew all the ins and outs of the social network of the RCC. She gave me the full scoop, and I appreciated the tips, especially the ones about the creeps who only came in to pick up girls. She also talked about who was dating whom and who were the best workers and the ones who just stood around pretending to work. She gave me some thoughts on breaks—where to kill fifteen minutes (out on the bench by the pond or under the umbrella in the north corner of the pool).

Then she said, "Hey, so you're friends with Jake? He's such a nice boy. You must know Chelsea then too?"

I shook my head and said, "Not really."

"She comes in here a lot when he's working. She and her friends lay out by the pool and swim. But they mostly spend their time harassing Jake. I'm sure he doesn't mind...what teenage boy would mind four bikinied beauties teasing you for hours?" I felt something tighten in the pit of my stomach. "Of course, me myself, I'm not such a big fan of Chelsea. Oh, I'm sorry—you're not friends with her, are you?"

I shook my head. "No, I really don't know her at all...I mean, I met her once on the soccer pitch, but it was just for a second."

"Good, well, the reason I ask is because I heard something about her recently..."

"You did? What?" My ears perked up.

"So, this might be total bullshit, I'm actually not sure, but one of the guys who comes in here all the time, Austin, told me that *he* was dating Chelsea."

"What?! No way!" My heart skipped a beat.

"Yeah, it was the strangest thing. The girls were all out by the pool doing their usual baking—you know, shake, spray, bake, flip, swim, repeat—and Jake's out there too, mind you, lifeguarding like usual. Then Austin comes in and asks me if

Chelsea's here, and I tell him yes and point to the pool, so out he goes. Then about twenty minutes later, he comes back and says thanks as he's about to walk out. I stop him and ask how he knows Chelsea, and he says, plain as day, like it's a given, 'She's my girlfriend.' So I challenged, '*Your* girlfriend? I thought she was Jake's.' He laughed at that, like I was stupid for even suggesting it. He says, 'Jake may think Chelsea's his girlfriend, and maybe Chelsea plays him like that, but believe me, Chelsea's all mine.' And he just walked out. What am I supposed to think of Chelsea after that? Either Austin's a total liar or Chelsea's a two-timing...well, you know the word. I know it can't be Jake—he wouldn't make things up like that."

My mind was racing...could this be true? Did Jake know? He must have seen Austin out at the pool with Chelsea. Didn't he notice? What was really going on? Was she really playing Jake?

"Did you tell Jake?" I asked suddenly.

"Naw, I didn't have the heart. He'll learn it soon enough on his own. I didn't want to be the one to break it to him. Plus, I can't corroborate what I heard. It might just be Austin puffing himself up. He's a big meathead—comes in every day to pump iron, always flexing in front of the mirror...you know the type. I thought maybe it was all in his head."

"Do you think so?"

She looked at me for a second and finally said, "No. I guess I believe him. Poor Jake...what do you think? Should I have told him?"

"I don't know...maybe not...I guess it's better if he finds out on his own."

"Yeah...exactly."

We sat in silence for a while after that. I felt like I'd been handed a top-secret CIA folder and wasn't sure what to do with it. The more I thought about it, the more I was torn. I didn't want Jake to be made a fool of—my heart ached to bring up the topic with him and see his reaction. Then I would know if it was true or not and how he felt about it. But I also realized it was definitely not my place to get in the middle of whatever was going on. I decided to leave well enough alone. Let it run its course. If there was one thing I learned from my *incident*, it was that having everyone know your dirty laundry (and provide commentary on it) made the entire thing much worse.

The rest of the day progressed quickly. It was busy because it was Saturday. Tina told me it wouldn't be as busy during the week and that I should bring a book so I'd have something to do in between checking people in. That sounded ideal—fifteen dollars an hour and I'd get to read books too! Didn't get any better than that.

Randomly, a guy I had played soccer with on the pitch came in. He said, "Hey, Slammer, you work here?"

Tina laughed and said, "Slammer?"

I winked at her and shrugged. I said to him, "Yep, just started today. What's your name again?"

"Gary. What's yours? Not that I'm gonna stop calling you Slammer."

As we grinned at each other, I said, "Delia."

"So, are you done with the pitch then?"

"No, actually, my schedule's pretty cool, I should be able to come next week."

"Awesome. I'll see ya there."

"Yup, okay, see ya."

As he walked away, Tina whispered, "Ohhhhwaaa, you'll be *seeing* him, will you? Sweetie, you sure do have a following. First Jake, then this guy..."

I shook my head and rolled my eyes at her insinuation.

"What, you think I'm blind? Don't be coy. Seems like all those soccer boys have a crush on you."

I rolled my eyes and said, "Definitely not."

"Whatever. Hey, when I was your age, I had all the boys after me too. Granted, now my poor husband is too tuckered out chasing after kids to chase after me much anymore except on the occasional date night, but I remember those days. You should cherish them—believe me, they're gone in the blink of an eye."

As Tina looked away wistfully, I thought for a moment about Mom. She was in her fifties now. Had the boys chased after her when she was my age? Had Dad been the one to win her and, if so, why had that not lasted? I wondered how it was going with Brian on their boat adventure. I was hoping she'd had "the talk" with him. After all, is it better to have a bunch of boys chasing after you or to have just one boy who really wanted you? Sometimes that whole happily-ever-after thing seemed so elusive. Maybe that's why so many people ended up divorced or with so many different partners. Look at Didi—she was totally in love with Paul but somehow ended up with Grandpa Ron. And look at Mom—she and Dad fell in love and then, a few years later, out of love. Even Tina seemed to be saying that love's not all it's cracked up to be. Or maybe she was just saying that love, just like all that potty training, ends up in the crapper sometimes.

But then Dad and Beth seemed happy. I caught them holding hands when they were doing the most mundane things, like sitting on the couch side by side watching TV or standing in the kitchen reading the mail. And now they were having a baby. That was certainly something to hang your hat on. And maybe Mom and

Brian would take it to the next level after all their slow-going reserve. That would be cool. And look at Jake's mom and dad—they seemed pretty happy. Maybe there *were* some great role models out there—you just had to look for them. Love was such a mysterious thing.

At the end of my shift, I gave Tina a great big hug and told her I was sad we wouldn't be working together. She said, "Me too. Believe me, sister, if I could stay here and work with you instead of going home and facing those twins, I would." I laughed and shook my head. On the drive home, I called Tyler. "Yo, yo, bro, what up?"

"Hey D-D-Deal-io, how've you been?"

"STU-pendous. You? Can you believe the news?"

"What? About the bambino? Mi hermano or hermana? Es muy magnífico, sí?"

"I think you may have just butchered at least two languages, but anyway, I don't know about magnífico…yes, I suppose…it is amazing that Dad's gun is still loaded with live ammo. Who woulda thunk?"

"Right?!" Tyler laughed. "Hey, what have you been up to this summer?"

"Well, cleaning the attic."

"The D.D.? Shit, girl. Fun. Kill the green slobber monster while you're up there."

"Already slayed."

"Cool. Actually, Mom told me about it…you must've done something extra wicked. Btw, how are you talking to me right now?"

"I have temporary custody of my phone and car—I'm working at the RCC, so she gave me a reprieve. I'm as shocked full of nuts as you. But don't worry—I'm on my best behavior. Absolute angel. Really. I've had a new chastity belt fitted, and it's squeezing me so tight right now that when I close my eyes, I pee a little."

He laughed, then after a second, he said, "Are you driving right now?"

"Um-hm."

"Ding-a-ling! You're gonna get a ticket. Get off, will you?"

"Chill. You're on speaker."

"Still…."

"Okay, whatever. Tell me quickly what you've been up to and when you're coming home. We need your mad field skills on the pitch."

"You been playing?"

"Uh-huh, with Jake and the guys."

He whistled and said, "Badass! You go, girl! So yeah, I'll be there soon. I'm finishing up this internship and then coming. I think I'm going to Dad's first, though—for the fourth. I might bring someone…" his voice drifted off.

"Wait. What?"

"A girl. I mean, a woman. Her name's Sara. She's coming home with me for a week. I've fixed it all with Dad and Beth. I hope you're coming out too so you can meet her."

"Whoa, Google alert! I didn't know…what's she like?"

"She's…nice. And she doesn't look bad either."

"Ha! Not kicking her out of the bed for eating crackers, eh? So, what's she doing with you then?"

"Funny."

"Where'd you two lovebirds meet?"

"Analytical physics."

"Wow, doesn't get any more romantic than that. It goes without saying, she's a complete dork like you?"

"Uh-huh, pretty much. Engineering major. The Borg says resistance is futile."

"Nice. Well, alrighty then, tomcat. I look forward to meeting her. Hey, you're going directly to Dad's…but I thought Mom was picking you up…?"

"Yeah, I need to talk to her…she doesn't know any of this…"

"She's gonna be pissed. She's mentioned it several times—I get to pick up Tyler in a couple of weeks…Tyler, Tyler, Tyler, my baby, my firstborn, my son, my precious, the fruit of my womb—"

"Enough…come on…you know I wear Calvin Kleins."

"Fruit of the *Loom*, haha, good one!"

"Anyway, you know you're her favorite."

"Yes, like bee stings and rectal thermometers. Anyway, what are you gonna tell her?"

"Same thing I just told you—that I'm headed to Dad's first, so it makes more sense for him to get me. She'll understand."

"Uh-huh, sure she will. You know she's been all down in the dumps lately. She's out boating with Brian today—I told her to have *the talk* with him."

"Did you now? That's cool—I like Brian."

"Me too—he's the first normal guy she's been with in a while."

"Word. Anyway, no worries—I'll talk to her soon."

"You better. And you better bring your girlfriend around to meet her, and quick. Otherwise, she'll be upset if Dad and Beth get more airtime than her."

"Yep, I'm on it. Alright, you better get off now. I'll see you in a couple of weeks."

"K. Later, gator."

"Bye."

Chapter XXII

I told Brian that I felt as though we had escaped to Fantasy Island together. Maybe his friend Peter would never come back and we could just live in his house on the lake forever. With Squiggy the cat. I thought that at any moment we might hear, "De plane! De plane!" It was such a wonderful getaway. I hadn't realized how it was going to feel to let go of all my worries and let someone else take care of me for a change. It was like sinking into a warm vat of cotton candy. At one point Brian even told me I was glowing! It couldn't have come as a bigger surprise to me. I hadn't looked for it or ever expected it, yet here I was—*in love at fifty-one!*

Of course, all good things must come to an end. Or at least to a pause. Brian dropped me off at the D.D. Sunday night, and I nearly cried in his arms to say goodbye. He agreed that it had been magical. But he said now, unfortunately, we must face reality. Brian kissed me tenderly on the lips and told me to stay strong and to call him anytime if I wanted to go to Fantasy Island again (in our minds, if only for a moment).

It was around eight, and as I walked in the front door, I waited for my perfect bubble of peace, happiness, and serenity to burst. I called Delia's name, and to my utter astonishment she hollered back. She was in her room. I went up and sat beside her on the bed. She was scrolling through her phone, but then (was this the same girl?) she put it down to talk to me.

"Don't you look like the cover of *Maxim* magazine!" Delia exclaimed, and I thought, yes, this was the same girl.

"What does that mean?" I asked, slightly confused.

"You know, all tanned and whored out," she answered.

I had to laugh. Of course, she was right. I guess she meant it as a compliment, so why not go with it? "Yes, that would be me."

"So, you had fun?"

"Yes, it was wonderful."

"You and Brian on the same page now?"

"Yes, we had *the talk* and guess what? Turns out he thinks I'm a gem."

She thought that was hysterical and said, through her giggles, "Like what, a diamond or a ruby, or maybe the one that has the dead mosquitoes in it? That's totally tops, Mom!"

I shook my head at her. "No, not amber. Anyway, grrrr, my child, enough about me—how are you doing? You survived the weekend? How's the new job?"

"I like it. Everyone's nice, and it's pretty easy work."

"And there were no...issues with the car?" I held my breath.

"What? Duh! No! Everything's fine. I told you it would be."

"What about the attic?"

"What about it?"

"Progress? I see there's still a mountain in the hallway..."

"Hey! Not a mountain—more like several odd-shaped gopher holes. It's not that bad...I worked on it a little. I sold a few things online. It's gonna take time for the rest. Hey, by the way, what do you want me to do with that rack of old coats? Should I try to sell those? I don't think they'll bring in very much..."

"Let me look at them first and let you know...isn't there a fur in there?"

"No. I mean, I don't think so. I don't remember that. Well, there's a wool coat with some type of mangy roadkill around the neck."

"You mean a stole?"

"I guess...whatever you call it. The rest of the coats are old and smelly. Honestly, I think we should just donate them or toss them."

"I think I remember the coat with the stole. It used to be Didi's. She wore it every winter. That thing must be seventy or eighty years old. She was rather stylish, you know. I don't think I ever told you that. I think she worked at some type of department store when she was younger..."

Delia looked at me funny and said, "Yes, I know. McCurdy's."

I laughed and said, "Yes, that's right. How did you know? OH! I almost forgot—of course, the diary. How's that going?"

She picked it up from where it was lying next to her on the bed and held it out to me. In my hand, I noticed the light, dainty weight of it with a strange sense of feeling Didi coursing through it and from it and into me somehow. I exhaled in surprise. It was so strange and wonderful. I opened it and said, "Wow, such tiny, perfectly neat handwriting!"

"Penmanship is next to godliness."

"Yes, it is!" I said, grinning. "You're enjoying Didi, aren't you?"

"Yes, I admit it. Although I'm rather stumped—so much is going on with her that doesn't add up."

"Is that so? Hmmm, well, let me look through it—maybe I can help you crack the case."

"I will, I promise, but not yet. I'm just finishing up. Probably be done tonight or tomorrow."

I handed it back to her. "Okay. I'll be patient and wait. You work tomorrow?"

"Yep, at seven. Speaking of that, will you make sure I get up in the morning?"

"Sure, okay. Don't stay up too late reading."

As I headed toward my bedroom, Delia hollered after me, "Mom, have you talked to Tyler this weekend?"

"No, why?"

"I think he was trying to figure out his dates for coming home."

Great—I wonder what that was all about. I thought we had that figured out already. "Okay, I'll give him a call."

I went into my room and unpacked my things. Delia talking about the diary made me think about the fact that I hadn't talked to my sister in a while. Mary lived in Colorado now—married with three grown boys. She lived down the street from the oldest son and his wife and babysat their children. She was always so busy, constantly posting pictures of the grandbabies on Facebook—seemed as though her life revolved around them. Well, good for her. I knew she rather scorned my life—the fact that I stayed here in the D.D., working at the P.O., surrounded by the same ol' townies and friends. Her goal when we were younger was to get the heck out of Dodge, and fast. Lord knows, she accomplished it. She went to college in Colorado, became an amazing downhill skier, met a ski instructor, married him, settled down, and stayed far, far away from the childhood memories that haunted us. I suppose in some ways I envied her. She didn't like the world we were born into, and she went and found a new one. All the more to her credit.

Should I call her? After all, it was only six fifteen there. But then again, I was tired. And I wasn't in the mood for a long ramble.

Instead, I called Tyler, and he told me he was having Johnston pick him up and bring him to his house before coming here. And he was bringing a girl home. I tried to hide the surprise and dismay in my voice. Didn't he know how much I missed him? Didn't he know how much I wanted to be the one to pick him up, bring him back here, make him his favorite dinner, do his laundry, sit up and talk with him into the wee hours of the night? Didn't he want me to meet his new girlfriend? Was he ashamed of me? This is what I kept hidden in my heart as he chatted on and on about how nice she was and how, after all, he'd only be at Dad's for a few days, and did I really mind, because it wasn't that big of a deal. I, of course, acquiesced quickly, "No, no worries, all good, you're fine—I'll just see you when you get here." What else could I do? It would have been wrong to scream into the phone, "Pick ME! I need you more! I want first dibs!" I know—petty, selfish, immature, stupid. And human.

I'll tell you what else: I shut up, hung up, and cried. Like a jealous teenager. Stupid fool. Why let it get to me? I guess it was because Tyler and I had always been best buds. He'd always been such a sweet, caring child. He'd even been kind to Delia when she was born. In his little toddler mind, he'd figured out that he had to be gentle with her and protect her. And he'd always been Mommy's little helper too. He would sit on the couch and rock Delia in his arms, talking to her, using those strange first words: "Baby nee appy. Baby goo Mommy. Here baby, ma baby. Deeya ma baby."

And now he was all grown up. In college. With a girlfriend! So why was *I* acting like the toddler now? Was it because if Tyler was getting older and finding his own way in life, it must mean that I was getting older and must find my own way too? Possibly. And maybe he wasn't going to be my best bud anymore. He had a new girlfriend now and was probably *her* best bud. Of course, after the weekend I'd just had and being with Brian and a potential career change, I was headed down a new path myself, wasn't I? Then why was I crying?

I changed out of my clothes and into my nightgown. I lay down on the bed and forced myself to do the thing I hated the most—to look inside myself, to examine my feelings. The dreaded word: *introspection*. Don't get me wrong—from a logical standpoint, I knew it was beneficial to assess my feelings once in a while to get to the root cause of my fears, anxieties, and pain, and then to fix whatever was damaged, button it up, and walk out again into the transparent light of catharsis and redemption. The problem was that emotions weren't always logical. Nor were they forgiving. Nor were they clean, easy, pretty, or welcome.

When I looked into my soul, here's what I saw: a child crouching in a corner, alone and afraid, wondering why the people she loved always left her. Mom, Didi, Mary, Johnston. And now Tyler. And later Delia and probably Brian. Then where would I be?

Once again, not logical. I knew in my mind that my children were with me for good—I'd given birth to them, and they would always be a part of me and my life, forever. But in my heart, *I* was the child seeing those suitcases and wanting to understand how to be a survivor with a titanium cocoon around my heart without losing the very marrow of my being in the process. It wasn't easy. Abandoned. Unwanted. Not enough.

I sat up and blew my nose. I was just being overly dramatic, right? Here's what it boiled down to: Tyler was going to stay with Johnston for a few days, or a week or two or whatever. Did it matter, the time? It was just the idea of him having quality time with them and his new girlfriend, and not me. And now Beth was pregnant, and Tyler would want to be around the glow of that. The hope of that. A new little brother or sister. And now Beth would have her own baby with its own baby talk that she would have to decipher, just as I'd had to with Tyler when he was a baby. And that baby would look up into her eyes with love and devotion just as Tyler had. And Tyler would also look into those same eyes and find a brother's love and devotion. As would Delia, with sisterly sass and bonding.

BUT—I forced myself to reverse course—the baby wasn't here yet, and at some point this summer Tyler *would* come here to the D.D. and be with Delia and me, and it would be like old times. We'd stay up late, talking around the firepit in the backyard, roasting hotdogs and s'mores. And who knew? Maybe Brian and his girls would come too, and Tyler's new girlfriend would be there, and she would be funny and nice. And maybe she'd ask me about our family traditions or maybe want to see the family photos. Maybe she would ask about my favorite recipes, and I'd give her Didi's recipe for blueberry scones, and we'd make them together sometime. Maybe we'd be-come friends and start new traditions like joint outings to the mall or liking and sharing each other's photos on Facebook. Okay, so I was getting ahead of myself...

I sighed. Yes, okay, good, Heather. Sufficiently off the ledge, I called Brian. As his phone rang, I almost hung up, thinking, would he mind me calling him? After all, I had just left the guy an hour ago. Granted, in our new state of coupledom, what were the rules? Maybe calling every night before bed was part of the package, or at least I was going to try to make it part of the package, starting right now. He didn't pick up. I didn't leave a message. Probably in the shower or getting the mail. So much for the package.

Instead, I called Donna and told her about my awesome weekend. She was happy for me. She talked for a while about Andy's ex leaving for Hawaii in five days and how they were reconciled to the situation. They'd even planned several mini trips with the girls, including a weekend at Darian Lake Waterpark. They were so excited, and Donna had spent hours with each of them at the swimwear store, buying new bathing suits in anticipation. After twenty minutes or so, Brian's phone popped up on the line, but I waited until Donna and I were finished, then hung up and called him back.

"Hi there," I said.

"Hey," his voice was warm, happy to hear from me. It gave me courage.

"I decided we should start a new routine."

"Oh, you did, did you? What's that?"

"A call before bed."

"Sounds like a plan. What should we talk about? Shall we give each other a breakdown of our day? Let me start. Hmmm, I went out boating with this totally hot, amazing woman. Then we grilled hamburgers for lunch and fished off the dock for a while, and then we, well, we...um, well, *you know*, which was magnificent. Ain't nothing like a little afternoon delight, is there? Anyway, sorry—I was distracted for a minute. So then we drove to the winery for a tasting and finally headed home after that. It was a great day. And you?"

He paused as I chuckled. How could I be sad with a man like this on the phone? I said, "Hmm, let's see. Ditto, to infinity and beyond." I could feel his smile through the phone. He waited. Finally I added, "Um, I kind of wanted to talk about something else...more serious...but...but I wasn't sure how you'd feel about that."

"Why?" he asked, curious. "Is it bad?"

"No, not bad, just...well, with our new...new commitment to each other—is that the right word? Anyway, with us dating how we are now, I wondered if you'd be scared or opposed to having some deeper conversations sometimes."

"Isn't that what we've been doing already?" he asked lightly, then added, "not including my daily review a second ago."

"Oh yes, I suppose," I answered quickly with a little laugh. "I guess I just wanted to make sure you were okay with continuing. I mean, I don't want to scare you off before we've even tested this…thing."

"Fire away, my dear. And also, let me be clear: that preamble you just gave me, please know you never have to do that again. Completely not necessary."

I exhaled into the phone, then said, "Okay," and smiled so wide that I felt the need to cover my mouth with my hand, even in the comfort of my own empty bedroom. It was the feeling of security and assurance that sent me to that special place with him—something I hadn't known in so long, if ever.

I proceeded to tell Brian about my phone call with Tyler and about my little cry, and he was so wonderful. He said all the right things about it being only natural that Tyler would want to go to his dad's first for a few days, especially if the rest of the summer he would be with me. And sure, the kids were growing up (his girls too!), but they would always be around, even if they went on to have their own houses and spouses and children. It was just the cycle of life. It didn't mean our lives were over because their lives were just beginning. If anything, it meant that we were due to start a new season, one in which the children weren't the center of our universes. How could that be a bad thing? We could go out without needing babysitters or groceries in the fridge or gas in the car. Our wallets would no longer work like malfunctioning slot machines—they would actually retain cash instead of losing it! Imagine that!

I had to laugh. So logical. Of course, he was right. It wasn't the end of the world—it was just the beginning.

Brian finally said, "Okay, then. You're alright? Not gonna stay up watching *Beaches*, are you?"

I laughed. "No. Maybe *You've Got Mail*, but definitely not *Beaches*."

"Okay, good. I feel better. So, hey, thanks again for this weekend—I had a great time motorboating you. Oh, oops, sorry, I mean, going out boating with you."

I chuckled—naughty boy. "Funny. It was a perfect weekend."

"It really was, wasn't it?"

"Yes."

"Hey, Heather?"

"Yes, Brian."

"I'm still mad about you."

"Okay, good. Me too."

"Good. Night."

"Night."

I hung up and put my phone down on the nightstand. Still with a big smile on my face, I sank down cozily into my bedsheets, turning onto my side as I cuddled my head into the pillow, never wanting the happiness of this moment to go away. In what seemed like thirty seconds, I fell into a deep, contented sleep.

Chapter XXIII

I WOKE UP FEELING STRANGE. It was that feeling when you wake up from a dream and you're halfway immersed in it, but you're halfway awake too. I was in that "other" place. Didi was there—she had popped up out of the diary and stood in front me. She was very urgent, pointing a finger toward the upstairs hallway. She looked young and fresh, like the photos of her with Paul in that scrapbook, but in my dream her face was all scrunched up in warning, urging me to listen to her. I laughed and rolled on my side away from her, attempting to recapture the dream world, but there she was again, tugging on my shoulder, whispering in my ear: "Delia! Get up!"

I shook my head, forcibly ignoring her. "Delia! Get up!" What on earth? Or in this case, what on another astral plane? I peeked one eye open and saw nothing in the room other than that it was pitch-dark. Ugh. My half-conscious mind remembered I had to get up early for work, probably in just a few short hours. Back to sleep, Delia—you want to be fresh for the new job, right? Shake off this silliness. I sighed and slid determinedly onto my stomach, willing myself back to sleep.

Goshdarnit! Not more than a moment later, or was it an hour? I wasn't sure—there she was again: my dream-state Didi. "Delia! Get up!" This time she put her hand over my mouth, and I couldn't breathe. That just pissed me off, right there. What was Didi doing? I woke up with a start, sitting up in bed and trying to take a deep breath. Suddenly, the hand was gone, the whisper was gone, the image was gone, but ALL of my air was gone too! A blast of smoke sent a searing pain up my nostrils and down into my throat.

I exhaled in a violent cough, screaming out, "Holy fucking shit!" The bedroom was filled with smoke!

My brain seized as if it had been slammed in a steel vise. My pulse raced out of control as my heart pounded loudly in my chest. Oh. My. God. What do I do? I sat for a full twenty seconds, stunned and completely at a loss. I couldn't think, couldn't move, couldn't react. It was as if I had been hit by a Taser.

Then I felt Didi again, forcing me to pay attention to her as she whispered in my ear: "Stay calm. Get out, but *stay calm.*" I breathed in again, and this time the air had been somehow purified for me, like mountain-fresh white air filling my lungs with courage and strength of purpose. I snapped back to reality and to a course of action. I remembered with sudden clarity the fire evacuation class we had taken in second grade. The first thing: Get down and stay down. I flung myself off the bed to the ground, trying not to notice the swirl of toxic smoke-filled air dancing around my head. Then I glanced at the dark, hovering mass of blackness slithering from the edge of my wall and out the cracked window into the inky night sky. I began to army crawl out of my room and toward Mom's. I was screaming bloody murder above the din of the fire, which I could now see was emanating from the floors below us, already engulfing portions of the stairwell and landing, and quickly moving across the threshold to the hall, lighting the piles of clothing and knick-knacks scattered there into huge balls of flames. Jesus, could we have set a better proving ground for fire acceleration than that?

I crawled into Mom's room and tugged at her bedsheets, a pillow tumbling over onto my head.

"Mom!" I screamed over and over.

Finally I heard her yell back, "Delia?! Oh my god, the house! The house is on fire!"

"YES! Come on!" I hollered, coughing up half a lung in the process.

"Delia!" she shrieked in my face as she lurched off the side of the bed and fell on top of me. As she rolled off, she quickly righted herself and asked, "Should we go out the window?"

"NO!" I don't know how I had the presence of mind to speak with such author-ity. All I knew was that I didn't want to go out that way. We were too far up the opposite side of the porch, with nothing to break our fall but the hard, grassy yard below. "Let's try the stairs—come on!"

As we crawled across the hall toward the stairs, I felt my fingers and knees burning as if prodded with red-hot pokers. I tried to get over or around the flaming piles, but they were mostly unavoidable. It was as if the house were in an angry, violent uproar, rearing its head up out of the jaws of hell. I had never seen or felt anything like it before. I was struck (in my half-sunk state of chaos and panic) by the awe of the scene and the power of the beast that was embodied in this mighty magnum opus of fire. I tried to repeat Didi's words in my mind: "Get out. Stay calm."

The ceiling was throwing down chunks of burning drywall and wood, the walls were covered in polka-dotted holes lined with orange rings, the floor was bubbling and buckling. The flames were beginning to lick across the attic door, which had been left open, and up into the cluttered stairwell. We crawled along as fast as we could, screaming out in pain at each movement forward. I felt portions of my clothes and skin frying, and it was as if my lungs were breathing in shards of glass. At some point, something scalding hot and stiff jammed into my knee. I cried out in pain and kept moving. Every inch seemed like a mile.

I looked back a few times to make sure Mom was still behind me. We'd started down the stairs, carefully testing each step, when a huge flying piece of flaming debris fell into Mom's hair. I swiftly turned to see it go up like a burning bale of hay. She went completely ballistic, writhing in shock and horror, attempting to squash the flames with her hands. I had a vision of her dying a horrible, gruesome death, and I inhaled a large smoked-infused sob. I willed myself to remain calm and to think. There was Didi again: "Stay calm, Delia."

I stood up and ran back to my bedroom, holding my hand over my mouth and holding my breath as best I could. My feet were in agony, but I kept going, yanking down the flaming sheet hanging from the opening of my bedroom. I grabbed a semi-damp towel from my laundry hamper (thank god I'd showered earlier that night). I rushed back to Mom's side, throwing the towel over her head, patting and rubbing until the flames finally dampened. She was screaming like a mouse suddenly plunged into a tub of boiling water. Finally, mercifully, I got the fire out, but I could still see that her face, head, neck, and ear were badly burnt. I couldn't let her know how bad it was. I needed her to focus. She was still wholly hysterical, and, in her panic, she tried to get away from me and go back up the stairs. I took her by the shoulders and slapped her across the face. I was horrified to feel pieces of her hair and flesh stuck to my hand. That slap got her attention, though. She stopped and stared, and I noticed even her eyes seemed to be on fire. I knew this couldn't be possible, but it was a blip in the middle of the carnage. I didn't have time to think or explain anything to myself or to her. I simply pointed and pulled her down the stairs with me.

Thankfully, the banister was still intact, so we could feel our way along the balusters, down, down, down. The sound of the fire was like a freight train whirring and whizzing through the air as windows shattered and items in the kitchen exploded like fireworks in the distance. When we reached the downstairs front foyer, also completely engulfed, I edged over to the door, trailing Mom behind me, and reached up for the deadbolt. I recoiled because it felt like a thousand degrees. I looked down helplessly at my singed hand and tried to think. Out of the corner of my eye, I saw a huge portion of the ceiling near the kitchen caving in, falling back into the basement stairwell. Then the upper banister, where we had just been seconds before, collapsed and tumbled down beside us onto the floor of the foyer. I pulled Mom to me and braced myself with a new determination, turning the deadbolt and the doorknob in two swift movements.

Like the starting gunshot of a sprint race, we burst through the door in a rush and toppled out into the wild, raging night. We stumbled down the porch steps and across the yard like two drunken apparitions. Finally safely away from the thundering monster, our wobbly legs buckled under us as we fell in a heap on the curb.

I didn't want to look back. I didn't want to know what we had just escaped. I closed my eyes and pressed them tightly together, pushing my knuckles against them to keep the wave of tears from coming, but to no avail. I sobbed hard and long and loud, which caused me to convulse in a fit of coughing. My lungs felt as though I had swallowed razor blades.

And I could still hear the fire. It was like an evil hissing, growling, cacophonous beast—a powerful cobra taunting us with its venomous roar. Mom was slouched beside me, her head inert on my shoulder. She was breathing hard but otherwise still. I peeked over her at the D.D., which was fully engulfed now. It felt like something right out of a movie, and I had a hard time processing what I was seeing. Was that our house? Was that the place we'd both lived in our whole lives? It didn't even resemble that place. The detached garage was the only thing not burning. On the porch we had just stumbled across, I saw the Nan (oh no, Didi's Nan!) swinging like a flamethrower's torch, swaying back and forth, then breaking off its chain and landing in the hole that used to be the front porch floor. The attic dormer window, which had provided my only fresh air during this past week of purging, exploded out of its opening and flung itself over the porch roof and down to the burning bushes below. The whole house was a strange shade of burnt amber and somehow black as night too, the smoke mingling with the flames. Loud popping and scraping sounds clipped the evening air as large chunks of the house's hull crashed down into the cavernous mouth of the foundation.

I was transfixed and horrified.

Then I heard sirens overpowering the sound of the fire, screeching in their deathly urgency. I hadn't even noticed until that moment that someone was on the ground beside Mom, talking to her, asking her if she was alright, if we were both alright. In slow motion, I recognized who it was—Mr. Freimuth, Jake's dad. I pulled away from Mom and tried to stand up, but inexplicably I fell back. Mr. Freimuth told me to stay down and that help was on the way. I heard him and sat back down, crying and coughing.

In a state of shock, strange, discordant thoughts raced through my mind, bubbling up from the depths of my broken heart. Is that truly the D.D. behind me, engulfed in flames? Shouldn't someone go back into the house and get the rest of our things? What's going to happen to that rack of coats Mom and I were just talking about? That wool one with the mink, hmmm, what did Mom call it—a mink scole? No, a stole, that thing—what would happen to that? And that full-length mirror—the one I had observed my full-length averageness in? What about Didi's bamboo shelf-thing, the what-not? And those old quilts in the cedar hope chest. Someone had hand-sewn every stitch of those! Not to mention, that hope chest had been Didi's mom's chest before Didi got it. And the Staffordshire china Mom had mentioned—I hadn't even gotten a chance to look at it—all the way from England, a hundred-plus years of serving tea in those cups. Dennis Diamond's cherry music stand, the yellow Depression glass bowl that Didi got at the movie theater when it was called vanity ware, the Kodak camera. OMG, the photos! Boxes and boxes of photos, a hundred years of Kodak photos. The Diamond family legacy, all incinerated, gone in the blink of an eye! Then I started to think about all of my stuff gone too...my cleats and shin guards (how would I play on the pitch?), my clothes and computer and phone and purse and toothbrush and hair straightener...on and on and on until—oh shit!

SHIT! Oh shit, shit, shit! Didi's diary! I would never know what happened to Didi and Paul and George and Frances and Burrows and Stella and Roy and Bernice and Sam and Honoree and James and Adelaide! Or what happened to her job or her friends or her family. I would never know if Didi and Paul got married or how she ended up with Grandpa Ron.

Then I had a strange thought. I remembered Didi warning me to get up. Whispering in my ear with that forceful plea. Good god—had she saved my life?! And Mom's! As I contemplated the mystery of things unknown and unseen, I felt something scratching my hip. I reached inside my singed and torn shorts, beneath my underwear, and pulled something out: the diary! I stared at it as if I were looking at a ghost. How did it get there? How had it stayed there through the torturous trek through the burning house? How was I holding it in my hands at this very moment, with chaos raging all around me, like a chalice of purified holy water?

I cried out loud, into the night sky, "Didi!"

Then I put my face in my hands and sobbed.

I stayed like that for what seemed like hours but, in reality, was probably only two minutes. When I finally looked up, I had this sense of being detached from my surroundings and from myself. Oddly, I had no pain, no connection to my physical body. I was numb. And yet I could still observe and comprehend the chaos around me: firetrucks, police cars, ambulances, firefighters, fire hoses, water shooting up in the air, neighbors staring and pointing, in their robes and pajamas.

I noticed with detached indifference a smell—an awful smell—of my own burning flesh, but also wood, plastic, household items. It was if the smell encased the loss—the spirit of the lives and objects and photos of an entire family, lost like the smoke that was billowing up, up, up into the unforgiving night sky.

A frantic fireman came over to me and shouted, "Is anyone else in the house?" I shook my head, staring at him vacantly. Except for Didi, I thought. And her childhood. And my childhood. And the lives of all the children and adults who had passed through this house in a hundred years. A parade of love and laughter and tears and tantrums and heartache and heartbreak and hope and happiness. Gone. Just like that.

A man in some type of uniform began administering to Mom, and then another came to work over me. He laid me flat on my back in the grass and talked to me while he checked me out. I didn't look at him—I kept my eyes on the fireworks show in the sky and that dark billow of smoke.

At some point, Jake was there. I looked at him and wondered why his face was filled with so much worry and fear. He said, "Delia, oh my gosh, Delia! You okay?" I nodded. I wanted to tell him not to worry, that I was fine, but as I opened my mouth to speak, I realized my voice was gone. Those sad green eyes! He said helplessly, "No, no, don't move, don't talk, okay? This gentleman here, he's...he's gonna fix you up...okay? Just stay still and do what he says...and um, Delia, stay strong, okay?" I was still trying to decipher why his face looked like that—so stricken, so helpless, when the medic suddenly moved into action, placing me on a stretcher and whisking me away. I looked back at Jake wistfully, thinking, don't worry, I'm fine. I feel fine.

Then I realized, actually, I feel nothing. Nothing at all. I am a speck of dust in the wind.

In a flurry, they were closing me inside the ambulance, and I suddenly thought, I have no idea where Mom is. I mouthed to the medic, and he told me she'd been taken to the hospital in the other ambulance. I nodded under the mask of oxygen he placed on my mouth. Then he tried to pry the diary out of my hand, but I held fast. I was not going to lose that—it was the only thing left of the D.D. He gave up, letting me keep it, and put the IV in my other arm.

Then we were off, the sirens roaring and our tires speeding away from the burning mass of pandemonium. I still had no pain or feeling of any kind, other than being desperately thirsty. I mouthed that I needed water, but the medic ignored me, saying to lie still while he took care of me. I obeyed because I started to feel an overwhelming sense of exhaustion. I closed my eyes and instantly felt myself falling into a dark, unconscious, blissful void, but the medic shook me awake, saying, "Hey! Stay with me!" I woke up and scowled at him. Why did I need to stay awake? How much I wanted to sleep! He began talking to me, forcing me to stay awake. It was the most annoying fifteen minutes of my life.

Finally we were at the hospital, and there were so many people talking to me and prodding me, like a swarm of bees. I lay back and watched them, mouthing my question again about Mom. A nurse pointed, and I saw Mom in the distance, with another set of bees working on her. Someone was fiddling with my leg, and that's when I felt the first bit of pain. I cried out. I looked down and saw what had caused my yelp—a piece of hardwood about four inches long and two inches wide, stuck out of my knee perpendicularly, secured there with a nail that looked like it had been shot into my knee with a nail gun. How had I not noticed that before? Then I looked at the rest of my body—completely scorched from head to toe with burn marks, charred skin, gouges, scrapes, scratches, gashes, cuts, blisters. I looked as if I had thrown myself through a burning plate glass window. That was around the time I began to moan.

One of the nurses said, "Be still, sweetie—we're gonna pump some good stuff in this IV, and you'll feel a lot better in a minute, okay?"

I nodded through a whimper.

After that, everything went foggy and faint.

Days went by, then a week or more—I wasn't sure. Mom was eventually put in the same room with me. Her hair was gone (oh, that thick, glorious red hair!). Her face, scalp, neck, and ear were a mangled mess of skin, welts, and charred remains. She was having trouble breathing and in a lot of pain—worse than me, but the nurses told me she would be fine after a while. A long while. She was wheeled away for various surgeries—so many skin grafts, I lost track how many. They'd put me under as well to remove the nailed-in piece of wood from my knee. They had the rest of my burns and scrapes stitched and wrapped, but at times I felt as though my lungs and skin were still on fire. In the beginning, I couldn't breathe properly without oxygen.

It was an awful, trying, painful, tiresome time.

I remembered people coming to see us. First, Dad and Beth—in a frenzy, asking me a ton of questions I couldn't answer about how I was doing and about the fire. Dad was blaming himself for not being there to protect me. I reassured him that I was okay, it wasn't anyone's fault, and luckily we had made it out alive. He nodded, but his face was strained and taut. They stayed for hours, or days—I'm not sure. I drifted in and out.

I remembered seeing Tyler for twenty minutes or so. He came with Dad—I guess Dad had gone and gotten him from school. The first words out of Tyler's mouth were, "I told Mom it would be easier to burn the house down than to clean the attic. I didn't know she would take me so seriously."

The tiny smile I gave him was my first since the fire.

Then he said, "You look like something out of *Hostel*. Or *Saw*. Or *Texas Chainsaw Massacre*."

My laugh turned into a cough, and then he felt bad and apologized, but I shook my head, letting him know it was okay and this was just par for the course. He stayed awhile, talking about his girlfriend and his internship, trying to keep my mind off everything.

One day, Brian and his two daughters came. They were so kind and friendly, bringing flowers and homemade banana bread. When Brian stepped through the door, I watched in awe as he stared at Mom and, with shining eyes of love and sincerity, said, "Hey, beautiful." She wept, floods of tears streaming down her horribly patched-up face. He took her in his arms, hugging her body carefully to his chest. His daughters came over to me to give them privacy, and we chatted for a while and pretended that everything was perfectly normal.

At some point, McKenzie came and told me we were the talk of the town. No one could believe we had escaped and lived—especially since the fire had happened in the middle of the night while we were asleep in our beds. She said the fire inspectors had been investigating for days. They said they had already determined that the smoke alarms weren't working, so they had no idea how we had woken up and gotten out. I didn't tell McKenzie about Didi. She probably would have thought I was making it all up, or worse, that I was crazy. McKenzie said nothing remained of the house except a few charred pieces of metal and debris lodged deep down in the foundation. They still didn't know what had caused the fire, but they suspected faulty wiring in the basement.

McKenzie told me that everyone was talking about how they couldn't believe the D.D. had burned down after so many generations of the Diamond family living there. She joked and said maybe ghosts had set it on fire. I tried to laugh with her, but all I could think was that maybe I had made the ghosts mad by cleaning out their attic, so I coughed violently instead. McKenzie left after that.

The next day, a bunch of kids from school came. They'd made a huge banner to hang in my room that said, "Get Well Soon, Delia!" and it looked as if the whole senior class had signed it. I cried a little when I saw it, but I tried not to let them see the tears. I think it was mostly because a few short weeks ago, those same kids hated me and had been happy to forward Greg's text to each other, mocking my body, my circumstances, my everything. Yet now they were here wishing me well. In my former screw-them-all state of being, I probably would have flicked them off and told them to get the fuck out, but I was weak and exhausted and spent, so instead I cried.

I think about twenty people showed up at that first visit, including those two girls from the diner, which made me have to hide my crying even more. They were extra nice, and maybe they felt a little remorse, so how could I not take that to heart? I began to feel as if Didi (and the house burning) had brought me a new lease on life. And only a few days after having told Jake's mom that I may have ruined my life forever! Who would have thought that such devastation and destruction could lead to something good?

I had this strange vision of how they would sometimes burn trees in a state- or federal-run forest. They called it a controlled burn when they purposely set fire to the trees, knowing that fresh, young saplings would soon take their place. That's what I'd needed (and hadn't even known it!), and here I was getting it: a restart button.

I sat in bed for long stretches, staring at the white walls and white ceiling and ruminated on my controlled burn and rebirth. A second chance at life!

Time passed slowly. Throughout the "Towering Inferno Show," I tried to be gracious to our visitors, saying thanks to everyone, but mostly I remained quiet, feeling a strange, overwhelming sense of gratitude and confusion over the about-face of my life and the attitudes of former enemies. Throughout each day, Mom and I talked, but neither of us brought up the elephant in the room—the fire or the D.D. or where we would live after we got out of the hospital (and after that). Nothing. She just kept telling me to "get better" and that "we both needed time to heal." I couldn't decide whether she was in shock or scared shitless, as I was.

Mom's friends were in and out. Donna came first, with the girls in tow. She stayed for a couple of hours until she had Mom in stitches, and not the kind that were plastered all over her body. It was good to see Mom smile and laugh again. Tanya and Christine came and brought flowers. They were nice but didn't stay long—based on their lack of eye contact with Mom, I think they were having trouble processing her messed-up face and head.

Aunt Mary flew in from Colorado. She spent every day in the hospital with us and stayed in a hotel across the street every night. She took charge, navigating complex conversations with the nurses and doctors and trying to figure out our treatment, insurance, and basic needs. Mom came to rely on her for everything and stopped making decisions for herself. I just sat and watched.

Jake came with his mom. Thoughtfully, he brought the Diamond family radio, all fixed and in working order now, and plugged it into the wall and turned it on. My mom cried for days about this, pondering small miracles in the face of abject devastation. Mrs. Freimuth spent a long time talking with Mom, letting Jake sit on a chair beside my bed, resting his hand on my arm. He gave me the first piece of good news from the outside world (that, for whatever reason, everyone else had failed to mention).

He said, "Hey, guess what?"

"What?"

"Your car's fine. Did you know?"

"Hell, no! It is? How?" I nearly jumped out of bed. Stupid, minor, ridiculous, shallow Delia! But so what? My CAR!

"They stopped the fire before it hit the detached garage. Don't ask me how. Some kind of crazy stroke of luck. Both of your cars are fine."

I hollered over to Mom and told her.

She was surprised and said, "Well, that's something…"

Mrs. Freimuth chuckled, and then I could see that Mom was sort of half laughing, half crying, losing it a little, so Mrs. Freimuth squeezed her hand and told her, "Everything's going to be okay." Then she paused and said, "I wanted to let you know that the ladies in the neighborhood have all raided our closets and our kids' closets, and we have a whole new wardrobe for you two. Don't you worry your little heads about any of that. And Sandy, MaryAnn, Rachel, and I went over to the mall and bought you both a few new pairs of shoes, undies, and bras—you know, the essentials. We had to guess on the sizes, but we saved the receipts, so if we need to make some exchanges, we can do that. Anyway, we have it all covered. Just focus on getting better, you hear me?" Mom nodded mutely, looking at me, tears in her eyes. I turned my head. I couldn't hear any more of that kind of talk. Jesus. What were we going to do?

Mrs. Freimuth deftly changed the subject and talked about how her girls were away at soccer camp. Mom was sufficiently distracted, so I turned to Jake. He paused and then said, "Tina's going to stay on at the RCC until you come back, so that's cool…they're keeping your job open for you…I mean, if you still want it."

"Yes, I do, okay, great. Thanks." I tried to smile. I tried not to look numb and dumb and vacant.

He sat for a second regarding my hopeless eyes. Then he reached down into his backpack and said, "I brought you some books."

"Oh, that was nice," I said half-heartedly.

"A little Hemingway, a little Dostoevsky, a little Chekhov."

"Wow, that's quite a mix. Talk about the depravity of the human soul. Are you trying to finish the job that the fire didn't?"

He chuckled, liking that my sarcasm was back. I grinned a little too. He said, "Yes, I'm killing you softly—a leisurely, meandering death through Hemingway's terse prose and the Russian's complex character development and plot twists."

"Or maybe just a paper cut?" I challenged back.

"Exactly. I've laced the pages with spit from a toxic mountain goat."

I couldn't help but laugh.

Without another word, as if in slow motion, he leaned over and kissed me on the mouth. It was soft and sweet and warm and wonderful.

Suddenly, I felt tears prick my eyes. Now, why had he done that? Before this, I had been holding myself together, even bringing on the jokes and irreverent banter. Now, like an unstoppable force, I was heaving in great gulps, the tears gushing down my face, and Jake was holding me in his arms. He stroked my hair as the tsunami consumed me. I had no control over it. I sobbed and sobbed until I finally lay limp, a hopeless, confused, weeping rag doll. He held me close and stayed there—inert, encircling, enveloping. Not a word. How did he know? How did he know I couldn't process another word, another thought, another feeling? This was it—just this, like quicksand, like a rock sinking into the depths.

What seemed like a year went by wherein I was lost to all external things. A cocoon of bliss. Then, awhile later, a jarring tap from his mom on his shoulder and he pulled away, telling me not to worry and that everything was going to be okay. I wanted to scream, "Don't go! Everything is NOT going to be okay!"

And besides, if I heard another person say that, I was going to punch them.

Snap! I sat up and stared wide-eyed at Jake's face, to which he grinned with a confused face. Did I really just think that? Did I really want to punch Jake? After he had just made my insides turn to mush? Maybe my flash of anger was a good sign. Better that than the numbing sensation I had been lost in for days.

I wiped away my tears roughly and said with a fresh smile, "Thanks Jake, for everything. I think I must be feeling better. You helped."

His eyes turned into those magical pools of green light as he said, "Good, I'm glad." He squeezed my arm and walked out, waving as he turned the corner out the door. I lay my head back on the pillow and stared over at Mom.

She paused a few minutes, regarding me with thoughtful eyes, and said, "You know what, Delia?"

"What, Mom?"

"Everything's going to be okay."

Ugh.

Chapter XXIV

July 1

(Friday) The weather was bad. Paul called and said he couldn't come because he didn't have money for the streetcar, and it was too far to walk in the rain. Mom, Dad, James, and I listened to the radio and played rummy. Dad offered to give Paul money, but I told him he wouldn't take it.

The radio! Jake and his dad saved it! Everything else is gone, gone, gone. Burned! So sad. And no news on the Paul job front either.

July 2

(Saturday) Horrible weather last night—shook the roof! The front page of the paper showed photos, said it was a tornado. Hard to believe, here in Rochester—wow! It was a good thing Paul didn't walk here. Everything was still open, though, so I went to work, then Paul met me, Roy, and Bernice at the streetcar stop at 6:00. I told Paul I had enough for the ride and a show (and he reluctantly let me pay). We went to see Niagara Falls. I told Paul it reminded me of the real Niagara Falls, which he didn't like because it reminded him of how I had left him for a whole weekend. Later we went to Roy's place and sat out on his back porch, where we heard a lot of fireworks in the distance.

A tornado in Rochester? Never heard of one before. Dorothy, we're not in Kansas anymore.

July 3

(Sunday) Glenys and Gail came over for supper. They had been reading in the paper about the new Democratic nomination for president, Mr. Franklin Roosevelt. They said he was "our ticket." The paper quoted him:

*"I pledge you, I pledge myself, to a new deal for the American people." We
immediately started planning our next Young People's Meeting. It certainly
does give one hope.*

Well, I'm glad she's getting back to her activism and other friends, as her mom
advised her, and FDR—good choice! Sounds like a foreshadowing of the New
Deal, which, of course, finally got us out of the Great Depression.

July 4

*(Monday) At work, everyone was talking about how Syracuse was going
to ban fireworks after that boy nearly lost his eye. We wondered if Rochester would do the same. It was surprisingly busy in the store because of the
holiday. I made 27 sales. After work, Mom insisted I sit down with her at
the kitchen table to checkmark the wedding list. We still have refreshments,
dress alterations, flowers, and the honeymoon. Everything else is done. I
talked to Paul on the phone, but he wasn't in a good mood. He didn't like it
that my parents were paying for everything. He also said he was lonely in
his place, all by himself with no job to go to. I felt bad for him.*

Okay, so the wedding's still on, I guess that's good. Or bad. I'm not sure.

July 5

*(Tuesday) Worked on the ledger all day with Sam. He's in love again with
Honoree and wouldn't stop talking about her. Bah! Paul called and said
he walked into 10 places today, but still no job. I told him to come to the
meeting on Thursday and we would try to focus on the positive—maybe
someone there would know about a job, and also maybe the new president
could lift us all up.*

July 6

*(Wednesday) Work was slow today, only 6 sales. Paul called, and I told
him he was being a crapehanger and that everything was going to be okay.
He said he didn't know how. He confessed he sold the watch but that he
didn't get much and probably wouldn't have enough food to last the month.
I told him to come to our house for food, but he said he didn't have a way
to get there. I told him I'd give him money or Dad would come pick him up,
but he said he didn't want handouts. He said he'd been a hard worker his
whole life, earned his keep, and never had to ask for a thing. Now he felt*

humiliated and ashamed, and found it a cruel injustice that an able-bodied man like himself should be forced to ask for charity when he was perfectly willing and able to work for a living. He said he thought his dad was rolling over in his grave. I cried for an hour. If only I could get him a job! Dad said there were no jobs in Rochester right now.

I had to look up that "crapehanger" word, and basically it described Paul—a gloomy, pessimistic fellow. But can you blame him?

July 7–8

(Thursday–Friday) Work was slow. At the Young People's Meeting, everyone was talking about Mr. Franklin Delano Roosevelt and how he was somehow related to the former president Teddy Roosevelt. The new Roosevelt has promised something new for America. Lord knows we need it! So many are out of work. We see Hoover flags everywhere now. Paul came to the meeting and talked to three other men who also lost their jobs. He said two were living with relatives now, and the other is living on the street because even though he begged his landlord to let him stay for another few weeks, he got evicted anyway. He said he had come to the meeting hoping there would be food (which there was). It's such a dire situation everywhere! We tried to be constructive, writing several ideas on the blackboard—things we could do to help get Roosevelt elected. At least that's a start.

Another thing I had to look up: "Hoover flags." Apparently before FDR got elected, Hoover was the president and people were starting to get pissed about having no jobs and no money and no food, so they turned their pockets inside out and walked around like that. Sort of like a symbol of how sucky Hoover was doing. Wow, never knew about any of this before. How did anyone survive? Makes me marvel at Didi and her family (my family!) even more. I do hope Didi and her friends can help save the day and the world—with Paul, with these young people, with the new course of our nation. Looking back now, it's inspiring how they didn't even think twice about whether they should help—they simply went into action trying to figure out how they could help. There's definitely a lesson in that. As I sit in my hospital bed, I think about what course of action I should take. I've been given a new lease on life, a second chance, and now I need to figure out what to do with it.

July 9

*(Saturday) Today all of us went to the beach to spend the day. The weather
was fine, and I forced Paul to come out and meet us (paying his way, even
though he didn't like it). I told him today is a day to have fun and get your
mind off your troubles, not to wallow in them. After a little convincing he
agreed, and we had the most wonderful day. We swam and lay in the sun
and took so many photographs that I lost track of how many. Frances and
George and Bernice and Roy walked down the beach a ways and tossed a
ball back and forth while Paul and I cuddled under the umbrella. It was a
perfect day, and I wouldn't have changed a thing.*

This must be the day of the photo—the one with Didi in the water with her
bathing cap in her hand. She did look spectacularly happy. I guess that photo was
gone now too—burned along with all the rest and, I suppose, along with Didi's
carefree smile.

July 10

*(Sunday) Bernice and Frances came over, and Mom made us stand still to
pin our dresses. She spent the next hour working on them, her head bent
over the sewing machine. Then we tried them on, and they're absolutely
perfect! Both Bernice and Frances began crying when they saw me in
my wedding dress with the veil over my head. Mom just waved her hand
and said, "Stuff and nonsense!" but then she cried too. James and Adelaide
came home with two quarts of cream. We had a hamburg roast and sat
outside to eat and then played horseshoes. Later I had to put Listerine on
my bug bites.*

July 11–14

*(Monday–Thursday) The days are flying by now. We finished the prepara-
tions for the wedding, but I haven't seen Paul since last Saturday. He only
called once to let me know that the phone had been shut off. He had to borrow
the neighbor's phone. I said, how will I get a hold of you? He said he didn't
know, but he would try to walk over to our house this weekend sometime.*

July 15

*(Friday) Sam and I worked on the ledger, and he suggested we go to the
Manitou with Honoree. I told him about Paul not having enough for the
streetcar or food. He said he would lend him some, but I told him Paul*

wouldn't like that and wouldn't take it. Just the three of us went to the Manitou. Several nice boys danced with me, but I told them I was engaged. One said, "Doesn't he dance?" and I said, "Not tonight." He thought that was funny for some reason. Paul called while I was gone and told James that he didn't want me to call back. James said he sounded mad.

July 16

(Saturday) Paul showed up at our door at 10. I kissed him and told him I loved him. He said he didn't care. He was sore about the dancing. Mom gave him some food, and he seemed a little better after that. We sat out on the Nan, and I told him we were going to be married in two weeks! He didn't really respond and kissed me instead. After supper, we put two chairs out in the backyard, listened to the cicadas, and watched the birds. Dad drove him home late that night.

Just a few days ago, I finally figured out what the Nantucket (the "Nan") was, and now that sturdy, perfect swing from Tell City, Indiana, was part of a pile of ashes. So many kisses snatched there, and all Didi's hopes for the future forged on those boards. What was to become of Didi's hopes and dreams—and my own?

July 17

(Sunday) Bernice came over to help me wash my head and style my hair. Minnie came with Ernest and Hotcha. Bernice and I took Hotcha outside to play with a ball. He can't pronounce Bernice's name and kept calling her "Berce." It was funny. Somehow he said "Didi" just fine. We played for hours, and then everyone went home. It was a nice day because it kept my mind off Paul.

July 18–22

(Monday–Friday) Paul called on Thursday and said he'd been waiting in line at the soup kitchen for three hours every day. I told him to come over and eat with us, but he doesn't have the money for the streetcar, and it takes too long to walk. He said he's too tired and hungry to walk. He asked if we should postpone the wedding, but I cried, "NO! I don't care about the money. I just want you!" He said he loved me but that we couldn't live on love. I said, "I can." He said, "You can do so much better than me." I disagreed, and we argued, and eventually he had to hang up because the neighbor needed the phone.

July 23

(Saturday) I decided to cheer Paul up, so I had Dad drop me off at his place. I had never been there before. It was a very small basement apartment. When I knocked on the door, he couldn't have been more surprised. He grabbed me in a big hug. I told him I was going to take him out for the day, and his smile was so big! We went to Durand Eastman to see the monkeys. We laughed at their funny faces. I brought a picnic lunch, and we sat on a bench and ate it together. I told him I couldn't wait to marry him. He kissed me and told me he loved me and that he didn't deserve me. It was a perfect day.

Chapter XXV

Wait. *What?! That was it? The end?* I flipped through the rest of the pages, looking for more words, but there were none. I even held the diary up by its spine and shook it out, thinking maybe something would spill out to explain. The only two things that fell out were the Young People's Meeting Flyer and the photo of Didi standing in the water at the beach. I looked at it and frowned. Oh, I guess that hadn't burned. But was she mocking me with her happiness and mystery?

July twenty-third, a week before the wedding. It was a perfect day, she had written, so confidently, so assuredly in her tight, organized, formidable cursive. Talking about the monkeys at Durand Eastman. The wedding was planned, paid for, buttoned up. She seemed so happy, despite Paul being a crapehanger and despite his lack of a job. She was working with Gail and Glenys on getting FDR elected. She had her dress altered and ready to go. She had just eaten ice cream outside with James and Adelaide.

My god, what happened?

It was four o'clock in the morning, and I didn't even care if what I did next woke up Mom. I threw the diary across the hospital room and watched it slide down the side of a wall until it landed with a thud on the floor. She didn't wake up. I almost wished she had so we could commiserate, even though I realized with a growl that she wouldn't have understood anyway—I hadn't told her I had the diary. I'd kept it hidden in my bedside drawer. I wanted to finish it first and then give it to her as a surprise. I thought Aunt Mary might want to see it too. I'd stayed up late, excited to finish it, so I could hand it over the next day.

Now I was left fuming. Seriously, Didi?! How could you leave it that way? No explanation, no understanding, no hint of what happened? Not another word? I felt as though I'd been cheated out of a prize at the carnival. Or worse, I'd been cheated out of an inheritance! Not the castle in Germany kind, but the kind where you learn about what made you who you are, and now you'll never know the full extent because the "you" that you thought you were suddenly vanished into thin air.

And of course, any other clues that might have remained for these ninety-plus years had all gone up in flames. What was that expression—"You can't get blood from a turnip"? Well, you can't get answers from an ash heap.

The D.D. wasn't the only thing that got burned. I was pissed. I felt cheated, robbed, taken for a fool.

Did they break up? Maybe one of them got sick at the last minute? Heck, it almost sounded as though Paul had tried to back out the week before, but Didi had refused him. Or maybe they really did get married and then got divorced at some point. Wouldn't be the first person to try to hide that. Maybe Didi never told Mom or Aunt Mary about it because it didn't work out, and divorce back then was so shameful. But then why would the diary stop when it did? Wouldn't she have written pages and pages about the wedding details and the honeymoon and everything else that happened after? She'd been so consistent, writing nearly every day for months and months, and now when it was about to be the most momentous day of her life, she stopped. It made no sense!

I hated to even think it, but I suppose it was possible that Paul died. Back then, people died, right? High mortality rate and all those communicable diseases. Maybe he had gangrene or tuberculosis or polio or smallpox or the plague or scurvy or something. He'd been eating the food from the soup kitchen—maybe there was some uncooked meat in it and he got Legionnaire's or E. coli or Salmonella or one of these diseases they didn't even know about back then. It could have been anything, right?

Didi was twenty at the time of the diary. Maybe she was getting to the age when a diary seemed like a chore or seemed immature. She was going to be a married woman. She would be a mature, responsible adult now. Diaries would be so last year, you know? Who was I kidding? I was grasping at straws.

There had to be a way to find out. I would ask Mom and Aunt Mary tomorrow. Maybe they knew. Or could find out. Maybe Aunt Mary was still in touch with the relatives mentioned in the diary. Maybe baby Hotcha had fifteen other baby Hotchas by now.

If only I had my phone, I could look up wedding announcements from back then. Surely it would be in the Democrat & Chronicle, right? They had sent a reporter to do an article about the dance marathon, so wouldn't you assume they had wedding announcements too? I was frustrated thinking about my lack of technology. Everything had been obliterated in the fire. I scowled. I'd gotten my electronics back for what, less than a freaking week, and now when I needed them more than ever, they were gone. I might as well have been in the 1930s with Didi, for shit's sake.

I got out of bed and picked up the diary, placing the flyer and photo carefully back inside the pages, narrowing my eyes at the outer cover. Such a betrayal! No answers! As I lay it aside and put my head down on the pillow, I tried to analyze why I was so annoyed. I thought it was because at this juncture in my life, I was looking for answers. How to move forward after *the incident*. Didi was a young woman, just like me, on the precipice of major life changes, just like me, and yet life didn't pan out the way she had planned. Or did it?

I mean, I had this new job and the SATs coming up and college visits and maybe something with Jake, and I thought, hey, if Didi can figure out this marriage thing and figure out this starting-a-new-life thing, then I can too. I'll get some lessons from her. She was probably worried about the wedding (and the wedding night—yowzah!) and living with the parents and trying to find Paul work and wondering how they would ever start a real life together—kids, house, independence, not to mention the FDR thing with that young people's group. Wouldn't it have been nice to learn exactly how she managed all that, and oh yeah, how that life trajectory somehow ended up in the tanker and moved onto Grandpa Ron? Again, I swore her name like an expletive: Didi!

Then I felt bad. She'd saved my life, after all. She'd saved Mom's life. And she'd bought me that rebirth that I hadn't known was possible and that I hadn't asked for but had needed more than anything else in the world.

Maybe she simply didn't want me to know what happened. Maybe it was better that I didn't know.

Feeling tired, trying to figure it out, not having answers, I finally fell asleep.

The next morning, I showed the diary to Aunt Mary while Mom underwent another surgery. Aunt Mary was so shocked that she cried, saying she had never seen it before and couldn't believe it had been saved from the fire. I explained that I was trying to figure out what happened to Didi. I asked her about Paul. She stared at me blankly. Never heard of him. Bummer. Aunt Mary offered to read the diary and see if she could glean anything from it. She sat in a chair in the corner of our hospital room and read the whole thing, cover to cover, or rather cover to nothing-ness. I was so hopeful that she would have answers. I stared at her the whole day, waiting so I could pepper her with questions.

My hopes were quickly dashed when she closed the diary and said, "Wow, I have no idea!"

My face fell. Didi's diary was an enigma wrapped in a black vortex. Aunt Mary went on to say she vaguely remembered seeing photos of Bernice (who apparently had been a bridesmaid in Didi and Grandpa Ron's wedding) and of James (who, of course, died in the war). She said Didi's parents were long gone before she and Mom were born. Not a word about Frances, though, who might actually have known what happened to Paul, being his cousin. She said she remembered Didi's family's friend Eddie coming to visit once when they were little girls. He was really old by then and living in Ohio. She said he was kind and brought them Barbie dolls. She remembered overhearing him talk to Didi about Hotcha and how he had just died of cancer the year before. But no other information on that front.

Then she said she remembered once that Didi talked about working at Mc-Curdy's and about helping get FDR elected ("She was adamant that, when we turned eighteen, we must vote because it was an honor and a privilege that had been earned on the backs of many others and was the best way to change the world"). She talked about the nostalgia of the diary ("I had forgotten all about the streetcars in Rochester. Of course, they had stopped running by the time we were born." and "Monkeys at Durand Eastman! I had forgotten that too—the park used to be a zoo. I had a girlfriend who lived in the neighborhood nearby and would hear the lions roar at night."). She talked about the clothes and games and expressions, but that was it. Nothing about Paul or what might have happened to him or to their love affair. Sigh. Total. Dead. End.

Well, that was that. Two days later, Aunt Mary flew back to Colorado, and the hospital discharged us. Mom still had bandages on her head and future appointments to finish the skin grafts. My knee was healing nicely—they were able to remove the nail without any major damage. Most of my scrapes and burns had turned a nice shade of Pepto pink, so the doctors were happy with my progress. And both of us were breathing normally again, no oxygen masks needed.

I went to Dad and Beth's house, and Mom went to Brian's house. It was strange being apart. Here we had just suffered the most horrific trauma (ain't nothing like a near-death experience to pull people together), and now we were going our separate ways. Another thing about almost dying: every person in your life becomes that much more precious. What if I hadn't awoken Mom? What if Didi hadn't awoken me? What if we had fallen through the floor? What if we had passed out from the smoke? What if I hadn't been able to put her hair out with that towel? What if…what if…what if…

We promised to call each other every day and to FaceTime as much as possible. Brian promised to take care of her and keep her wounds clean. I hugged her as hard as I could (trying not to upset her bandages), and we looked into each other's eyes, saying more than words could, knowing we had each other's back no matter what and we were never going back to the way things had been before.

When I got in the back seat of Dad's car, he asked how I was doing ("good") and then, "Is your mother going to be okay?" I gave a small smile. I knew he still cared for her.

"Yeah, I think so. She's pretty banged up, or burned up, but the doctors think she'll be alright."

"Who's the guy?" Beth inquired, looking at the Jeep pulling out of the hospital parking lot.

"Her boyfriend, Brian Napier."

"Well, that's good. What's he like?" she asked.

I thought it was odd that she was so interested, but maybe she figured that since she was with Dad, it would make her feel better if Mom was with someone too. Who knew? Anyway, I responded, "He's nice. I like him. He has two daughters about my age. They're nice too."

Dad jumped in with, "Guess what?" Time to change the subject (apparently).

"What?"

"Beth has made your favorite mac 'n' cheese for dinner tonight! And we're doing Zweigle's white hots on the grill."

"Awesome—that sounds great."

Dad added, "Yeah, poor Beth is a real trooper." He grabbed Beth's hand and kissed it. "She wasn't feeling well, and the smells coming from the Crock-Pot (which, mind you, smell like heaven to me!) were just about killing her."

"Oh," I said, the whole baby thing hitting me like a bomb. I hadn't thought about it at all in light of recent events. "Sorry about that! Morning sickness, eh?"

"Yeah, well, they should really call it all-the-time sickness," she replied dolefully. "It must be an old wives' tale that it only comes in the morning. Come to think of it, it probably was some twisted old wife trying to mess with the young wives: 'Oh yeah, it's only in the morning, I swear.' Not funny. Seriously."

"Bummer. That stinks. Well, thanks for cooking—I really appreciate it. It'll be great to have something other than hospital food for a change."

She smiled at me and leaned her head back against the headrest while Dad drove along silently.

Out past the city streets and into the rolling countryside, I had the strangest sense of déjà vu with a hint of muddled fog. For seven summers, I had taken this drive—off to Dad's house for my summer visit. Part of the custody agreement,

I suppose (although I'd never actually seen the custody agreement and was unclear of the exact rules), was that I would be ushered here and there and everywhere throughout the years. Here I was on my annual pilgrimage, yet I couldn't quite wrap my head around the fact that I wasn't being picked up from the D.D., and I didn't have a bag with me, and that was because I didn't have any clothing or belongings or a phone or a pot to piss in. To further the fog, I wasn't sure where I would end up. We hadn't talked about that yet. Would I stay with Dad indefinitely?

Don't get me wrong—Dad's place was great. He and Beth owned one of those super-sweet farmhouses out in Pittsford. They had about ten acres and a couple of horses, not to mention a huge wraparound front porch with a swing and a backyard deck complete with a grill station and an in-ground pool. It was like peace on earth, and I loved my summers there. Dad loved family time, so we spent most weeknights and weekends laying out by the pool, riding the horses, grilling out, playing cards, watching the sun set and the stars rise. My average reading mileage added up to about three or four books a week. It didn't get any better than that. It was an idyllic setting for home and family.

And Dad and Beth were very chill as far as their parenting. Unlike Mom, they didn't helicopter me half the time and ignore me the other half. They simply let me be. I mean, what kind of trouble was I going to get into out in the middle of nowhere? When Greg and I got together last year, I'd been at Mom's, and I guess that was why Dad had missed out on the colossal detonation otherwise known as *the incident*. Well, I doubt he would have used the word *missed*, but anyway, he knew the whole history, told through Mom's jaundiced eye, and yet here he was—taking me in despite this past year's antics, ready to take in the teenager with the checkered past and even more checkered future. Don't get me wrong—he obviously wasn't totally clueless about my breakdown—after all, I'd stayed with him for a month in the middle, but it hadn't worked out. I was still a hot mess back then, and eventually I was brought back to the D.D., much to Mom's chagrin.

As we pulled into the driveway, I had this alarming thought: what would happen at the end of the summer? I knew the drive to Franklin was too far for Dad, so would I be transferring schools? Going to Pittsford? What about my friends? McKenzie and those kids who had made me the banner? What about work? And soccer? I was planning to try out for varsity, if the coach would have me. What about Jake? Hey, don't get me wrong—I knew that kiss and hug in the hospital were merely a sympathy vote, and I certainly didn't want to get in the middle of the Chronicles of Chelsea (much like the *Chronicles of Narnia*, they involved a wardrobe, except Chelsea's was filled with peep toe pumps and strappy sandals—all pointed at my head!). But then Jake's green eyes still sent me over the moon, and those soft lips...

And how would I know about anything if I didn't get back into town? Would I be stuck out here with all of the Pittsford kids? OMG, can you imagine—what would they think of me? I was hardly an inner-city girl, but I wasn't Designer Delia either. In fact, at this very moment, I was wearing a truly heinous flowered T-shirt and baggy sweatpants, thrown-off charity giveaways from the neighbor ladies. What would the Pittsford pretties think of that?

I groaned. Dad asked if I was okay, and I took a deep breath and said, "Yep, I'm fine."

"Good," he said, "because we're here, and I have a surprise for you!"

I got out of the car and said, "More than mac 'n' cheese, you mean?"

"Yes, more than mac 'n' cheese!" He laughed, and I followed him out back behind the house while Beth went in to check on the food. When he kept walking toward the barn, I began to wonder if he'd bought me a chicken or goat or something. I looked at him quizzically. He just laughed and finally pointed.

WHOA. There it was—my car! None the worse for wear. Like a shiny new black pearl. I hugged him. "How'd you get it?"

"Can you believe it made it through the fire? And I had always hated that detached garage when I lived there. Crazy...anyway, actually, it was a little complicated to pick it up. Had to go over there with a dealer guy so they could make a new key since yours was lost in the fire. And you'll need to apply for a replacement driver's license. I looked it up—you can order it online from the DMV, and it should be here in a week or so. No driving until then, though, okay?" He stopped to look at me. I was nodding, my eyes wide and glowing. Then, he saw me start to get weepy, so he put his arm around me. "See, you'll still be connected with your friends now. Jake called and told me about the job at the RCC and about soccer. And McKenzie said she would drive over and see you this weekend and stay over, if you like. What do you think of that?"

I just nodded and cried like a stupid baby. He smiled and hugged me to his chest. Then he said, "Look in the console."

I opened the front door. A new iPhone! Okay, so I might have been momentarily transported because I screamed out like a spoiled rotten, materialistic, phone-loving Designer Delia!

Dad said, "They were able to load everything from the Cloud, so your contacts, photos, everything, it's all there."

"Wow!" I couldn't believe it. I hugged him again and started scrolling through my texts, which were like, um, holy crap, a thousand or so. Apparently, everyone and their grandmother had my number and had sent me sympathy texts about the fire, get-wells, and best wishes for a speedy recovery.

Dad broke my frenetic perusal with, "Listen, take ten minutes out here, then come inside and eat, okay? And I want you to go to bed early tonight. I promised the doctor we wouldn't let you overdo it this first week. Got that?"

I nodded absently. I heard him, but only out of one ear. He laughed, shrugged, and walked away.

I was grinning like a crazy fool. I sat down in the driver's seat of my car and read everything.

Then I texted Mom on Brian's phone, *"Hey Mommy, what up? How's it going?"*

She wrote back, *"Got your phone back, I see. That's good. Everything here is fine. Brian's daughter gave me a new scarf to wear over my head. It's pretty. We're just about to sit down to dinner. You okay?"*

"Yep, all good. I gotta bounce. I'll check you tomorrow, k?"

"OK. Love you, Delia."

"Love you too, Mom."

I put the phone in my lap and stared out over the fields behind the house. The sun was still a bright yellow circle in the sky, casting a gleaming golden hue over the grassy slopes. I sighed.

Maybe everything *was* going to be okay after all.

CHAPTER XXVI

I STARED IN THE MIRROR, looking at my grotesque face and head. Good god! How could Brian even look at me? He kept telling me I looked beautiful, but was he just blowing smoke up my ass? Of course he was, the foolish, blind, ridiculous man. To tell the truth, I felt rotten about the face staring back at me. Okay, so maybe I was being vain and superficial and self-absorbed, but holy shit, I looked like Freddy Krueger!

It took my breath away—this feeling that you take everything for granted until it's ripped away from you without warning or recourse. For instance, let's start small. I'd always had a huge wave of red hair. I used to call it my lion's mane. The longer I let it grow, the bigger it got. I had been growing it out for years—a great tumbleweed of curly dark auburn tresses spilling down the middle of my back. It wasn't uncommon to have a complete stranger say to me during any given day, "Wow, you have the most beautiful hair." It was part of my identity. In high school, the boys used to call me Pinky Tuscadero. That was my hair—my token, my fetish, my idol, my me-ness. And now it was gone. Shot up in a ball of flames in one blasted, horrendous night like a rocket ship sent to hell, taking half of Earth with it. I was bald and burnt and barren and bereft.

It had been weeks, and I hadn't been sleeping. I was still having nightmares—always back in the D.D., being screamed at by Delia, pulled out of bed, into the hall, and down the stairs until a flamethrower shoots a spear of fire into my head. Sometimes the house is a maze, and no matter how hard Delia and I try to get out, exits are barred as we frantically stumble down random passageways, my head aflame, trying every door, tightly grasping each other's hands, but with no escape, no egress.

In other dreams, I'm back at the D.D., and it's bright and sunny. I'm sitting on the front porch with Didi and Mary, sewing or reading or shucking

corn, staring out at the neighbors' houses and yards when, without warning, we're engulfed in flames and tearing down the street in a panic. In one
dream, I'm in the backyard chasing a cat. I have this feeling that someone
left me in charge of the cat, but it's gotten out and I can't catch it. I'm helpless, looking at the D.D, wanting so much to grab the cat and run back into
the sanctity of the house. I try chasing it, then coaxing it, coming up slowly
on one side of it and then the other, but it's always just outside my grasp. I
feel the end of its tail on my fingertips, its whiskers on my arm. Time passes
and the cat is hungry, meowing and crying, so it finally comes to me and I
snatch it up in my arms, run with it as fast as I can into the house, closing
and locking the door behind me, and release the cat to the floor, pouring
food and water into its bowl. Then just as I sit down on a barstool, exhausted
but satisfied in my accomplishment, the cat turns to stare at me, and its tail
is suddenly on fire. The frightened cat jumps into my arms, clawing its way
up my chest, face, and head until I'm on fire too, and covered in scratches
and burns.

I wake up and my head tingles. My fingers move gingerly up to my face
and neck, where my wounds are still bumpy, scaly scabs, some bandaged,
some not, some throbbing, some not. Then I realize swiftly and with an
overwhelming sense of gratitude and grace that I'm safe and sound, tucked
in a bed beside a strong man who loves me despite my hair, or lack thereof,
despite my box-of-melted-crayons face, despite myself. I stifle my sobs and
get up quietly, go into the bathroom, and cry.

Don't get me wrong—on any given day, my first feeling wasn't usually
gratitude. In fact, quite the contrary. There is no worse pain than burn pain.
It was like being continually stabbed with a thousand angry knives into every
sensitive nerve you possessed, simultaneously. It was torturous. I cried for
that too. The pain pills made me foggy and groggy, so I tried to go as long as
I could without taking one, but sometimes the pain was simply unbearable
without them. I tried (for Brian's sake) not to complain too much, but good
god, there were days when I wished I were dead, or in a medically induced
coma, or under some type of semipermanent anesthesia. I began to crave and
look forward to my skin graft surgeries because at least I could get a few hours
of deep unconsciousness with no pain and no dreams and no me. Oh, the
sweet, inviting black void when the nurse pushed the liquid oblivion into my
IV. Ahhhhhh. Was that a bad thing? Bowing down to the Propofol idols...
crazy, I know, but can you blame me?

And besides the physical pain, there was the emotional pain. And general confusion too. How can life change on a dime? One minute, you're tootling along doing the usual daily grind—work, drinks, friends, family, home, sex, TV, sleep, social media, groceries—and the next, you're a disembodied alien sent to a foreign land where you haven't yet been taught the language or the customs or a way to be yourself, your *new* self.

This new foreign land was me—the new, half-burned version of Heather—but it was also Brian and his house and his life. On the one hand, Brian and his daughters had been great. How could I not be grateful? They took me in when I had nowhere to go. But still, it was kind of...awkward. That was the rub, really. I wished with all my heart that it wasn't that way, but it was. I had been living in the D.D. essentially my whole life, and the bones of that house were ingrained in my soul. That was something you couldn't just shake off quickly.

Not to mention, Brian's house was a three-bedroom, one-bath ranch. It was tiny. Or at least my feelings about the situation were tiny. No, not the square footage. It was the fact that Brian and I were in the same bed every night with those fresh, impressionable teenage minds right next door. And I don't mean sex—there wasn't much of that going on. I mean that I was basically a stranger. Who was I to them? Some woman their dad had been dating on and off for years. Why had they never met me before? And now I was living with them. Oh, don't get me wrong—Brian had been aboveboard at the hospital when they'd come to visit, told them how I didn't have a place to live and wanted to make sure they were okay with me coming to stay with them for a while. Of course they said yes. They really were the nicest girls, and I was grateful—I was.

But still, I was such a charity case! I hated that feeling. I had always prided myself on my independence. Back when my sister and I were young, it was my job to keep us safe and sound, just the two of us on a boat together out on the big, wide ocean facing the storms and sea monsters together, my arm around her shoulders. Even with Johnston, there was never a thought of me not keeping my job. I wanted my own life, not just to be an appendage of his life. Granted, it worked out that I also took care of the house, the kids, the groceries, the cooking, the cleaning, and of course, Johnston too. I'm not saying I did a bang-up job. All evidence to the contrary, in fact, but I tried. I wanted that role—to be strong, to be the leader, to make decisions, to take care of everything and everybody, to live without help or handouts. Didi taught me that. She lived that way too. Grandpa Ron was overbearing, but Didi was in charge.

Now here I was, relying on everyone else, and I hated it!

And everything was so unfamiliar. I knew it sounded ridiculous, but the smallest things made me frustrated. Brian used a different toothpaste from me. I couldn't find the light switches at night. I didn't have a garage door opener, so I had to get out and press the button and jump over the sensor. I know, I know…petty, stupid, superficial things! The kitchen layout was completely confusing to me—why was the silverware drawer by the stove instead of the sink? And why, oh why, were the coffee mugs in the cupboard over the microwave? That made no flippin' sense—they were hard to reach and nowhere near the coffee maker! And that was the other thing—they had one of those Keurig machines, didn't even own a coffeepot! I had no idea how to operate that contraption, and when you're a total insomniac, trying to function in the morning without coffee can just about set you over the edge. Do you see what I mean?! DO YOU?!!!!

Simmer down now, Heather. Okay, sorry. So yes, I felt like a complete idiot. And to make matters worse, they got up every morning and ate breakfast together, like the Cleavers, and what's more, at the dining room table! Who does that? I couldn't remember the last time Delia and I had sat across from each other at the table for any meal. And he asked them about their homework and their friends and their lives. Super civilized. I felt like the worst, shittiest mom ever. He was a great dad *and* mom! And I sucked. They were a perfect little family unit, and I was this sad little outcast add-on, like a wet, broken bird brought in from the rain that no one knew how to feed or care for.

In my mind, I kept thinking it's me and it's them. No, not me versus them—not that bad—but more like me on the outside looking in. They were cohesive, well-oiled, in sync, and I was just this other blob spinning out here on my own island, watching enviously through a keyhole.

And I lamented the loss of the D.D. every hour of every day. It had been my home, and my family's home, for generations. And now, in the course of an hour, it was gone. Just like that. A hundred years of memories, up in smoke. It wasn't only the memories, of which there were many—as varied as they were long—it was the sense of home, security, identity, and of *me*. Wrapped up in the Diamond family legacy. Obliterated, in a heartbeat.

After I got out of the hospital, Brian drove me over to see the remains of the D.D., which weren't much. Except (miraculously) the garage and our cars and Dennis Diamond's carved words in the cement floor in the basement: "D.D. c. 1900." The rest was total decimation. Nothing else salvageable. Not even a lonely shoe. Not even a fork or bed frame or photo or book. Not even my heart. Or Didi's heart, which probably perished with the house.

So instead of focusing on that, I did what little I could. I followed a new routine—faced each day fresh, and each night woke up from the nightmares, snuck out to the couch, turned on the TV, and tried to self-talk my way through the pain, the depression, the lack of direction and understanding. I would say (in my mind) the most inept platitudes: This too shall pass, my dear. Buck up! You can take it. Everything's going to be okay. You're strong, smart, and crafty, and you can make this new reality work. Besides, things aren't all bad. You survived a fire—that's got to count for something. Not everyone does, you know. You should be grateful and in awe of the miracle that is life—your life.

And I was.

That's just not all I was feeling. Maybe one day I would get there, though, and that's what I was counting on.

On a brighter note, Tyler was home and was staying at Johnston's, along with Delia. I met his girlfriend, Sara. She was tall, quiet, and shy, bringing me an adult coloring book, telling me how therapeutic they were. Very thoughtful. And apparently Delia was doing well. We'd been talking on the phone every day. She was fully recuperated now, back working at the RCC, and playing "a little" soccer, she said. The doctor told her to be careful with the knee, but I wasn't so sure she was listening. Essentially, everyone was back in their routine, and life was stable again. I was going out to dinner with Tyler and Delia that evening—that would be nice. And as of last Monday, the doctors told me I could go back to work because I was done with surgeries for a while. They wanted these latest grafts to heal up before we started the next round. I would miss my Propofol, but I knew the time had come for me to face the music, and that was exactly what I was going to do.

Throughout the whole ordeal, Brian had been calm and caring—really careful with me. He knew I was a fragile piece of spun glass, so he was handling me with kid gloves, thank god. Really. God bless that man. On this particular day, the day I was set to meet Tyler and Delia for dinner, I had woken up to a nightmare. It was just after three o'clock in the morning. I'd shaken off the sweat and fear and tiptoed into the living room to watch TV. Brian came in a few minutes later, and I nearly jumped out of my skin.

"Oh, sorry about that," he said, lifting up my legs from the couch to sit beside me, placing them on his lap.

I said with a pout, "You scared me."

"I know—really, I'm sorry." His face turned sober. He stroked my hand and asked, "Can't sleep?"

I shrugged mutely.

He hesitated and then commented, "Maybe you should go see someone."

I rolled my eyes and looked away.

"Heather. Sweetie. Come on. It's not normal to only get three hours of sleep a night. You look tired."

"Well, thank you for that!" I said, a little too sharply.

He shook his head, calmly hurting me with his patience. He said, "Listen, that's not what I meant and you know it. I'm just trying to help."

I said as bravely as I could, "I don't need help. I'm fine. It's just…well, it's just a…phase."

"A phase? Come on, Heather." He grabbed both my hands and said, "Listen, I'm no shrink or anything, but this pattern or phase or whatever you want to call it…it's not healthy."

I frowned.

He continued, "Listen, you say you're fine, but when I wake up in the middle of the night, you're never in bed anymore. Instead you're here, watching this."

He pointed at the paused *Grey's Anatomy* on the screen. I had been binge-watching old seasons, starting with season one. I was up to season three.

"Why, what's wrong with this?" I asked flippantly. So what if I'd become overly obsessed with the lives of Meredith and McDreamy, Little Grey and McSteamy, Stevens and Karev, Yang and Burke, O'Malley, Bailey, and the Chief. Did this mean I was broken? Did this mean I needed to "go see someone"?

Brian answered, "Well, it doesn't seem normal, that's all." He sighed and kissed my hand, looking at me with those wonderful, kind brown eyes. "You seem somewhat…detached, that's all. I'm no expert, and maybe this is the way things go after…well, after what you've been through, but still, at some point, you need to come back into the world of the living—here." He leaned into my face, giving me a kiss and pleading, "I need you, Heather. Your kids need you. My kids need you. I know beyond this island you've been living on for the past few weeks, there lives an amazing woman full of love and life and imagination and fun. I mean, why don't you look into that real estate license thing again? Or…or we could go on a weekend hiking trip or something… get outside…enjoy the summer weather. We could go back to the lake for a day or two. Something. What do you think?"

I shrugged. If only I had his energy to do things. Lately, all I wanted to do was sleep, and then as soon as my head hit the pillow, I was up again. It was so frustrating, like a luscious, big, ripe orange I couldn't quite figure out how to peel. So I watched *Grey's Anatomy* and escaped into the complicated story lines. It was comforting. Characters so jaded and damaged, going through such divisive and rotten situations. My pathetic little life paled in comparison.

But here was Brian, worrying about me. I didn't want that. I wanted my island to myself! I didn't want him on the island. That would just drag him down, and he was on a beautiful, unblemished mountain peak. I needed him to stay there.

I said, with as much energy as I could muster, "Hey, stop worrying. I'm really fine. Really. I don't need to see anyone. I know I seem…withdrawn, and I'm sorry about that. And yes, maybe I've been watching too much TV, but I only allow myself small doses when I can't sleep, and in between the real stuff, like you and the kids, and my favorite thing—talking on the phone with the insurance company."

He regarded me skeptically, then playing along, with a smile, asked, "How's that going?"

"Well, the investigators have ruled out arson."

"What?!" he exclaimed.

"I know!" I replied, shaking my head. "They just told me that yesterday on the phone. Can you believe they were even looking into that? As if we would (or someone else would) set our house on fire *while we were in it*. Freakin' ridiculous. But they assured me it's standard protocol. Anyway, they think they've determined the source of the fire, which was faulty wiring in the basement and too many big things plugged into the outlet down there."

"Hmpf. Interesting. Sounds about right."

"Yep. Anyway, I just can't deal with them anymore. I have a few outstanding calls, but they can wait, as far as I'm concerned…"

He nodded thoughtfully, probably not wanting to push me on that. Instead, he asked with hesitation, "So, so…have you decided…what you're going to do?"

Brian knew I hated this question. It forced me to think about my future, when I was perfectly content to sit and think about nothing at all. I answered, "No."

"Do you...want some help?"

"What kind of help?" I asked doubtfully.

"I've been thinking about it, actually. Don't worry—I'm not trying to dictate your life or anything...and, it's totally up to you, but I wanted you to know that you're welcome to stay here for as long as you need to." Then, rather sheepishly, he said, "Forever, in fact, if you like."

Ohhhh, how to react to that?! I decided funny was the way to go, for now anyway. I said shrewdly, "You're appreciative of the possibility of steady sex, aren't you?"

He laughed and kissed me, saying, "Bingo." He pulled away and said, "No, seriously, on the constructive side, have you tried to make a list?"

"A list?" I frowned. I was still on the sex topic—we had already tried so many different positions over the years...what purpose would a list serve?

He laughed and popped my bubble. "Not a sex list, you hot, unpredictable vixen. I mean a list of pros and cons. For the house. Like, is rebuilding better or worse than cashing in the insurance money versus buying another house. If you'd like another option, you and I, well, we could build another house *together*. Sell this place. Sam's a senior this year, then she'll be off to college, and Nancy's a junior, so...timing-wise, it would make sense. I'm not sure what your plans are for Delia...but she'd be welcome to stay with us too. Have you talked to her about your plans? Or Tyler?"

"Nope. Like I said, I haven't even thought about it. Plus, I don't want to freak them out before I need to." I sighed and lay back. It was such a swirl in my mind to think about the bureaucracy—all the forms, questions, and phone calls. I wanted to crawl in a hole.

Brian squeezed my hand and added, "I think it would be helpful to talk it over with them tonight."

"Okay, I will. You wanna come?" I asked hopefully.

"I would, but...I think you need some quality time with them...alone. They may have their own ideas about what to do."

"Yeah, I suppose..."

Brian kissed me once more and then went back to bed. I finished the episode where Meredith falls into Puget Sound and goes drifting down, down, down into the water. I tried not to watch with longing and envy.

Chapter XXVII

THE SUMMER HAD FLOWN BY. Nothing like a one-eighty from the end of school until now. I had trouble wrapping my head around it. It was the end of August already. In June, I was leading a life of imprisoned leisure back in my tiny room with no door—grounded, reading, assigned to dusty, godforsaken attic duty—and now I was busy, happy, healthy, with a new zest for life. Yes, I *did* just use the word *zest*. So shoot me. It felt good. I felt good. Better than I had in a long time—heck, maybe ever.

I woke up on a Wednesday and went for a ride on Buckeye, Beth's chestnut mare. Beth was afraid to ride her. I told Beth surely the baby wouldn't slide out of her womb just by being jostled on a little trot. No, not having it—not taking any chances. No riding for Beth. So instead, I took Buckeye out most mornings myself. Buckeye loved the fresh country air, and I loved the blush of the early morning dew on my boots as her flanks got soaked by the tall grass. We had fun. Sometimes I would set her off on a canter and she loved that, but we didn't have enough land to make it a long chase, so inevitably I'd pull her up and we'd trot along for a while, admiring the cornfield off in the distance and the hum of the crickets. We were in sync, me and Buckeye, two peas in a pod, so much so that I talked to her. She was my confidante. She responded in turn, and I found her to be an exquisite conversationalist.

On this muggy August morning, I said to her, "Buckeye, can you believe this summer? It's been awesome! Well, minus the whole thing with the D.D, but otherwise, totally stellar."

Heavy breathing.

"I mean, sure, I nearly died and Mom nearly died, but then it all ended up being a blessing in disguise, didn't it? Crazy I should say that or even think that, but it's true. All those years being afraid of the D.D.'s ghosts—the ding-dongs and goings-on up in the attic—and lo and behold, the ghost of Didi saved my life. Maybe the only resident ghost all these years was Didi. Maybe she was my Casper, my friendly ghost."

Snort, grunt, chew.

"Anyway, remember when McKenzie came and stayed over that first weekend and she rode you? You were so confused, not having Beth on your back (or me, for that matter). Sorry about that—you know my knee was still healing back then. Someone had to lead you around the paddock. We had so much fun, although, I know, McKenzie's a horrible rider. What can you expect? She wouldn't know a horse from a hole in the wall. Yes, McKenzie, your hair will get messed up, and your clothes, and your makeup, and your sunny disposition. Shit, you can take the girl out of the city, but you can't take the city out of the girl—you see what I'm saying, Buckeye?"

Nod.

"I'll never forget what McKenzie told me at that first sleepover. About Jake and Chelsea. McKenzie's sister had filled her in on the whole scoop. It had all gone down while I was in the hospital. How Chelsea had dumped Jake. Can you believe it? *She* dumped *him!* Stupid, idiotic, asinine girl! Who would ever dump Jake? But I guess the cat was out of the bag—like out of the bag and into the toilet. Her cheating with Austin came to light, and apparently her three-timing both of them with some other dude named Mark came to light too. My god, she was busy, wasn't she? Who has time for three dudes? The girl needs to get a life. Or slow down on a life. Anyway, she's finally settled on the third dumbass and broke up with Austin and Jake. And if I were them, I'd be like, good riddance, spawn of *The Devil Wears Prada*."

Loud snort.

"Word. But seriously, Buckeye, sorry not sorry. Her loss has been my gain. Isn't Jake wonderful? You've met him—remember when he brought you those three carrots? He knew the best way to your heart, didn't he? That's kind of been my experience too. All those books he's been bringing me. That week when I was still recuperating and had finished the Hemingway and the Russians, I nearly went stir-crazy. And there he was like a knight in shining new book covers. He knew I'd resorted to those romance novels Beth reads, but there's only so much you can take of Guillermo's 'pulsing passion' being thrust into Jane's 'valley of desire.' Am I right or am I right?"

Chew, chew, shake.

"Thank goodness. An entire set of Willa Cather—wow! I thought I was living and breathing in Nebraska. How did he know that was exactly what I needed?

In fact, Buckeye, sometimes when I'm riding you, I imagine I'm there, conquering those wide-open prairie fields—lost in the wild and in my quest to save the world from evildoers. Here I am, straddling you out on the back paddock, and yet in my mind, I'm overlooking the vast slopes of wildflowers and flowing wheatgrass. I carry a doubled-barreled rifle in your saddle because that's what people did back then to protect themselves, ready to shoot if anyone threatened their charge. You are my faithful sister—yes, you, Buckeye—and we're going to get to the next town, even if we have to kill twenty men along the way. But of course, we always make it safe and sound—who could possibly catch us? We ride like the wind."

Whinny, neigh.

"Once we're in town, I tie you to one of those railings with a water trough underneath, and you start chugging away as I walk into the general store wearing a tight corseted dress, ribbon-tied garter stockings, and a feathered hat. Don't ask me how I've managed to stay neat and clean even though we rode forty miles to get here. Let's just say you have to suspend reality for a bit, Buckeye. Anyway, who's there to meet me at the door but one hot, steamy, sexy cowboy sashaying up to me as I promptly slap his face, to which he grabs hold of me in a long embrace and an emblazoned kiss that makes my knees go weak. My handsome cowboy has sandy hair and dark green eyes, of course. Well, can you blame me? I can totally see Jake back then—out on the open range, ruling the town—women wanting him and men wanting to *be* him. Or hating him because they're jealous. After all, he's fearless and the quickest draw in the West. What would he have been called, Buckeye? Hmmmm. Quick-draw-Freimuth? Come-hither-cowboy? That-old-rake-Jake? Take-the-cake-Jake? I-wanna-make-it-with-Jake? Take-me-for-my-sake-Jake?"

Jingle, thump, thump.

I sighed. "Anyway, Buckeye, you get the idea. So, what, maybe Beth's romance novels have kind of leaked into my Willa Cather fantasies. Or it could just be Jake. I guess I never realized before how a boyfriend could be strong and loving at the same time. Is it crazy that I didn't know before? I was a fool! Or temporarily insane. Anyway, my head and my heart are screwed on right and tight this time. And I'll be seeing Jake on the soccer field this afternoon, and maybe I'll get a kiss or two in between wind sprints. If I have any air left, that is."

I was back at the barn taking off Buckeye's gear, filling her water and food pails, and brushing her down. It had been a nice chat. I gave her a kiss on the nose and told her, "Until tomorrow, mon amour."

I walked back to the house, finding Tyler at the breakfast table eating a bowl of cereal.

"Nice ride?" he asked, chewing.

"Yep, Buckeye loves me."

He nodded. "Well, you feed her," he said sarcastically. Then, "What time are we meeting Mom tonight?"

"Not sure—five-thirty, I think. I have tryouts until four. I'll have to come back and shower and change. She said she'd come our way. Where you wanna go?"

"I don't care...maybe Label 7."

"Okay, sounds good," I said, thinking about something else. "Who's driving you back on Saturday?"

"Dad. Why? You wanna come?"

"Puh-lease, negatory. I'm working." I paused and then said, "But I think Mom might want to take you."

"Really? Why?" Tyler asked with barely a glance up from his bowl.

"She hasn't been able to do any of the drop-offs or pickups yet, and I think she really wants to, that's why," I said. Then, more thoughtfully, "Listen, I don't think she's been so well since the fire. I'm not exactly sure what's going on with her, but she seems...sad and kind of broken."

That got his attention. "Yeah?

"Yeah, I mean, her house is gone and all the stuff—you know, the legacy of the D.D.—and then recovering from the burns, and moving in with Brian and his girls, and going back to work...it's a lot in a short period of time. And we're just about all she has left, you know, and I think we should kind of be cognizant of that, don't you?"

He sat listening with concern on his face. He said slowly, "Oh." He put the spoon down and I could see the wheels turning in his head. Maybe because he hadn't been in the fire, he hadn't really thought through all of the ramifications until now. "Okay, I'll ask her tonight. It would be good to show her my place and maybe she can meet Sara's parents too."

I smiled. "There you go. Make a day of it. Good." I felt better. I think Mom needed to feel us close right now, and since Tyler was leaving soon, that responsibility would be falling on me soon, which was fine, but I really wanted Tyler to assist as best he could while he was still around.

I went upstairs and got ready for soccer. I was trying out for varsity, which in theory should be a slam dunk but instead had been a hard-ass romp through drills, foot skills maneuvers, never-ending scrimmages, and two-and-a-half-mile cross-country treks at an eight-minute-mile pace. Not that these "fun" calisthenics weren't for every player, but Coach Andrews was especially punishing on me.

She was testing me, trying to make sure I passed muster this time. Served me right. I suppose since I'd ditched the team unceremoniously mid-season last year due to the Greg-control-freak debacle, I had to prove I was serious this time and in it for the long haul. In it to win it. So, no matter how out of breath I was, or how much my muscles were pushed to the limit, at the end of a drill, coach would holler, "Elliott, three more—yes, you, hop to it!" Aarrrghh. I wanted to die.

Today Coach Andrews was cutting five girls. The ideal team number was twenty, and unfortunately or fortunately, twenty-five had tried out. It wasn't going to be easy for her. There were a lot of great players, and more importantly—or rather, more obnoxiously—there were a lot of annoying, whiny-ass parents. Based on the look on Coach Andrews's face, I'd say she was wishing she could cut the parents instead. All those busybodies showing up at tryouts to "have a chat" with her after we were done—wanting to "share their thoughts" on how Janie could be used better if she played defense closer to the goal or how Janie could pass a lot more accurately if she had a better right wing to receive the ball or how Janie would be a much better player if she only had more playing time on the field. You get the idea. Delusions of grandeur. These girls (the ones with the annoying parents) were always (inevitably) horrible players. I didn't envy Coach, that was for sure. Thank goodness neither of my parents bothered with the persuasion, bribes, or cajoling. Or to show up, for that matter, and that was just fine with me. I mean, this was just tryouts, not the actual games. There was really no need for parents to be there at all. What those other parents didn't realize was that if your kid was good, no parental intervention of any kind was required. Just f-ing play and leave the decisions to Coach, would you?

But still, I felt bad for Coach. Thank goodness she was tough as nails. She would listen politely to the pestering parents, and I could see her nodding her head, sure, uh-huh, right, makes sense, but then when push came to shove (literally and figuratively), she would walk away, and if a girl sucked, she was out. After all, that was why they hired her. She had taken the girls to state three times in the past five years. And I was fully in agreement with her decisions, come what may. In reality, we all knew it was counterintuitive to kick the ball to a dud on the field who had no more idea what to do with it than a cat with a pogo stick. Nothing made life more wretched than a rotten teammate. She would weigh down the whole team like an insidious weed taking over a field of flowers. Power to you, Coach Andrews—may the force be with you, and may those parents eat crow and be gone.

At the end of practice, Coach announced the five girls. There were angry words of indignation and gnashing of teeth (on the part of the parents) and tears of defeat (on the part of the five girls), but Coach stuck to her guns and that was that.

I took my gear off and walked toward my car, where I found a pleasant surprise waiting—Jake, looking like something out of a teenage vampire romance movie, leaning against the hood, grinning.

"Hey," I said, smiling.

"Cut?" he asked, wrapping his arms around me and kissing me.

"Funny," I replied and then protested the kisses jokingly, saying, "Hey, watch out—I'm sweaty."

"Me too. Salty and sweet—my favorite combo," placated the foolish boy.

I dumped my bag in the trunk and asked, "You cut?"

He grinned and said, "Why bother asking?"

"Cocky," I teased.

"Well, seriously, like that's gonna happen." he said wryly. Then he asked, "Can I bum a ride? Mom needed the car for the girls' physicals today."

"Sure. I have to rush, though—having dinner with Tyler and Mom before he heads back."

"You can open the door and push me out as we drive by."

"Perfect." On the road, I glanced over to see Jake watching me. He did this sometimes. "Stop staring!" I protested.

"I can't help it. You're so pretty with your hair all messed up and your face all tan and gritty."

"Yeah, yeah, lean over and give me a kiss, you green-eyed monster." He obliged, and I had to keep myself from swerving off the road. Oh, I could write a novel about Jake's eyes—like green pools of light, the kind you see in a drop of water on a green leaf on an early summer morning. And those kisses! Sometimes cute and kitschy, sometimes long and lingering, sometimes sweet and soulful, sometimes hot and bothered. I liked those last ones the best.

After our diverting interlude, Jake asked, "Is everything settled for this weekend?"

"Yep. Moving my stuff over to McKenzie's Sunday night. Sadly, all my worldly possessions are contained in one rather small suitcase."

"How are you feeling about the whole thing?"

I pondered that for a moment. "I'd say about an eight on the one-to-ten scale. Don't get me wrong—I'll miss Dad and Beth and especially Buckeye, but still, not so much that I'd stay and go to school in Pittsford. I mean, who starts their senior year at a brand-spanking-new school with a bunch of brand-spanking-new cliques? How can I rule the school when I don't know the existing military regime or pedigree?"

"Good point. Well, you won't get any objection from me. I want you close enough to smell."

I smiled at him and squeezed his hand. And he really meant all the crap he said to me—that was what was so sweet. After a minute, he asked, "How's your mom doing with the whole switch-a-roonie?"

"Hmmm, not sure—hard to tell. I think she kind of wanted me to move in with her and Brian, but I didn't want his girls to have to double up in one of their rooms just for me. Not exactly the way to start a semi-sibling symbiotic relationship. Plus, McKenzie's mom's been great—she met with Mom and squashed all her fears. You know Mom—she was worried I could wig out like I did before. But I told her things are completely different now and everything's going to be fine. Mrs. Allen told her the same thing—she said she'd let Mom know right away if anything went awry."

"That's good. I mean, I can kind of see why your mom might worry…"

"Hey! I thought you were on my side!"

"I am, I am! It's just, there aren't sides anymore, are there? I mean, I've been around you a lot more these past couple of months than your mom has. She hasn't witnessed Delia 2.0. She's still a little stuck on Delia 1.0. She thinks…well, she wonders if you might slip into some of those bad behaviors again."

"Yeah, I know you're right," I admitted. "I'll need to build a mountain of trust on that island before she'll see there isn't a volcano waiting for her. And I agree, there are no sides. In fact, I really want her to know she can count on me now. This isn't like before when we were stuck in the roles of jailer and prisoner (which, granted, was a situation I basically forced into being). I'm actually going to try to be the mature, hands-on daughter I was always meant to be. Whaddya think?" I laced my hands under my chin and grinned.

"That's the spirit," he agreed.

"Seriously, though, I am. I've been texting her and calling her a lot more, you know, just to check in. And Mrs. Allen reassured her she had strict rules about homework, bedtime, and the morning wake-up ritual. And no boys allowed except in the living room with a chaperone. It cracked me up—as if Mom ever had any rules like that. But there was Mom, nodding her head as if everything was totally expected and copacetic. I think she's had a bit of an awakening herself and is beginning to see a new way forward. And I'm ten minutes from Brian's house and ten minutes from you. Best of both worlds. By the way, please thank your mom for me—she's been going over to see Mom, and I think she's really helping."

"Yeah, Mom told me. She thinks your mom's going through a bit of post-traumatic stress syndrome. Remember Mom used to work with those veterans at the rehab home? She said she sees some similarities."

"Wow," I said, looking over at Jake with slight alarm. "Is it that bad?"

"Well, heck, I don't know—that's just what Mom said."

I sighed. Poor Mom. "Yeah, maybe..."

We were at his house, and he leaned over to kiss me goodbye, then told me he'd call me tonight and asked, "What you want next? Japanese? Or the Brits? Or the New Englanders? Or the Southerners?"

"Hmmm, maybe a New Englander."

"Hawthorne it is."

"That would be divine."

"I'll bring it Friday."

"Okay, great, love you." My salty, smart, caring, literary boyfriend.

"Love you."

Chapter XXVIII

I rushed home to Brian's to get ready for dinner with the kids. I wasn't looking forward to the drive to Pittsford in rush-hour traffic, but oh well. With Delia in tryouts all week for varsity, this was the best time and place to get together. As I pulled up to the restaurant, I saw them both getting out of Delia's car and walking in. Delia looked tan and cute in cutoff overalls and a pink tank, and Tyler looked tall and handsome in a light blue polo and beige shorts. I put my hands up to my head, feeling self-conscious about the royal blue bandanna tied there to cover my scars. The hair was growing back in patches now, but I still looked like a cross between a troll doll and Shrek. I hoped they wouldn't notice the dark circles under my eyes. I'd used a lot of concealer. I exhaled and plastered a smile on my face.

We met at the entrance and Tyler said, "Hi-de-ho, Mommio—what's shaking?"

I answered, "The cellulite in my ass at the moment, and you?"

"TMI, thank you very much," he said, laughing and giving me a hug. "Me, I'm hoping some spicy buffalo sauce on my wings in about fifteen minutes." That boy! More and more like Johnston in both looks and personality. Besides my red hair—he still had that. I sighed.

I hugged Delia and asked about soccer, which garnered a cool and confident thumbs-up.

We got seated and ordered. As soon as the waitress was out of earshot, Tyler asked quickly, with a strange glance toward Delia, "Mom, can you drive me back to school this Sunday?"

Wow, that came out of left field. I said, "What? Oh sure, I think so. I thought your dad was driving you."

"Well, he can, but I'd really like you to see my new place, and I think it would be good for you to meet my roommates, and Sara's parents, who are dropping her off at her place the same day."

"That would be great. How many roommates do you have?"

"The house is a three bedroom, and there are six of us, so we're jammed in there pretty good. Two per room. And only one bathroom."

Delia chimed in, "Essentially a smelly bathhouse filled with athlete's foot, moldy towels, and an eighty-inch TV."

"Jealous?"

Delia rolled her eyes and said, "Uh-huh, totally."

Tyler ignored her, turning to me again and asking, "Well, can you?"

"Sure, what time? I'll borrow Brian's truck."

"Let's leave at eight, if that's okay."

I nodded. My heart felt a little less leaden. I smiled. A whole day with Tyler! I couldn't remember the last time we'd spent quality time together.

Our drinks and food came, and we were munching away when Delia asked, "So Mom, how's it going? How's Brian, and Nancy and Sam?"

I answered reflexively, "Fine, everything's fine. All good."

"I heard from Jake that Mrs. Freimuth's been stopping by."

"Yes, yes, that's true. She came over the other night after she put the girls to bed. It was nice seeing her." I began to wonder what Jake's mom had told Jake and what Jake had told Delia. Sure, the two mothers had commiserated on their children having found "young love" with each other. Jeepers, a few years ago, neither would have seen that coming, and here they were, madly in love! After reveling in that for a while, they had ventured into some deeper conversations. Sharon Freimuth was one of those people you find yourself telling your innermost secrets to (not to mention thoughts and feelings) without really realizing you're doing it or *why* you're doing it. It was disconcerting and oddly comforting at the same time.

"I'm glad. She's a good listener," Delia said significantly. So, Sharon must have played the telephone game with Jake. Who knows what Delia had heard. I sighed. Oh well. It wasn't as though I'd cracked open the shell that wide. I'd only scratched the surface. She knew about my insomnia and about my fears for the future and about my indecision about the house. She hadn't said much, but she'd listened and given me a huge hug before she left. I still felt that hug lingering in my heart. She was a good woman.

Delia continued slowly, "I mean, I'm glad you have someone nice to talk to. I think it might help you...figure things out...you know?" She was beginning to sound like Brian. Just what I needed—my boyfriend *and* my daughter worried about my well-being.

I repeated, "Thanks, but I'm fine—I'm really fine." I chewed for a few minutes, trying to think of a way to redirect the conversation. Tyler was elbow deep in his wings and couldn't tear himself away. I said, "Actually, I have some good news to tell you both."

"What?" Tyler managed to mutter.

"My buddy at the P.O., John—remember, the one who sells junk on eBay every week? Well, I gave him a box of stuff to sell from the D.D. before the fire."

Delia said, "Oh yeah! I'd forgotten about that. Did he have any luck?"

"As a matter of fact, he did. You could have pushed me over with a feather."

Tyler jumped in with, "Are we rich? Can I quit school and buy a yacht?"

"Yes, dear—make it three, one for each of us. Naw, it was only a box of old jewelry and watches and knickknacks and things, but yeah, we made a few hundred bucks, so that was cool."

"Nice," Tyler said. "Better than a kick in the pants."

"Yep," I agreed. Then I said woefully, "Of course, in retrospect, I wonder if I should have tried to get it back from him—it was, after all, the only stuff left from the D.D., and now it's gone too."

Tyler shook his head absently while Delia looked at me funny. After a minute, she said, "Not the only stuff, Mom."

"Huh?"

"Well, you have me!"

"Yes, Delia—yes, I have you," I said, smiling into her pretty face and patting her arm. "That's really all that matters, isn't it?"

"Yes," she continued casually, "and don't forget Dennis Diamond's radio."

"True, true," I nodded.

Then Delia dropped this bomb. "Oh, and Didi's diary."

"What?!" I cried, completely flabbergasted. "No—you don't!"

She pulled it out of her purse and held it up. I gasped. She said, just as casually as can be, "Oh yes, I do. I was reading it, *that* night, and I guess I shoved it into my shorts when we crawled out. Don't ask me how it didn't fall or get destroyed. Some type of miracle or otherworldly shit going on, but what can I say, here it is."

Without warning—without even a second to breathe or take it all in—I burst into tears. Tyler was so shocked, he dropped a wing on the floor. I was absolutely overcome with emotion. How was it possible?

There was something left of the D.D.!

And of Didi!

My surrogate mother, the woman who had raised me, who had been there for Mary and me when no one else had been. The woman who had shown me how to stay strong and be a good woman and a good mother, and how to carry on the family legacy.

I choked out, "How...? Why didn't you...?"

"It's okay, Mom," Delia said, giving me a side hug. "Didn't you hear me talking to Aunt Mary about it in the hospital?"

"No, I guess not. I was kind of in a daze...all those surgeries..." I put my hand to my mouth, shocked and awed. She placed the diary on the table in front of me, and I picked it up, cherishing it like an idol. After a minute, I opened it and leafed through the pages. A photo fell out onto the table. It was Didi, in a bathing suit, standing knee-deep in Lake Ontario, young, grinning, without a care in the world. I sobbed. Didi! Back from the dead and so alive!

Delia smiled and said, "Yeah, I wondered if you had ever seen that photo before. Doesn't she look amazing?"

"Yes!" was the only word I could get out between my sobs.

Tyler looked at the photo, smiled, and said, "Cool."

Delia said, "I wanted to give it to you sooner, but I had some research to do first. You see, the diary...it's sort of a mystery. I won't give anything away until you've had a chance to read it, but it has *no ending*. It just...stops...on July 23rd, 1932. For no reason. Without warning. Very frustrating. It was driving me bonkers, not knowing what happened, so I did a little research online, and I've found out a few things. I'll tell you more once you've read it."

I couldn't speak. I just nodded. All I could think was that this was a piece of the D.D., and a piece of Didi, and a piece of Delia and Tyler, and a piece of me.

And maybe *a peace for me.*

✻ Chapter XXIX ✻

I DROVE HOME TO BRIAN'S, thinking about my dinner with the kids and how great it was. I thought, you know what, Heather? The kids are alright—*we're all alright*. I sat and talked with Brian on the couch for a few minutes, telling him I felt better, and he said he was glad and that I even *looked* better. I showed him the diary. We kissed and I went into the bedroom, lay down on the bed, and cracked open Didi's diary.

1932
Delia "Didi" Marie Diamond
Birthday: February 29, 1912
12 Spencer Street
Rochester, New York

January 1

(Friday) New Year's Day. Decided to start a diary. New Year's is a time for new beginnings, right? I hope it will be for me. I've been stuck in a rut lately. Work, family, friends, life. It's been a year and a half since I graduated Franklin, and now I'm looking for a new adventure. I think Mom and Dad would like for me to meet a nice boy and settle down. I would like that too. We had company last night (Harold, Vera, baby), which was fun, but then when I woke up this morning, I looked out the window at the snow and wondered what the future would bring. I went to Frances's in the afternoon and met her cousin Paul. After a while, we went to the Riviera and saw Rich Man's Folly *and* Sidewalks of New York. *Not exactly fireworks for the start of 1932, but at least I didn't sit home and cry.*

I stayed up all night reading the whole thing. At one point, Brian came to bed, and I moved to the living room couch so I wouldn't disturb him.

My first thought was, wow, what a different picture of Didi than I remembered from my childhood. Isn't it funny, though, how, as a child, you don't really see the adults in your life? Sure, they direct your actions, feed and clothe you, discipline you, teach you, but they're almost like inanimate objects swirling around innocuously in your orbit. Your whole sphere of existence is in your own mind, your own self-absorption, your own forming of yourself. You love the adults, but you also resent them for telling you how to be you. It's a natural instinct to embrace the guidance they give you but also to resist it. Made me think a lot about my relationship with Delia.

The Didi of my youth had been a strict disciplinarian, laying down the law of Grandpa Ron but also letting us know that she loved us unconditionally. She was there to parent us, not to be our friend. She was the master of that balance. Mary and I knew exactly wherein lay the limits of her tolerance, and we tried our darnedest to stretch to the precipice without careening over the edge. Sometimes we succeeded and sometimes we failed, but we knew that no matter what, Didi would never abandon us, never sacrifice us to the wiles of the world or our own stupidity. She had pulled us out of foster care (in defiance of Grandpa Ron), and she was going to be there for us from that point forward, even if it was difficult or challenging or if (let's be honest) we didn't appreciate her.

And yet, here she was in the diary—young and fresh and hopeful. Tackling the world head-on! I realized (duh to me!) that she had once been just like any other girl—the whole world ahead of her and dreams of what could be. I had only ever thought of her before as the Didi of *my* youth, not her own.

Lo and behold, Didi really was an entity in and of herself. Didi Marie Diamond! A girl growing up in Rochester, New York. A working girl, during the Depression, going out with friends, getting involved in the community, dating and dancing with handsome, eligible young men, hanging out with her little family unit in the D.D. and with friends coming to visit. Taking trips to Niagara Falls, joining card games, group dates, dances, shows, radio hours, picnics, birthday parties. Living a full and happy life.

I could feel her excitement—her expectations for life. Twenty years old, in many ways still a child under her parents' roof, yet striving for adulthood. Trying to make a difference in the world, find a man, settle down.

It reminded me of myself back when I was twenty as I finished up college, dated and married Johnston, explored career options and then motherhood. Up until that point, my main goal had been to get away from Grandpa Ron and his overbearing rules and discipline. When I met Johnston, I figured—probably just like Didi—that was my only way to independence, to have something of my own, to start my own life. Unlike Didi, though, I didn't stop to think about the fact that maybe I was pushing forward for all the wrong reasons and was ill-prepared for marriage, managing a household, or being a mother.

What happened to Didi? Did she do the opposite of me and actually stop to think before marrying Paul? He was out of a job, and his family was gone. Shacking up with her parents probably didn't sound appealing, especially as newlyweds. They loved each other, but was love enough to sustain them? Didi, oh Didi, what happened to you? And to Paul? I named my daughter after you—for your courage, for your strength, for raising me and my sister when you were past your prime and when we probably didn't deserve your charity (especially after everything Mom put you through). You could have walked away. I know that would have been easier, but you didn't. You stood up to Grandpa Ron, probably at great detriment to yourself, and you never let on, never let us see that we were a burden. What happened to you all those years ago, before any of us were a twinkle in your eye? What happened to the bubble you portrayed in 1932? The bubble of youth, fun, love, life, happiness. What happened?

I wanted to call Delia and see what she had found out, but it was two thirty in the morning. I went to bed for a few brief hours of sleep before work, trying to wipe the images from the diary out of my mind until I had more time to process them. The next two days at work flew by. I think I was still in a trance—lack of sleep, leftover trauma from the fire, and my questions about the diary—a recipe for fogginess and lackluster movements through space and time. This was my world lately.

I had arranged to meet Delia on Saturday when her shift was over at the RCC. I was dying to know the rest of Didi's story. We arrived at Joe's Pizza at 12 Corners at the same time, parking next to each other and getting out and hugging. Sometimes I had to stop and pinch myself. A few months ago, hugging Delia would have been more foreign to me than a shark hugging a seal. Wow, how our world had changed, and it made me smile. My precious baby was back in my arms like old times.

We ordered and sat down, and Delia said, "Two times in a week, Heather? To what do I owe this pleasure?"

"Don't be cute, Delia. Let's get down to brass tacks."

"No 'Hi, how are you, Delia?' Nada? Besides, what does that expression even mean anyway? Am I supposed to pound brass tacks into a wooden board or something? How does that have anything to do with talking business? I'm confused…"

I sighed. Maybe I'd jumped the gun on my sentiments about the hug. After all, this was still my wisecracking, irreverent daughter. "Okay, sorry, yes, please tell me how you're doing," I replied dutifully and sat as patiently as my body language would allow.

"Well, as a matter of fact, I have my first soccer game tonight. You coming?"

"Sure. Home game? What time? I'll ask Brian and the girls too. You feeling ready?"

"Yes, home, eight o'clock. And as far as me being ready, like you have to ask."

"Your modesty touches me."

She shrugged and grinned widely.

"No, what I meant was, how's your knee?"

"Oh, that. Fine. Tip-top. No worries on that front."

"Well, good." We sat and stared at each other, smiling. I couldn't help but think with pride, this was my daughter—confident, strong-willed, gritty, cheeky, sassy, and sweet. It was beyond my comprehension how she'd survived *the incident* with that prick and now also the fire, and still sat here grinning about an upcoming soccer game. Talk about resilience! I swear, I could take a page from that girl. Maybe I had done something right with her, or maybe it was all her and I had nothing to do with it. Either way, she was quite a marvel.

Speaking of *the incident*, what she said next floored me.

She pronounced nonchalantly, "Jake got in a fistfight for me last night."

"What?! With whom? Why?"

"Yep, for reals. With Greg, the fucker."

"Delia—mouth, please."

"Well, I'm sorry, but he is—there's no better word for him."

I wasn't about to split hairs. I said, "Okay. Tell me what happened." All thoughts of Didi went out of my head.

"Jake and I had a date night—you know, to celebrate soccer, and well, because we've never really been on a quote-unquote date before. Anyway, so I was all dressed up and put makeup on—like, put some effort into my look, you know? Jake told me I looked beautiful and that he loved me and how pissed he was that he couldn't watch my game because men's varsity has an away game at the same time, and of course, since he's their star forward, it's not like he can miss, not that he would, just for me, or that I would ever ask him to, because that's not how we roll. Anyway, I couldn't help but notice he was wearing his green T-shirt, my favorite, which makes his eyes stand out. I told him his eyes looked better than the grass on the soccer field. He said that was the best compliment he'd ever gotten."

She stopped to laugh, and I rolled my eyes and said impatiently, "I get it. You're crazy about each other. Glad to hear it. Now, would you *focus*, please, and tell me what happened?!"

"Yeah, yeah, I'm getting there. So anyway, we went to dinner and split a steak, like, the best steak ever. Thick and juicy with a little pink in the middle—"

"Delia!" I was about to strangle her.

"Alright! Remain calm, Mummy. After dinner, we drove out to Charlotte and walked down the boardwalk. I was holding Jake's hand and watching some dogs play in the water, not a care in the world. Right as I turned to ask Jake about getting an ice cream, guess who we see? Greg! The dickhead is there with some slut with her hair so high and her skirt so short, I could see Mars and the Moon and a little bit of Uranus."

"Delia!" I exclaimed again, sighing and shaking my head.

She ignored me and continued, "Greg's immediately in Jake's face—like an inch away from his nose. No provocation, not a second to think, and he's there, grabbing his wrist and yanking him away from me. I get in the middle, screaming, 'Greg! Back off!' but Greg's still got a hold of him. He's yelling at Jake, 'Who the fuck are you?' as if he has the right to ask or to talk to me or Jake in the first place. Totally fucking delusional. Asshole!

"Just as Jake shakes him off, without warning Greg clocks Jake upside the head. When he did that, I saw red. I ran at Greg's face with my fists out and my feet kicking. I was like the Tasmanian devil. Just by virtue of his surprise, I got a few good punches and knees in before Greg grabbed my wrists so hard, I thought he broke them. As Greg's holding on for dear life, Jake turns him and punches him right in the jaw. Greg lets go of me and goes after Jake. Instantly, somehow, they're both off the boardwalk and rolling around in the sand like two pythons in a death match.

"I'm watching and feeling like I'm going to puke. Mind you, there's a crowd of people watching, and Greg's slut is standing there with her hands on her hips cheering Greg on (the stupid skank—I'm sure she doesn't even know what the fight's about). I jumped down in the sand with Greg and Jake, trying to pull them apart, but they're completely ignoring me and slamming each other from every angle. I can't tell who's winning—they both seem to be breathing hard and leaving marks all over each other's faces. At some point, in the midst of the melee, I reach in and get a rogue fist to the ribs. I go down like a sack of potatoes. Jake turns to check on me, and poor boy, gets slammed in the eye for his kindness. That made me so mad, I forgot I was hurt. I jumped up and kicked Greg right in the head—I'm talking my best shot on goal. Greg lay back for a second, just long enough for Jake to stand up, holding his eye, and pull me away before I set up for another kick.

"Then, as I'm protesting to Jake, I see out of the corner of my eye two cops walking up to the scene. Jake has a hold of my arm and is running me out of there as fast as he can. We don't look back—we just keep going until we reach the car and jump in. I was still shaking as I put the car in drive and sped the hell out of there."

She paused and looked at me with her huge brown eyes, breathing hard. I said, "Good god, Delia!"

She regarded my horror and said simply, "Prick."

"What is wrong with him? And poor Jake, in the middle, defending your honor. Were you both okay?"

"Oh yeah, fine. I mean, I think I broke a rib because it hurts to laugh or cough or move. And Jake's got a black eye, but otherwise we're good. He said it ought to give him an edge in the game tonight—I mean, who's gonna approach a player with a shiner like that?"

I just shook my head. "For heaven's sake, Delia. What a nightmare. By the way, how are *you* going to play tonight?"

"Oh, I'll be fine." She shrugged.

"Huh. I don't know…you worry me, you really do."

"What? It's cool. I mean, thank god I was with Jake, you know? He's amazing. And Greg is such a control freak—I haven't even seen him in months and he still thinks he owns me! I don't care…I'm not going to be afraid or intimidated by him anymore. He can say and do whatever the fuck he wants."

"Delia," I said, grabbing her hand, "are you sure?"

"Yes," she said definitively. "I don't know why, but I feel like maybe this is it. Maybe that fistfight finally showed him that he's never getting me back. Plus, he's graduated now, out of school, probably working at the county junkyard or saying, 'Would you like fries with that?' Whatever. I don't give a shit. I'm away from him now, and I'm not wasting another ounce of energy on him anymore. End of story."

Her eyes were glowing, and I knew she meant it. I squeezed her hand and said, "Okay, Delia. That's good."

We got our pizza, and as we ate, Delia began with, "So you want the full digs on Didi?"

"Yes! I have a thousand questions."

"Well, me too, but I've managed to figure out a few things."

"You have? Like what? Paul? What happened?"

"Hmmm, how should I break it to you?" she said tentatively, then bluntly, "um, sadly…he died."

"Oh no!" I couldn't believe it. I wasn't expecting that. I figured he just broke off the engagement. "He *died*? But how?"

"Hit by a streetcar. Six days before the wedding."

I nearly choked on my pizza. "No! That's awful! Poor Paul! Poor Didi!" I repeated, shaking my head. Well, that explained why Didi never talked about it, never mentioned a word.

"Yeah, I found it online. I was on Dad's computer, searching under Paul Miller from 1932, and I found his obituary, which said something like Paul Miller, age twenty-one, of Rochester, New York, was killed instantly when a streetcar on Lyell Avenue struck him. Witnesses said he was attempting to cross the street when he ran out from behind a truck and the streetcar coming from the other direction didn't see him and slammed right into him."

"Whoa…," I said sadly, shaking my head.

"Yeah…," Delia responded. We stared at each other, thinking about how horrible that must have been for Didi. Then I noticed Delia raise her eyebrow just a hair.

I said soberly, "Are you thinking what I'm thinking…?"

She simply nodded, her mouth a thin line. After a few moments, she said quietly, "Suicide." She paused and we looked at each other solemnly. "Of course, we'll never really know. I suppose Didi never really knew either. Which would have been torture—the not knowing. I can't even imagine…"

"No," I agreed. "It's so odd how it started off so hopeful and wonderful—their meeting through his cousin Frances and dating and falling in love. All the group outings—it seemed so innocent and ideal. Like something out of a black-and-white movie. Then, over time, I noticed how things were turning...slightly sour...as if a darkness had descended. It's amazing Didi had a job and that her family was doing so well, but I could see where Paul's past, family, and lack of work were causing the struggle. When the Stand closed and his mom and brother moved back to Pennsylvania, I couldn't figure out how Paul was going to make it work—on his own or with Didi and her family. I suspect he wasn't sure either..."

"Exactly," Delia said, frowning. "Everything must have looked hopeless. He didn't want to take money from Didi or her dad, so how was he going to be okay totally living off them after they were married? And with Didi working and him not working, how was that gonna fly? Wasn't that basically unheard of back then?"

"Pretty much."

"So, what could they have done?"

"I don't know."

"Right," Delia confirmed sadly. After a pause, she asked, "Didi never told you about Paul? What about the other people? Frances, George, Burrows, Bernice, Roy, Sam, Honoree? Anyone?"

"Nope, no one. I didn't even think to ask about her early life. Mary and I were having so many struggles of our own with Mom being institutionalized and Dad dying and then Mom committing suicide, I guess we didn't have the time or inclination to ask. Plus, Grandpa Ron was so domineering that it wasn't as though we had a lot of time alone with Didi. She was expected to keep the household in order and follow his rules, and we were expected to toe the line. Between the chores and school and punishment, there was very little time for chitter-chatter or anything else."

"Hmmm," Delia said thoughtfully. "I guess it make sense, though, doesn't it? She fell in love with Paul, and that didn't work out. In fact, that ended in just about the most horrific way possible. Then, like eight years later—Aunt Mary told me Didi and Grandpa Ron were married in 1940—Didi goes for eight years without a guy, so she must have been nearly thirty. No—hmm, twenty-eight or twenty-nine. Regardless, that was like old maid territory. She probably thought Grandpa Ron was her last chance. I bet all her friends were married and had kids by then, which might also explain why she wasn't in touch with any of them anymore."

"I suppose," I answered slowly. "I never thought of it before, but yeah, it was pretty rare to get married and start a family that late in life. Maybe she was...kind of desperate."

"Did she ever say how she got together with Grandpa Ron in the first place?"

"I think she told me once that they met through her dad. Grandpa Ron worked at Kodak and so did Dennis Diamond, so that makes sense. And I remember Didi told me my mom was born when Grandpa Ron was overseas at war and that she had some type of trouble during the delivery, which is why she couldn't have any more children after that. Can you imagine? Having a baby by yourself and there are problems, and you're home alone with a newborn while your hubby's over in Europe or who knows where fighting Nazis. It must have been horrible."

Delia shook her head. "Yes." We were both quiet for a while. Then Delia said, "You know, I think Didi was a fixer. That's what she was. Maybe she tried to fix Paul and couldn't, so then she found Grandpa Ron and lord knows he needed help, and she thought she'd try her hand at him."

I said slowly, "I really don't know. If so, I don't remember it working. In all the years I was around them, I don't think I ever witnessed him giving her one kind word. And I certainly never saw them touch each other—no holding hands, kissing, pats on the back, nothing." I thought back in my mind to the foggy images, the ones that weren't completely obscured by trauma and merciful blackout.

I continued, "I do remember they had a sort of stable routine together, though. A certain rhythm in the way they lived. She'd make the meals, and we'd all sit at the dining room table together and eat, no matter what was going on in our lives. She'd leave the morning paper by his coffee, and he'd read it with his breakfast, and we weren't allowed to interrupt him. She'd set out his clothes on the bed while he got ready in the bathroom before work. While he was gone, we'd get home from school and were expected to help Didi clean and vacuum and dust and get the table set. Grandpa Ron came home, and she made sure he had a drink—a Manhattan—and a fresh cigar in the ashtray, perfectly lined up next to his recliner in the living room. We were told to be quiet or to go outside while Grandpa Ron was 'decompressing,' and believe me, we listened to that advice. We knew enough not to tick him off, especially when he first stepped in the door from work. Even if we were starving, we would go outside on the porch swing and kill time."

"But Mom…," Delia asked, "Was he mean to Didi?"

I tried to search my memory banks and finally said, "No, I don't think so. I never saw him be outwardly aggressive toward her. He would huff and puff, if

you know what I mean, but it never went beyond that. She seemed to understand his limits, and vice versa. He was definitely more physical with Mary
and me, for whatever reason, but he left Didi alone. Maybe I'm remembering
this wrong, but I think she once told me that when she first met him, he was
basically a good guy, if a little formal, but that something happened to him
in the war, and after that he was testy and angry. Regardless, when he was
'in one of his moods,' she was the only one who could deal with him. Mary
and I just stayed away, withstood his punishment, or cowered in our room or
outside, trying to weather the storm."

"So, Didi never really fixed Paul or Grandpa Ron then, did she?"

"No, not really, I suppose—or my mom. But then she did alright by Mary
and me—well, the best she could anyway—and that really meant something.
I'll never forget her or what she did for us."

"Me either," Delia replied sincerely, seeming to include herself in that mix.
I gave her a small smile, and we both sat staring at each other mutely.

Sensing the clock ticking, Delia finally asked, "Mom, how did Didi die?"

"Sadly, she had Alzheimer's."

"She did?" Delia said, shocked. "Oh, I didn't know. What was that like?"

"Awful," I answered flatly. "Grandpa Ron tried to take care of her at home
for the longest time, but eventually he had to put her in a nursing home. Mary
was living in Colorado by then, and your dad and I were living a few miles
away in an apartment, with two little babies and working, so we really weren't
much help. It's a devastating disease. Eventually she lost the ability to swallow
and became very thin, so when a strain of the flu went through the nursing
home, she caught it and died within a day or two. She's buried out at Mount
Hope, right next to her parents, her brother James, and Grandpa Ron. He
died just a few months after her of stomach cancer. That's when I inherited
the D.D. and your dad and I moved in. It was a crazy, long, confusing year."

"Wow, so tragic..." Delia said with a faraway look in her eyes.

I nodded sadly and said slowly, "Yeah, whenever I hear that Dixie Chicks
song about a silent house, I think of her. I can't remember the exact words,
but it's something about how everything that was made by hand, everything
that was known by heart, I will carry on and let her forget. That's sort of how
I feel about Didi, especially now that I've read her diary. I think we'll let her
rest in peace, and we'll carry on and let her forget. What do you think?"

Delia answered, "Totally. But I guess I feel a little sad about it all. Don't
you?"

"Yes, I do," I agreed. "Of course, every life has its hardships. You still have to keep plugging away, don't you? What other choice do you have? That's what Didi did. And that's what we're gonna do too."

Delia nodded, but then she pinched her mouth up and inquired, "Mom?"

"Delia?"

"Do you think Didi burned the house down?"

"Delia!"

"Well, I was just thinking as you were talking, wondering if she wanted us to erase the D.D. from the map—have it all be done and buried. You know, like you said, let her forget. Or let *us* forget. Gone, obliterated—the whole thing. Slashed out of existence. A clean slate."

I chuckled. My crazy, clairvoyant daughter. I said, "Come on..."

"Yes! I'm serious," she replied adamantly. "I think Didi wants us to re-member her as she was in 1932—young, naive, hopeful. Unblighted, you know? And maybe...just maybe...she wants us to learn from her—to walk away from the past. To not carry it like a weight around our necks, like she did. To move on, move forward. Yes, we keep a piece of the past with us—it's who we are—but it's not everything. We don't want to repeat our mistakes, but we gotta live for the present. She's basically channeling a message to us: listen, I got a second chance at life and I still screwed it up (if you consider Grandpa Ron a screw-up), but you two don't have to. Do it right—don't screw it up! I'm totally down with that. What about you? I'm taking my life by the balls right now and running with it!"

I had to laugh at her enthusiasm and the mixed metaphor. I said, "Alright, Confucius, pipe down. That visual is confusing me and making me cringe." I tapped her on the nose with my finger, saying, "However, I do think that's sage advice, my dear, especially coming from a very wise seventeen-year-old rebel *with* a clue like you."

She nodded her head, confident in her vast knowledge of the world and ignoring my sarcasm.

As we left the restaurant, I handed her back the diary, saying thank-you with a hug. Then I said, "Delia, you know what?"

"What?"

"I'm really proud of you."

"Thanks, Mom—I'm proud of you too."

What a world of difference one summer can make. As I drove away, I sud-denly had a vision pop into my mind. It was of Didi tucking me into bed

one night many years before, a lifetime ago, when I was a young child. As
her warm brown eyes hovered over me, she said earnestly, "Heather, I want to
tell you a story, and I want you to remember it. Can you do that?" I nodded,
thinking she was being very serious for a random school night in the dead of
winter, but I agreed.

She began, "Once there was a little girl who lived in a big city. In this city,
the weather was harsh in the wintertime. Unlike other cities, snow was mea-
sured in feet instead of inches. This was called lake-effect snow because when
the nearby lake looked across the landscape at the gray sky, mucky fields,
and dreary houses, it would cover the wintry blight and brown decay of that
view with a blanket of white tears. The lake knew the only way to remove
the sadness that permeated the landscape was to overlay it with a crisp white
layer of snow. The lake understood that the more tears there were, the more
rejuvenation.

"The little girl thought this was a particularly beautiful image and asked,
'Lake, why then do people curse the snow?' The lake shivered and said, 'Because they are afraid of the melt.' The little girl didn't understand and asked,
'The melt?' The lake responded easily, 'Yes, you see, once the snow melts,
the landscape must begin again. People fear having new beginnings without
knowing the outcome. Sometimes they prefer to start back where they began
(before the snow came), but in reality, the old topsoil is gone—it has washed
away. They must start over, no matter how afraid they are.'

"The little girl nodded and asked, 'What about the earth underneath? Will
that still be there?' The lake smiled at the little girl's intuition and replied,
'Earth is made up of bedrock that can't be melted away. This bedrock is
strong and part of the deepest layers of the ground—the part that has been
there since the beginning of time and will continue long after we are gone. It
is only the top layer of the soil that must be renewed after the melt. This layer
is more fragile and will fall away many times in a lifetime.'

"The little girl crinkled her forehead and finally said, 'I want it to snow.'
The lake grinned and swept in a huge snowstorm during the night so that
when the little girl awoke the next morning, the city was covered in a thick
layer of white tears. She went outside and played for hours, thanking the lake
for her new snowman and her new snow angel and her new igloo."

At the time Didi told me this story, I didn't understand it. Sure, it was
a visually stunning parable, and maybe it made me appreciate Rochester's
winters, but I didn't get the significance until just this moment in the car ride

home from the pizza place.

Life was filled with new beginnings. We couldn't be afraid of them, and we couldn't allow ourselves to get swept away by the trials that led us to them. After all, we're all made of bedrock too. My guilt stemmed from the fact that I hadn't listened back then, and if I wasn't careful, I would miss Didi's lesson even now.

It was time for my new beginning, my second chance, my new snow angel. And this time I was going to stand on the bedrock of my family and my strength and my fortitude, and I wasn't ever going to fear the tears of snow or the melt again.

❧ CHAPTER XXX ❧

How to Slash the Spunk out of Punk:
So, how *do* you slash the spunk out of a punk?

Step One: Exile the deviant to her bedroom. Well, not really *her* bedroom. The bedroom she now shares with her best friend, McKenzie.

Step Two: Take away all forms of reminiscing and musings about past year of hell wherein shitty ex-boyfriend wreaked havoc over optimistic teen spirit, and all familial sense of stability in the form of ancestral home burned down.

Step Three: Confiscate anything or anyone that might stand in her way. Otherwise, watch out—she will plow through.

Step Four: Fill remaining dialogue with sarcasm, irreverence, irony, and oh yeah, once in a while, thoughtful kindness.

Step Five: Set social media to start over and think before you post, or better yet, bounce and go read a book.

Step Six: Push everything and everyone off that doesn't lift her up, make her think, get to know her, or care.

Now you ask, did it work? Was this the proper formula? Did the alchemist mix the right fixins and stir in the right amalgam to sock it to the sicko? Were all forms of rebellion stripped from the defiant child? Was the lobotomy complete? Was the spunk sufficiently removed from the punk? Was she back to her untainted, unblemished form—white and pure as the driven snow?

Hmmm…um…NO.

So yeah, I'm still a punk. With a bit of spunk.

Didi would be proud.

❦ Chapter XXXI ❧

Life has its own mind. And so do my granddaughter and her daughter, and that's what I love most about them. Things don't turn out the way you plan, but they do turn out the way they're meant to.

Would I do anything differently? Surprisingly, no. I am the fierce, unabashed survivor and matriarch of this family, and yes, I went through hardships and pain during my time on Earth, but I made sure my girls knew where they came from and how to pull themselves up by their bootstraps when the going got tough. They learned how to dig deep, and no matter how deep I am below the ground now (six feet or otherwise), I will always watch over these two strong, independent, willful, determined women with pride, love, and admiration—for the rest of their lives and for the rest of time.

The End

About the Author

Amy Q. Barker holds a BA from Syracuse University and an MBA from Rensselaer Polytechnic Institute. She grew up in Spencerport, New York, and currently lives with her husband in Indiana. She is the author of *Rue* and *Punk*.

Made in the USA
Monee, IL
11 November 2021